I0654889

Resurrection

A novel

Paul L. Hall

Libero Press

A Division of Partners Publications

RESURRECTION

Copyright © 2014 by Paul L. Hall

All rights reserved. No part of this book may be used or reproduced by any means, graphic, electronic, or mechanical, including photocopying, recording, taping or by any information storage retrieval system without the written permission of the publisher except in the case of brief quotations embodied in critical articles and reviews.
This is a work of fiction. All of the characters' names, organizations, and dialogue in this novel are either the products of the author's imagination or are used fictitiously.

ISBN-978-0-9770415-0-3

CONTENTS

Ling'ring perdition - worse than any death

Can be at once - shall step by step attend

You and your ways;

The Tempest

PROLOGUE

So, if this were a movie, it might start like this:

Scene A

FADE IN:
INT. OLD, SPANISH-STYLE CATHOLIC CHURCH

The church is traditional with rows of pews and altar and confessionals in the traditional style. It is a late Saturday afternoon in winter and the church is deserted. The period for the priest to hear confessions has expired about a half-hour earlier.

DISSOLVE TO:
CU PRIEST'S FACE

We understand that he is still in the confessional. He is dozing, probably because 1.) he is old, and 2.) he's had a few drinks before assuming his confessor duties for the day. In any event he does not wake up as we hear someone quietly enter the confessional. Thirty seconds elapse.

Slowly, the old priest seems to sense that he is not alone and begins to wake up. He seems confused for a few seconds, unsure of his surroundings and what he should do. Tentatively, he starts to rise from his seat, then sits back down. After a few more seconds of hesitation, he seems to remember why he is there. He slowly reaches for and slides back the little door covering the screen that separates his face from that of the potential penitent. He begins speaking the required prayer, but before he can even get three words out, a large knife comes crashing through the screen and into his temple, killing him instantly.

Scene B

EXT. PIAZZA NAVONA IN ROME-DAY-ESTABLISHING

Amid hundreds of tourists on a brilliant November day, a man sits at an outdoor table drinking an espresso. He wears a large brown Borsalino safari-style hat and sunglasses and smokes a cigar. The man is not Anthony Hopkins, although you may be forgiven for making that connection. It is clear that he is watching someone across the square at the outdoor table of another restaurant. His attention is complete; he never takes his eyes from the object of his surveillance. After a few minutes, the man he is watching—a middle-aged white man dressed casually in Levi's and a black long-sleeve T-shirt who has been nursing a glass of beer—gets up from his table and begins walking across the piazza toward Corso Rinascimento. The man in the Borsalino hat arises unhurriedly from his seat and follows his "prey" at a discreet distance. A sort of leisurely travelogue ensues down Corso Rinascimento to Corso Vittorio Emanuele, across Largo di Torre Argentina (where the man being followed stops briefly to observe the vagrant cats lounging in their sanctuary amid the ruins) to Ponte Garibaldi and over the Tiber into Rome's Trastevere section. This casual pursuit continues for a few more minutes as both men walk down Viale di Trastevere. When the man in the Levi's turns onto a side street, Mr. Borsalino watches from the corner as the object of his pursuit reaches the stairwell at one of the residences and descends. The man in the Borsalino waits a few minutes, then walks to the residence where he has seen the man in the Levi's open the brass-plated front gate and enter the building. The man turns his gaze to the address registry with the names of the occupants of the building and doorbell buttons beside the names. The man's eyes scan the list of names, seeming to stare at the registry for a long moment. From his POV, we see that all of the names are Italian except for one. That name is Greene. He looks at the name for nearly a minute before he looks up at the façade of the building for another long moment. Then he walks back up the street towards Viale di Trastevere.

MARCH 2004

ONE

REUNITED

I got it in my head to repaint my apartment. That was the easy part. Not so easy was the drive over to the Home Depot in a snowstorm that wasn't exactly blinding. It was more like clogging. Slow. Infuriating. People driving around in desperation, looking like they'd spent their lives in a closet, maybe with a sibling murdered in childhood. They have THE LOOK etched into their faces. This look says, "I take this snow seriously, but I take it personally, too. Why have I not found some productive or at least plausible life in a tropical location?"

Of course, this is one of those questions that has no answer. But constant questioning makes us feel better about ourselves, don't you think?

My last memory of interior house-painting: I am twelve years old. It is 1963.

My father and I were in the pre-stages of painting the living room of the ranch house from which we somehow avoided eviction despite notices and foreclosure warnings and threatening calls that eventually turned my father against all forms of personal communications, like it was the telephone's fault or the postal service's fault that we didn't have money for the mortgage payment. We had money for other things. Plenty of money. My father was a tradesman, but he worked so much overtime that we were as affluent as any executive's family was likely to be in 1963. We had enough money for a late-model car and a summer cottage near Caseville and three televisions (one color, two black-and-white) and a stereo and for carryout food every Friday night.

But we didn't have money for the mortgage payment because my father objected to mortgage payments. He refused to explain why he hated paying rent, although I once overheard him say to his brother-in-law, my Uncle Daryl, that all ownership of property was basically a legal fiction. To spare us from homelessness, my mother would walk the mortgage payment to the bank without my father knowing about it (this was actually common practice in that quaint era), until my father found out about this little subterfuge and expunged my mother from the checking account.

So, anyway, my dad and I were going to paint the living room eggshell white to cover the wall's previous neutral colors. We put bed sheets over all the furniture except for the TV, which was constantly on. White drop cloths covered the floor.

For some reason, I was not in school. For some even more inexplicable reason, my father was not at work, although this may have been one of those periods during his working life when he had opted to work midnights.

My father was superlatively proud of the precautions he took to prevent paint from reaching any surface it was not intended for. In addition to coverings, the entire room had been meticulously outlined in masking tape to prevent paint from getting on windows or moldings or the ceiling, doorframes or baseboards. It had taken us two days just to achieve this level of preparation and when it was done, the room looked like a miniature set for a movie about Antarctica—*Them* (the John Carpenter version) or maybe *Ice Station Zebra*. Before we began painting, my father took time to admire the aesthetics of his precautions. He was not a dainty man. He was big, and, well, slovenly doesn't do it. How about disheveled? He always looked like he had been caught in the middle of getting dressed. But I remember how dapper he looked on *this* particular day. Dad, ready to paint. Dressed all in white, his shirttails tucked away, an undersize virgin painter's hat on his head, something maybe Curly of The Three Stooges would wear. Not that my father was ever a stooge.

We had applied maybe half a dozen paint strokes when the news broke on TV about President Kennedy being shot.

Did I mention that my father worshipped John F. Kennedy?

He sat down on the covered couch with the paint roller in his hand, paint dripping to the drop cloth at his feet, and did not move (except to go to the bathroom) until Kennedy was buried. All he kept repeating was, "This has gotta be a joke," as though the president might pop back to life any minute, that Zapruder film might rewind. The room never did get painted. My father said that any activity interrupted by an event of that magnitude was not meant to be completed, an assertion I did not question until I realized a few years later that Kennedy's death had interrupted a great number of activities and not all of them had been suspended indefinitely. When you consider the range of human commotion underway at the instant those shots rang out, it's hard to imagine what kind of world we would inhabit if it had become The Day the Earth Stood Still. Think about it: bridges and roads were being built. Patients lay under surgeons' knives. People somewhere were having sex. Famous people, people who have since made great contributions to society, might never have been conceived. People, say, like George Clooney. He's probably about the right age.

So, at the Home Depot, I'm presented with my first challenge, if you don't count the drive to the store through the snowstorm. The new challenge has to do with color, as in, What color do I want to paint the various rooms of my apartment? I'm still in the neutral color mode that I've been in since time stopped four decades ago. But I'm here to tell you that interior decoration has moved on. Now, many of the same designers who create expensive sartorial fashion lines every year so that commentators at the Oscar Awards show will have something to say about the various celebrities attending—like the aforementioned George Clooney, no doubt—these same designers now have lines of interior house paint.

What genius came up with this idea? I have been in the homes of a few friends and acquaintances in my time and during these visits I never have had occasion to ask whether the paint on their walls was Ralph Lauren or Tommy Hilfiger. I intend to ask this the next time I'm in a house respectable enough to warrant it, but I haven't been in the homes of too many other people lately. I've been, uh, reclusive, for the past few years. More on that later. Maybe in the next chapter. It depends. But I promise I'll get to it. It's important. It's the reason I'm writing this book, actually. So, if I forget, just let me know. You can email me at fargo@gofuckyourself.com.

Speaking of computers, at the Home Depot the salesperson who was "working with me" was able to pull up on the computer all these examples of rooms that had been painted in colors concocted by all these famous fashion designers. "French Pink" was the color the salesperson, a perky brunette, tried to foist on me when I told her I was looking for something "off-white."

I wasn't falling for it.

"You know what would really be helpful?" I said. "If you would come to my apartment and kind of look things over. Make some recommendations." But *she* wasn't falling for *that.* She was attractive in a bubbly sort of way. She resembled a knock-off Dorothy Hamill. That same short brown, wedge haircut and those sparkling eyes. Actually, my tastes in women run to the less wholesome variety, but when you think about it, those Dorothy Hamill types have dark, secret lives, too. Maybe even darker and more secret than any number of, er, sluts, that I've been involved with, not including my former wives.

"I want something like an eggshell," I told her. "I'm very conservative that way." I think I added that last tidbit to reassure her somehow, to render myself less threatening.

She pondered for a moment, although, I couldn't imagine what there was to ponder about. By this time, my enthusiasm for repainting my apartment had pretty much dissipated. And by the time she finally came up with a few paint samples of eggshell variations (who'da thunk it?) I'd decided to abandon the project. Dorothy took it very well.

I wandered around the store and bought several items that I will never use. I bought a little device that you affix to your power drill to saw circular holes up to two-and-a-half inches in diameter. I bought some paraphernalia for hanging pictures on the wall. I also bought a power screwdriver. I couldn't remember the last time I had used a screwdriver, but the point-of-purchase display for this particular power screwdriver was so compelling that I couldn't imagine getting through the rest of my life without it. This is why it's dangerous for me to be in places like Home Depot. I'm a marketer's dream. I envisioned loading up on all sorts of things I would never use: leaf blowers and power sanders and miter boxes.

I sprinted to the checkout line, where the worst thing that could possibly happen happened. I ran into Someone I Knew.

I heard his voice first, asking the cashier about the price of an item he was buying. Unmistakable, a deep baritone that said "broadcaster" with every tonal modulation. It belonged to Barry Justice, a former news correspondent for one of Detroit's local TV stations. I'd known him casually back in the days when I had been a political consultant and he had been the station's Lansing bureau chief. He was a big, bearish man with an outsized personality to match his physical dimensions—a loud, profane, gregarious, mustachioed guy who fancied himself in the mold of Ernest Hemingway. A man's man. Big eater, big drinker. All of this, of course, was off the air.

He had left broadcasting in the early nineties—his style no longer fit the slick, hi-tech environment the news channel was trying to promote. I'd also heard he had landed a job as a corporate communications person, or perhaps a lobbyist, in private industry. But he still had that voice. I'd heard that he'd been a serious stage actor in an earlier career and had developed that voice over countless live performances of Shakespeare even before he'd gone over to the dark side of entertainment to do TV news.

I turned to sneak out of line, but a queue of customers had already formed behind me, and to make a break for it now would call more attention to myself than I wanted.

This would be a good time to tell you the first thing you should know about me:

I'm alive.

Of course, you're alive, you are no doubt thinking. But it's not that simple. See, I'm *presumed* dead. I arranged my own disappearance a few years ago by embarking on a solo sailing trip to Bermuda on a sailboat I had bought and learned to operate. It was extravagant, melodramatic, even. There are easier ways to fake one's death. It would have been especially easy for me because I have no close family or friends. I could have hopped a bus for somewhere and taken up a new identity and a new life in some galaxy far, far away

But I've had weird experiences of running into acquaintances in unlikely places. Once, I stopped for lunch at a combination bakery/restaurant run by Mennonites just outside of Artesia, Mississippi, and bumped into an old college professor of mine. His name was Chance Summers, a name more appropriate for a gunslinger or a utility baseball player. But what can you do? That was his name. He was an Elizabethan scholar I'd taken a class from. I was behind him, too, in line. And the first thing I heard was his stentorian voice as he corrected the unfortunate, bonneted Mennonite girl behind the counter asking him what kind of salad dressing he wanted.

"Italian?" she had said, repeating his order, pronouncing it "Eye-talian.

"Italian," he said, using the proper pronunciation. He was a relentless pedant.

He had not seemed nearly as surprised as I had about meeting in that place.

"There are a finite number of places in the world, Mr. Fargo," he had told me. I realized that. "Combine that fact with the dizzying array of conveyances available to us and it would be more unusual *not* to be running into people you know all the time, everywhere."

I'm not likely to run into Professor Summers anymore, though. He truly *is* dead, murdered by his jealous lover, a man named Derrick Means, who had been one of Summers' graduate students (he had also claimed, to anyone that would listen, that he was the illegitimate son of Neal Cassady).

Still, Summers was right about the possibility of running into almost anyone almost anywhere. This prompts a question: if I was so concerned with running into people I knew, why did I return to the same geographical area of the country—Detroit—where I had spent almost my entire life? And why go to a damn Home Depot on a whim? To buy paint that I was never really going to use?

I must have been giving off the stink of anxiety because Barry Justice abruptly turned around and looked me in the face. My eyes darted to everything else available in my field of vision except Justice, as if I could deflect his scrutiny by avoiding his eyes.

"I don't believe it," he said. "You're supposed to be dead." He said it with that voice, and the fifteen or so people in the immediate vicinity instantly turned their attention to me. I felt my face flush. Perspiration sprung from strategic areas of my body like a sprinkling system going off on a lawn.

"You must be mistaken," I said.

"About you being dead?" he said. "Well whose fault is that?"

The woman at the register gave him a credit card slip and a pen to sign, which he did with a flourish. Big B, Big J, almost obliterating the rest of his signature. He accepted the shopping bag from the woman and moved to the exit, where he waited for me.

I felt suddenly foolish with these ridiculous, incongruent purchases. Years of careful planning, ruined. My elaborate effort to disappear and achieve total obscurity and anonymity exploded by the impetuous notion that my apartment needed painting. I went through the transactional ritual with the checkout woman, forgetting to take my change until she reminded me, then almost walking off without my precious gadgets. Justice still hadn't gone anywhere. I was going to have to talk to him

"I gotta hear this story," he said when I was beside him at the exit. "I'll buy lunch."

This can't be happening, I thought. One moment I'm living in perfect seclusion, no one aware of my existence. The next, a former TV reporter, a man who numbered his media contacts in the thousands, was bullying me into lunch. Doing lunches with people like Justice was one of the reasons I had dropped out in the first place. Still, I couldn't just let him wander off on his own and start crowing to everyone he met that he had run into the late Stephen Fargo. That could suck me into a vortex of accusations and explanations—not to mention legal entanglements—that I would never be able to deal with. I would have to buy myself another boat and lose myself at sea all over again, for real this time.

I wondered if any of the implements I had just bought could be used to murder Barry Justice.

TWO

SNOWPRINTS

"This is, like, fortuitous," said Justice. We had finished lunch. I had tried to eat a Reuben sandwich, but my stomach was too jumpy to permit proper digestion and I'd only gotten through a couple of bites. Justice ate as though he had to keep Ernest Hemingway's reputation for his appetites alive, even forty years after the great man's death. Or maybe it was Elvis's reputation. He plowed through a huge steak and baked potato—we'd gone to Morton's, where no entrée on the menu weighed less than five pounds—as well as salad, soup, a carafe of wine and an Irish coffee with strawberry cheesecake to round things off. Had I eaten that much, I *would* have died. Seriously. My stomach would have become so distended that it would have compressed major arteries, stopping blood flow to the brain.

Justice did most of the talking, initially avoiding the topic of my "disappearance." He brought me up to speed on mutual acquaintances, talked about himself extensively, and held forth with various waiters and waitresses, bartenders, patrons and even the busboys in an almost uninterrupted monolog. He seemed to know everyone in the place and everyone knew—and deferred to—him. I was thinking I might get through this without having to explain myself.

"You had your reasons, right?" he said. He had lit some foul smelling cigar and was waving the smoke away from his face.

"Uh, yeah," was all I could come up with.

"Well, I don't need to know them," he said. "Like I said, our meeting like this is fortuitous. I believe that everything happens for a reason. How about you?"

I believe that things happen for no reason at all. If you start thinking that things happen for a reason, pretty soon you start wondering what those reasons are. And before you know it, you're looking for meaning in life. And I happen to know that there is no meaning to life.

"I believe in the chain of cause and effect going back to the Big Bang," I said.

"Right," said Justice. "Things happen for a reason."

"You're talking about our running into each other?"

"Correct," he said. He laid the cigar down on the saucer of his coffee cup. "Timing is everything."

How many clichés were we going to use?

"I need you to find someone for me," he said. "That's what you do, right? Find people?"

"There's been a lot of misunderstanding about that."

"I don't think so," said Justice. "I know about you. I was a member of the Fourth Estate, remember? I know about the Blessings and about that mess with Eric Crowe."

He was talking about my Adventures in Detective Land. The first had taken place when I had unearthed—literally—the secret of the great auto magnate Draper Blessing back in the early eighties. I had written a book about that experience called *The Blessing Cipher*, which had been made into a forgettable movie. But I had made quite a bit of money on the book and movie—enough to make me financially independent, although, just to keep my hand in, I dabbled in the world of politics as a consultant for a few years.

The second event Justice referred to involved my efforts to find the husband of the daughter of an old friend. This had led me to the criminal activities of Detroit talk show legend Eric Crowe, serial murder being at the top of the list of those activities. It also happened that the Eric Crowe thing was related to the Blessing thing. So, okay, maybe things do happen for a reason. But my embarking on a third great escapade to find someone wasn't going to happen, for a very good reason. I didn't want to do it.

"The misunderstanding," I told Justice, "is that finding people was something I did as a living or a vocation. Those were isolated incidents. I'm not a cop. Not a private investigator. I'm retired, in fact."

"That disappearance-at-sea trick was pretty neat," said Justice, ignoring my protests. "The reporter in me would really like to know how you pulled that off. You had to be working with someone, right?"

I said nothing.

"Well, anyway, that would be the reporter in me wanting to know that," he said. "I'm not a reporter anymore. I'm a corporate flack. So, I don't care how you pulled it off. I just know you had your reasons and you probably don't want people to know that you're back among the living. Am I right?"

Well, yes. He was right. But I was ambivalent about it. If I wasn't, why had I returned to the Detroit area? I was free to go anywhere. I had spent two years in the Bahamas, and three more in Rome.

But I had gotten homesick, if you can believe that. Homesick for the Motor City. For the past six months, I had been living under the name of

Stephen Greene in the apartment that I had decided to repaint. Was that whole thing a subconscious need for exposure? To be found out? Just as I had found out about Blessing and Crowe? Was my foray into the world of interior decoration a cry for help?

"I'm prepared to keep your secret," said Justice. "But only if you'll agree to help me."

"Help you what?" I said. No, it wasn't a cry for help. It was an unfortunate occurrence. I liked the fact that Stephen Fargo was dead. I liked my anonymity. I liked seclusion. I liked my freedom as Mr. Greene. Mr. Greene had a driver's license and a social security number and even a history. He had attended grade schools and high schools and had graduated from college and law school and had become a patent attorney in the bowels of corporate America and had taken early retirement. He had never married, never defaulted on loans or failed to pay taxes. As a fictional character, he was as innocuous as they come. He had lived the kind of boring life that had maybe been possible in the 1950s—maybe had even been aspired to in the 1950s—but which, today, would be almost impossible.

And that was a problem. Mr. Greene's life was so sanitized and low-profile that he stood out. It was something I had thought more frequently about, especially since returning to Detroit. I had taken the gutsy step of applying for a credit card, which the bank issuing the card couldn't send to me fast enough. I had also bought a computer and signed on with Yahoo!. I had an email address and I frequently surfed the Web, just like any other patriotic American. In these troubled times, the last thing I wanted to do was arouse suspicion because of my obscurity.

"Help me find someone, of course," said Justice, irritation in his voice. "My wife has disappeared."

"You sure she hasn't just left?" I asked, not too diplomatically.

"I'm telling you she's disappeared," said Justice.

"You know what I mean," I said. "It might not be a disappearance so much as a departure, if you know what *I'm* saying."

"Yeah, I know what you're saying. But it would be out of character. Lashona isn't the retiring type. Even if she was leaving me, which I don't believe, she would make a point of telling me why in specific detail for about an hour before she left."

Ah, I remembered now. Lashona Webber. She had been a reporter at the same station Justice had worked for. She had been a rising star, a beautiful, talented, intelligent and tenacious journalist who also happened to be African-American. She played well in Detroit, which was ninety percent or so black. I remembered that Justice had fallen hard for her. He'd left his wife and kids and had pursued Webber relentlessly. The affair scandalized the town for about a year, off and on, until the two eventually married and respectability set in.

Justice was right about Lashona Webber. She wasn't the retiring type. I had met her socially once or twice. She had serious presence. She had a one-thousand-watt smile and a way of talking to you like you were the only person in the room and all she wanted to do for the next three or four hours was listen to you ramble on about your pathetic life. She was tall and athletic—she bore a passing resemblance, in fact, to Venus Williams, but without Venus's hint of gangliness.

I was on the verge of asking Justice how long Lashona had been AWOL. I wanted to know, but I didn't want to ask. Asking that, or almost any other question, would invite Justice to assume that I was on the case. And I didn't want to be on this or any other case.

But Justice was way ahead of me.

"She's been gone for three days," he said. "And I've heard absolutely nothing." I offered the most tentative, noncommittal nod I could give. "And, yes," said Justice, "I've called everyone I could think of. Her family lives in Florida. A mother and an older brother in Bradenton." I studied the fingernails of my left hand. "She's got a few friends, none you would call close. I contacted all of them. None of them had a clue. They could have been lying to me, but I doubt it. They seemed to be as surprised as I was that she had disappeared. How come you're not asking any questions?"

"Because I don't want to get involved in this," I said.

"You're already involved," he countered. "I told you. If you don't help me, I'm going to tell some key people that I ran into you. I can make you the lead story on three local affiliates, Live at Five, today. I've still got friends in the business." I groaned. "On the positive side," he continued, "I'll pay you to find Lashona and I'll keep your little secret."

"The problem is," I said, "there won't be any secret if I start this. I'll have to talk to people, get in circulation. And given the circles Lashona traveled in, I'm not going to be able to maintain my anonymity for ten seconds."

Justice blew a couple of smoke rings, marveled at the integrity of their forms until they began to disperse. Then he replaced the cigar in the saucer and looked at me hard.

"I told you," he said. "I believe things happen for a reason. You and I running into each other like this right after Lashona's disappearance . . . it's like God is up there moving pieces around on a chessboard."

Oh, Jesus, I thought.

Justice continued: "Now, I'm appealing to your humanity here. Lashona could be in trouble. She could have been kidnapped. She is, after all, a highly visible public figure."

"Then why don't you go to the police?" I said. He didn't answer. "There haven't been any ransom demands, right? No contact from these alleged kidnappers. You don't think she's been kidnapped at all, do you?"

Justice picked up his cigar as if he was going to take another pull from it, then put the cigar back in the saucer.

"The day before she disappeared," he said, "I got home early. Lashona wasn't home, but, at that time of the day, she usually wouldn't be."

"What time of the day are we talking?" I said, realizing that, there, I had done it. I had asked The Question. It was all over. I had allowed myself to be sucked into this thing.

"About three-thirty," said Justice. "Lashona would be at the studio by then. Did I tell you she's now co-anchor at WEEE?"

"No," I said. "Please extend my congratulations when she shows up."

Justice grimaced. He took a drink of his coffee and used a napkin to wipe some of the coffee out of the ends of his mustache.

"I'm about ready to shave this thing off," he said.

"Gee," I said. "That would be a shame. It's kind of your trademark, isn't it?"

He shrugged. "It says too many of the wrong things in the corporate world."

I wondered what exactly those things were, but I didn't ask.

"As I was saying, the day before she disappeared, I got home early. It had just snowed. I was standing at the kitchen sink, having a rare drink of water. I looked out the window to our backyard, which stretches for about a hundred yards back to a wooded area. That's when I saw them." He stopped. He wasn't going to make this easy for me. I almost sighed.

"Okay," I said. "I'll bite. That's when you saw what?"

"Footprints," he said. "In the snow. Leading away from the house."

I thought about it for a moment, although there wasn't a lot to think about. Someone had left the house and walked towards the wooded area leaving footprints in the freshly fallen snow.

"So, they obviously weren't *your* footprints," I said, just to keep things moving. "And I'm assuming they weren't Lashona's, right?" He shook his head.

"Lashona ever take walks in the woods?" I continued.

"Not that I'm aware," said Justice. "She hated being out in the cold. She couldn't tolerate cold."

"Should I infer anything from your use of the past tense?" I said. A look of surprise came over his face.

"I didn't even realize," he said, awestruck by the betrayal of the tenses.

"Well, what if, just this once, Lashona *did* decide to take a walk? It's not totally out of the question, is it?"

"I guess not," said Justice. He scanned the nearly deserted restaurant, then spotted our waitress standing at the bar with another waitress, talking to the bartender. Justice got her attention with a big, sweeping arm gesture. When she got to the table, he ordered a Stoli straight up.

"You want one?" he said to me.

"Ah, I'll have a Bud," I said. I didn't feel like drinking, but I wanted to be sociable.

"Don't forget about us over here," Justice said to the waitress as she turned to retrieve our drink order. The tone was not jocular.

"Were you and Lashona having any problems?" I asked when the waitress was out of earshot.

"Have you ever lived with a big personality, Fargo?" he said.

"I thought *you* were a big personality," I said.

"Yeah, but I'm not high maintenance."

"Lashona was high maintenance?"

"Stratospherical," said Justice. "It's exhausting after a while. So, yeah, we had our little irritations. Lashona's got this hybrid Baptist-slash-Islamic religious thing going, so she didn't, *doesn't*, drink. There was a lot of friction about that."

"Let's get back to the footprints," I said. "They weren't yours and you're pretty sure they weren't Lashona's." He nodded. "So who does that leave?"

"I don't know," said Justice.

"Were they, like, adult footprints? I mean, could you tell that? Is it possible the paperboy or someone like that took a shortcut?"

Justice shook his head. "Nothing like that," he said. "They looked like adult footprints to me."

We were both dancing around the real issue here, the "I" word.

"Okay," I said. "Who do you think the footprints belong to? A secret lover, maybe?" I tried to make it sound light, to indicate that a secret lover was out of the question.

"That was my thought, too," said Justice. "But I tried to reconcile that idea with the pure concept of Lashona, and I can't make it work. I mean, why wouldn't this secret lover drive a car? I can't see some Lady Chatterley's Lover thing with Lashona. The fact is, she can get down when it comes to sex. She's no prude, her religious affiliations and devotional tendencies notwithstanding. But Lashona's fastidious to a fault. I can't see her slumming with some gardener."

I thought about this for a moment. Justice could have been right, but in my experience, men typically knew less about the sexual nature of their wives—their proclivities, including the potential for kinkiness—than they cared to admit. Or else they were just deluding themselves.

"Sticking with the secret lover theme for a moment," I said, rather diplomatically I thought, though I could see some irritation in Justice's expression, "is it possible this lover just made a quick getaway to avoid detection? It wouldn't be the first time a boyfriend on the side had to leave hastily by the back door."

"Don't get cute with me," said Justice. "I'm not saying Lashona wasn't fucking some guy. I just don't know. But she didn't have no backdoor man. If Lashona wanted to have an affair, she'd probably parade the guy right past me while I sat on the couch watching Sports Center. She might not be above infidelity, but she's above being ashamed of it. She didn't run off with some guy and not tell me about it. Not her style."

A man misunderstanding his wife's style fell under the same category as misunderstanding her sexual needs, in my opinion. But I let it pass.

"All right," I said. "So what else is there? Was your house burglarized? Anything valuable missing?"

Justice shook his head, then leaned back from the table as the waitress arrived with our drinks. Before she had even left, he had finished off the shot of vodka. I'd not had time to take the first sip of my beer.

"One more," he told the waitress. "And that's it." He smiled, his earlier irritation at her lack of attention all but departed. Jeez, I thought, talk about high maintenance. I tried to imagine what the ambience must have been like around the Justice/Webber household. Lots of tension in the air, I imagined. I took a long drink of my beer. It tasted good. Alcohol always tastes welcome in the company of fools.

"I guess we've come full circle back to the abduction scenario," I said. "Maybe someone was casing your home in preparation. But that seems risky, doesn't it? To be so obvious about it? Leaving your footprints in the snow like that? That seems careless for any self-respecting kidnapper." Justice shrugged. "You know, it's also possible that there's no connection between the footprints and Lashona's . . . ." I didn't want to say disappearance. That had too many negative connotations.

"Lashona's disappearance," said Justice.

I was out of ideas. This smelled of something that could drop me into some abyss of the warped psyche that I didn't want to enter, someplace where the drawings on the cave wall weren't something that I particularly wanted to discover.

"What have you told the station?" I said. "It must be disconcerting to them that their star anchor isn't showing up at six and eleven."

"You got *that* right," he said. "I told them that she got called to Florida suddenly to take care of her sick daughter. Station management wasn't happy about it, but luckily Lashona's daughter does have a legitimate health problem of some sort. I don't know really what it is, something mental. Maybe autism."

"You didn't mention a daughter," I said.

"Not too many people know about her," said Justice. "Lashona had the kid when she was fifteen or sixteen. Lashona's thirty-two, so that would make the kid about sixteen or seventeen. She lives with Lashona's mother and brother. Lashona doesn't talk about her much. I've never met her. As far as I can tell, the kid's never been out here to visit her mother. Her name is Venetia. I wouldn't say Lashona was ashamed of her, per se, but Venetia doesn't fit in with Lashona's image. And the truth is, she's not the maternal type. Still, it's not as if she outright abandoned the kid. She keeps in touch with her mother, follows Venetia's progress, although I don't think there's been a lot of progress to keep up with."

"What about the father?" I asked. Justice made a dismissive gesture with his hand.

"Out of the picture. Some gangbanger. We're not talking about a love affair for the ages, here. The guy's probably dead or in jail."

The waitress returned with Justice's "last" shot of vodka. This time he didn't drink it right down. Instead, he played with the glass. Something was on his mind.

"There's one more issue," he said. "It's sort of a timing thing, as in bad timing." He continued turning the glass in his hand.

"A timing thing?" I said. He nodded.

"We took out an insurance policy on Lashona about a month ago. Five million."

I nodded. His reluctance to involve the police made more sense. My God, I thought, whatever possessed me to walk out of my apartment this morning to look for off-white paint? How could such an innocuous impulse warrant such cruel punishment? Things happen for a reason, my ass.

"I'm guessing you didn't take out a policy on yourself at the same time," I said. Justice shook his head.

"There wasn't much point. Lashona's the one who makes all the money. Problem is, she spends it as fast as she makes it. How come the Baptists and the Muslims don't have prohibitions against shopping? Shopping ruins more marriages than alcohol and infidelity combined." He wasn't smiling, so I didn't allow myself to chuckle. "Of course, I help her spend it," he said.

"You must make a pretty good salary," I said. "I remember how much money those lobbyists make."

"I don't make nearly as much as I need," said Justice. "They basically hired me for my marquee value, and that was not all that high to begin with. They don't really give me much to do and they pay me accordingly."

"So, the idea behind the insurance policy was . . . what?"

"To provide for Venetia, mainly," said Justice. "But, as Lashona's husband, I would be the executor until such time as Venetia gained some level of competence that would allow her to take over the trust fund, which is not likely to ever happen, or until Venetia died."

"Don't take this the wrong way," I said, "but why make you the executor? Why not a family member?"

"First, I *am* her husband," said Justice, somewhat defensively. "Second, her mother's got her own health problems. She's got emphysema. Walks around all day hooked up to an oxygen tank. Still smokes, too. And as far as her brother is concerned, Lashona doesn't trust him." Justice shrugged. "I met him a couple of years ago when we visited her mother. Know what we did?" I couldn't imagine. "We took her and her oxygen bottle to the fucking dog races and sat there for a couple of hours while she made bad bets and smoked cigarettes and sucked on her bottle. The old woman sleeps with a rifle. No shit. She inherited it from her father. Apparently, her grandfather was lynched somewhere down south and his son bought a gun, swearing never to allow himself to suffer the same fate. He handed the gun down to Lashona's mother." Justice paused to mull that over. Then he abruptly shifted gears. "Tell you what, I don't see what all the fuss is about when it comes to dog races. You ever been to the dog races?"

I told him that I hadn't.

"Don't go," he said. "Horse racing, that I can see. That's exciting. But you can't win enough money to make a dog race worth watching. That's where I met Desmond, Lashona's brother. He didn't seem like too bad a guy to me, except that I could never figure out what he did for a living, unless his mother paid him to push her around in her wheelchair and make sure she stayed stocked up with oxygen bottles. The way Lashona explained it, he was into something like Amway sales, some multilevel swindle or other. She was ashamed of him. I don't think she thought he was living up to his potential. I think he was also involved in some disability litigation relating to Gulf War Syndrome. He was over there. Got gassed or whatever it was that happened to those guys. I guess the major point here is that the guy's a loser and Lashona didn't want to put him in charge of five million dollars to watch over it for her daughter. He could probably run through that money faster than one of those Greyhounds could do a lap around the track."

"Well, just how much do you stand to gain here?" I said. "I mean if Lashona dies."

He looked at me as if I didn't know a dog race from a monster truck show.

"Five million," he said. "Haven't you been paying attention?" I almost told him that it hadn't been real clear, but I figured, what's the use. "But it just looks bad, is all. The timing of the thing. I mean, there is no way in the world I would harm Lashona. I love her. She's high-strung and exasperating, but I love her very much."

I believed him, not that it made any difference.

"Barry, you don't need me for this," I said. "You need the fucking CIA. I don't have the resources, not to mention the interest, to take this on. It wouldn't be fair to you. I really think you need to go to the police right now and tell them everything. The longer you wait, the harder it's gonna be to find Lashona. And if the police do learn that she's disappeared and you knew about it and said and did nothing, how do you think that's gonna look to them? I'll tell you. It's gonna look like you had a good reason not to tell them."

Now Justice *did* polish off his drink, after which he slammed the glass down on the table.

"We've already covered this," he said. "I can't go to the police. I'm not going to the police. I don't even like police. I don't trust police. And, believe me, Lashona had no use for them either, and vice-versa. You remember that scandal a few years ago when the police chief got canned? Lashona helped break that story, and she was always on their case about police brutality. She was the investigative reporter on that recent case about the Detroit cop who's shot about a dozen citizens, you know, the one they keep trying to fire."

I gave Justice a helpless look.

"Oh, that's right," he said. "You've been dead for a couple of years. Well, lucky you."

I should have stayed dead, I thought.

"Okay," I said. "Where do you suggest I begin?"

"If I knew that, I would have done it myself," he said. I pondered that for a moment, looking out the window. Except for a few flurries, the snow had subsided, but it had been one of those Detroit snowfalls that dumped about eight inches in two hours. Cars were barely negotiating the parking lot outside. Just in front of the restaurant, three tow trucks were working the lot. I had about a ten-mile drive back to my apartment and I would be lucky to make the trip in less than an hour and a half.

"I guess I could take a look at the house," I said. Justice didn't seem to know at first what house I was talking about. Then he got it.

"Oh, yeah, sure. No problem. Whenever you want."

"But I want to do it alone," I said. "I don't want you around. If I have any questions, I'll call you."

"Sure," he said again. And again, "No problem." But he didn't seem real genuine a bout it.

THREE

RECERCHE DE LA FEMME PERDU

Okay, things happen for a reason. But that doesn't mean that the reasons are good. This encounter with Barry Justice, for example. This was *not* a reward. If this was a karmic episode, it was more on the punishment side of the ledger. He had threatened my exposure if I didn't help him. But, really, who was I kidding? I was threatening my own exposure by coming back to Michigan. Was it possible that I really wanted to be exposed, to be revealed as the fraudulent dead man that I was? Did I secretly want to merge once again into the stream of life, humbled by my own deception, scorned for my lack of resolution, people disappointed in me because I wasn't dead?

Barry Justice lived in Bloomfield Hills, one of the more affluent neighborhoods on the planet. In the days before the collapse of the American auto industry, it's where many of Detroit's robber baron auto execs lived, and where many still do. CEO country.

Compared to other homes in the area, the Justice/Webber abode was a modest affair. We're talking houses with six-car garages and horse stables and tennis courts—homes where the rooms could have different zip codes. Barry and Lashona had opted for a smallish, four-bedroom colonial that, in a different community, would have cost a third of what they had likely paid for it. The home had no more than half the floor space of the two homes it stood between. Still, it was a big house.

Inside, it had a distinct non-lived-in look and feel to it. It was tastefully, if sparsely, furnished and not much was out of place, which was typical of a home only infrequently inhabited by two busy professionals. The absence of children was obvious. The absence of pets was obvious. The absence of microbes was obvious. There weren't even any houseplants. The place was not hospitable to sentient life.

So, it went without saying that visitors made rare appearances, indeed. Except for the mystery guest who had left the tracks in the snow a few days earlier, I was probably the first visitor to set foot in the house for weeks.

Justice had insisted that I go to his house immediately after our lunch. He probably figured that if he gave me time to think about it, I would once again slip back into that obscure mausoleum that had become my existence, and he'd never hear from me again. He'd asked for my telephone number, which I at first refused to give him, until he started again with his not-so-veiled threats about exposing me to the world for the fraud that I was. As I've already suggested, this threat was losing its potency, but I caved anyway and we exchanged cell phone numbers. I had promised to call him later that evening. Justice claimed that he was heading back to work after our lunch, but I didn't see it happening. He had put away a good deal of alcohol, and, besides, he probably didn't have any work to speak of to go back to. I know all about how those corporate communications jobs work. And in Justice's case, since his position was largely ceremonial, he no doubt had less to do than most corporate flacks.

I'd chosen to visit the Justice/Webber residence first because, well, I didn't know how else to proceed. I thought I could get a sense of the couple's domestic lives, pick up some vibes that would propel me in some direction as I sought to discover Lashona Webber's whereabouts—or fate. Not that I expected to find physical evidence. We are not talking Mr. CSI here. I've never won a game of Clue, a game I despise, by the way. You can tell a lot about people by the kind of board games they like. I like to play computer chess alone at home against imaginary opponents. So there.

But I wasn't picking up too many vibes. This place was like an exhibit at Epcot, maybe the Spaceship Earth ride, minus the crowds. I passed quietly through the *Architectural Digest* living room and den. The bookcase lining one wall of the den was full of books, all right, maybe even books that human beings had once read. There were hardcover copies of John Grisham and Tom Clancy novels, that kind of fare. Half of the bookcase was taken up with DVDs. Lots of action/adventure movies. No chick flicks, unless you count the first Terminator movie, which, I guess, some chicks would. I didn't think Barry and Lashona spent a lot of time cuddled up on the couch here watching movies.

So, I was learning something after all. Maybe this marriage wasn't the fairy tale—despite the scandal, the passionate courtship, the hasty nuptials—that the media had portrayed it. Or maybe all that had cooled off soon after the marriage. I mean, it usually takes about thirty seconds, right? Or maybe Lashona really did like action/adventure movies—Arnold and Bruce and Jean-Claude and Steven rampaging across her field of vision during her down time.

Predictably, the kitchen looked as if nothing had ever been cooked in it. I couldn't detect the slightest residual odor of food preparation. The only sign of life, a bowl of fruit, sat in the middle of the island counter. I squeezed one of the oranges. It seemed fresh, as did the apples and bananas. Had Justice called ahead after I'd left the restaurant to have someone plant the fruit there? See, this is the twisted way my mind works.

I moved upstairs to the bedrooms, hoping to find actual artifacts of habitation. One of the rooms had been converted into an office, with a computer, phone, fax, printer and such on a large desk. I hit a key on the computer keyboard, but the screen didn't jump to life. A three-day-old copy of *The Detroit News* lay next to the mouse pad with an ABC television network logo on it. I tried to remember if the local station Lashona worked for was the ABC affiliate, but I hadn't paid much attention in the past few years. I had been dead, after all, although not as dead as local news. It looked as if someone had put the newspaper there for effect, the kind of touch you would see at a museum display. I started getting the creepy feeling that the entire house was non-functional, that if I started flipping switches or punching buttons or twisting dials that lights would not illuminate, no whirring, humming, rattling, buzzing or clanking would take place. Almost panicking, I hit the light switch on the desk lamp. It ruined the whole Twilight Zone effect by lighting up instantly. God, it was scary what I could talk myself into.

Two of the other bedrooms appeared to be guest rooms. Their closets held no clothes, their bathrooms were devoid of the usual bathroom essentials. I continued my Goldilocks tour to the master bedroom and was relieved to find that it, at least, had a lived-in look to it. Someone had made a half-hearted attempt to straighten up the covers on the king-size bed and a white terrycloth robe lay on it. The tag on the robe's collar read XXL. Justice's, obviously. I saw no other haphazardly strewn clothing.

The master bedroom had two closets; one was a huge walk-in affair that rivaled in size the two guest bedrooms. Lashona's closet. Even given its cavernous capacity, she had managed to fill it. Forty or fifty business suits hung from racks, along with various slacks, blouses, skirts, evening gowns and sweaters in a dizzying array of colors. One of the walls was a shoe rack. Lashona had a long way to go to be serious competition for Emelda Marcos, but she was working on it. By my quick calculation, more than one hundred pairs of shoes occupied the wall. I'm sorry. I don't care what your station in life is, if you have more than one hundred pairs of shoes, you need to get some help.

It seemed clear that Lashona hadn't packed much before leaving. I opened a few drawers on one wall. These held various undergarments, stockings, workout attire, bathing suits and nightgowns. Some of the underwear was the naughty stuff—Victoria's Secret and Frederick's of Hollywood items—thong panties and other things that looked too insubstantial to be serviceable. I was starting to veer into voyeurism territory. I pushed the drawer shut, took another look around the closet, and stepped out.

Justice's closet was more modest—cramped by comparison. He, too, had quite a few business suits. He also had lots of shoes, only a fraction of what his wife owned, but, again, more than he needed. A clothes hamper stood at the back of the closet with a few items in it, but my particular form of voyeurism didn't extend to examining the dirty laundry of middle-aged men.

In the master bath, I saw indications of recent human activity. The sink contained old soapy water with black and gray whisker hairs floating in it. A disposable razor lay on the counter next to a can of shaving gel, the cap of which had not been replaced. Towels were strewn about various surfaces. All this casual havoc was male in origin. I could see nothing to indicate that a female had used the master bath recently. I went quickly through the drawers of the vanity and the linen closet. I found some of what were surely Lashona's personal items, which told me nothing more than what her closet had told me—that she had, indeed, shared this home with Barry Justice. Duh!

Well, I couldn't leave without the obligatory ransacking of the medicine cabinet. And here's where things got a little more interesting. The Justice/Webber household was a major consumer of prescription meds. Some of them I recognized—being a lay connoisseur of pharmaceuticals—mostly the pain medications and the anti-depressants. Oh, and the Xanax and the Valium. Lashona Webber's name was on all of these. There were four or five heavy-duty painkillers, including Percocet, Vicodin, and Demerol. This was the kind of stuff you would find in the medicine cabinet of an ex-football player, not in that of a beautiful local news co-anchor. The prescribing doctor's name on the label of the antidepressants and painkillers was Robert Astrachan. I took out a pen and a small pad of paper I had taken from my glove compartment for just this purpose and wrote down the name. I thought of helping myself to a few of the painkillers—maybe just one from each vial. I just love those things. Doesn't everybody? But I resisted the urge.

I also found a few vials with Barry Justice's name on them. They were mainly for physical ailments, as far as I could tell. Inderal, probably for high blood pressure. Lipitor for high cholesterol, I thought. Nitroglycerin for angina. Like I said, I know prescription drugs.

So, Mr. Justice had some serious heart problems and here he was eating like a twenty-year-old and smoking and drinking like a condemned man. In the back of the bottom shelf, I found an unopened package of birth control pills. Do women travel without their birth control pills? I didn't think so.

I was getting a clearer picture of domestic life in the Justice/Webber household. Amazing what a little pharmacological research will reveal. The picture was one of a marriage perhaps strained by drug abuse and depression, perhaps exacerbated by the risky behavior of one of the partners in the marriage whose health was already compromised. Justice was committing slow suicide and Lashona was agonizing over it.

Or . . . Lashona was already drug dependent before she met Justice. Was her mental health unstable enough for her to just book? End up wandering around the streets of a strange city asking Kenneth for the frequency?

Possibly, and especially if she'd suddenly gone off her meds or had suffered some psychological trauma that had undermined her already fragile psyche. Jesus! Listen to me . . . psychoanalyzing this woman, this marriage, based on the contents of a medicine cabinet that probably didn't differ much from what would be found in the bathrooms of three-quarters of the population of the United States.

I had been in the Justice/Webber residence for almost an hour, and I had probably seen basically what Barry had wanted me to see: that the disappearance of his wife was mysterious, indeed. I did a quick tour of the rest of the house. Nothing indicated a struggle. The last place I looked in was the garage. It contained one vehicle—Lashona's, no doubt—a silver Cadillac Escalade. It was so large that it looked like Lashona would need a stepladder to get into it. What was it about women and cars like this? I owned an SUV myself, a Jeep. So I knew the attraction from a male point of view, but Jeeps weren't exactly elegant. Maybe it was a power thing.

The car's interior smelled new. I went through the console and found the window sticker, which, along with carrying an obscene manufacturers suggested retail price, also confirmed that the car had been delivered only a couple of weeks earlier. This was supported by the fact that the car was almost antiseptically clean. Besides the owner's manual and proof of insurance slips, the only other thing I could find was a sheet of paper that had the same ABC logo as the mouse pad in the office and the words "From the desk of Lashona Webber" printed at the bottom. On the sheet of paper, someone had written the name "Bob" and a local telephone number. I pulled out my pad and pen and wrote this information down, wondering if "Bob" referred to Dr. Robert Astrachan. I, myself, have never called any physician with whom I had a doctor-patient relationship by his or her first name, but that was just me.

I got out of the car and did a quick walk around the vehicle. No scratches or dents to indicate that someone might have tried to run the car off the road. Now, if you were leaving your husband in the aftermath of some domestic squabble, you might abandon your clothes temporarily, but why would you not take your brand spanking new SUV? Was it possible Lashona thought her husband would try to track her down through her car? Give the police her license number? That would indicate a dynamic in this relationship that I hadn't considered. Did the fact that Justice likely hadn't taken these steps, that he wanted to keep the police out of it, in fact, indicate that he had been abusing Lashona? It didn't seem likely. For all his exterior Hemingwayesque, he-man persona, I had never gotten the sense that he was a violent man. I'd never heard any stories about brawling, no complaints from former wives. And, given the fact that at one time he had enjoyed celebrity status in this city, that kind of thing would inevitably have gotten out. And Lashona, from what I knew of her, was no pushover. She had grown up in tough neighborhoods, she had clawed her way to the top of one of the most competitive fields there was, and she projected a sense of confidence and power that would have been hard to fake. Would she take any crap from a guy like Justice? I didn't think so.

But, then, I wouldn't have thought she was a candidate for Zoloft, either. You never know what goes on in people's private lives. It was possible that Mr. Hail-Fellow-Well-Met was beating Ms. Ball Breaker in the Corner Office like a rented mule every night.

I wasn't dressed for it, but I decided to take a walk around the outside of the house anyway. The fresh snowfall had left a good six inches of snow on the ground and the snow removal service that Barry and Lashona undoubtedly employed had not yet made its way to the house. I was wearing running shoes, and, halfway around the house, my feet were already freezing. Around the back of the house, I saw the expansive back yard. It looked as smooth as the icing on a sheet cake. At the far back edge of the yard, I could see a line of trees. I saw no man-made structures, no indication of vehicular traffic. I wondered, probably just as Justice had, what anyone could be attempting to reach by walking in that direction. I was tempted to just start walking toward the trees to find out, but, like I said, I wasn't dressed for it. The snow was deep and, well, I just don't like to be cold. I wished I had questioned Justice a little more closely on the area's geography.

I trudged back up to the front of the house. I had parked my car in the driveway, thinking that the city snow removal crew would arrive at any moment to plow the streets. They hadn't arrived yet, but a kid who looked to be about sixteen was using a snow blower on the sidewalk of the residence adjacent to the Justice/Webber house. I walked over to him and pantomimed my way through a greeting and an indication that I wanted to ask him a question.

The kid shut down the snow blower and that unique, right-after-the-heavy-snowfall silence re-asserted itself. I introduced myself as a friend of Barry Justice, using my Stephen Greene identity. The young man's name was Stephen—or Steven—as well.

He thought it was "cool" that we were both named Steve.

"I was named after Stevie Yzerman," he said. "You probably weren't, right?" I assured him that I *wasn't* named after Steve Yzerman, not withstanding my admiration for the captain of the Detroit Red Wings. I explained to Steve that Mr. Justice had asked me to give him an estimate on some interior decorating. The kid seemed totally unimpressed with this information.

"I was just admiring the layout here," I continued. "What's behind the wooded area out back?" The kid shrugged.

"Not much," he said. "About a hundred yards more to the right is the golf course. The rest is just mainly woods until you get to Lahser Road." Of course, Bloomfield Hills Country Club. That's what would be back there. But there would be little reason to walk there in winter.

"Do kids play back there in the winter time?" I asked. "Any ponds for playing hockey, that kind of thing?"

He looked at me funny. "Outside?" he said. He didn't say, "Are you nuts you fucking Neanderthal you?" but he didn't have to. The expression on his face said that. This kid had grown up in the modern era of indoor ice rinks and four a.m. hockey practices. The idea of playing hockey on a frozen pond, outdoors, would be foreign to him. I was about to drop it when he spoke up again.

"Some people cross-country ski back there. You know, on the golf course." I thought about it for a second. Then I thanked Steve and turned to walk back to the rear of the house. I heard him pull the starter rope on the snow blower and it fired up.

Cold or not, I decided to retrace the mysterious footprints that Justice had seen a few days before. Of course, it would only be an approximation, since the new snow had buried any trace of the old tracks. I started from the rear entrance and made my way towards the trees. My toes were numb halfway there and by the time I got to the tree line, I was starting to think about frostbite. I looked back at my trail and was surprised to find that I had not exactly walked a straight line to my current position. Close, but not straight. I made my way through the trees until I reached a clearing. To the right, about a hundred yards off, I could see the softly rolling, snow-covered landscape indicating the golf course.

Since my feet were already frozen, I proceeded to walk the rest of the way to the boundary of the course. I remembered playing this course once back in the early nineties when I worked as a political consultant. But I couldn't remember anything about its layout or the circumstances of our round. I couldn't even remember who my host was or who I played with. I know people who can remember every stroke of every round of golf they've ever played. I think that's an amazing talent, but I usually can't remember what I had for breakfast. I usually don't want to remember. To me, memories are highly overrated.

As I stood there pondering these deep thoughts and wondering how many toes I might lose to frostbite, I caught movement to my left. I turned and saw a woman on skis making her way towards me. She wore black tights like runners wear outdoors in winter. She also wore one of those quilted parka vests with no arms over a white turtleneck. She had a red ski cap and red gloves. She also had wraparound sunglasses. She was very styling.

I waved vigorously to get her attention. At first I thought she was going to ski right past me, but at the last moment she veered in my direction. She stopped about five feet from me and took off her sunglasses.

"Hi," she said, flashing me a smile. Close up, I saw an attractive woman with high cheekbones and dimpled cheeks. Her face had taken on a ruddy hue from the wind and cold, except for where the sunglasses had protected her eyes. She pulled off her gloves, then removed her hat to reveal short, dark hair. She shook her head vigorously, then put her hat back on. I noticed that her earrings were tiny earth globes. I'm not kidding. Tiny turquoise spheres with little green continents and white polar regions.

"Sorry to interrupt you," I said.

"No problem," she said. "I'm grateful for the break." I had the feeling she was indulging me because she thought I might be a local resident, a neighbor.

"I was wondering about the cross-country skiing," I said. She was still smiling, but she tilted her head a bit as if she was having trouble following me. Then a strange look came over her face and I thought she was about to say something. I almost thought she blushed, but it was hard to tell. Had I caught her breaking some law, trespassing or something?

"I mean, skiing on the course," I continued. "Do you have to be a member?"

She laughed.

"I hope not," she said, regaining her poise. "I'm not one. I've got better things to do with a hundred and fifty thousand dollars or so." She was pulling her gloves back on.

"So, anybody can ski the course?" I asked. She gave me a strained look.

"Not really," she said. "I think they just turn a blind eye to it, to the few of us who live nearby and ski the course. Officially, it's probably forbidden." Then, after a pause, "Do you live in the area?"

"No," I said. "I'm just looking." She gave me a look I couldn't interpret, somewhat disapproving, maybe impish.

"Well, have a nice day," she said. Her eyes narrowed again as she looked at me. Then she put on her sunglasses.

"Wait," I said. She stopped and smiled again. "You live around here then?"

"Yes," she said. I paused for an instant, wondering just how deep into this I wanted to get.

"I'm thinking of buying a home in the area," I said. She was still smiling, although she was smart enough not to encourage me beyond that.

"You'll love it," was all she said.

"Well, that's what my real estate agent says," I told her. "But I'd sure like to talk to someone who lives in the area, you know, to get the inside skinny on the neighborhood."

"I think you should talk to your agent," she said. "I'm sure he or she can recommend a local resident you can talk to." She gripped her ski poles and pushed off, shuffling smoothly across the new snow. She had excellent quads and superb gluts.

I could have persisted, but it would have been at the expense of my feet, which, I imagined, were turning black right about now. I took one last look at the retreating figure of the female cross-country skier and turned to make my way back to the Justice house.

While I was looking at the house, I suddenly saw the blinds in one of the upstairs rooms—I guessed it was the master bedroom—close. Someone was in the house. My first thought was that it had to be Barry Justice. The possibility that it was Lashona Webber was too much to hope for. That would mean I was done with this bullshit and could return to my life of obscurity. Yet, my heart sank a little when I thought that. The life of a recluse wasn't all it was cracked up to be and maybe my foray to the Home Depot *had* been a cry for help, after all. Here I was in my mid fifties, still healthy, still in good shape (assuming they could save my feet), relatively well off financially, though certainly not rich, and I had virtually no idea what to do with myself from one minute to the next. Ah, sweet freedom, you might be thinking to yourself. But it's a burden, too. You tend to fall into apathy, you know? Not much really impacts you on a day-to-day level because you're not engaged. Life starts to imitate art, so that, in this case, the contrivance of my death was being parodied by my day-to-day life. So, in some small way, I was hoping that Lashona wasn't home.

I reached the house and once again let myself in with the key Justice had given me. I stomped the snow off my running shoes and tried to move my toes within them. I stopped and listened for sounds of another occupant in the house.

"Hello," I said, giving the greeting a carefree, musical sound. No answer. I walked to the foot of the stairs in the foyer and looked up the staircase that led to the bedrooms.

"Barry?" I said. "You up there?" Again, no response. "Lashona?" I wondered if I had been seeing things with the movement of the blinds. Or, since it had taken me thirty or forty seconds to cover the distance from the golf course to the house, maybe whoever had been in the house had left. Or fled. Or maybe it was simply a matter of someone being in the bathroom where he or she couldn't hear me.

I started up the stairs, not loudly, but not tiptoeing either. At the second floor, I paused and again called out for Barry or Lashona. And again, my calls were met with a thundering silence. I walked into the master bedroom. The room was empty and at first glance I could see no signs that anyone had been in the room. I saw that the window blinds were, indeed, closed. Had they been closed before? See, this is why I don't belong in the private detective business. I'm not a trained observer and I don't have gobs of talent for it. I mean, when you can't even remember whether the blinds were open or closed—

My eye caught something. A glitter on the hardwood floor beneath the window. At first I thought it was a piece of glass, but as I stooped to touch it, I realized it was a small lump of snow. It was melting fast, and, now that I was down there on the floor, I could see a few other small puddles. Whoever had left the snow couldn't have departed more than a minute earlier.

Or maybe they hadn't left at all.

My heart was pounding and a bead of sweat ran down my back. So, why aren't my feet getting any warmer, I wondered. I walked softly to the master bath. It was empty as well, and I saw no evidence of a snow trail in there. I did a quick tour of the other bedrooms, but to no avail. Whoever had been upstairs was either downstairs now, or they had managed to get out of the house without my seeing them. I was pretty sure it was the latter.

I retreated down the stairs and did a quick walk through the rooms of the lower floor, then through the basement and the garage. Everything looked as it had before. As I walked back into the foyer, my cell phone rang.

"Hello," I said. I was greeted by the voice of Barry Justice.

"So?" he said. "Anything to report?"

"Uh, actually, I'm still at the house, Barry." I looked through the pane of glass in the front door to the porch and walkway beyond. I saw footprints, mine, of course, but it was hard to tell if someone else's were there as well.

"That doesn't mean you don't have something to report."

"Nothing yet," I said. After all, what I knew—the drugs, the evidence of a less than blissful marriage—he knew that better than I. It hit me that maybe Barry's call was a ploy. Maybe it had been him in the house, spying on me, and this call was just to throw me off.

"Where are you?" I asked.

"I'm at work," he said. "Where did you think I was?"

"I don't know," I said. "Don't get so touchy. It was just a casual question. Look, if you're going to call on the hour to ask about my progress, this just isn't going to work."

"Okay, okay. It's just like I was telling you. There's some urgency involved."

"I understand," I said. "You can always hire someone who can do this job quicker."

"Nice try, Fargo," said Justice. "But you're my man. I'll try to restrain myself." He sounded like he was about to hang up.

"Hey, Barry," I said. "Who else has a key to your home?" A few seconds of silence.

"Other than you, all I can think of is the cleaning service."

"You mean, like a maid?"

"No, I mean like a cleaning service, a crew. They come once a week, Friday, I think. Lashona hired them. I don't know who they are."

"Not even a name?"

"No. I can get it for you, though. Lashona writes them a check once a month. They'll be in her check register. Wait, what am I thinking of? It's right there in the top drawer of the desk in the upstairs office."

"Lashona's checkbook?"

"Well, it's actually a joint account, but she wrote the checks for all the bills. You know me, I'm strictly a cash man." I remembered that he *had* paid the lunch tab with a hundred dollar bill.

"Okay," I said. "I'll look at it."

"Why do you ask?" he said.

I didn't want to get into the episode of the apparition at the bedroom window. First, it was possible that I had not seen what I thought I had seen. Not likely, but possible. Second, I didn't want to set Barry off. Telling him what I had seen might build up in him an expectation that the phantom I had seen was Lashona. I saw no reason to give him that kind of hope at the moment.

"I was wondering if someone you had given a key to could account for the footprints you found. You know, someone doing work on the house or a service guy. A realtor, maybe."

"Why would I give a realtor my key?" said Justice. "We weren't planning on selling. Are you fucking with me?" Justice was likely slipping into late afternoon hangover mode, and in my experience, that phase of the drinking cycle made for a bad mood.

"No," I said. "I'm just throwing out examples of other people who might have extra keys to the house. Like, you know, sometimes people give family members keys so they can watch the house when the occupants are out of town." A brief silence ensued. "Barry?"

"Yeah, I'm here. I'm thinking." He paused for a few more seconds. "No. Nobody else had a key. Just the cleaning people."

"Right," I said. "I'll look at the check register, maybe give them a call just to touch that base, see if they might have seen anything unusual."

"Fine," said Justice, apparently over his little snit. "Look, just keep me informed, okay?"

"You got it, Barry," I said. He hung up without saying goodbye.

The checkbook register was right where he said it would be. That seemed convenient, but maybe I was just being paranoid. When I had been married I never would have been able to tell you where my wife's checkbook was. In the case of my first wife, it was because she didn't trust me to have that information. In the case of my second wife, I trusted her so completely that I didn't care where the checkbook was. My first wife divorced me. My second wife died as a result of a freak accident. Go figure. At the present time, I didn't have a checking account or a wife. Before I had faked my death, I had liquidated everything and put most of the cash in a safety deposit box and had taken the rest with me on my "voyage." I had since gotten a credit card using my alias, but no checking account. I reasoned that opening a checking account would put me too much at risk of exposure. Don't ask me why. A man who fakes his own death doesn't have reasoning skills of the first water.

I leafed through the check register, at first hoping to find the name of the cleaning service. But it was like looking up a word in the dictionary. You get so distracted by so many other words, that you forget the word you originally intended to look up. So, as I was looking for the name of the cleaning service, I was paying more attention to the other check payments. Lots of them were routine. Checks to the mortgage company for the house payment. And a hefty one it was, too. More than twelve-thousand per month. It would have brought my father to his knees. I saw entries for utilities, phone charges, cable bills and car loans; checks to American Express and to other credit card companies. There were several stubs for Desmond Webber. Finally, I came across an entry for Stellar Cleaning Services. These seemed to have been paid on a monthly basis, as Justice had indicated, so I assumed it was the service that cleaned the Justice/Webber residence. I made a note of the name.

I took one last look around the house, then left by the side door. I sat in my car for a few minutes, waiting for it to heat up. From outside, the Justice/Webber home looked normal, I mean if you consider a house worth a few million dollars covering about ten thousand square feet in one of the ritziest neighborhoods in North America normal. It was a quiet neighborhood, or maybe it was the heavy blanket of snow that made it seem that way. Somewhere, I heard the drone of a snowblower motor.

A snowplow had cleared the street, pushing a huge berm of snow across the driveway behind me. I looked both ways down the street, dropped the car into reverse, then floored it, blasting through the snow berm and into the street. These are the kind of cheap thrills my life has come down to. But if you're going to own an SUV, you have to pull these guerrilla vehicular maneuvers every once in a while to justify your choice of transportation. I drove the rest of the way home like I was leading a funeral.

FOUR

MAUDE GONNE LIVES!

Barry Justice called at eight o'clock the next morning.

"I wanted to call you last night," he said. "I thought I would hear from you by now." He almost sounded hurt.

"Look, Barry," I said. "We've been over this. The way this works is that I call you when I have something significant to tell you, some major development. Or if I need to ask you a question. I'm not going to give you a play-by-play. If you want that, I suggest you hire someone else for this."

"Once again, nice try," he said. I could almost see him jauntily poofing out a smoke ring.

"So, I'm assuming you still haven't heard anything from Lashona," I said, hoping against hope.

"Niente," said Justice. "So, what's your next step?"

"I haven't decided yet. Maybe I haven't made myself clear. You're going to have to quit interrogating me on the process. I don't exactly work according to an agenda. I go a lot on instinct. By the way, you mentioned yesterday about paying me, but I don't recall that we discussed the specifics of that."

The other end of the line was as dead as potted meat.

"You do recall that, right?"

"Sure," said Justice. "Just send your invoices. Whatever your rate is is fine with me. My priority is finding Lashona." How noble.

"Keep in mind," I said, "that the meter's running every time we talk."

"Okay, Fargo. I get the point. Just keep me informed, okay? I've got a lot of balls to keep in the air on this. The faster we can make some progress, the more comfortable I'm going to feel."

By "balls in the air" I assumed he was talking about queries from the TV station concerning Lashona's status and the need to keep the police at bay.

"I forgot to leave your key," I said. "All right if I just slip it in your mailbox?"

"Whatever," said Justice. Then he hung up.

After dropping off the key, I pulled into the Starbuck's parking lot not too far from Barry's house. Inside, I ordered a regular coffee from the freckle-faced young woman behind the counter and sat down at a table by the window. A few minutes later I saw a Jaguar the color of a cabernet wine pull into the spot next to my Jeep and a woman with a familiar face emerged from the car. It was the babe I had seen cross-country skiing the day before when I had been out reconnoitering the woods behind Justice's home.

She wore form-fitting jeans and a brown leather bomber jacket and she looked great. She had that blue-black hair that shimmered in the sunlight and flawless olive skin. She wasn't wearing makeup, but I don't think she needed any. She pushed through the door and walked right by without appearing to notice me. I didn't turn to look at her, but I heard her conversing with the girl behind the counter.

Finally, I couldn't resist. I turned in my chair and looked up to the counter. She was standing there looking back at me as she waited for her coffee. When I met her eyes, she smiled. I smiled back and lifted my head a bit in greeting. The girl came back to the counter with her coffee and the woman dug into the front pocket of her jeans for money. I turned to look out the window again.

"Any luck with the house-hunting?" She was standing next to my table now, coffee in hand.

"Uh, no," I said. "Not yet."

"You know, people who live around here, maybe you don't know this, but they don't typically advertise that they have a home for sale."

"Is that right?" I said.

"Yeah," she said. "It's like beneath them to put a for-sale sign on the front lawn, you know?"

"Do they think the wrong element might inquire about their house?" I asked. "There would go the neighborhood?"

"Something like that," she said, smiling. "But your realtor should know that."

"Right," I said. "Well, the fact is, I'm not really working with a realtor." She raised an eyebrow. "I can explain."

"I can't wait to hear it," she said.

"If you'd care to join me, I'll tell you all about it." She hesitated for a moment and looked at her watch.

"I only have a few moments," she said. "But since it looks like we could be neighbors . . . ." She put her coffee down and pulled out the chair across from me.

Suddenly, I wondered what the hell I was doing. Her comment had reminded me that "neighborly" was the last thing I wanted to be. Any conversation we were about to have would be nothing but lies and evasions on my part and could lead to absolutely nothing. Hell, this woman could be married, for all I knew, although I didn't see a ring. Then the old paranoia began to creep into my soul again. How convenient was it, after all, that we had both just walked into the same coffee shop at ten-forty-five on a weekday morning? How coincidental was it, come to think of it now, that she had been out skiing yesterday when I had been snooping around the neighborhood? Well, okay, neither incident by itself was significant. But to run into each other two days in a row? And for her to nonchalantly accept my offer join me at my table? It was probably all totally innocent, except that I didn't believe in innocence any more than I believed things happened for a reason.

"Maud Gonne," she said, offering her hand. I shook it.

"You're kidding, right?" I said.

"About what?"

"About being Maud Gonne."

"No," she said. "But, then, only one in a thousand people I meet even know that there was an historical Maud Gonne, so I usually don't have to explain."

"What do you do that you meet that many people?" I asked.

"I own an art gallery. In Birmingham. One in a thousand is probably an exaggeration. How about one in five hundred?"

"Who's counting?" I said. I took a drink of my coffee.

"I didn't catch *your* name," she said. I hadn't thrown it at her.

"Stephen Greene," I said.

"Stephen Greene, huh?" she said. I didn't like the way she said it. A chill ran through me.

"Yes," I said. "Greene with an 'E.'"

"So, Mr. Greene with an 'E', how is it that you happen to know about Maud Gonne?"

"I was an English major in college," I told her. "And I used to teach English literature. Uh, in high school. In California." Please, please, please don't ask which high school in California.

"But you don't teach anymore, right?"

"Not for years," I replied. "Decades, in fact."

She peeled the plastic top off her coffee cup and took a careful sip.

"Well, I didn't have a clue who Maud Gonne was until I married a man named Conor Gonne. I was named Maud for my grandmother. I hated the name all through childhood. It sounded so, well, grandmotherly. Then I married Conor and people started telling me that Maud Gonne was this famous Irish woman. I was a business major, myself, so I knew like nothing about literature. I didn't want to know anything about literature. I never got it when it came to literature, although I'm a voracious reader now." She gave me a look that revived the chilly sensation I'd had a few minutes earlier.

"And you run an art gallery," I said, desperate to change the subject.

"Yes."

"What kind of art?"

"Mostly modern," she said. "But we're pretty eclectic."

"So, like impressionists and cubists—stuff like that?"

"Some of that, yes." She blew on her coffee and took another sip. "So, are you really looking for a home in this area, or are you just casing out particular homes?"

I laughed at this. It was one of the more inauthentic laughs you'll ever hear.

"I'm looking," I said. "I just thought I'd do some research at ground level before I committed to the neighborhood. I didn't want to rely on the party line regarding the area." She gave me a penetrating look, but didn't say anything for a few seconds.

"These are very private people," she said finally. "They have a lot of money. New money, mainly. We're talking mostly self-made men who've ascended the corporate ladders. In addition to being rich, they're very sensitive about their privacy. They're mainly a bunch of untalented bureaucrats who've gotten lucky. You know, latched on to the right corporate patrons, ingratiated themselves with the right boards of directors. I know the breed. I used to be married to one."

"Would that be the aforementioned Mr. Gonne?"

"It would," she said. I found all this to be profoundly revealing coming from someone I had just formally met three minutes earlier.

"I guess I'm not sure what you're telling me," I said.

She leaned closer to me. "This is an exclusive neighborhood, Mr. Greene. A discriminating neighborhood. Quite frankly, you don't look like you would fit in."

Well, I was taken aback by this. And what about the use of that word "discriminating?" Was I supposed to read that as code?

"You don't know anything about me," I said, with what I considered the appropriate level of indignation. She smiled and sat back in her chair. She took another sip of her coffee without taking her eyes off me. I felt the corner of my left eye begin to twitch.

"I know your name isn't Greene with an 'E,'" she said.

I didn't know what to say, but I think my expression must have revealed my shock or trepidation, or whatever it was.

"If you're about to protest, forget it. And don't worry. I'm not a cop or a lawyer. I'm an art dealer."

"Right," I said. "Maud Gonne, art gallery owner." I had not planned my exit strategy well, here. I might not have looked like I was squirming, but I sure felt like it inside. Suddenly, she threw her head back and laughed. A genuine laugh.

"I'm sorry," she said. "This is just so unbelievable." She laughed again.

"What is?" I said.

"You're not Stephen Greene. You're Stephen Fargo," she said.

FIVE

THE CALL

There was triumph in her voice. The coffee churned in my stomach. Any second, I expected it to erupt back up my throat. Had someone placed a "Hello, I'm Stephen Fargo. Expose me" sign on my back?

"Well, you don't have to answer," she said, leaning forward. "I know you are. I knew it when I saw you yesterday."

"So, what, you've been following me?"

"No," she said, surprised. "You mean, follow you here?"

"You recognize me yesterday and you just happen to run into me today in this coffee shop?"

"I come to this coffee shop every weekday between ten-thirty and ten-forty-five," she said. "I grab a cup of coffee on the way to the gallery, which I open at eleven a.m. Ask Ashley." She nodded towards the girl behind the counter. She sounded convincing.

"So why didn't you mention that you knew who I was yesterday?" I said.

"I don't know," she said. "I guess I was a little bit shocked. Maybe I wasn't completely sure. I thought you were dead. And, like I was saying, around here you respect other people's privacy. I've lived here almost ten years and I've been thoroughly conditioned."

I thought about this, trying to recollect our encounter of the previous day. Had I missed some sign of recognition in her face or voice yesterday? I could recall nothing.

"So, I'm fascinated," she continued. "What are you doing around here? Have you been here all along? Why pretend to be dead?"

"Am I going to be expected to answer those questions in order?" I said, trying to lighten the moment. The moment probably didn't feel particularly heavy to Ms. Gonne, but I was experiencing some serious compression.

"Sorry," she said. "I just got carried away."

"Don't worry about it," I said. The jig was probably up anyway. Two days, two recognitions. This was unbelievable. Maud Gonne sipped her coffee and looked at me expectantly. "I'm not sure I know what to say," I said. "This is a little embarrassing."

"Don't be embarrassed," she said, putting her hand on my wrist. "I think it's exciting. I won't tell anybody if you don't want me to. I'm a big fan."

A big fan?

"How did you recognize me?" I asked her. "I'm not exactly a celebrity."

"Oh, I've followed your career forever," she said.

That was interesting. I hadn't really had much of a career since the mid 80s. The way she was looking at me seemed to indicate that I was supposed to be flattered.

"So, you read the book and saw the movie, right?"

"Oh, well of course. And I also read the one by Claude Nickle."

Claude Nickle was a writer I'd met in Italy during the Blessing affair. After my "death" he'd published my original version of *The Blessing Cipher*, which I had called *Our Father*, before the editors had gotten their cannibalistic mandibles into it. I remembered reading about the book's publication. But, being dead at the time, I was in no position to comment on it publicly. Believe me, the book did not approach bestseller status.

So, what was this creature sitting before me? A thirty-five-year-old groupie? If so, she was part of a very select group.

"I just don't know what to say," I said.

"Yes, you've already said that."

Was the writer/investigator/adventurer hero already diminishing in her eyes in the face of the sobering reality that I was a middle-aged white guy with not much to say who had not even been able to die correctly?

"So let's talk about me," she said. That was fine with me. "Guess where I grew up?" she said. I didn't have a clue.

"Bloomfield Hills," I said, not even stopping to realize that she had just told me moments before that she had only lived here for ten years. She shut her eyes and slowly shook her head. I think my answer disappointed her.

"Grosse Pointe, silly," she said. She said "silly," but I could hear some serious reprimand in her voice. "Now, guess *where* in Grosse Pointe."

I hate these guessing games. I have debilitating performance anxiety.

"I just don't know," I said.

"Across the street from the Blessing house," she said.

Well, I thought, *somebody* had to live across the street from the Blessings. When I didn't go into shock at this disclosure, Maud Gonne seemed a little disappointed. She was right about her name, by the way. Every time I thought of her name, the Bea Arthur character from the old seventies sitcom jumped into my head. It really was an unfortunate name for such a fetching lady.

"So," I said, "you knew the Blessings?" She shook her head.

"*Nobody* knew the Blessings," she replied. "Not in any kind of neighborly way. Everybody knew *about* them, of course. Especially after your book and the movie came out. But they were secretive, for reasons that you know better than I. I was twelve years old when all that stuff happened. To me, the Blessings were just some mysterious old couple that the neighborhood kids made fun of."

I nodded. But I couldn't think of much to say. As profound an effect as the Blessings incident had had on me—I had found the love of my life during that time—it was still ancient history. I'd been trying to get past all that for more than twenty years.

Maud looked at her watch.

"I've got to get to the gallery," she said. She gave me a look that I took to be apologetic. "Folks aren't exactly breaking down the door to get in, but I've got this obsession with being on time. Like, you know, the one day I'm not on time, the gallery is going to burn down or get robbed." She smiled.

"That's pretty severe," I said, lame as usual.

"Why don't you stop in sometime?" she said. She stood up and smoothed the front of her jeans by sliding her palms down them. It was a gratuitous gesture. Her jeans fit like shrink-wrap. Then she picked up her coffee cup. Definitely no wedding ring.

"Sure," I said. "I'll do that." She stood motionless for a moment.

"Do you want to know where the gallery is?" she said.

I shrugged. "Downtown Birmingham isn't that big," I said. "I'm sure I can find it."

"Why do I get the feeling I'm not going to see you walking through the gallery door?" she said. Then, before I could answer, she said: "As a teenager, I was fascinated with Denise Raccette. I used to fantasize about her."

Denise Raccette was my deceased wife, the woman I had met during the Blessing episode. She had died a few years earlier after falling during a sightseeing tour we'd been on in Sedona, Arizona. I'd had a number of people comment to me over the years about various aspects of the Blessing experience, but no one had ever expressed such sentiments about Denise.

"I'm not talking about anything sexual," said Maud Gonne, interrupting my thoughts. "I just liked her so much when I read your book that I wanted to be like her." She looked at her watch again. She wanted to leave, but I got the feeling that she also didn't want to let me out of her sight.

"I could be free for lunch today," she said. "That is, of course, if you've got nothing going on." She gave me a dazzling smile. She was trying real hard, and, while I found it flattering, it also bothered me. My paranoia always ran just below the surface.

To give myself something to do, I took a drink of my coffee. It was growing cold.

"I'm actually in the middle of something right now," I said.

"Oh," she said, stepping back awkwardly, as if I had just told her I had the ebola virus. She smiled again.

"Well, it was very nice talking to you," she said.

"Same here," I told her.

When she had gone, I took my coffee cup to the waste receptacle and dropped it in. Then I went to the counter and ordered another coffee to go.

When I got outside, I found a business card under my car's driver-side windshield wiper. I wondered how she knew the Jeep was mine, until I realized it was the only car parked in front of the coffee shop now that she had left. The card read: "The Birmingham Gallery, Maud Gonne, owner and proprietor." The card also had the address and telephone number of the gallery. Below these, written in purple ink, was another telephone number, presumably Maud Gonne's home or cell phone number.

I'm not the ugliest guy in the world, but rarely do women come on to me. Especially since I passed the age of fifty. Especially after I died. There was something about Maud Gonne's urgency that was unsettling. I had an impulse to throw the card away, but I stuck it in my wallet. I had every intention of returning to the life of Stephen Greene, retired gentleman. Lashona Webber would show up, or my lack of progress would frustrate Barry to the point that he would seek help elsewhere. And Maud Gonne? Well, I could just chalk that up to a bizarre coincidence. She didn't know where I lived. If she wanted to tell someone she had run into the famous Stephen Fargo (which would mean nothing to most people), let her. Hey, it would be just like all those Elvis sightings. I was still safe. I could still return to being dead. Cool. I was starting to feel better. Things were going to work out after all.

I got into my car, cleared some space for my coffee cup and pulled out of the parking lot, looking forward to returning to my apartment, even with its dreary walls.

My cell phone rang and I froze. The caller ID told me that the call was from out of the area, whatever that meant. I let the phone ring until it stopped. I watched for the little envelope to pop up on the screen indicating that I had a voice mail message, but it didn't happen. I started out of the parking lot, and my cell phone rang again. This time, the caller ID read "Barry Justice."

Once again, I was tempted not to pick it up. But I didn't want Justice getting squirrelly on me without my knowing about it. I hit the talk button.

"Yeah, Barry," I said. "What's up?"

"Mr. Justice is indisposed," said a male voice I didn't recognize. "Is this Mr. Fargo?"

"Who wants to know?" I asked.

"I have some information about Lashona Weber," said the voice, ignoring my question.

"Well, I'm sure Mr. Justice will want to know about it," I said. "Why don't you tell him?"

"I told you," said the voice. "Mr. Justice is indisposed."

"Okay, so tell him when he's not indisposed," I said. I heard a chuckle on the other end.

"He's indisposed forever," said the voice.

SIX

CHOP, CHOP

"Justice is dead?" I said. "Is that what you're telling me?"

"Justice, chivalry, God, all those cherished concepts. All dead."

"I mean *Barry* Justice," I said. "What did you mean when you said that he was permanently indisposed?"

"Did I say that?" said the voice.

I pushed the "end call" button, then threw the cell phone into the passenger seat. Then I started retracing my route back to the Justice residence. The phone rang again almost immediately. The caller ID screen once again read "Barry Justice." I grabbed the phone and hit the "talk" button.

"We must have been cut off," said the voice.

"Put Justice on the phone," I said.

"Tell me, Mr. Fargo, are your fingerprints on record with any law enforcement agency?" Needless to say, I didn't like the sound of any of this. "And I'm assuming you didn't *walk* to Mr. Justice's house. Perhaps one of the neighbors saw your car. Perhaps you even spoke to one of the area residents." I thought of the kid next door whom I had interrupted in his snowblowing the day before. Then there was Maud Gonne. "Maybe one of those residents even got a license number. I understand they have a very robust neighborhood watch program in this area."

Neither of us said anything for thirty seconds. Then I heard the voice again, almost as if the speaker was musing to himself.

"Of course, the fingerprints would be the real problem. I guess you could drive back over to the Justice house and wipe down everything you touched. But the police might already be there. That could be awkward." I started thinking about what in the house I had touched, realizing that I would never have time to wipe everything down, even if I could remember everything I had touched.

"Who is this?" I said.

"This is the voice of reason," the voice responded. "I think you've gotten yourself into something you'd be better off ignoring. I could take the time and effort to try to find you, Mr. Fargo, but I'd rather come to an understanding with you."

"What kind of understanding?"

"You disappear, forget about whatever business you had with Justice. And I'll see to it that your name doesn't come up in the matter of his, his, well, death."

"Did you kill him?" I asked.

"It doesn't make any difference who killed him," said the voice, almost soothing in tone. "What's important is who the police *think* killed him."

I had reached Justice's subdivision. I turned slowly onto his street and looked for cars. It was not a neighborhood where residents parked in the street. Anyone parked in the street would likely be visiting.

"Don't let the absence of police cars give you false sense of security," said my buddy on the phone. "Just because you don't see them now doesn't mean they won't be there any second."

Whomever I was talking to must have been able to see me right at that moment, perhaps had been tracking me somehow, maybe since I had been at the house earlier that morning.

"Hmmm," said the voice. "Now here's a discrepancy. Mr. Justice had entered your name in his cell phone as Stephen Fargo, but I see that your car is registered to Mr. Stephen Greene. I'm sure you didn't steal that vehicle. Did you borrow it, perhaps?"

I didn't say anything. As I rolled past the Justice house, I could see Barry's dark blue Cadillac Seville in the driveway. I saw no other vehicles. Maybe he'd come home for an early liquid lunch. I heard a chuckle.

"I just remembered where I heard your name," said the voice. I almost groaned. "You wrote the book, right? But I heard you were dead. Some accident."

"You must be thinking of someone else," I said.

"Maybe," said the voice. "As I recall, the Stephen Fargo I'm thinking of had a bad habit of poking his nose into other people's business. Some kind of private investigator, I think."

"That isn't me," I said, maybe a little too quickly. A pause on the other end.

"All right, kitty cat," said the voice, finally. I should have hung up right there. I should have driven to my apartment to pick up—to pick up what? There was nothing that I had to have. I should have gotten on the freeway and started driving. They would never have found me. But I didn't do any of that. Instead, I did something a lot worse. I asked a question.

"So," I said. "Who am I talking to?" A heavy sigh on the other end.

"I'm very disappointed in you, Mr. Fargo, or Mr. Greene, if you prefer." I was disappointed in *myself*. "Why would you want to know that?"

I, of course, had no good response. I pushed the "end" button, then held it down to shut off the phone. I wanted to hang around to see who emerged from the Justice house, but I couldn't just park across the street and sit there until someone came out. I would be far too conspicuous. I drove on slowly to the end of the block, where I stopped at the intersection. Still no movement, no activity around the Justice house. I considered calling the police, but I wasn't sure what I would tell them. And I also remembered what the guy on the phone had said about my fingerprints being all over the Justice residence. No, the police, for the time being, were out of the question. I then considered driving back to the Justice residence and knocking on the front door, just to see who would answer. Whoever was there would be a fool to shoot me there on the front porch, assuming whoever was in the house meant to do me harm. But even if he didn't shoot me, I would clearly be signaling my intention to "stick my nose in." And that was sure to piss him off enough to look for less public ways of disposing of me. I turned left onto Lahser Road, then left once again when I got to Long Lake Road. Within a few seconds, I was rolling up the driveway of the Bloomfield Hills Country Club.

The parking lot had more cars in it than I had expected. It was probably getting near lunch time, but I thought country clubs usually closed down for the winter. Yet, notwithstanding the snow, we were actually late into March. In fact, officially, it was springtime, a concept you could never quite grasp if you came from Michigan, where spring actually began sometime in mid-June—if you were lucky. Ask anyone who's ever been to an Opening Day at the old Tiger Stadium.

I parked my Jeep between a couple of luxury numbers and got out. I saw no one—no security guards, no friendly cross-country skiers. Certainly no golfers.

My feet still ached a bit from my previous day's trek through the snow, and I was no better prepared today. We hadn't gotten any more snow. If fact, it had heated up to the mid forties, and a lot of the stuff was melting. But snow still covered the golf course.

Well, I couldn't stand there forever. I walked past the clubhouse and towards what I assumed was the first hole. I tried to walk purposefully, like I actually had some business out there in my lightweight green windbreaker with the white Michigan State Sparty logo and my running shoes. Like I hadn't just escaped from one of those homes in the middle of residential areas where they try to mainstream severely retarded alcoholics who had faked their own suicide/death.

I made my way towards the Long Lake side of what might have been a fairway. Who could tell? About two hundred yards out, I cut diagonally toward the area where I guessed I had been standing the day before when I met Maud Gonne out there skiing. Yes. Hmmm.

Why had she been out there skiing? Why hadn't she been at the art gallery, where, she had insisted, she arrived every day at 11:00 a.m.? It must have been the middle of the afternoon when I had run into her. Who had been minding the store?

My paranoia about Ms. Gonne returned, compounded by this new development of the mystery threat at Justice's house. Were Maud and the voice on the phone working together? How plausible was it, after all, that I had met someone who was actually named Maud Gonne? I had come back to life for *this*? I decided that right after this current little errand of mine, I was going to pay Ms. Gonne a visit at her gallery after all.

I continued walking parallel to the property line of the course for another hundred yards or so, until I reached the area where I had encountered Maud Gonne the day before, which I determined by the tracks from her skis. I took a quick look around, saw no one, and started walking toward the Justice/Webber residence. I followed the tracks made by my running shoes the day before back to the grounds of the Justice house, where I halted to consider my next move. I was going to be awfully exposed just walking across the backyard to the house. If took that approach, I would have to hope that whoever might still be in the house, other than Justice, that is, wouldn't happen to look out the window. I didn't think the guy was a complete idiot. Don't ask me why. Something in his voice, maybe. He would anticipate this stealth maneuver. So, why didn't I think of that when I was back in my warm car?

The Justice residence was separated from its neighbor to the north by a rough line of pine trees. It wouldn't provide complete concealment, but it was the only cover available. And it wasn't bad.

I walked over to the pine trees and started towards the house next door to Justice's. I half expected to hear the report of small arms fire as I hustled along the tree line, and by the time I got to the house, sweat was dripping from my chin in spite of the chilly temperature. I paused at the corner of the house and looked over to the Justice residence. Everything seemed peaceful, normal, just as I had seen it when I had dropped off the key earlier that morning. I tried to detect any movement behind the windows, but I was unable to do so. What to do, what to do?

Finally, heaving caution to whatever wind there was, I sprinted across the common area between the two dwellings, arriving at the garage door of the Justice residence.

I tried the walk-in door to the garage, which opened like it had been waiting for me. Inside, Lashona's SUV stood where it had been parked the day before. I walked to the door that led to the house. Again, no problem with any locks. I tried to remember if these doors had been locked the day before, but in my preoccupation with the search of the house, I hadn't paid much attention to whether the door to the garage had been locked. Another problem with being dead: you don't pay as much attention as when you're alive.

I had the sickening thought that whoever might be waiting for me inside had just unlocked all the doors to facilitate an ambush. But my leaving at that point would have been bad form. I took a deep breath, blew it out slowly. Then I pushed the door.

It creaked—and I didn't remember a creak from the day before, either—and I continued pushing until it met with resistance from the wall. I could see through the kitchen to the dining room. There was no sign of Justice, no blood that I could see.

I walked slowly across the hardwood floor through the kitchen and into the dining room. At first, everything seemed okay. I took in the periphery quickly. Nobody seemed to be lurking in the shadows, no stiffs lying on the floor.

Then I noticed something that *was* different. A covered skillet sat incongruously on top of the highly polished cherrywood dinner table. It was one of those weird, ornate tables with intricate pearl inlay detailing along the sides and carved elves for legs. A very heavy table for a very heavy eater. You could fit a spit-roasted boar nicely in the middle of it with plenty of room to spare. But, you get it—the skillet just didn't belong. Of course, somebody had put it there just so I would take the cover off. This thought occurred to me, unfortunately, after I took it off, although, I must say, that something told me not to remove that lid. But did I pay attention to that small inner voice, that oracle of good sense that all of us know and should heed?

I did not. I lifted the lid and, for a second, I didn't recognize what I was looking at. Then I sort of gasped-gagged and dropped the lid clanging to the floor. In the skillet was a human penis and a pair of what it took me a minute to realize were testicles, swimming in a sauce of blood and who knew what other kind of vile fluid.

Surprisingly, I neither puked nor fainted. The display in front of me was almost beyond revolting. It was more like fascinating. You don't see those things detached very often. I did feel a little weak in my own groin area, the kind of feeling you get—or at least I get—in the testicles when looking down from a great height. But give me some credit. I didn't blow chunks.

Instead, indulging my fascination for a moment, I walked around the table, observing the gory sight from all angles. I made no move to touch the skillet. They didn't make tongs long enough for that. Once I had satisfied myself that I was, indeed, looking at a man's, er, package, I started to think about its former owner.

Jesus! Barry Justice. My first uncharitable thought was, there goes the voice. Forget returning to broadcasting.

Forget returning to anything, I knew in my heart.

Justice wasn't far away. Whoever had done this to him had propped him up in the La-Z-Boy in the den. He still had his shirt and tie on, although the shirt, reaching to mid-thigh, was stained with blood at his midsection. His pants had been pulled down to his ankles. Blood from his groin area had pooled on the leather seat of the chair and, now, I *was* beginning to feel ill.

The phone rang suddenly—loudly—and I let it ring six or seven times, until it stopped. A few seconds later, I heard Justice's cell phone ring. At first, I couldn't make out the phone's location, but then I realized it was in the pocket of his overcoat, hanging from the back of one of the chairs in the kitchen. I walked back to the kitchen, tried not to look at that skillet, and dug Justice's cell phone out of his coat pocket. The caller ID read "pay phone." I let it ring until it stopped, but it only stopped for a few seconds, then started up again.

I pushed the talk button, but didn't say anything.

"Hey, Fargo," said a now-familiar voice. "I knew you wouldn't be able to keep your nose out of it." I remained silent. I didn't want to speak. I didn't know what to say. "Hey, Fargo," the voice repeated. "I know what you're wondering." A pause. "Before or after, right?"

"Before or after what?" I said, immediately wishing I hadn't.

"You're wondering if the equipment was removed before or after he died, right?"

I hadn't been wondering that, but I started to now.

"Well, it was before," said the voice. "I mean, I don't go in for mutilation of corpses and all that. Those fucking guys, those necrophiliacs, they're sick. I'm not interested in fucking with dead people." He paused again. "Are you catching my drift, Fargo? What I'm trying to tell you is, I'm so happy you're once again back in the land of the living."

SEVEN

WHO CARES?

I had to regroup. Obviously, the thing for me to do, now that events had gotten completely out of hand, was to bring the police in on this. If Justice had taken my advice and done that, he wouldn't be sitting there now, like some grotesque couch potato in a pool of his own blood, neutralized, in more ways than one. But I sure didn't want to call the police. Truthfully, I just didn't want to get into the narrative of my life over the past two days. And I didn't want to have to explain my faked death and reappearance, because, frankly, I didn't understand it myself. Meanwhile, I sat there with the late Barry Justice as his body, most of it anyway, progressed to rigor mortis.

I had known one former police officer I could trust. Retired Detective Jules Lazard of the Detroit Police Department. He had been involved during the Blessing case and to a lesser extent, during that business with Eric Crowe. But I didn't even know if Lazard was still alive. I certainly didn't have his phone number with me and, besides, I know what his advice would be: call the police.

Jesus! The police. What the hell was I thinking? They might materialize at any minute. The voice on the phone had indicated that he had tipped the police off to the carnage at the Justice residence. I had to get out of there.

I considered wiping down everything I could remember having touched, but decided against it. I pocketed Justice's cell phone. I would get rid of it someplace else.

I made my way out of the house the same way I had entered. When I got to the garage door, I peeked out, saw nobody, then retraced my steps through the snow to the tree line and, from there, to the golf course, across the snow-covered fairways and back to my car. I started the Jeep and slowly drove out of the parking lot and onto Long Lake Road. I was tempted to do one more drive-by past the Justice residence, but I decided that would be pushing my luck. I wondered if my apartment was safe. The voice on the phone had somehow learned that my car was registered to my Stephen Greene alias.

How had he managed *that* so quickly? Did he have some kind of inside track to the Secretary of State's office, or the Department of Motor Vehicles, or whoever it was that had that kind of information? And if the ease with which the owner of the voice had discovered my new identity was any indication, I had to believe that he had also discovered my address. He might even be there now, waiting for me. He didn't sound like he had the most innocent of intentions regarding me when he had ended our last phone conversation with that cryptic statement about being happy I was alive—so he could, what, have the pleasure of killing me? Still, he could have already done that had he wanted to. He could have killed me at the Justice residence, I realized, only then understanding how foolish my last visit there had been. So, why didn't he?

Well, first, because I was no threat. I didn't have the slightest idea who the guy was, nor did I have a clue as to his motive for killing Justice, especially in such a gruesome fashion, although one would have to think there was some element of revenge or retribution involved. What a weird thing. Cut off a man's genitals and put them in a skillet. Why a skillet? Was this some disturbing Hannibal Lecter scenario? Somehow, I couldn't even imagine old Hannibal munching on sautéed . . . Well, maybe that was the closest receptacle at hand.

I drove south down Woodward Avenue, trying to make sense of all this. First (at least as far as I could tell, it was the initial event in the sequence), Justice's wife, Lashona Webber, a popular and highly visible local TV news co-anchor disappears amid curious circumstances. Justice encounters me in the Home Depot and presses me into service to help him locate his wife by threatening to go public with the hoax about my death at sea a few years earlier. I snoop around, meet a gorgeous art gallery owner out cross-country skiing when she should be hawking Chagalls, or whatever hangs on the walls of her place. Then, less than twenty-four hours after I run into Justice, he is castrated and murdered by someone who knows who I am and threatens my life. Just another fun-packed day in the lives of Stephen Fargo/Greene.

Thinking about Maud Gonne gave me an idea. I got into the right-hand lane for Old Woodward and downtown Birmingham. The Detroit suburb of Birmingham is normally a place where I wouldn't be caught dead, if you'll pardon the little play on words. It's full of overpriced real estate, pretentious boutique shops, snobbish inhabitants and wannabes. I suppose every large metropolitan area has its own version of Birmingham. It's sort of a second rate Beverly Hills. The place doesn't have enough integrity to be bohemian, not enough class to be Georgetown, not enough character to be Soho. I guess the best thing you could say about Birmingham, especially downtown Birmingham, was that it was stylish, which, of course, meant nothing to me. However, downtown Birmingham was where Maud Gonne's art gallery was. So that's where I had to go.

The day had heated up considerably. It had to be approaching sixty degrees and the snow was melting at such an accelerated pace that you could see steam rising from the mounds that had been plowed up against the curbs. It was so warm, in fact, that joggers, which Birmingham has in a supply of disproportionately high numbers, were running through the streets in shorts, T-shirts and sports bras. It's the irrational way that Michiganders respond to warm weather in spring, even those whom experience had taught that tomorrow it could once again snow knee-deep and the temperature could plummet by forty degrees.

I spotted Maud Gonne's gallery on the east side of Old Woodward, the main drag in downtown Birmingham. Of course, there was nowhere to park nearby. There never is. I turned off on one of the side streets and parked in a structure several blocks from the gallery.

I sat in the car and considered how to approach Maud on this thing. Since I didn't completely trust her, I didn't want to just come out and spill the beans about Justice. On the other hand, I didn't want to arouse her suspicions by pumping her for information without a good rationale. As I sat there, the unavoidable idea began to emerge in my feeble brain that Maud Gonne might be the only ally I had in the world. That is, if she wasn't allied with the enemy.

I got out of my car and walked down the stairs of the parking structure to the street level.

As soon as I hit the street, I knew he was there.

Parking was not allowed on this particular street, but down about a hundred feet and stopped on the other side was a sleek black car, something foreign, although I was too shaken at the moment to even worry about identifying the make or model. The car had its flashers going, but I could see it wasn't in distress. The windshield and side windows were tinted—not that opaque black tint that absolutely obscures the occupants—more like a light hue that rendered the occupants into shadows. And of these occupants, I saw only one. It appeared to be a man. He sat still behind the wheel. Don't ask me how, but I just knew that this shadowy form belonged to the voice that had been taunting me earlier.

I stopped in my tracks and made a big show of patting myself down, meaning to indicate that I had forgotten something in my car. I turned and retraced my steps up the stairs to the second level of the parking structure. When I got there, I went into stealth mode, dropping into a crouch and inching along the wall to get a look down to the street below. I stuck my head up over the ledge of the wall and looked down. The black car was still there, its emergency flashers still on.

It hadn't even occurred to me that someone might follow me. Boy, I was way out of practice, and probably way out of my league. The last thing I wanted to do was lead this guy to Maud Gonne, to get her involved in this, assuming she wasn't already involved in some sinister capacity. Unless I could lose him, walking to her art gallery was out of the question.

I scanned the parking structure and saw a red exit sign diagonally across from me about fifty yards away. Bent at the waist, I made my way slalom-style through the parked cars until I reached the exit stairs. I hurried down the stairs and headed for the exit, which dumped out onto a different street that ran perpendicular to the one on which the car with the flashers was parked. I crept around the building, thankful there were no pedestrians around to observe what they would no doubt consider strange behavior on my part.

When I got to the corner of the parking structure, I peeked around and saw that I was now behind the car, about seventy-five feet away. The driver seemed not to have moved a muscle, as if a mannequin had been planted behind the wheel. The flashers were still flashing. I turned back and hurried down the street, out of sight of the car's occupant.

Just to be sure that I wasn't being followed, I stopped at the windows of a few stores as I made my way to the art gallery. I came to a coffee shop, where I entered and downed a quick espresso as I sat at a window seat watching both the pedestrian and vehicular traffic. Nothing seemed amiss. I saw lots of black, expensive looking foreign cars, but none of them seemed to have the simmering menace of the car I had seen by the parking structure, a car which I now convinced myself had been a Mercedes. And the people walking by the window seemed innocent enough. Of course, what was I expecting? Something out of "Spy vs. Spy?" A man in an oversized Fedora and a black overcoat with a neon sign hanging from his neck that blinked "Bad Guy" off and on?

I left the coffee shop and walked another few doors to a bookstore, where I stepped in. I pretended to go over the magazines, while I again watched out the window for anything that seemed out of the ordinary, my heart pounding hard enough to set my entire frame into rhythmic motion. Fortunately, or unfortunately, depending on your opinion of Birmingham, things seemed fervently ordinary.

I bought a *Time* magazine, left the store and headed directly for the art gallery without further evasive tactics. Unlike some of the other establishments in Birmingham, the art gallery run by Ms. Gonne looked small from the outside and actually was small once you entered it. None of that false modesty stuff here. The gallery smelled like some sort of incense, and I immediately wondered if burning incense had any effect on the artwork, although, for my money, if a few of the things Maud Gonne had hanging on the wall accidentally went up in smoke, the art world wouldn't be that much poorer.

I recognized none of the paintings, nor did any of them seem to possess the stylistic tendencies of the painfully few artists I knew about. No Monets, no Picasso's. No DeKoonings. Many of the paintings *did*, however, seem to be stylistically and thematically related. Lots of bold, primary colors, lots of intensity, and lots of what appeared to be Christian imagery. One large canvas which dominated the room, for example, portrayed a crucifixion scene. Three crosses in the foreground with emaciated forms hanging from them, lots of dark, foreboding atmosphere, all seen from a somewhat elevated perspective. Crowds huddled around the base of the crosses, looking like so many cockroaches standing on their hind legs.

Then, if you looked real hard, the crosses seemed to be telephone poles with telephone lines extended between them, and, I couldn't be completely sure, but it looked like some of the onlookers in the painting were holding cell phones up to their ears. I looked at a little card in the bottom right-hand corner of the painting. It read "Juxta-poison-nation" by William Bleak.

Maud Gonne? William Bleak? What the fuck was going on here?

"Do you like it?"

It was Maud. She had made her way noiselessly behind me. I turned to see her standing with her arms crossed over her chest, smiling.

"It's a joke, right?" I said. "William Bleak?" She shrugged.

"Good question. William Bleak, whoever he is, is very shy. I've never met him. I work exclusively through his agent." I looked around now and noticed that most of the paintings I could see were by William Bleak.

"Do any of these things actually sell?" I said.

"Oh, yes," said Maud Gonne. "Almost all of them. Mr. Bleak has quite a following."

I looked again at "Juxta-poision-nation." I wasn't much of an art critic, but I didn't see much in terms of talent here. The technique was not even good enough to be primitive and I saw nothing novel or fresh in the subject matter. And if the guy *was* trying to imitate William Blake, he was doing a poor job of it.

"So, is Mr. Bleak trying to tell us something about, what, the dangers of cell phone calling plans here or something?"

Maud laughed. "I try not to interpret them," she said. "I just sell them."

"Who in their right mind would buy something like this?" I said, almost exasperated. These were truly bad. Even their unintentional humor couldn't save them. They had that sense of earnestness and mission that's just deadly to art, at least so far as I was concerned. I imagined Mr. William Bleak to be the Ted Kaczynski of the contemporary art world, slaving over canvases in some shack in Montana.

"I take it you're not in the market, then," said Maud.

"Art can't be possessed," I said. "It can only be appreciated." A look of mock alarm came over her face.

"I hope you won't tell that to any of my clients," she said. I looked around, not seeing any clients.

"I'll restrain myself," I said. She smiled.

"I actually didn't think you'd take me up on the offer to visit the gallery. At least not so, well, immediately."

Well, telling her I just happened to be in the neighborhood probably wouldn't work. And she could plainly see I was no art aficionado. I paused. We both paused. It started to get uncomfortable.

"Do you know a man named Barry Justice?" I said.

"Of course," she said immediately. I looked to see if her face betrayed anything at all, but I saw nothing. "He's a neighbor. His wife is Lashona Webber, the newsperson. What about him?"

Well, I thought, he's sitting at home in his living room about twenty feet from his genitalia, which is not a good situation for a man.

"When we ran into each other yesterday at the golf course . . . " I paused. Her eyes narrowed.

"Yes?" she said.

"Is it normal for you to go cross-country skiing during the middle of the workday? I ask because I don't see anyone else around here." She considered for a moment.

"I'm not sure what my work schedule has to do with Barry Justice, but, okay. I'll play." She walked to the front door and opened it, then beckoned me to where she stood. When I got there, she pointed to the sign on the door displaying the gallery's hours of operation. "You apparently missed this on the way in," she said. The sign indicated that the gallery was open from 11:00 a.m. to 7:00 p.m. Tuesday through Friday, 11: 00 a.m. to 9:00 p.m. on Saturday, and from noon to 5:00 p.m. on Sundays. The gallery was closed on Mondays, kind of like the barbershops of my youth.

"Oh," I said, getting it. "Yesterday was Monday, right?"

"According to my calendar," said Maud. I felt my face heat up.

"Well, that explains it then," I said. Then, feeling the need to be a little more expansive, I said: "The days kind of run together for me."

"So, my alibi is satisfactory, then?" she said. I hung my head and sighed.

"I wasn't accusing you of anything. I was just trying to clear up this discrepancy."

"So, now it's cleared up," she said. "What does my work schedule have to do with Barry Justice?"

I didn't answer right away, but clearly I was going to have to bring her in on this. I had piqued her interest. As soon as she heard on the news or from some other source what had happened to Justice, she was going to remember this conversation. She would certainly remember that I was in the vicinity. But the *real* reason I decided to bring her in was, I needed an ally. I needed someone else to know what was going on in case I was arrested or otherwise detained. And I also needed help. I couldn't do this alone, whatever *this* was. I was a dead man, after all.

"We need to talk," I said. Then I walked to the window and looked outside. I didn't see anything suspicious, but you could never tell. Maud looked at her watch.

"How about lunch?" she said.

"That would be great," I said. "But can we take your car?"

"There are good restaurants within walking distance," she said.

"I'd rather get out of Birmingham," I said. "I'll explain at lunch." She shrugged.

"I'll get my keys," she said. She put one of those little signs on the front door that read "Be back at" then showed a clock face with hour hands. She adjusted the hands to 1:30. Then we left.

All the way to her car—and once in her car—I kept a lookout for the black Mercedes. And, of course, before I knew it, I was seeing black Mercedes everywhere.

"You're jumpy," said Maud Gonne from behind the wheel.

"Someone has been following me," I said. "Someone in a black Mercedes."

"In this neighborhood it would be hard *not* to be followed by somebody in a black Mercedes," she said.

"So I'm learning. But the guy in this particular black Mercedes is not a nice man." I saw a look of amusement come over her face. She peered intently into her rearview mirror.

"Well, I don't see anything that looks like a black Mercedes behind us. So, where do you want to eat?"

We ended up at a Mexican restaurant in the neighboring suburb of Troy. Maud ordered the taco salad and a huge margarita. I had the chimichanga and a Dos Equis. The food arrived in about thirty seconds and I watched as Maud ate about two mouthfuls of the salad. Then she put her fork down and didn't touch another bite. I, on the other hand, found to my amazement that I was hungry beyond belief. Maud sipped her margarita and watched me eat with what was probably something bordering on concern. I was concerned myself. I kept shoveling the food in with abandon. I think I even started to eat faster the fuller I got. When I was finally finished, my plate was clean. I looked at it.

"I don't normally eat like this," I said. Maud nodded over the lip of her margarita glass.

"But you're under stress, right?" she said.

"You could say that."

She put her glass down, put her hands on the table and interlaced her fingers.

"I'm listening," she said.

I told her everything that had happened since my fateful decision to venture out of the house for paint. She listened impassively for most of my story, although she did make a face when I told her about what had happened to Justice. When I was done, she picked up her margarita glass and drained it. I did the same with my Dos Equis.

"Could we get another round?" she asked. We could, indeed.

After she was settled in with her second margarita, she began with the questions.

"Do you think this man on the phone—and, presumably, the man driving the Mercedes—wants to kill you?"

"If he can find me," I said.

"Right," she said. She pondered for a moment.

"You need a place to stay," she said. "And I have plenty of room at my house. So that's settled." I grimaced a bit. "It can be totally platonic," she said with some haste after seeing my expression.

"I appreciate the thought," I said. "But that's not what I'm worried about." She cocked her head, confusion, maybe a hint of embarrassment in her face. "This guy on the phone is a stone killer. Based on what I saw of his handiwork with Justice, he likes his job. He may have already killed Lashona Webber, too. I don't think he's going to have any scruples when it comes to me. Or you, either, if he finds out you're involved."

"How would he find that out?"

"Well, you do live relatively close to the Justice house."

"Right," said Maud. "That's why it's perfect. He'd never expect you to be staying that close. As long as he doesn't see us together, he'll never figure it out."

"He may have already seen us together," I said. "Anyway, even if he hasn't, he will figure it out. This guy's no dummy."

"Neither are you," she said. I almost said, don't be too sure about that, but I managed to keep my mouth shut. Actually, her idea about my staying at her place made some sense. The guy on the phone had no reason to believe that I knew any of Justice's neighbors and if he didn't already know my current address, he soon would. He seemed to have connections. If I were to take up residence in another apartment or in a hotel—someplace where I had to give my name and park a car in the lot—he would probably be able to track me down.

But how would he know about Maud Gonne? I hadn't even known about her twenty-four hours earlier. She was right. Unless he saw us together or perhaps overheard a telephone conversation or had some other form of intelligence that I didn't know about, there would be no way for him to connect me to Maud Gonne.

"Okay," I said. "We'll give it a try. But at the first sign of any awareness by this guy that I'm hunkered down at your place, I split."

"Agreed," said Maud. I looked at her closely. She paused as she raised her glass to her lips. "Really," she said, her eyes narrowing in earnest. "I'm not a martyr."

"I'm not saying you are," I said.

"Then what *are* you saying?"

"I wasn't saying anything."

"You're thinking something."

"No," I said, "I wasn't. Honest." But I *was* thinking something. I was thinking she was too eager. She was trying to hide it, but she was excited about getting involved in this—almost giddy about it.

"We just need to keep in mind that this isn't a game."

"I know that," she snapped. "I'm not that twelve-year-old who wanted to be Denise Raccette anymore," she said. "And my infatuation days are over. Marriage cured me of infatuation."

"Okay," I said. "We just need to stay on an even keel. Both of us. We have to be methodical and think things through." She nodded, then took her belated sip of the margarita.

"So, why didn't you just disappear?" she said a few seconds later.

"What do you mean?" I asked.

"I mean why are you getting involved in this stuff with Justice and Lashona? Once you learned that Justice was dead, you were off the hook, right? He wasn't going to reveal your secret anymore. You could have just dropped it and left for a fresh start someplace else. But you didn't." Her eyes seemed to bore into mine.

"I've been asking myself the same question," I said, trying to laugh off her inquiry. But she wouldn't be laughed away.

"Do you want me to tell you what I think?" she said.

"Why do I think I should answer 'no' to that question?" I said.

"Is that a 'no?'"

"No," I said. "Please tell my why you think I'm getting involved." She sort of rose and settled in her chair, almost like a sprinter easing into her blocks.

"You wouldn't be able to live with yourself knowing that this was hanging out there," she said with certainty. "It's not the morality of it, so much. It's not like you want to crusade against evil. You're not an avenger."

"You got *that* right," I said, trying to make light. She seemed slightly irritated, as though she resented my commentary.

"But you have this sense of order, of things having to be justified." This time, I said nothing. "It was a passage in *Our Father* that made this clear to me. The part where you talk about having this need to know things."

"I haven't read the book," I said.

"You *wrote* it," she protested.

"Claude Nickle may have taken editorial license," I said. She shook her head.

"I read the book. Your voice comes through loud and clear." She brought her hands together, palm to palm, and closed her eyes, almost as if she might go into prayer. Then she bounced her fingertips against her pursed lips. "You try to portray yourself as humble, reclusive. And to some extent, I think you are. But there's another side of you."

"Uh, are you getting a transmission from somewhere right now?" I asked. She opened her eyes and smiled.

"You don't like to be analyzed, do you?" she said.

"I just don't know what value there is in it," I said. "I don't see its relevance to our current situation."

"Everything's relevant," she said without hesitation. "Don't take this the wrong way, but at the same time you try to project this image of self-effacement, you're also sending these powerful vibes of arrogance."

I have been called a lot of things, but I couldn't remember ever being accused of arrogance.

"Not that that's bad," she hastened to add. "But don't you think there's something arrogant in assuming that the universe should reveal all its secrets to you? That just because something is unknown that you should know it? Like this stuff with Justice and his wife."

"I think you're mistaking common curiosity for arrogance," I said. "Besides, I've mellowed since I wrote that book. If I expressed a concept that seemed to you to suggest arrogance, I'm sure I've been cured of it." She peered intently at me for a few more seconds.

"I don't think so," she said, finally. "You know why?"

I didn't, but she didn't wait for me to tell her that.

"Because of this whole episode of faking your death," she said. "That to me says arrogance, too. It's like saying, not only can I control my own fate, but I can control others through this action."

"You could say the same for suicides," I said.

"Exactly."

I kept quiet. I didn't see any point in continuing this line of discussion, so I took a drink of my beer.

"You're irritated, aren't you," she said. I told her I wasn't. And I really didn't think I was. Maybe she was right, after all. Maybe it was arrogance that prevented me from just dropping the whole Justice thing and re-disappearing. Maybe it was anger. In my opinion, I do anger much better than I do arrogance. But I saw no point in getting into that discussion at the moment.

"Is it possible," she said, "that at some point I might get the story behind your disappearance?" I shrugged.

"I suppose so," I said. "Not that there's much to tell." She nodded slowly without taking her eyes off me.

"Well, the first thing we need to do is make arrangements to visit Lashona Webber's family in Florida," she said.

"See," I said, "I'm bothered by this disappearing act of Lashona's just a little."

"Act? You think she only pretended to be abducted?"

"The problem is, I don't know," I said. "What if she's somehow involved in what happened to her husband? What if, for example, he was fooling around on her and she wanted to teach him a lesson?"

Maud shook her head.

"That's way too simplistic," she said. "I'm assuming you're talking about the castration. But if she was going to hire someone to castrate her husband because she was enraged at his infidelities, what lesson does he learn if he's killed? Who is she trying to send this message to?" Maud had a point.

"Except that the killer suggested he had separated Justice from his genitals before he killed him. Maybe that was the plan. To let poor Barry just sit there for a while and appreciate the error of his ways before killing him. I imagine there might be some satisfaction in that. Maybe Lashona was even in the room when it happened."

"Ohwww," said Maud, her face registering disgust.

"I'm not saying she was," I said. "I'm saying it's one possible scenario. I'm also bothered by the domestic touch. Using the skillet to display the, uh, parts."

"Maybe the killer just has a sick sense of humor," said Maud.

"I still don't think we can rule out Lashona," I said. "Her disappearance doesn't make a lot of sense to me yet, and since we don't know the motive for Justice's murder, I can't cross her off my list. And maybe her family was in on this."

"Okay," said Maud. "Let's assume, for the moment, that we *don't* start with Lashona's family. What's our next move?"

I thought about this for a few seconds. The truth was, I didn't have a plausible alternative. We both sat silent for a few minutes. Then Maud said: "The medication angle is interesting." I had been thinking about my conversations with Justice, trying to review them for something I had overlooked, and her statement surprised me.

"Medications?" I said.

"Yes," said Maud. "The antidepressants prescribed for Lashona Webber."

"I don't know," I said. "Everybody takes antidepressants these days."

"Still," said Maud, "I'd like to know what she was depressed about. Here she was this successful, polished, well-paid, respected professional. From what I know of her, she was popular with viewers and well regarded among her peers. Not that I follow the industry that closely."

"Plenty of people at the pinnacle of their careers with, ostensibly, every reason to be happy are depressed. After all, if you buy into the current thinking on depression, it's all about imbalances in brain chemistry. And keep in mind that Lashona's childhood was probably pretty grim. There could be lots of residual problems that could resurface as depression in her adult life. And she has a sick child."

"I know, I know," said Maud. "I'm still thinking it would be interesting to find out why a doctor prescribed antidepressants."

"Well, it's not likely that he'll tell you or me. There's that doctor-patient privilege thing. I'm sure he's professionally bound to confidentiality regarding his patients. Hell, they don't even have to give cops that information. Don't you ever watch 'Law and Order?' You think this doctor's just gonna blurt it out for you and me?"

"No," said Maud. "I suppose you're right." She had a look on her face that suggested *she* was going to need massive doses of Prozac any second.

"You know, maybe the best thing to do is just go to the police," I said. As much as that would cause major embarrassment and disruption in my life, it was beginning to look like the only practical option. But Maud was fiercely against it.

"We can't do that," she said. "For all we know, the police might be responsible for this. Well, not the entire force, but some rogue element. Lashona made some major enemies there. It could be payback time."

"So why kill Justice? He didn't engage in any crusades or exposés against the cops."

"Yeah, but we don't know how much he might be involved. Lashona probably told him things, I mean, pillow talk kind of stuff."

That didn't ring true for me, but I had to admit that in the unlikely event that the police were involved with Lashona's disappearance, they might be motivated to eliminate her husband as well. Make it look like the result of some domestic upheaval. I drank what was left of my Dos Equis. Maud looked at her watch.

"I need to get back," she said. She took one of her business cards and a pen out of her purse and wrote something on the back of the card.

"This is my address," she said. "And my cell phone number." Then she detached one of the keys from her keychain. "Park in the garage. There's plenty of room and that way the car would be less visible should our friend decide to revisit the general area of the scene of the crime."

"I think we ought to forget this whole thing," I said, twisting her house key in my fingers.

"You might want to stop and buy yourself some clothes," she said, ignoring me. "I don't have much in the way of men's clothes in the house. Conor didn't leave anything behind, which I have to say, I appreciate."

"You're not listening to me," I said.

"I heard what you said. I'm just not responding to it. You know what I think? I think you have more insight into this than you realize. You faked your own death. I think you believe Lashona pulled off some similar stunt. I think people take the extraordinary approach of faking their own deaths for good reasons. Well, maybe not good reasons, but reasons. We need to look at that. We need to look at why you did this. It might give us some insight into Lashona's motivation, which, in turn, could lead us to where she's at and to some rationale for the murder of her husband."

"Just like that, huh?" I said. She looked at me intently.

"You don't want to go to her family. The doctor won't tell us anything, according to you. The police are out of the question. So, no, it's not just like that. I don't know what else to do. Besides, I want to know why you did it. With the heat you've got on you, who knows how long you'll survive. And somebody needs to bear witness to your story."

"Bear witness? Nobody gives a shit, believe me."

"Well, I do," she said.

EIGHT

PLAN B . . .

Well, I'm a sucker for a beautiful woman's worship. I admit it. I had promised to discuss the faked death incident with her when she got home from the gallery that evening. The problem was, between now and then, I would have to do some serious introspection into those motives. And I had a feeling Maud was likely to be disappointed. If there were any grand and noble—or even ignoble—reasons for what I did, I certainly didn't know what they were. But, what the hell? It was only two p.m. I had five or six hours to come up with some rationale.

Maud had offered to drop me back at the parking structure, but I thought that, as unlikely as it was that the occupant of the black Mercedes was still staking out the place, it was better to minimize any chances that Maud and I be seen together.

I walked from the gallery to the parking structure, where I was relieved to see that the Mercedes was gone. Even so, I scanned for the vehicle as my car nosed out of the parking structure and I kept a lookout in the rearview mirror for its reappearance for the rest of the day.

I went to a mall not too far from where Maud and I had gotten lunch and did some shopping at a Nordstrom's. Not a complete wardrobe. A week's worth of underwear and socks, several shirts and three pairs of Levi's. Just the basics. I used my credit card to pay for the stuff, then did a quick tour of the inside track of the mall, neck-and-neck with those wacky mall walkers, stopping every once in a while to look in a storefront, and, surreptitiously, to see if I was being followed. If someone *was* following me, they were doing a good job of it, because I didn't see anything or anyone that looked suspicious.

I was concerned for my own safety, of course, but I was also worried about leading any of these degenerates back to Maud's residence. Relatively convinced that I wasn't being followed, I left the mall, got in my car and drove to Maud's house, which, indeed, turned out to be in the same general vicinity as Justice's home.

I drove past the house first, without slowing down and without letting my head swivel in the house's direction. I checked the rearview mirror. Not a car in sight. I went around the block and approached Maud's house again. This time, I pulled into the driveway. As Maud had instructed, I got out of my car and used the key she had given me to open the side door of the garage. Once inside, I found the switch for the garage door and hit it. The door opened with a loud grinding noise, that, it seemed to me anyway, would have gotten the attention of someone three blocks away. I jogged back to the Jeep, got in, and pulled it inside, where I shut off the car, quickly jumped out and hit the switch for the door. As it was about halfway down, I saw a black car—it could have been a Mercedes, but I didn't see it that well—pass by. My heart sank. So this was how it was going to be, huh?

I found a bottle of cabernet sauvignon—not my first choice in alcoholic beverages, but the only thing Maud had around the house. I had considered going out for a six-pack, but the thought of that black car cruising the neighborhood made an excursion to the liquor store seem foolhardy. So I opened the bottle of wine and sat down to watch the feverish coverage of the war in Iraq, flipping back and forth from CNN to MSNBC to FOX News just to see how these various networks tried to outdo each other. The war was in the alleged mop-up phase, during that giddy time of the premature confidence of "mission accomplished," and the really juicy stories were getting harder to find. At the moment, I was watching Wolf Blitzer salivate over the capture of one of Saddam Hussein's half-brothers or some such nonsense.

The little digital clock in the corner of the TV screen reported that it was 3:58 Eastern Time when I heard the garage door grind into operation. This was earlier—a lot earlier—than I had expected Maud to get home, and I tensed up for a moment. What if The Voice had found me? But, no. Those were definitely high-heels clicking across the kitchen floor.

"Is this how you investigate a crime?" said Maud a moment later, standing in the archway of the door leading from the kitchen to the dining room.

"Do you run your art gallery from long distance?" I replied.

She threw her purse and her bomber jacket on a chair in the dining room and stepped out of her shoes.

"I closed up early," she said. "This is much more exciting than selling art—or not selling art. Besides, while you've been indulging your teenage war fantasies, I've been doing productive things." She walked over and turned off the TV.

"Hey," I complained. "This is an historic moment. They've just captured Saddam's half-brother."

"Again?"

"Yeah, again."

"Maybe this one knows where the weapons of mass destruction are."

"You call yourself a patriot?"

She picked up the ten-ounce tumbler that I was using as a wine glass and took a drink.

"I *do* have the appropriate glasses for this," she said. "I just want to get that on the record." She sat next to me on the couch, not exactly close to me, but on the same piece of furniture. I tried not to read anything into this. She looked absolutely radiant. Slightly breathless, a bit flushed in the cheeks. She gave the glass back to me and I noticed that she had left a lipstick imprint on it. When I didn't immediately put the glass down on the coffee table, she took it from me and deposited it there herself.

"I need your full attention for this," she said. She swept a stray strand of black hair out of her eye.

"This better be good," I said. "I'm missing history in the making."

"It's *very* good," she said. "I know how to get Lashona Webber's psychiatric records." I didn't say anything, waiting for her to continue. "Well," she said, "aren't you impressed?"

"I'll let you know," I said.

"The only problem is, we may have to do something that isn't strictly legal."

"Why did I know that?" I said.

"No worries. This has to work out. It's too weird not to."

"I'm listening," I said.

"When you mentioned the name of Lashona's psychiatrist, it sounded familiar. Turns out, his office is right in downtown Birmingham, about half a mile from my gallery. Astrachan is like a celebrity psychiatrist on a minor scale, a shrink to the stars. I mean, it's not the kind of thing he brags about, but he doesn't mind it when he's referred to that way in the media, either. He never identifies his patients, but it's pretty well known that he caters to Detroit's elite. He's worked with a couple of the Detroit Pistons with drug problems and he's done some work with the Detroit Police and Michigan State Police on solving some high-profile murders over the years. Apparently, he also treats several of Detroit's media stars."

"If he's so confidential about his patient list, how do you know who he treats?" I said.

"Because my source has seen them going into and out of his office. Remember the guy who had the sex addiction problem he went public with? Oh, that's right. You've been dead. A few years ago, one of the local TV reporters went public with a problem he was having with addiction to computer porn or something like that. Apparently, the police picked him up when they found out he was setting up an appointment with a thirteen-year-old girl through some Internet chat room. Of course, the thirteen-year-old turned out to be a police detective. The police never charged the guy because he agreed to get treatment and, I guess, because he never really met with any of his computer correspondents. *And* because redemption is as American as Lotto tickets on the night of the big drawing. Anyway, the shrink who treated him was Robert Astrachan."

"And you know this because your source saw this reporter in Astrachan's office," I said.

"Basically, yeah."

"Who is this source?" Maud hesitated. She took another drink from the wine tumbler.

"We have to be careful, here," she said. "We're talking about a person's livelihood."

"I won't tell," I said. "There's nobody that I particularly want to talk to. I'm dead, remember?" Maud smiled and nodded.

"The woman's name is Maria Vejar. She cleans my gallery. Well, not just her. She and a group of her relatives. She has a little office-cleaning business. She cleans several of the establishments in Birmingham. She's very good. Completely reliable and discreet." I raised my eyebrow.

"She *is*," Maud protested. "I totally had to drag this information out of her."

"What led you to her?" I said.

"A hunch. Like I said, she cleans several offices in the area. I called her and asked if she cleaned Astrachan's office and she told me she did. She was less forthcoming on the other information about his patients, but she eventually told me. I've done her some favors in the past."

"What kind of favors?" I said.

"Is that relevant? I think you're missing the bigger picture, here."

"What bigger picture?"

"I'll get to that in a minute," she said. "I asked Maria when was the next time she would be cleaning Dr. Astrachan's office, and here's where the good part comes in. She told me she hadn't cleaned it for a week because Dr. Astrachan was out of town, but that she would be cleaning it again starting tomorrow when he returns. Can you believe it?"

"Believe what?" I said. "That Astrachan is out of town?"

"No," said Maud, slapping her thighs in frustration. "Can you believe our luck?"

I was beginning to understand, and I didn't like where this was going.

"This brings us to the part about doing something that's not strictly legal, right?"

"Right," she said. "We need to pay Dr. Astrachan's office a visit so we can take a look at his files."

"That would be breaking and entering," I said. "For starters."

"We wouldn't be breaking in," said Maud. "We'd have a key."

"Which we would no doubt get from Señora Vejar," I said. "I think it's still breaking and entering. And why would Vejar risk this for you?"

"I told you, I've helped her out with a few things. And she wasn't exactly thrilled about this."

"I noticed that you didn't mention trustworthy when you were running down her character traits."

"That's not fair," said Maud. "The woman is trustworthy. But she's also not an ingrate." Maud sighed. "A few years ago, when I was still married to Conor, I got him to help out Maria with a deportation issue. One of her daughters. And I've also gotten her a few clients. Listen, I had to swear on my life that I would not take anything from the good doctor's office and that I would never reveal that she had let me in. The woman was in tears when she agreed. We went through a significantly emotional episode while you were sitting here guzzling my wine and watching George Bush's storm troopers squash Iraq."

Storm troopers? Squash Iraq? That seemed a little harsh.

"Maud," I said, putting on my best voice of reason. "We can't break into Astrachan's office and steal his files."

"Why not?"

"Because it's illegal," I said.

"And murder and kidnapping aren't?"

"Are you saying that Astrachan had something to do with Lashona's disappearance and Justice's murder?"

"No," said Maud. "What I'm saying is we have no other options. Astrachan never has to know that we were in his office. We won't actually take the files, just look at them. What are you afraid of? You're a dead man, anyway. I'm the one who would be taking the greatest risk, and I don't care. I'm going into that office with or without you."

This was nuts. In the space of a day and a half, I'd created a monster in Maud Gonne.

"When?" I said, trying to infuse that one syllable with as much resignation and defeat as I could.

"Mr. Enthusiastic," said Maud. "Tonight. It has to be tonight. Astrachan will be back tomorrow and then it really does get too risky."

"Can we at least wait until dark?" I said.

"Absolutely," she said, springing forward on the couch and kissing my forehead. It was too spontaneous a gesture to be anything more than pure exuberance. I had no reason to think that sex would be on the menu tonight.

"Oh my God," she said suddenly, as if she had read my mind. "I forgot that I had food in the car. I stopped at P.F. Chang's." She jumped up from the couch and headed back toward the kitchen. When she got to the archway, she stopped and looked back at me.

"Don't look so forlorn," she said. "This is our big break."

It didn't feel like it to me, but at least it preempted the need for me to tell the story of my disappearance at sea.

NINE

. . . & E

We had eaten our dinner of orange-peel chicken and rice, had roughly planned our assault on Dr. Robert Astrachan's office and had waited until about 8:00 p.m. before hopping into Maud's Jag and heading back to Snobville, USA. I was now about to spend more time in the quaint, if pretentious, burg of Birmingham, Michigan, in one day than I had in the last twenty years of my so-called life.

Astrachan's office was in a plaza of medical suites on the north end of downtown Birmingham. Psychology seemed to be the predominant specialty of the office complex, although I did notice an ophthalmologist and a dentist on the lobby directory. Every other name on the list appeared to be a therapist, or family counselor or "life coach." And, unfortunately, many of these offices were still open, as indicated by some pretty significant lobby traffic.

"Maybe we should come back after office hours," I ventured. After all, wasn't that the reason we had waited until dark?

"Relax," said Maud. "Just act like you belong here."

Boy, did I *ever* belong there. I didn't even have to act.

The lobby directory indicated that Astrachan's office was on the second floor. I started toward the elevator, but Maud yanked my arm toward the stairs.

"I will not, on principle, take an elevator to the second floor," she said firmly.

"I'm just trying to blend," I said.

We took the stairs to the second floor and found Astrachan's office at the end of the hall. On the way there, we passed the offices of several other therapists. A few of these were still open for business and I saw patients sitting in the waiting rooms. They all looked the same. Expressionless, subdued, defeated, like they were waiting to see the principal.

"Have you ever been in therapy?" I asked Maud as we walked down the hallway to Astrachan's office.

"That's kind of a personal question, isn't it?" she said. "You *are* focused on our objective, here, right?"

"Sure," I said. "Just making conversation."

At Astrachan's office, Maud didn't hesitate. She had the office key in her hand and she used it to open the office door without even checking to see if we were being observed. So *I* checked. The hallway was empty, but my heart suddenly sank as I looked up to the corner of the ceiling and spotted a surveillance camera. I tapped Maud on the shoulder—for some reason, I now thought it was important to maintain silence—and she turned around, the door already ajar. I pointed to the camera. She looked at it, then back at me.

"You're acting way too suspicious," she said. "A little audacity is what's called for in this situation." Well, excuse me, Nancy Drew. "The camera's not working now," she said with conviction.

"And you know that how?" I said, recovering my voice.

"Do you see a little red light?" she said. I looked, but I didn't see one.

"Are you sure all surveillance cameras have little red lights?"

"Yes," she said. "Definitely."

"And how do you know that?" I said.

She didn't answer. Instead, she grabbed my arm and pulled me through the door, shutting it behind us. We found ourselves in a small waiting room with three steel-legged chairs, a couple of end tables with very utilitarian lamps on them, illuminated even now, and a magazine rack affixed to one wall. The rack held mainly golf magazines, with a couple of *People* issues thrown in the mix. Next to the magazine rack a small sign on the wall indicated that payment for services was appreciated at the time of the patient's appointment. Maud was already opening another door, mostly likely to the inner sanctum, where all the magic happened.

"You didn't answer my question," I said.

"What question was that?" she said, stopping to look at me, the key in the lock, her hand on the doorknob, ready to turn.

"How you know that all surveillance cameras have little red lights?"

"You want to discuss the arcane technology of security equipment now?" she said. "A security consultant told me, okay? I was thinking of having some cameras installed in my gallery, so I had a guy come over and look at the place. He told me about the little red lights."

"You're lying," I said. "You just made that up." She rolled her eyes.

"I'm not going to take that personally," she said. "You're under a lot of stress. Whether the camera is working or not doesn't make a lot of difference at this point, does it? We're already in."

"Yeah, but what if it's a realtime situation, you know? With a direct feed into the police station? They could be on their way right now." Maud sighed.

"Okay, leave if you want," she said. "I'm going in." She pushed the door open and walked through.

Well, I couldn't let a girl outdo me in the audacity department, so I sucked it up and followed her into the room.

Maud hit the light switch and the room sprang into view. I saw a large desk of some sort of polished wood, a bookcase full of weighty tomes, and the obligatory couch. It was orange and of a hard, modern design. It didn't look comfortable. Next to the couch was an end table with a small lamp and a box of tissues.

I didn't see a computer on the desk and mentioned it to Maud.

"Most therapists don't have them on their desks, out in the open like that," she said. She said it with authority. I had no idea if she actually knew what she was talking about. Just how many therapists' offices had she been in? My confusion must have shown on my face.

"It's threatening to the clients," she explained.

"Do you just make this stuff up?" I asked. I hadn't expected an answer and I didn't get one.

Overall, the office had a low-rent golf motif working. Behind the desk, a large LeRoy Neiman painting of some golf scene dominated the wall. The golfers appeared to be Jack Nicklaus and Arnold Palmer on the green. The golf course could have been Pebble Beach, if the suggestion of ocean next to the green was any indication. Astrachan's desk itself was very tidy. Let's not suggest any disorder to the nutcases. He had a coffee cup sitting on the desk with a 1996 U.S. Open logo on it. I remembered that that was the year the Open had been held just down the road at Oakland Hills. Birmingham was in all its glory that year. The desk also contained a bronze paperweight, a replica of the Pinehurst logo—a statue of a young caddy addressing a golf ball with a club. I deduced that it was the Pinehurst logo because it read "Pinehurst, 1895" on the base. In a corner of the room behind the desk stood a putter and several golf balls along with one of those plastic golf hole/ball return gizmos.

"I don't know," I said. "I'm not sure his décor sends the right message to the patients."

Maud said nothing. She was probably still pissed that I had called her a liar. She made a big show of going right to the file cabinet, which, of course, was locked. I gave her a "see, smarty-pants, told you so; now what are we going to do?" look, which she fought to ignore.

She walked behind the desk and opened the middle drawer. A few seconds later she was dangling a key in front of her eyes.

"What would be the point," I said, "of locking the file cabinet, then leaving the key to the file cabinet in an unlocked desk drawer?"

"You give people way too much credit," she said. "I, myself, am kind of surprised the key wasn't in the keyhole of the cabinet just waiting for us to turn it."

"You're assuming that key fits that file cabinet," I said, pointing to each in turn. She walked to the cabinet, inserted the key, turned it, and pulled open the top drawer.

"Oh, Ye of little faith," she said. I watched her rifle through a few files, then shut the drawer and open the bottom drawer. After a quick scan of the files, she pulled out a manila folder.

"Bingo," she said, her eyes sparkling.

Unfortunately, the file didn't contain much. There was a new-patient application on which Lashona Weber indicated that she was seeking help for depression, but there was no indication of the cause of the depression. The file also contained a few insurance forms and a bio of Lashona Webber, which appeared to have been prepared by the PR department of the TV station where she worked. It wasn't especially helpful. Born in Bradenton, Florida. Attended Florida State University on an academic scholarship. Stints in various small media markets, primarily in the southeastern part of the country. Hired on as an urban affairs reporter at WEEE, and recently moved up to the co-anchor job at six and eleven. I noted that Lashona had won a local Emmy two years earlier for her exposé of the Detroit Police Department's problems with the excessive use of deadly force.

She was doing well, career-wise. A rising star. So why was she depressed?

"I wonder where he keeps his session notes?" said Maud, looking around the room.

"Maybe he keeps those at home," I said. "It would explain his casual security with the files."

Maud wasn't paying any attention to me. She replaced the manila folder in the file cabinet and walked back around Astrachan's desk. She picked up a picture frame from the desk, looked at it a moment, then turned it around for me to look at. The photo showed a man and a woman on a beach somewhere. The man—I assumed it was Astrachan—was about forty years old in the photo. He wore a pair of those ridiculously skimpy Speedo bathing trunks that men should never allow themselves to be talked into wearing, or certainly not photographed in. He was bald except for black hair over his ears and he was heavily tanned. He had thin arms and the narrow, hairless chest of a twelve-year-old boy above the beginning stages of a beer belly. He was smiling broadly. No doubt the reason he was smiling was the bodacious blond standing next to him, his arm around her waist. She looked like something out of a suntan lotion ad, or an MTV Spring Break show. Big blond hair, circa mid-1980s style, pink thong bikini and huge breasts. She, too, was tanned and had a big smile on her face. It was as if the photographer had just told them the funniest joke they had ever heard.

"How can anybody take this guy seriously as a therapist?" I said. Maud shrugged.

"Therapists aren't supposed to have fun?" she asked.

"Not so demonstrably. I mean, they're not supposed to be so in-your-face with it. They're dealing with fragile emotions here, people with real problems."

Maud rolled her eyes and pulled open the desk drawer to her right. While she busied herself with the drawer's contents, I leafed through Astrachan's appointment book, which he had conveniently left sitting on his desk. I wondered if the guy had violated any professional ethics by leaving all this stuff lying around.

The appointment book was chock-full. Astrachan appeared to keep very regular office hours. He had appointments starting at 10:00 a.m. and running until 6:00 p.m. The names of the clients were cleverly disguised by using their initials. As I flipped through the previous few months, I saw the initials L. W. several times. It seemed her therapy wasn't the intensive, total immersion variety, but more like a maintenance situation. This indicated to me, confirmed layman that I was, that her mental illness wasn't in the acute stages. I flipped the pages back to the current week. Astrachan had blocked it out and had written "Southern Cal., Psych. Conf., San Diego" across the entire week.

"I believe our boy's in San Diego," I said. Maud didn't seem impressed with my deductive prowess. Or else she was getting frustrated.

"I've found a tape recorder," she said. "But no tapes."

"I'm telling you, he's not going to leave those lying around for people like us to find. He has a responsibility for protecting his clients' confidentiality. Can you imagine what would happen to his practice if information like that got out? The liability? I mean, he's got a pretty elite clientele here. He'd be ruined."

Maud ignored me. In the back of the bottom drawer of the credenza behind Astrachan's desk she had at last found a cache of audiocassette tapes. She pulled one out and showed it to me.

"I don't believe it," I said.

I walked around the desk and peered down into the drawer open in front of Maud. In it were hundreds of audiocassette tapes, the microcassette kind, neatly aligned in rows. Shelves and shelves of them. "This guy is just begging for a lawsuit," I said.

Maud was going through the tapes, looking for Lashona Webber's.

"We can't just sit here and listen to all the tapes of her sessions," I said.

"I don't think that's what they are," she said. "He probably just summarized the sessions at the end, you know, two or three minutes of recap. Ah-*ha*."

She pulled out a cassette. "Lashona Webber," she read. "December 2001 to, well, I guess to present. See? All his summaries of Lashona's sessions must be on this tape." She put the cassette in the pocket of her bomber jacket and closed the drawer of the credenza.

"What are you doing?" I said.

"Taking the tape," she said. "You're right. We can't sit here and listen to the whole thing. It's a ninety-minute tape."

"You can't take that tape," I said. "What happens when he finds out it's missing?"

"I don't know," said Maud. "What happens?"

"You know what I mean," I said.

"No, really, I don't. Do you think the first thing Dr. Astrachan is going to do when he gets back is inventory his tape file? We'll take it and listen to it tonight, then return it tomorrow night. He won't even know it's been gone."

Well, audacity was one thing, but this seemed plain foolhardy to me.

"How do we know he won't be meeting with Lashona tomorrow on his first day back?" I said, realizing immediately how stupid that question was.

"Stephen, the woman is missing, remember?"

"Yeah, but she may be missing selectively, you know? Maybe she just re-emerges to meet with her shrink."

Maud shook her head slowly. She had a small grin on her face.

"Well, you've got the appointment book right there. Let's see if Lashona's on the agenda tomorrow."

I could feel my face flush. Of course. I had been looking at Astrachan's past appointments up to the current blank week. I had not thought to look forward to see when Lashona might be scheduled for a visit. Feeling sheepish, I scanned through Astrachan's appointment book, looking for the telltale L.W. I didn't find any L. W. entries for the next day. Nor the next week. Not even the next month. In fact, for as far as his appointments went, I saw no indication that Lashona Webber would be returning to Dr. Astrachan's office.

"That's weird," I said.

"What?" said Maud.

"Lashona's not scheduled at all."

"Astrachan knows!" shouted Maud. I motioned with my hands in a palms forward, slightly downward-facing, noise-suppression gesture.

"Knows what?" I said softly.

"He must know what happened to Lashona," said Maud, still excited.

"You're jumping to conclusions, kind of one of those "Wide World of Sports" agony-of-defeat ski jumps." I said.

"I don't think so," said Maud. She thought for a moment. "When was the last time Lashona was here?"

I referred again to the appointment book.

"Last Wednesday," I said.

"Two days before she vanished," said Maud. "And now Astrachan has no more appointments scheduled for her. I find that mighty strange."

I had to admit that I found it mighty strange, too.

"I think the final entry on this tape is going to be very interesting," she said, tapping her jacket over the pocket that held the tape. "We need to hit an electronics store before they close," she said. "I don't have a tape recorder for these kinds of tapes."

We didn't find an electronics store. Birmingham's zoning ordinances probably didn't permit anything as practical as a Radio Shack to set up shop within its borders. However, I happen to be a chronic 2:00 a.m. shopper and I knew exactly where a 24-hour Meijer's was.

"They sell tape recorders at Meijer's?" said Maud.

"Are you kidding?" I said. "You could buy the components for a hydrogen bomb there. Well, not really. But you can buy things you wouldn't expect from a glorified supermarket. Agricultural equipment, furniture, you name it. It's great. You don't get out much, do you?"

By the time we got back to Maud's house, it was almost 10:00 p.m.

"I'm going to make some coffee," she said.

"Where should I . . . park myself?"

"Oh, I'm sorry," she said. "I got so excited about the tape. Come on." She led me downstairs to what I assumed had once been a basement, but was now fully finished into a bedroom, complete with its own bathroom and study.

"Nice," I said. Maud shrugged.

"Conor built this as a home office for himself. Then, after he started spending more and more time down here working, he eventually turned it into sort of a guest room. Problem was, he was the only guest. I should have seen it for the omen that it was. He was just leaving me in stages." I nodded slowly, not knowing what to say. "Anyway, the bathroom should be fully stocked, but if you need anything, let me know." She opened a sliding door. "Plenty of closet space." She laughed. "I sound like a real estate agent."

"It's a big house for one person," I said.

"Yeah, I know. Conor relinquished the place to me out of guilt, I think. At first, I thought there was no way I could stay here alone with all those memories. I thought I would just sell and get something a little smaller. This house would go for a couple of million. But then I thought about it more and realized that, it's just a house after all. And I'm dug in here, so to speak. I don't dislodge easily. Even filling out a change of address form would be traumatic for me. I know that's not rational, but what can I say?"

"Hey," I said, "you don't have to defend your decision to me." She smiled.

"I know about you, Mr. Fargo," she said. "You're the rootless type. I feel the need to explain myself to you, my attachment to place. I'm actually a pretty adventurous person."

"So I've noticed," I said.

"Meet you upstairs," she said.

I took a shower and changed into some of my new clothes. By the time I got back upstairs, Maud was sitting at the kitchen table sipping a cup of coffee. The new tape recorder was standing in the middle of the table, loaded with the cassette.

Maud had changed from her jeans and top to a long sleeve, white T-shirt that read "Please Don't Touch the Works of Art" across the front. In smaller lettering under that was the name of her gallery. I, of course, was looking at the works of art themselves. She had obviously taken off her bra and her nipples were hard. Maybe it was the stimulation provided by the prospect of listening to the tape. She had replaced her Levi's with a pair of running shorts that showed off her legs. They were nice legs, blemish free, with long, smooth muscles. She'd removed what little makeup she'd had on, but that only accentuated her large eyes and pale, full mouth. Maud was one of those rare women who looked much better without all the packaging than with it. I poured myself a cup of coffee and sat down.

"This is so exciting," said Maud as she depressed the play button on the tape recorder.

TEN

LET'S GO TO THE AUDIO

A high-pitched, nasal, almost effeminate voice issued from the tape recorder, not the voice I thought would emerge after having seen Astrachan's photo on his desk. Then again, there was the troubling matter of those Speedo bathing trunks. Maud and I glanced at each other, then redirected our gazes to the tape recorder as if it were some sort of fetish. Astrachan was giving a rundown of his first session with Lashona Webber.

" . . . African-American female, thirty-one; occupation, television journalist. Patient complains of periodic fatigue, weight loss and indifference to her job and family, as well as acute episodes of despair. Could assign no cause to these feelings. Reports a stable marital relationship, although she finds herself less committed to the relationship than in the past. Reports a strained relationship with her mother and a brother." I looked at Maud.

"No mention of the daughter?" I said.

"Stephen," she said, "we're only thirty frickin' seconds into the tape." We continued listening.

"Patient indicated that she never before experienced the symptoms she describes and, in fact, prides herself on her energy and determination. Patient exhibits significant defensiveness about her professional life. I explained that her symptoms indicate severe clinical depression, which the patient rejects. I explained that it is a relatively common affliction and doesn't reflect on her sanity or any moral deficiency on her part. She continued to resist the idea that she is depressed. I prescribed Zoloft and twice-weekly therapy sessions."

The next entry is six weeks later.

"How come six weeks later?" I ask Maud.

"He probably didn't conduct her actual therapy sessions," she said. "He probably assigned her to a clinical psychologist for that. He probably just saw her periodically to monitor her progress and adjust her meds."

"So, you *have* done this therapy thing," I said. She shrugged.

"For a while, around the time of my divorce."

We listened to several more entries, none of which was very compelling. Astrachan mentioned having discussed Lashona's case with her therapist, a woman named Genevieve Brace. Apparently, Brace had tried some hypnosis and other techniques, which Lashona resisted. I got the impression that her therapy wasn't going well. Lashona was a strong-willed person who didn't like being told what to do, even if it was for her own good.

Around the time of Lashona's third visit to Dr. Astrachan—by this time, she was four months into the therapy—tensions seemed to be rising. Lashona had been reassigned to another therapist, a man named Warren Priest, and it was going no better with him than it had with Genevieve Brace.

"Patient continues to demonstrate extreme hostility to therapy," Astrachan reported toward the end of this period. "I am recommending a hiatus on sessions and a change in medication to Paxil to address PTSD."

"If you can't beat 'em, drug 'em," I said. "What's PTSD?"

Maud shushed me and scowled at the tape recorder. "This is telling us nothing at all," she said. She reached over and pushed the stop button on the recorder.

"What's PTSD?" I repeated.

"I think it's post traumatic stress disorder," she said.

"Really? How would you know about that?"

"When I was in college I used to work at Common Cause, you know, the crisis center? I used to get a few calls from Vietnam and Gulf War Vets who suffered from it."

"I don't recall seeing anything about military service in Lashona's bio," I said.

"It doesn't have to be military related," said Maud. "Sometimes woman who get assaulted, you know, rape victims, suffer from it."

Hmmm.

"I didn't hear any reference to a traumatic event," I said.

"Neither did I," said Maud.

"Of course, we haven't heard the whole tape," I said.

"These don't even sound like a real psychiatrist's session notes to me," she said. "There's something about this that doesn't make any sense."

"You think Astrachan is a fraud?" I said. "That kind of thing is hard to fake. I mean, it's easy enough to check a person's credentials. And, by the way, how many recorded session notes have you listened to, anyway?"

"None," she said. "But I don't know . . . I have met with psychiatrists and therapists. They were very professional. There's way too much . . . melodrama in these tapes, don't you think?"

"I don't know," I said. "I guess most psychiatrists assume their notes and recordings are confidential. Protected. They might let their hair down. Although given the state of Astrachan's hair, that might be difficult."

Maud ignored my pathetic attempt at humor.

"Something's not right," she said. She turned the recorder back on. The summaries continued in much the same vein, until the final summary, the one for two days before Lashona's disappearance. It was very abrupt.

"Treatment terminated by mutual consent," was all Astrachan said. He didn't sound real happy about it. Maud and I looked at each other again.

"Can he do that?" she asked. I shrugged.

"Sounds like they agreed to it," I said.

"I would think there would be more of an explanation, some concluding remarks from Astrachan," said Maud. "Just for his own protection, you know? In case of a malpractice suit or something."

"Well, I guess you can't force a patient to continue therapy," I said. But something Maud had said bothered me. Then I realized what it was. The malpractice thing. I slapped myself in the forehead.

"What?" said Maud, a look of alarm on her face.

"She was doing a *story*," I said. Maud said nothing for a moment. She seemed to be searching my face for an explanation.

"What do you mean?" she said, finally. Then I saw it begin to dawn on her. "You mean she was, like, undercover?"

"Something like that," I said. "That was Lashona's forte, right? Exposés? Investigative reports. I read in her file that she won an Emmy for investigative reporting of the police department. Maybe the mental health profession was next on her list."

"Well, it would certainly answer a few questions," said Maud. "Maybe Astrachan was a fraud and she knew it, or found out about it during her so-called therapy." She paused. "Hey," she said excitedly, "how's that for a motive for killing Lashona?"

"We don't know that Lashona is dead," I reminded her.

"Still, Astrachan would be highly incented to keep her quiet," said Maud. "You should have seen some of the names in his file. We're talking the social elite of the southeastern Michigan area. And not only that. He's got clients on both coasts. Business leaders of nearly legendary status."

"I wonder why Lashona chose Astrachan," I said. "I mean, assuming she was investigating the mental health industry. I can see it if the guy's ripping off average Americans with some kind of psychobabble scam. But who cares if a bunch of rich people are stupid enough to give their money to a quack? Lots of people would get satisfaction out of that. Another skirmish won in the never-ending class war. Where would be the outrage, you know?"

"Good point," said Maud. Then a moment later she announced: "We need to find out why Lashona was seeing Dr. Astrachan."

"I'm not breaking into a TV station," I said.

"I'm not suggesting that," she said.

"What are you suggesting?"

"I'm not sure yet," she said. "But something will come to me. Now I'm wishing we'd lifted a few more session tapes. Maybe find out why some of Astrachan's other patients need therapy. You know, those aren't usually the kind of people who go to therapists, even it they need it." I nodded.

"So we'll do it?" said Maud.

"Do what?"

"Find out why she picked Astrachan. See what she was up to."

"Well," I said, "that depends. Lashona's dealings with Astrachan might have nothing to do with her disappearance and the death of her husband. It could be a coincidence that she was working on this story." Even as I was telling Maud this, I was having a difficult time believing it. She was right about the people she had found in Astrachan's file not being the kind of people who go to therapists. There was something just not right here.

"What about this," said Maud. "Tomorrow, we call Lashona's office and ask to speak with her. We'll tell them that we have some important information for Lashona about the medical health story she's working on. They'll tell us Lashona's not there, unless she happens to turn up overnight, so then we'll ask to speak to her producer."

"And what do we tell this producer?" I asked. Maud pondered this for a moment. "And while you're thinking about that, see if you can also come up with some way that this ploy is going to do us any good at all."

"Maybe we could at least confirm that Lashona was working on an investigative report about Astrachan."

"I already assume that's the case," I said. "So, how does that help us?"

"Okay," said Maud. "How about this: I call up Astrachan and tell him that I've been referred to him for some psychiatric help. You could do it, but it would be more credible coming from me."

"Especially given the fact that you're alive," I said.

"I'm part of his target market," Maud continued, ignoring my remark. "I could even tell him that I was referred by Lashona." She smiled and straightened her posture. She seemed pleased with herself for coming up with this idea. So, along comes Mr. Buzz Kill.

"I highly doubt that Astrachan is going to discuss his work with other patients simply because you claim to have been referred by one of them," I said.

"Do I look completely stupid?" said Maud.

"Not at all," I said. "And I appreciate your imagination. It's just that I don't see the point."

"The point is, it gets us close to Astrachan. Maybe he'll give himself away unintentionally."

"Assuming he has something to give away," I said.

"Well," said Maud. "We won't know until we try, will we?" She got up and retrieved the carafe of coffee. She poured us each another cup, then sat down and gave me the sort of penetrating stare that I sensed was the prelude to Heavy Communication. I braced myself. "I'm sensing resistance," she said, finally. "Do you want to do this or not?"

"I thought you already had me figured out in that regard," I said. She looked down at her coffee cup.

"I'm starting to have my doubts," she said. I stared at *my* coffee cup. The answer wasn't *there*, either.

"Maud, this whole thing is interesting, like figuring out a crossword puzzle is interesting. But I really didn't know Barry or Lashona all that well. It's not like I feel the urge for revenge, here. And I'm not a cop. I've run things like this down before. They tend to consume your life. They also tend to become dangerous. You don't encounter the best of humanity. I guess what I'm trying to say is that this is no game."

"I know that," said Maud. "But we are talking about human beings, here. One who has been brutally murdered and another who could suffer the same fate unless we do something about it."

"She may have already suffered the same fate," I said. "And if she did, it really is a call for the authorities."

"Except," said Maud, "that in this case the authorities may be involved."

"We have no proof of that," I said. "Police departments don't murder news reporters because of exposés. The police department is just another bureaucracy. People are always writing stories critical of the police department. They respond with more incompetence, not murder."

"You're forgetting that this exposé ruined a couple of careers."

I shrugged. "It still seems unlikely to me, and I'm more paranoid than most."

"Well, the police don't know what we know," said Maud.

"They can figure it out," I said.

"But it may be too late by then if Lashona Webber is still alive right now."

I took another drink of my coffee. This was a bad idea, drinking so much coffee this late at night. I would probably have trouble sleeping. My tolerance for caffeine has decreased as my tolerance for alcohol has increased. Maud seemed to be watching my every move with intense interest. I smiled at her. She did not smile back at me.

"Do you want to hear my theory on why you pulled this stunt of faking your own death?" she said. I had had no idea that anybody thought that was worth theorizing about.

"What does this have to do with Barry Justice and Lashona Webber?" I said.

"It has to do with you," snapped Maud.

"I'm sensing some hostility here," I said, trying to keep it playful. She didn't back down a bit. "Okay," I said. "No, I don't want to hear your theory, okay?"

She continued to stare at me. I replayed in my head the previous few minutes of our conversation, trying to remember what I might have said to put her in whatever kind of mood she was in. Was it because of my reluctance to jump into this Barry/Lashona mystery with both feet?

"Stephen," said Maud, "you can't run away. You might as well get involved. I think it's your fate. I'm a big believer in fate."

Yeah, and Barry Justice was a big believer in things happening for a reason. Look where it got *him*. I hoped that, at least, he died for some noble reason, but I doubted it.

"I mean," said Maud, "don't you find it weird that you should run into Barry Justice in a Home Depot while you're supposedly a missing person, and he tells you about a missing person and before you know it, he's dead?"

"Yes, I do think it's weird. But it's not my fault. And it's not my responsibility."

"But that's my point," said Maud. "In a cosmic sort of way, it is."

In a cosmic sort of way?

"Look, Maud," I said, "for me to get involved in this means that at some point, probably sooner rather than later, I'm going to have to resurface, you know, publicly. That's going to be awkward, but it's not going to be as bad as how upset some people are going to be, some dear friends, whom I've led to believe that I'm dead. Not to take myself too seriously here, but, they've gone through their grieving process or whatever they've gone through as a result of what they thought happened to me. They're going to feel, I don't know, betrayed."

"Well, they *were* betrayed," said Maud. "But you know what? They'll get over it. That's not the reason. The reason goes deeper. You sure you don't want me to tell you?"

"No," I said. "I've had enough psychology for one night." Jesus!

"I'm sorry," said Maud. She started fidgeting with her coffee cup again. "I'm nagging, aren't I?" Then, before I could respond: "It's just that I'm one of those people who feel betrayed."

Gulp. I was out of clever or even self-righteous things to say.

"Well, I'm sorry, too," I said. "But we don't—didn't know each other."

"Right," said Maud, abruptly. Goddamn, this evening was just disintegrating into a nightmare right before my very eyes.

"Look, we're both tired. Or at least *I'm* tired. Maybe we can talk about this in the morning." Whatever "this" was.

"I don't want to talk about it in the morning," said Maud. "Let's just forget it. But whether you go ahead with this or not, I'm not going to let it go. Somebody needs to help and I can't just sit around until I read in the paper that they've found Lashona Webber's body someplace. I wouldn't be able to live with that."

The implication being, of course, that only the worst kind of an excuse for a human being—namely me—*could* live with that.

We went to our separate beds, but my chances of sleep were almost nonexistent. First, I was in a strange bed, and my "rootless" soul notwithstanding, I could never sleep well in a strange bed. Second, there was the issue of the coffee. I never sleep well when I drink coffee in the evening. Never. And now, to top off those two major impediments, I had to deal with the unresolved issue of how we were or were not going to proceed.

All of this weighed on my mind when I finally got out of bed at 4:30 a.m. I showered, then went upstairs. I washed out the coffee machine and made a fresh pot. If Maud had heard me, she wasn't in any hurry to get downstairs. I heard no evidence that she was even stirring. I poured myself a cup of coffee, and, being the old print-oriented bastard that I am, I started to feel the itch to read the newspaper.

I looked out through the front door. It was still dark outside, but I saw a newspaper on the driveway, wrapped in yellow cellophane. I ran out in my bare feet to retrieve it. The temperature had dropped to the high thirties or so and my feet, which hadn't recovered from my hiking experience behind the Justice/Webber house, immediately went numb.

Then I got back inside, read the lead headline on the front page, and all of me went numb.

I don't know how long I stood there, but at some point Maud arrived on the scene.

"Stephen, what's wrong?" she said. I must have looked bad. Her voice contained alarm. I turned the newspaper around and showed her what I had been reading. I watched her eyes get big and her mouth fall open.

Prominent Local Psychiatrist Found Murdered, the headline read.

ELEVEN

THE PLAY'S THE THING

"That does it," said Maud.

"Does what?" I asked. She looked at me in disbelief.

"Maybe I misspoke," she said. "Maybe I should have said that *should* do it, for any normal, compassionate human being."

"Do what?"

"Should make your mind up about your involvement in this case," said Maud. "We've got a serial killer out there. You can't ignore it anymore." I wondered if two murders constituted a serial situation.

"I wasn't ignoring it," I said.

"You know what I mean."

I was trying to work up some indignation, but it was pretty hard. Maud looked great. She had changed her T-shirt. This one had a picture of Marilyn Monroe on the front, after the famous Andy Warhol painting. Under the picture were the words "Dumb blondes love the Birmingham Gallery." She also wore black tights and running shoes. The tights accentuated her slim, muscular body; she could see that I was staring. She pulled on a sweatshirt, gave her head a shake, then pulled on a pair of white mittens.

"I'm going for a run," she announced. "I'll be back in an hour. That should give you time to think things through. I want to talk about this, but I'm absolutely fanatical about getting my run in before I get involved in the day. If I don't, it's too easy not to do it."

Having been a runner myself off and on back when I was still alive, I could appreciate this. I didn't like the tone of ultimatum in her voice, though. Maud fitted a pair of white, furry earmuffs over her head, looked at me and gave a sad shake of the head. She was an absolute vision. I was almost ready to take up running again just so I could accompany her, watch her in action. A moment later she was out the door.

I poured another cup of coffee and sat down at the kitchen table to read the story about the unfortunate Dr. Astrachan.

He had been found stabbed to death in his hotel room. The San Diego Police stated that Dr. Astrachan had attended a panel discussion the afternoon of the previous day and had joined several of his colleagues for an early dinner and drinks. The concierge at the Manchester Grand Hyatt Hotel, where Astrachan had been staying, said that Astrachan had requested a 6:30 a.m. wake-up call. The police found a printout of a boarding pass in the room, indicating that Astrachan was scheduled to fly back to Detroit on the morning he was found, which, I realized, was yesterday, the day we had ransacked his office.

According to the police, nobody had heard sounds of a struggle, nor had anybody noticed suspicious behavior. Astrachan's wallet was found in the room with his cash and credit cards still in it. No immediate motive, no immediate suspects.

The rest of the story was a rundown of Astrachan's career, focusing on the upscale client list he was purported to have, including information that he had counseled numerous "show business and sports celebrities," especially in the area of substance abuse. In fact, the topic of the panel discussion Astrachan had been part of was "The Pressures of Celebrity and its Relationship to Substance Abuse." Poor babies, I thought.

After reading the news story, I turned on the TV to see if I could learn anything more about the murder on the local news, but after flipping through about fifteen infomercials on Bowflexes and coral calcium and other health and beauty aids ad nauseam, I still hadn't seen anything about Astrachan. I drank another cup of coffee, then decided to make a fresh pot so that Maud would have some when she returned. I had to do some serious ingratiating with that woman.

Maud returned twenty minutes later. She poured herself a cup of coffee—no doubt noticing that I had gone to the trouble to make another pot. She didn't mention it, though. She stood at the kitchen counter, still in sweatshirt and tights, drinking her coffee and reading the story on Astrachan. Any second, I expected her to demand my answer on what I was going to do; instead, she set the newspaper and her coffee cup down on the table and announced that she was going to take a shower. I thanked whatever deities might be hanging around for this reprieve, then resumed thinking how I was going to respond.

I still hadn't come up with an answer a half hour later when Maud reappeared in the kitchen. She looked ready to go to the gallery, even though it wasn't yet 7:30 a.m. I braced myself. It absolutely had to be coming now—the lecture on my civic and moral responsibility. She poured herself another cup of coffee and looked at me over the cup's lip as she drank.

She was wearing black satiny slacks and high heels. Her top was a three-quarter sleeve, scoop-necked number that was kind of a shimmery silver. She looked about as good as I could ever remember anyone looking, and that included my deceased wife, Denise, whom I had thought nobody could ever outdo in the looks department. The high heels emphasized Maud's height and the slender muscularity of her legs. She had thin arms and beautiful long fingers. She still did not appear to have put on any makeup. Her full lips looked pale, but by no means unattractive. I was still waiting for her to launch into the sermon on My Duty as a Human Being.

"Somebody is watching the house," she said. For a moment, I thought maybe she had taken a run by Barry Justice's residence and had seen someone parked in front of it. But almost immediately I knew she was talking about *her* house. And immediately after that, I realized that her reserved behavior was a result of concern. "A black Mercedes," she said.

"We need to get out of here," I said. "Now."

"And go where?"

"The nearest police station," I said. "This has gone far enough."

"No," she said.

"Maud, the operator of that black Mercedes is almost certainly my phone pal, you know, the one who killed Barry Justice. He obviously knows that I'm involved and he also, obviously, knows that you're in the loop, too. I think we're next on the list. Then you really *would* have a serial killer. We need to get the police involved."

"Why?" said Maud. "Do you think the police are going to protect us? I can tell you about police protection. I had a restraining order against Conor. You know how the police enforced that?" I didn't say anything. "They didn't enforce it at all. Conor harassed me continually. Finally, one day he showed up and decided maybe he could pummel me into submission, which just shows you how little he knew about me. But he did manage to put me in the hospital overnight, which was longer than Conor spent in jail for the assault. He made bail and was out before dinner. It's been a year and a half and a trial date still hasn't been set. So don't tell me about the protection I can expect from the criminal justice system. I'll take care of myself." She was trembling slightly, but I could see rage and determination in her face. No sense trying to talk her out of whatever course of action she had in mind. Not at the moment, anyway.

"Sorry," I said. "I guess I got the impression that it was your husband who left *you*." She looked skyward and blew air between her lips in a clearly derisive way.

"Let's just say he was conflicted," she said. "Like most men. He didn't want me, but when he made that clear, I was still supposed to want him." She looked at me for a moment. "You don't get that, do you?"

"Yeah, I get it," I said. "Why wouldn't I get it?" Maud didn't answer. I got up from the table and walked to the window in the living room.

"He's not there now," said Maud. "He was there when I left for my run, and he was still there when I got back. When I realized what was going on, I decided to have a little chat with him, but before I could get close enough, he drove off."

"What?" I said. "Are you crazy?"

"I will not be intimidated," said Maud.

"I don't think intimidation is what he has in mind," I said. "He thinks I won't go to the police. He thinks he can keep me quiet by threatening to expose me, and implicate me in Barry's death. But now he'll be worried about you. He might be worried that you *will* go to the police." Maud said nothing, but her eyes still said, anger, anger, Will Robinson.

"How about a compromise?" I said. She gave me a suspicious glance. She would not be intimidated, and, apparently, would not be compromised, either. "We don't go to the police, at least not now. But we need to find someplace else to stay." Now her expression shifted to skepticism.

"He can follow us to a hotel," she said.

"You're absolutely right," I said. "He can. How many suitcases do you have?" Maud twisted her head a bit and looked at me.

"I don't know," she said. "Three or four."

"Okay," I said. "Pack one of them with things you absolutely have to have." She was already shaking her head.

"What?" I said. "Don't you get it? We need to get out of here."

"Stephen," said Maud. "I just can't take off for a few days. I need to be at the gallery. I have a life. I don't have the luxury of everybody thinking I'm dead."

"If you don't listen to me," I said, "you may have that luxury sooner than you think." She started to say something and I put up my hands. "I know, I know. You won't be intimidated. But that doesn't cut any ice with our friend out there. You mean to tell me you have nobody you can call to cover for you at the gallery? What happens when you get sick? When you have to go out of town?"

Maud smoldered for a moment and didn't answer.

Finally she said, "And just what are we going to be doing while this person covers for me?"

"I don't know," I said. "But it will give us a little breathing space. I think better when I'm not being surveilled."

"*One* day," said Maud, firmly. "I can call someone who helps me out now and then. She's an art student at the Center for Creative Studies. But for one day only. If you haven't come up with something by then, I resume my normal activities."

"Deal," I said.

Maud made the call to the art student. They conversed for about ten minutes, and I heard Maud laugh a few times.

"Okay," she said when she walked back into the room. "That's taken care of. Now what?"

"Now," I said, "pack the one suitcase like I said. We'll put it in the car while the car's still in the garage. When we pull the car out of the garage we'll load the other suitcases in it, you know, making a big show of it."

"Stephen," said Maud, "I told you, the guy's gone."

"Guys like that are never gone," I said.

Maud did what I said, not quite reluctantly, but not eagerly, either. She retrieved a set of luggage from a storage room. Three matching suitcases by Ralph Lauren. Jesus, that guy was into everything. Paint, luggage. He'd be doing designer handguns next.

Maud went upstairs to pack one of the suitcases. While she was gone, I called the Townsend Hotel in Birmingham. The Townsend was one of the more elite hotels in the area, certainly the most elite in Birmingham. Lots of celebrities stayed there, especially entertainers with gigs at the nearby Palace of Auburn Hills where the Detroit Pistons played. Don't ask me why they aren't called the Auburn Hills Pistons.

I reserved a room for that night. All they had available was a luxury suite at $365. It was a small price to pay, I thought, to evade a psychopath. I put the reservation on my Stephen Greene credit card. I asked what time check-in was and the nice reservations lady told me it was 3:00 p.m., but that maybe we could check in earlier if our room was ready.

"Can I check our bags this morning?" I asked. "I really don't want to leave them in the car all day."

The reservations lady paused a beat, probably wondering what was wrong with leaving bags in the car all day, then told me that, yes, we could certainly check the bags and that someone would even put them into our room just as soon as it was ready. I thanked her and hung up.

A few minutes later, Maud was back downstairs with a suitcase in her hand.

"That goes in the car," I said. "Here, I'll take it. What I need you to do is fill these other two suitcases with towels or something, anything to give them some ballast." Maud looked at me like now she was convinced she had made a mistake sitting down at my table in the coffee shop.

"Ballast?" she said.

"Yeah," I said. "Something to give them some weight, but that won't shift around. So the baggage guys at the hotel won't think they're empty."

"God forbid they would think that," she said.

"Trust me," I said. "And let me have your keys." Maud shrugged and gave me her car keys. Then she went looking for ballast.

I carried her packed suitcase out into the garage, where I loaded it into the trunk of the Jaguar. Then I opened the garage door and backed the Jag down the driveway to the front of Maud's house. I got out of the car and gave a furtive look up and down the street. No sign of the Mercedes. But I could feel its occupant. He was around somewhere.

I went back into the house and helped Maud pack the two other suitcases with towels and bed sheets and a few table clothes and blankets.

"I'm going to get this stuff back, right?" she said.

"Sure," I responded automatically. I told her the plan. We would drive to the Townsend and drop off the two suitcases with the towels and blankets in them.

"With the ballast," Maud corrected me.

"Right," I said.

"So we're really going to just pretend to check into the Townsend," she said.

"Right, again," I said.

"Then what are we going to do?"

"Then we're going someplace else," I said.

"Where?"

"You'll see," I said.

"You're treating me like a six-year-old," said Maud. "Don't do that." She wouldn't be intimidated, compromised or, I guess, condescended to. I was hoping she could at least be reasoned with.

"We're going to my house," I said.

"You mean, your apartment?" said Maud.

"No, I mean my house." Maud said nothing for a moment.

Then she said, "But what's to keep the bad guy from just following us to your house?"

"The convincing nature of our performance," I said.

TWELVE

REDUNDANT HOUSE

We carried the two "ballast bags," as Maud was now referring to them, out the front door and made a big show of depositing them in the back seat of the Jag. Then we drove to the Townsend Hotel. On the way there, Maud grilled me for more specifics on the plan. Unfortunately, I didn't have much in the way of detail to give her.

"Okay," she said. "So the idea is to make Mr. Phone Voice think we're checking into the Townsend. For our safety, right?"

"Right," I said.

"Then we really don't check into the hotel at all?"

"Not necessarily," I said. "We probably should check in. We're just not going to *stay* there. Hey, can you kind of keep it within shouting distance of the speed limit?" We were traveling down Woodward Avenue, where the speed limit was forty-five miles per hour. Maud was inching it up to seventy.

"I can't help it," she said. "I've always had a lead foot." She backed it off to about sixty, but she was an impatient driver. She didn't like driving behind slower cars. She didn't like stop signs—which she tended to roll through by lifting her foot off the gas pedal but not necessarily applying it to the brake. And she didn't like traffic signals. Or, she didn't like *red* traffic signals.

"How many points do you have?" I asked, referring to moving violations on her driving record.

"I don't know," she said. "A few. Quit changing the subject. So, we check into the hotel, but we don't actually stay there."

"I think that's the way to go," I said.

"And then what?"

"I told you. We go to my house."

"*The* house?" she said. I nodded. "The one with the secret passages?" I sighed and nodded again. "The one Claude Nickle referred to in *Our Father*?"

"The very same," I said. She started driving faster again.

"I can't believe it," she said, a smile breaking out over her face.

"Neither can I," I said.

"So you never sold the house," said Maud.

"Nope."

"You knew you might need it, right?"

"Something like that."

The house, the one my old buddy Claude Nickle had apparently described for all the world at the end of *Our Father*, was a paranoid's dream. It was everything that Claude had said it was. It was built for a man—myself—who intended never to leave the house and who wanted to make sure it was invasion-proof. The house had what, for the mid-to-late 80s when it was installed, had been state-of-the-art electronic security equipment. There were redundancies everywhere. In fact, that's what my wife, Denise—rest her soul—called it. Redundant House. There were backup security systems, several bathrooms, a fully stocked panic room, a room that could only be called an armory, an underground area that most people would consider a basement, but that was actually a bunker that could withstand significant bombardment short of a direct nuclear strike.

There were also secret escape routes. What can I say? At the time I was flush with cash from the book and the movie deal. I was also convinced that some malevolent force out there was enraged by my success and what had spawned it—basically, my revelations about the Blessing family—and wanted to exact retribution of the most extreme form. Denise used to laugh at me, but she was also an indulgent creature, a person who truly did live by the tenet that you have to let other people be who they are (despite what people will tell you, there are precious few like Denise in the world). We spent several glorious, rapture-filled years in that modest fortress, until we took that fateful vacation out west.

I continued to live in the house right up until the time I "died" in the boating accident on the way to Bermuda. But I didn't think of it as a safe house for nothing. Before my "accident" I'd taken the precaution of signing a quitclaim deed for the place over to a good friend of mine—Mr. Stephen Greene. Then I'd contracted with various maintenance outfits—landscaping, snow removal, a cleaning service—to keep the place up. I explained to these various groups that Stephen Greene would be traveling frequently and living at other residences for large parts of the year, so that the house would often be unoccupied. Under Greene's name, I had retained all the security contracts, including the direct notification lines to the police and fire departments. All of this took some finessing and at times I wondered if it was worth the effort and the expense. Now, I knew that it was.

When I had returned to Detroit, I had been tempted to take up residence—again, as Mr. Greene—in my old house. But I realized it would be risky. I might be recognized. That's why I rented the apartment and just kept my house as the mother of all safe houses. Now it was going to come in handy.

Maud broke into my reverie with a question that had been proving thorny to me, as well.

"How are we going to get to the house without someone following us?" she said. "I mean, okay, we get to the Townsend, we unload our bags, pretend to check in or actually check in, but we don't stay. Instead, we're just making someone think we're staying there, but, actually, we're going to your house, which, presumably, the bad guy doesn't know about." She paused. "Or does he?"

"He didn't seem like the type that might have read *Our Father*," I said. "And even if he did, we're still safer there. The fucking Marines on their best day couldn't penetrate that house."

"Okay," said Maud. "That aside, how do we get from the Townsend to your house without being followed or noticed?"

Well, I was on shaky ground here. My hope was that Mr. Phone Voice, or whoever was working for him in the capacity of a tail, would assume we were taking up residence at the Townsend for the duration. They would either relax their vigilance or try some other approach.

"We let the valet take the car," I said to Maud, thinking aloud. "Then we get the concierge to rent us another one. Have it delivered to the hotel. Then, somehow, we make it to the rental car without being seen." Maud was nodding, indicating that she thought the plan might actually have some merit.

"If they could park it in the structure that adjoins the hotel, we could get to the car without going outside," she said. "And they would be looking for the Jag driving out of the structure. And if we left at night, they would have an even harder time seeing us."

"We can't wait until dark," I said. "We've got too much to do. We'll have to take the chance that they'll be looking for the Jag."

"Okay," said Maud. "I like it."

We made it to the Townsend without killing any innocent motorists or pedestrians and without damaging the Jag. We had the valet guy take our bags into the hotel and let him take the car to park it. Inside, we checked with the young man at the registration desk, a guy who looked like he was out of some Spanish movie of the thirties. He wore a black suit, black tie, starched white shirt and he had black hair combed back and so shiny that it looked like a beetle's back. He also had one of those mustaches that were in two parts—pencil lines drawn vertically from each nostril then diverting left and right at a ninety-degree angles horizontally over the upper lip. I looked at it closely. It really was hair. I wondered how long it took him to shave every morning.

He informed us that, indeed, we couldn't actually check in yet, but we could store our bags and they would be moved into our room when it was ready.

"You know, they have really nice rooms here," said Maud as we made our way over to the concierge's station. "Maybe we should think about staying the night." I shot her a look as we walked. What did she mean by *that*, exactly?

"It's an interesting thought," I said. "But as I mentioned, we've got too much to do."

"Yes," she said. "Just what is it that we're going to be doing?"

"I'll tell you when I know," I said.

We approached the concierge—this guy was more of a surfer type—and I explained to him that we wanted to rent a car because we didn't like the way the Jag was running. I was about to explain more to him about the specific problem we were having—plausibility seemed very important to me at that moment—when he looked at Maud and said, "Good morning, Ms. Gonne. So nice to see you again."

"Hello, Matt," said Maud. "How are you?"

Well, they went on like this for a couple of minutes with their displays of faux cordiality. Finally, Maud took up the discussion of the need for the car. "Mr. Greene and I are doing sort of an art tour today," she said. "Mr. Greene is a dealer from New York." Matt looked at me without much expression but a small, grudging concierge's smile and nodded his head. Apparently, all the big time art dealers like me showed up in jeans and a T-shirt. I looked more like Jackson Pollock than Al Taubman, but when you say those magic words "New York," it doesn't make much difference how you're dressed to a concierge in the Great Midwest, even the concierge of a swanky place like the Townsend.

"No problem at all," said Matt. "We have an agreement with Hertz and keep several cars on site. I can have one at the door in a matter of minutes."

"No," said Maud, touching Matt's arm. "We're going to have breakfast. Could you just ask them to park it in the structure?"

That probably came as an odd request to Matt. Most of the people who stayed in the Townsend had spent about as much time in parking structures as they had in sewers. Most of the people who stayed at the Townsend probably never walked more than ten feet to get into their cars. And they never retrieved their own cars. Still, there was something in the way that Maud made the request that encouraged Matt to agree to it without even the raising of one hair of his blond eyebrow. The weird requests of rich people. What could you do but humor them?

By the time we were finished with breakfast, Matt informed us that our car, a brand new silver Mercedes, was waiting for us in the, ahem, parking structure. He gave us the keys, handing them to Maud after asking once again if we were sure we didn't want the car brought around. We assured him that we didn't, thanked him, and headed off toward the parking structure.

"You and Matt go way back, huh?" I said as we settled into the leathery front seat of the car.

"I use the hotel for when guests and business associates come in from out of town," said Maud. "I give them quite a lot of business, actually. I'm sure they appreciate it."

The Mercedes was a helluva car, and I took some delight in the irony of a Mercedes being stalked by a Mercedes. Or, we now hoped, not. I sat behind the wheel and fired up the car. Vroom, vroom. Maud looked at me and rolled her eyes.

"We aren't going to be challenging teenagers to drag races, are we?" she asked.

"You should talk," I said.

Before pulling out, I took a look around the parking structure. I couldn't see anybody. I pulled the car slowly out of its parking space and made my way to the exit. When I got there, I pulled slowly out to the narrow side street where the Townsend Hotel stood tucked away from the main drag. I couldn't see the black Mercedes, which didn't mean much. But it made me feel better.

"Hey," said Maud. "What if *he's* changed cars, too?" That made me feel *worse*, but the prospect was so ridiculous that the feeling passed quickly. Within five minutes, I was tooling along Woodward Avenue in a northerly direction, glancing occasionally into the rearview mirror. No black Mercedes. Maybe we had pulled this off.

Less than half an hour later, I was exiting I-75 to Clarkston. I hadn't spent much time in the area for five years and things had changed somewhat. More office buildings, a few more strip malls. It occurred to me that this could be a problem. Could new right-of-ways and easements have interfered with my escape routes?

Maud had another problem on her mind.

"Why haven't we heard anything about the police finding Justice's body?" she said. I hadn't really given it a lot of thought, but now that she mentioned it, yeah, I wondered why, too.

"Do you think he's still sitting there in his living room?" said Maud, a sort of queasy look on her face.

"I suppose he could be," I said. "Especially with Lashona not being around to find him. And I had a sense from talking to him that they didn't really miss him much at the office when he was gone. He could sit at home for a while." Maud nodded.

"Just like Astrachan could have," she said. "The only reason they found him was because they had to clean up the room."

"Right," I said.

"Which is why," said Maud, "I'm having a problem with this being some kind of message killing. You know, with the castration and everything."

"It might not be a message," I said. "The killer could just be some sick fuck with a weird sense of humor." I paused for a moment. "Hey, do you suppose there's a support group for maids who find murder victims and other dead bodies in hotel rooms?"

Redundant House looked the same. The landscape guys had done a good job of keeping up the exterior of the house. I turned into the driveway and around the side of the house to the garage. I didn't have the remote garage door opening gizmo, of course, so I had to get out of the car, unlock the side door to the garage and open the garage door from the inside. As I walked back to the car, I looked around for the black Mercedes. Redundant House had been built on a large lot of nearly an acre-and-a-half. The houses in the area were not close together. There also wasn't much traffic because the subdivision was basically a loop. Normally, the only people in the area were residents, delivery people and motorists who had gotten lost. I couldn't see any cars now.

I pulled the silver Mercedes into the garage and closed the door behind us. We unloaded Maud's suitcase and walked from the garage into the house. Inside, everything looked pretty much the same. Maud looked around quickly, dropped her suitcase and did what most women do when they enter a new domestic environment. She asked me where the bathroom was.

"The nearest one is through the hallway on your left. If you get to the laundry room, you've gone too far. It's a purely functional bathroom, however. If you're looking for something a little more extravagant—and I use that term loosely—the master bath at the top of the stairs is worth seeing."

"Functional will do for what I have in mind," said Maud. "Anything I should know about the local wildlife before I wander in there?"

"Nothing you haven't seen before," I said.

"I'm not so sure." Maud headed off to the bathroom and I did a quick check on the security systems. Everything seemed to be intact and operating. The phone was even working. I had set up an account in the name of, you guessed it, Stephen Greene, for which the phone company automatically charged Mr. Greene's credit card.

Maud returned to find me in the living room. She plopped down on the couch, abruptly arched up to remove an empty beer can that had wedged itself between the cushions, and sat back down.

"Only you could have a place where sitting down could be dangerous," she said.

"Well, don't sit down, then," I said. "Come on. I'll give you a tour. She got up with a show of some weariness, I thought, and followed as I headed upstairs.

"Here's a guest room," I told her when we got to the top of the stairs. "You're welcome to use it, or I have a couple more."

"Just how long do you think we're going to be here?" she asked.

"I don't know," I said. "At least one day, right?"

I showed her the master bedroom and the "extravagant" master bath. She basically just stuck her head into these rooms; she might have even been giving them the odor test. I couldn't be sure.

"The place really is clean," I told her. "A cleaning crew comes through it once every two months, whether it needs it or not. They don't do any deep leaning, if you know what I mean, but they get the surface stuff."

"That would explain the beer can," said Maud.

"I suspect cleaning the place got to be pretty much a matter of going through the motions," I said. "You know, with nobody here to get it dirty."

"It feels so lonely," said Maud. I thought she might be going through some profound disillusionment. After all, she had read and heard about Redundant House. And here she was touring a pretty normal dwelling, notwithstanding the fact that "Trading Spaces" would have a field day redecorating every room in the house.

"Try to keep up," I said to Maud, who gave me a sickly smile in response. "The fun stuff is still to come."

I led her to a storage room at the end of the hall. I opened the door and showed her the false panel behind the stacks of boxes and bicycles and unused exercise equipment. I slid the panel back to reveal a keypad onto which I punched a code, which caused another panel to slide open just behind the false panel. That redundancy thing, again.

"Wow," said Maud. "It's just like *Panic Room*."

"Well, it's not quite as good as that. It's not totally assault-proof. But it will buy us time if we need it."

She followed me into the room and I showed her some of the emergency equipment—flashlights, two-way radios, flares—"Don't light these in here," I told her helpfully—first aid kits, water in plastic jugs, Army MREs, the modern version of C-rations, bought from military surplus stores—"These are actually quite tasty," I told her. She turned up her nose.

"Are these real?" she said. I saw her pointing at one wall where I had hung a couple of handguns and grenades. "As far as I know," I said. "I've actually never used them, but the guy I bought them from was pretty reliable; that is, he came highly recommended."

I showed her a small bathroom with a shower stall.

"Talk about functional," she said. I nodded.

"The guy who built this for me was the former head of security for the Israeli consulate in Detroit."

"What the hell are they worried about it Detroit?" said Maud.

"Oh, when the Arab-American community here began to burgeon, they, well, I guess you could say they took extra precautions. They brought in the head of security for all of the Israeli embassies around the world and had him work on some modifications to the consulate here. Detective Lazard—you remember who he was, right?—he got to know this security guy somehow, probably because the police were involved through some kind of notification system. When Lazard found out I wanted to secure the house, he recommended this guy, whose name, unfortunately, I can't remember. It was one of those names I could never get comfortable with, so I didn't put a lot of effort into memorizing it. I don't think it was his real name, in any event. In fact, for all I know the entire tale was bogus.

"Anyway, my budget was somewhat smaller than the consulate's, and this stuff isn't state-of-the-art anymore. Not by a long shot. But it does provide some reassurance in these troubling times. Come on. One more thing to show you."

I took her to another keypad at the back wall and punched in another code. That panel slid back to reveal a door. I opened it and the light beyond the door switched on automatically, revealing stairs leading down.

"You're kidding," said Maud. "Nickle was right about the secret passages."

"Yeah," I said. "I showed him. He'd helped me out in Italy with the Blessing thing, and I trusted the guy. So, I gave him the same tour I'm giving you. Whoda thunk he was going to capitalize on it the way he did?" I turned and faced Maud.

"*You* aren't going to write a book, are you?" Her magnificent cheekbones reddened, but she recovered quickly.

"I don't even like to write a shopping list," she said. "I hate writing. I don't know how authors do it. It would make me crazy."

"Authors *are* crazy," I said. "Time to go down the rabbit hole." I turned and started walking down the stairs. Maud seemed to hesitate at the top. "You coming?" I said.

"Where does this go?" she said.

"I thought you liked the challenge of the unknown," I said. "The sense of adventure."

"I'm not sure I know you this well," she responded.

I reached back, grabbed her hand and gently yanked her forward. We descended the metal stairs, our footsteps echoing off the stark walls. After several flights of stairs, we came to the tunnel.

"Brrr," said Maud, hugging herself. "It's cold."

"Yeah," I said. "Well, the idea wasn't to spend much time in the tunnel, so we never got around to heating it."

"Did your wife ever come down here?" said Maud, picking up on my use of the first person plural.

"Never," I said. "Oh, I think she came down here once when it had just been built. But she basically thought that I was, well, paranoid. She used to laugh about it."

"She was probably right," said Maud. We continued walking through the tunnel until we got to another door, a walk of exactly one hundred and five yards.

"Ready?" I said.

"I guess," said Maud, but she didn't sound too ready. I pulled the door open and led her out of the tunnel and into the interior of a cinder block structure.

"Where are we?" said Maud.

"It's sort of a boiler room," I replied.

"Yeah, but for what?"

"A school. Stephen T. Mason Middle School."

"A school let you build a tunnel from your house to their building?"

"Well," I said, "they didn't actually know about it. They were closing down the school, you know, consolidating the district. So, they sold me the building."

"So, nothing happens here?" said Maud. "It's just an empty building?"

"Not exactly empty," I said. "Come on."

Our footsteps again echoed as we walked across the concrete floor of the school's basement storeroom/maintenance room/boiler room to another set of stairs that took us up to the main level. The school was one of those dreary one-story utilitarian structures that states had probably built by the thousands in the mid-50s as the wave of the Baby Boomer generation crested. I hadn't done much to change the building. The floors were still tiled a uniform gray; the walls were painted a pale yellow. I'd even left the student lockers intact, although I had cleaned them all out. What a collection of flotsam and jetsam *that* had been.

"Don't you worry about vandalism?" said Maud. "Kids breaking in and such?"

"No," I said. "This building has the same state-of-the-art security equipment my home has. Or maybe I should say what state-of-what-the-art was."

"What were you going to do with this place?"

"Nothing," I said. "It's another redundancy. In case I needed to get out of my house and find somewhere else safe to stay."

Maud looked at me carefully. It was a look of serious concern.

"How many more of these do you have?" she asked.

"What do you mean?" I said. "You think I'm crazy? I can't afford to buy buildings all over town." She wasn't convinced. "This is the only one I have."

"The only former school building," she said.

"The only other building besides my home," I said. I quickened my pace a little, more in an effort to discourage Maud from asking additional questions than anything else.

I led her to what had once been the faculty lounge. I had slightly reconfigured the space into a respectable, if not glamorous, living area. It had all the basics. Hot and cold running water, a TV hooked up to cable, telephones, a kitchen alcove and a partitioned area for use as a bedroom. I had stockpiled the same rations, water and emergency equipment here as was found in my house. Maud was looking more and more distressed.

I was about to explain myself, but I decided that anything I said would only perplex her more. After all, how do you tell somebody that for ten years or so, your entire life was devoted to securing the survival of yourself and your wife against, well, against those who would end that survival? And just because I couldn't put my finger on exactly who these people were didn't mean my efforts were wasted. Denise used to tell me that I was still living the Cold War, still anticipating the hard rain of nuclear ordnance. I don't know. Maybe I was. I used to tell Denise of my fantasy of ensuring my immortality by being hooked up to every diagnostic instrument known to medical science and having a cadre of specialists at my side 24/7. At the first sign of disease or degeneration, the medicos could spring into action, my feeling being that the only reason illness and death prevail is because we don't arrest their insidious overtures early enough. Neglect, I theorized, was death's opportunity. Denise used to laugh at me. She laughed at me a lot, not maliciously, but almost like I was her personal comedian, her Jerry Seinfeld or something.

"You can't be too careful," is what I would say to Denise when she would start her gentle ragging on me for my protective zeal.

"You're careful enough for both of us," she would reply. But neither of us was careful enough when it came to her falling to her death from a rock in Sedona.

"I just wanted to make you aware of this," I said to Maud. "You know, in case of the need for a speedy evac." Maud nodded, but I think she was still pondering what kind of man would actually go to the lengths I had gone to in the name of precaution.

"If someone breaks into your house, couldn't they just follow you here if you fled?" she asked.

"Good question," I said. "And the answer is, not if I don't want them to. The doors would seal immediately behind us as we left. They'd need the code to open them. They could break them down if they had some major demolition equipment or explosives, but most of the time people don't carry that stuff around. They could probably figure out at some point that we'd escaped to the school here, but by that time, we'd be ready for them."

"I don't even want to know what that means," said Maud.

"Hey," I said. "If we're lucky, we won't even need to worry about it. And once this is over, I'm going to dismantle all this stuff and sell the buildings. I can use the money."

"I think that would be a good idea," said Maud.

We retraced our steps back through the school hallway to the door leading to the tunnel. Maud didn't have much to say all the way back to the house. Maybe she was having second thoughts about getting involved with a full-blown paranoid. Well, I had tried to discourage her from playing detective. By the time we were back in my home sitting at the kitchen table, Maud was ready to talk again.

"So, now that we're here, what are we going to do?" she said.

"Do battle against evil," I said. "Make the world safe for democracy."

THIRTEEN

NOTES FROM UNDERGROUND

Maud went upstairs to the guest room to stash her clothes and whatever else she'd brought. A few minutes later she was back downstairs.

"Let's call WEEE," I said. "See what happens." I pushed the phone towards her.

"What if they want to know who I am?"

"Tell them," I said. "Say Lashona had ordered some piece of art from you and you wanted to get in touch with her about it."

It was weak, but Maud was the kind of person who responded to a challenge. She picked up the phone, dialed directory assistance and waited while she was connected to the WEEE newsroom.

"I'd like to speak to Lashona Webber," she said. Then, a second later, "Maud Gonne. Thank you." She drummed her fingernails again for a few seconds. "Yes, hello. My name is Maud Gonne. I own the Birmingham Gallery in Birmingham, of all places. Ms. Webber had inquired about a work she was interested in and I was just getting back to her with some information."

Maud listened to the person on the other end of the line, occasionally nodding her head. "I see," she said finally. "Well, if Ms. Webber should call in for messages, please ask her to call me." Maud then recited her cell phone number. She thanked whomever she was talking to and hung up.

"Well?" I said.

"If they suspect she's missing, they're not letting on," said Maud. "The second woman I spoke to claimed to be her assistant. She said that Lashona is on special assignment."

"Well, maybe she is," I said. "But there has to be some kind of contingency for emergencies. And why wouldn't she tell her husband she was on assignment?"

"I didn't give them an emergency," said Maud. I nodded and reached for the phone.

"My turn," I said. But I had even less success than Maud had. I first called the TV station where Barry had worked to get the phone number for his new position. They told me it was company policy not to disclose such information without the consent of the departed employee. And Barry hadn't given such consent. I didn't believe this, but they weren't about to budge on it. Then I started calling all the utility companies in the area, which comprised a short list. On the third call, to Michigan Co-Energy Company, I learned that that was where Barry had landed, but all they were authorized to do was direct me to his voice mail. And, well, I didn't think voice mail worked where Barry was.

"What were you saying about this being where all the action is?" said Maud. I didn't respond. I didn't think it warranted a response. "Are you sure you don't want to hear my theory about why you faked your own death? We seem to have a break in the action."

"I'm going out," I said, standing up and retrieving my jacket from the back of the kitchen chair.

"Out where?" said Maud. She stood up with me, and I could see a slight look of alarm on her face. "You're going out *now*?"

"I need to get a charger for my cell phone," I said. "It's run down."

"Well, we all have our priorities," said Maud. Then a second later, she asked, "What kind of phone is it?" I told her.

"I have the same kind of phone," she said, getting excited again. "Maybe my charger will work."

"You carry it around with you?" I said.

"Sure. Doesn't everybody?"

She went back upstairs and returned a minute later with the charger. I plugged it into my phone. A perfect fit. Which was just a little disappointing, since I had been looking forward to a few minutes alone. Maud was pleasant enough company and she was certainly not hard to look at. What can I say? Sometimes I need my space, you know?

The phone's display area showed the little envelope icon, which meant that I had a voice mail message. I went through the rigmarole of getting to the message. It was from my friend, Mr. Phone Voice. Right. As if someone else would be calling with a message.

"That was a pretty neat trick," said the voice without worrying about the niceties of a preamble. I assumed he was talking about how Maud and I had slipped the surveillance on us.

"What's he saying?" said Maud. She looked like a kid on her way to Disneyworld. I waved her quiet.

"You might be able to stay underground indefinitely," said the voice. "But I think the woman has a business to run. You made a mistake getting hooked up with her. I can wait you out."

"What's he saying?" said Maud, much more insistent this time.

“He said he can wait us out,” I told her.

“Wait us out?” she said, confused. Then, awareness. “He knows we have to surface at some point. He knows *I* have to surface.” She gave her head a small shake, almost as if she was admonishing me. “We need to do something, Fargo. And I don’t mean make any more telephone calls.”

FOURTEEN

JUAN AND THE CASUAL HOSTAGES

Whoever Mr. Phone Voice was, he had the advantage of us.

"We need to find out who this guy is," I said to Maud. She gave me a slow, non-committal nod.

"How do you propose to do that?" she said.

I could only think of one way. I went through my cell phone menu until I found the "incoming calls" category. I hit the "okay" button and the list of calls recently made to my cell phone appeared. The top few entries on the list read "Caller ID Unavailable." So much for my idea.

"He's shy," I said, turning the phone to Maud so she could see the screen.

"I imagine he'll be calling again soon enough," she said. "He seemed to want to talk to you." I nodded, but I didn't want to wait around for that.

"I think I need to draw him out," I said. Maud thought for a moment.

"We could go to the gallery. I'm sure he's watching it. Or has someone watching it."

"I think you should stay here," I said.

"No way," said Maud, shaking her head.

"What if this guy just decides to shoot on sight?" I said. "One of us has to stay alive to tell the police what happened."

"I'm not going to sit around twiddling my thumbs while you draw his fire," said Maud. "I couldn't stand that. It would drive me crazy."

"Okay," I said. "Then I'm open to suggestions."

"Actually, I don't think you are," said Maud.

"What do you mean?" I said. "Of course I am. I'm fresh out of ideas."

"You make a couple of phone calls and you're out of ideas?" said Maud.

I needed this?

"I just *said* I would try to draw him out," I said.

"Is this the famous Fargo ingenuity?" said Maud.

"What's going on here?" I said. "There *is* no famous Fargo ingenuity. The famous Fargo is dead. And he was never too ingenious in the first place. He basically just stumbled into things." It felt weird to be speaking of myself in the third person.

"Not the Fargo I read about in *Our Father*," said Maud.

"That was a character in a book," I said. "You didn't think I was going to make myself look bad, did you?"

"So, you're saying that was an embellishment," said Maud.

"Why are we talking about this?" I said. "We have more important things to worry about."

"I'm not sure we do," said Maud. "I think it's time we talked about my theory of your phony death."

"I don't think you're qualified to talk about that," I said. I could feel my ears burning and sweat collecting at the small of my back. "Is this some ploy to get a rise out of me?"

"Ploy?" said Maud. "Of course not. I'm trying to help you."

"Yeah," I said. "Let's talk about that for a moment."

"About what?"

"About your effort to help me."

"What about it?"

"What do you care whether I pursue this Justice thing?" I said. Maud gave me a theatrical sigh.

"We've already discussed this," she said. "It's part of your makeup. I'm just trying to bring you to an awareness of your own desires."

"My own desires?"

Maud's turn to redden. She dropped her gaze to the tabletop. She fidgeted with the cell phone.

"What you want out of life, I mean," she said without looking up.

"What I want out of life? I don't want anything out of life. In fact, I want out of life. That's why I killed myself."

"No, it's not," said Maud, shaking her head slowly, but not looking up from the cell phone, which she spun slowly, using her index finger. "You have a lot of anger."

"Is this a therapy session?" I said. "Of course I have a lot of anger. You get to be my age, hell, you get to be ten years old, you're going to have a lot of anger."

"I don't," she said, finally looking up and giving me a level stare.

"Is that right?" I said. "What about Conor? You didn't sound too magnanimous about him."

"I'm not angry at Conor," said Maud, defensively, I thought.

"Right," I said. "Can we return to the issue at hand?"

"This *is* the issue at hand," said Maud. I was now fully regretting that I had brought her here to my house, had opened up about the secret passages, had gotten her involved in my "investigation." It's amazing how quickly almost any relationship between a man and a woman can go bad. Not that we had a relationship.

"The issue at hand," I said slowly, deliberately, "is how to flush out Mr. Phone Voice. My psychology doesn't enter into that."

"Yes, it does," said Maud. This stubbornness of hers was getting tedious and making her less and less attractive.

"What about you?" I said. The question seemed to take Maud by surprise.

"What *about* me?" she said.

"You'll forgive me," I said, "but I haven't had the benefit of reading about your exploits, you know, seeing them up there on the silver screen. All I know about you is that you grew up across the street from the Blessings, that you used to be married and that you run an art gallery in Birmingham. Not a lot to go on."

"You know more than that," she said.

"Okay," I said. "I know you live in Bloomfield Hills. I know you drive a Jaguar. I know you like cross-country skiing and Starbucks coffee. I know you don't read the newspapers." Maud continued to look at me.

"You know more than that," she said. I started to speak, but before I could get another syllable out of my mouth, the cell phone chirped to life there on the table between us. Maud snatched her hand back from the phone as if it were a dead bird come back to life. We both looked at the phone for several seconds, then at each other.

"It's *him*," said Maud in a whisper. "It has to be."

I picked up the phone and read the screen. Caller ID Unavailable. I hit the talk button and said hello.

"Ah," said Mr. Phone Voice. "So we've resurfaced, have we?"

"Who is this?" I said.

"You know who this is," said the voice. "We talked earlier. I left you a message."

"No," I said. "I mean, who are you?"

"So, what have you been up to?" said the voice, ignoring my question.

"I asked you first," I said.

"I thought we already went through all that," he said. "It doesn't make any difference who I am. What matters most is what you are going to do. All these evasive maneuvers and this new alliance with the woman are troubling. They suggest some intention on your part that might not be compatible."

"Compatible with what?"

"Compatible with other intentions, let's just say."

"I think we should meet," I said. "You know, clarify a few things."

"Clarification is good," said the voice. "Meeting would be good. The world needs all the interpersonal communication it can get, don't you think? There's so much misunderstanding in the world, don't you agree?"

I was about to ask him if he wanted me to put Maud on the phone. Those two could probably have a great chat, all about anger and misunderstanding. Maybe clear up that Middle East thing.

"Do you have a location in mind for this tête-à-tête?"

Tête-à-tête? Was this guy kidding? The same guy that castrates his victim before murdering him is using the term, tête-à-tête?

"Not off the top of my head," I said. "Or my tête."

The man on the other end of the line laughed mirthlessly.

"That was good," he said. "I'm assuming we're talking about a meeting with just the three of us, right?"

"The three of us?" I said, looking at Maud. She had crossed her arms over her chest and almost seemed to be holding her breath.

"Yeah, the three of us. You, me and Ms. Gonne."

"No," I said. "Just you and me."

"I'm afraid that won't work," he said.

"Why not?"

"Because I need to know where her head is on this. I need to look her in the eyes. You understand."

"Actually, I don't," I said. There was a pause on the other end.

"I think you don't trust me," said the voice, finally, feigning injury.

"I think you're right," I said. Another pause.

"So we'll meet in a totally public place," he said. "Somewhere where you and Ms. Gonne will feel safe."

"I can't imagine where that would be," I said. Didn't he know he was talking to a man who had faked his own death just to try to achieve some basic level of safety? "Maybe we should just handle this over the phone."

"We could meet for lunch," he said.

"No. Restaurants aren't safe. People get killed all the time in restaurants. Haven't you ever seen *The Godfather*?"

"Is this the famous Fargo humor?" said the voice.

"I don't know what you're talking about," I said. "My name is Greene. With an 'e.'"

"Sure it is," said the voice. "This is getting tiresome. As I said in my voicemail, you can probably stay underground forever, but Ms. Gonne has to attend to her business at some point."

"Haven't you heard?" I said. "It's a digital world. You'd be amazed at how much you can accomplish over the phone and through cyberspace these days."

"I remind you, Fargo, or excuse me, Greene with an 'e,' that you're the one who wanted to meet."

"You're right," I said. "I'll tell you what. Why don't you give me your number and I'll call you back in five minutes."

"No," said Mr. Phone Voice. "I'll call you. Five minutes. Have a place in mind." He hung up.

I hit the button to end my side of the call and looked at Maud. She still sat tensely and only seemed to exhale now that the call was done.

"He's agreed to meet," I said. "He wants you there, too. I'm not crazy about that."

"I'll be fine," she said.

"This isn't about chivalry," I said. "If you weren't there, it would be like insurance. But it doesn't matter. He doesn't sound like he's going to cave on this point."

Maud said nothing. Maybe the reality that she might soon be sitting across from a man who had brutally murdered Barry Justice and may have also killed Robert Astrachan and Lashona Webber was finally settling in.

"We need to think of a public meeting place," I said. "He's calling back in five minutes." I looked at the clock displayed on the phone. "Four minutes," I said.

We decided on the Starbucks not too far from Maud's gallery in Birmingham. It was her idea.

"They have security cameras," she explained.

"Security cameras in a coffee shop?"

"Sure," she said. "Security cameras are everywhere these days. We could do it at the gallery, as far as that goes, but it's really not public enough. He could blow us away in there and just take the security camera tapes with him. But he'd have a hard time doing that at Starbucks."

"Wait," I said. "I thought you didn't have a security camera at your gallery."

"Did I say that?"

He called himself Juan, although he didn't look Hispanic, nor did he betray an accent. He also didn't give us a last name. Just Juan. He was short—maybe five-eight, tops, and that was in heels. Really. He wore these black leather boots with what used to be called Cuban heels. His hair had been bleached blond and he wore it short on the sides and fuller on top. He had a dark unibrow over dark eyes, a delicate nose and a small mouth that wasn't much more than a slit, room enough to slide a postage stamp in there, maybe. He had tiny hands, almost like a child's, with well-manicured fingernails and several rings, including one on his left thumb. He was refreshingly free of piercings. But he had lots of bling. A couple of chains hung from his neck, one a gold crucifix. I always find it so endearing when a brutal murderer sports the icons of his faith like that. He also wore one of those copper bracelets that golfers wear to ward off tendonitis or arthritis, or whatever. His black polo shirt had the collar turned up and his tight black jeans were adorned by a very narrow black belt with pearl inlay in the buckle, just like they used to wear in the fifties.

His mouth was so small that it seemed to almost hurt him when he smiled, although he tried to smile often. He seemed to have a pretty good temperament, for a killer. Or maybe he was just flirting with Maud, whom he looked at more than he looked at me, even when he was talking to me. He also had nice manners.

"Mr. Greene," he said, bowing just slightly, almost, it seemed, because he might be hard of hearing and he wanted to make sure he caught my response.

"Yes," I said reflexively shaking his hand, then wondering what the hell I was doing shaking the hand of a murderer. I wasn't as bad as Maud, though, who actually suffered the little creep to take her hand and kiss the back of it when I introduced her.

Maud and I were each drinking coffee. Juan had not bothered with anything to drink. He had slid into the chair across from us and was twisting one of the rings on his right hand with the thumb and middle finger of his left. I noted that he had quickly glanced around the room and had noticed the security camera before sitting down.

"You chose this place because of the cameras, right?" he said.

"What difference does it make?" I said, trying to be tough.

"Just trying to make conversation," he said. "But in the future, if you have one, you should choose someplace like an open area, a park or something."

"That would leave us too exposed," I said.

"True," he said. "But it takes a lot of innocent people out of the equation." I looked at Maud.

"*We're* innocent people," I said. "And, anyway, that was the point."

"What was the point?" he said, inclining his head a little. "You mean you assumed that because this was a public place with a security camera you would be safe?"

"Well, yeah," I said. I didn't like this guy's attitude. He leaned in closer to me.

"Don't look now," he said, "but there's a skanky-looking bitch and a geeky-looking fucker sitting at the table about ten feet to your right." So much for the good manners.

"I'll take your word for it," I said.

"Good," he said. "Now, would you prefer that the geek or the bitch be executed?"

I heard a slight hitch in the throat that wasn't quite an audible gasp coming from Maud. Now I *did* look at the table Juan had indicated. Indeed, a geeky-looking guy in a faded blue T-shirt that was too small for him sat chatting with a young woman with shocking purple hair streaked with pink, cut short, and not very stylishly. She also had shockingly white skin. She was slightly chunky and plain, sipping at her frappacino, or whatever it was, through a straw. I turned my attention back to Juan.

"I think I get the point," I said. "You've got a partner in the area."

"Very impressive deduction," said Juan. "Now which one dies?"

"Nobody has to die," I said. "You've made your point."

"I don't think I have," he said. "I don't think you take me seriously."

"We do," said Maud. "Please don't kill anyone." Juan looked at her for a long moment.

"I'll think about it," he said finally. "But only 'cuz you asked so nice." He looked to the table where the young couple sat. "Cute," he said. He turned his attention back to me.

"The people I work for want me to kill both of you," he said, smiling, or trying to.

"Can we change the subject?" I asked.

"Actually, I don't want to do that, although, in your case, Mr. Greene," sarcastic stress on the surname, "it would be redundant. But I'm a businessman, and I thrive on discipline. Killing you entails an unnecessary risk. I don't know what you know and I don't know who else you may have involved in this, who else you may have invited into the circle, so to speak."

"Good thinking," I said.

"They are especially worried about you, Ms. Gonne," said Juan, ignoring my remark. "They didn't tell me why. Perhaps you could enlighten me." We both looked at Maud.

"I have no idea what you're talking about," she said. Juan simply stared at her for a few more seconds. Then he turned his head again to the table where the young couple sat.

"I think the woman should go," he said. "She's not very attractive, so I can't see her making much of an overall contribution to the gene pool. Not that the guy is much to look at, either. But, he probably has a better-paying job than she does and contributes more to the national economy. Not that I'm being sexist. I just want you to see how complicated my life can be. You probably think, what's so hard? Someone wants someone else killed, they hire me, I kill the person. But every act is a decision at some level. I have to go through each day making hard choices, just like everyone else."

"What made you decide to castrate Barry Justice?" I said. "That seemed a little excessive."

He gave me a look that wasn't exactly smiling, but it was close. "But we were talking about our BFFs at the next table," he said. "Tell me, Ms. Gonne, have you ever seen anybody shot in the head with a high-powered rifle? I mean, close up, not like the movies." Maud said nothing. "It's not a pretty sight," said Juan.

"I have no idea why anyone would be worried about me," said Maud. Juan studied her for a few seconds, then turned to me again.

"I choose to believe you," he said. "But these youngsters aren't out of the woods yet." He glanced to their table again. "They don't appear to be in a hurry to leave," he said. "Maybe they just met at the pathetic office where they work and they've stopped here for a coffee after their lunch. Maybe it's a budding romance. Yes. I think they might linger for a few more minutes." He looked at me again. "So, how did you two meet?"

"Juan," I said, "is this really why we're here?" He held up a hand to stop me.

"This entire conversation is under my control," he said. "I thought I had made that clear. We're here because I want us all to be here and I'll determine the agenda." He paused. "You know, I really think you need a demo. I think I've pretty much decided on the girl."

"Okay, okay," I said. "I met Ms. Gonne in the process of doing some work for Barry Justice. Then I met her again at a coffee shop. Like this one, as a matter of fact. We just kind of hit it off." I looked at Maud, then put my hand on top of hers. She reddened at the throat a bit and smiled.

"So, this is a romantic situation?" said Juan.

"Exactly," I said.

"The timing seems a little weird to me," said Juan.

"You never know when love will strike," I said, squeezing Maud's hand.

"Yeah," said Juan. "Just like death." Mr. Sunshine. He looked at his watch. Was he running late for a 2:00 p.m. killing? "Will you excuse me for just a moment?" he said. Without waiting for an answer, he got up from his chair and walked to the table where the young couple sat. I watched him shake both their hands and engage them in conversation. He spoke with them for several moments, lots of smiling and even some laughs between the parties.

"What's he *doing*?" said Maud in a whisper indicating a high level of stress.

"I don't know," I said.

"Maybe we should just get out of here," she said.

"Somehow, I don't think that would be a good idea," I said.

"Do you really think he has a partner someplace, watching us right now with a high-powered rifle?"

I shrugged. I guessed the threat was credible enough. An image of the young woman's face exploding in a pink cloud of vaporized tissue passed before my mind's eye.

A few minutes later, Juan was back at out table.

"The delightful couple's names are Greg Mineo—just like the late movie star—and Leia Fountain. Ever notice how girl's of a certain age, there's a lot of them named Leia. It's from Star Wars." He waited a few seconds for us to appreciate this nugget of trivia. When we didn't, he continued. "They do, in fact, work not too far from here for the same auto supplier. He does tech support and she's an administrative assistant to the head of marketing. Nice folks."

"They told you all that?" said Maud.

"Sure," said Juan. "You'd be surprised how most people will open up to you. So. Now Mr. Mineo and Ms. Fountain are your responsibility."

"What do you mean, our responsibility?" I said, although I had a pretty good idea what he meant.

"It won't be hard for me to find out where they live," said Juan. "I guess you could call them hostages, in a loose sort of way. Casual hostages. If I don't get what I want from you, or if I hear reports of you guys getting too interested in what happened to Barry Justice or Robert Astrachan, Greg and Leia will never see their wedding day, not that they had mentioned setting a date yet. But you can tell when two people"—he looked deliberately from me to Maud—"well, you can just tell when two people are destined to be together." He looked again at his watch. "I'd love to continue this," he said. "But I've got to run. Let's chat again real soon."

"Little prick," said Maud when Juan had left. I'd thought about pressing him to stay, to perhaps get some more information out of him, since we'd gotten precious little, but he didn't seem like the type that was going to "open up."

"Think he would make good on his threat, killing those two?" said Maud, looking at me, but motioning with her head to where Greg and Leia sat oblivious, sipping their drinks and flirting awkwardly.

"I don't know," I said. "I don't know anything about this Juan."

"This was a bad idea," said Maud.

"It's not like he gave us much of a choice," I said.

"Well, I think he's an arrogant little prick. I don't think he ever killed anyone in his life, unless it was in a video game."

"Are you willing to bet their lives on it?" I said, butting my head toward the table of the young lovers.

"You can't be serious," said Maud.

"I think we have a moral dilemma here."

"*You* have a moral dilemma," said Maud. "I think he's bluffing."

"So we call him on it?"

"I don't say we do anything overt," she said. "We just keep on looking into things."

"It's not like we have resources," I said.

"We've got a face," she countered, "and a name. Juan. I know it's not his real name, but people choose what they want to be called for a reason." I didn't know where to go with that. I had called myself Mr. Greene after my "death." Did Greene mean anything to me? Not that I could think of. Maybe a few decades of analysis would dredge something up. I was worried about Greg and Leia despite Maud's breezy dismissal of the threat to them.

"I don't know, Maud," I said. "It seems to me we're being given the opportunity to just let this drop. We've got a plausible reason. The lives of Greg and Leia are in our hands."

Maud took a sip of her coffee. "That's convenient," she said.

"Convenient?"

"Yes. Little Juan makes an empty threat and you close up shop, absolve yourself of all responsibility in the case."

"First of all, this is not a case. Second, I have no responsibility."

"What about your promise to Barry Justice?"

"Promise?" I said.

"Yes. Your promise to find out what happened to his wife."

"I'm not sure I promised any such thing. I may have acquiesced under pressure. But Barry's dead. I don't owe him anything, if I ever did."

"We've been over his already," said Maud. "We can't let this go. I can't let it go."

"Okay, okay," I said. "Let me think."

"I'm going to get another cup of coffee," she said. "I think better on massive doses of caffeine. Can I get you one?"

"Sure," I said. I was thinking that what Starbuck's needed to do was get a liquor license for all its coffee shops so they could serve some really interesting concoctions. Maud returned a few minutes later with two cups of coffee.

"Think of anything yet?" she asked.

"I was thinking I wish this place served liquor," I said.

"There are plenty of bars in Birmingham," she said.

"Let's finish our coffee," I said. "I need to keep a clear head at least until I decide our next step." Maud was blowing across the surface of her coffee to cool it.

"I've already taken care of that," she said, still holding her cup at lip level.

"Oh, yeah?"

"Yes. I asked the man at the counter if he recognized the guy we were sitting with."

"You *did*?"

"Yes. And it just so happens he did recognize him."

"From where?"

"You're not going to believe it," she said.

"I'll try," I said.

"He thinks he went to high school with him."

"Did he have a name?"

"Philip," said Maud. "Philip Beste: B-E-S-T-E." She pronounced it *beast.*

"Is he sure about this?"

"He seemed pretty sure," said Maud. "He said Philip Beste was a year ahead of him at Brother Ignatius."

"Brother Ignatius the Catholic high school? The one right here in Birmingham?"

"That's what he said."

It didn't seem right to me. "How long ago?" I asked.

"How long ago what?"

"How long ago did they go to school together?"

"Ten years," said Maud. "The young man at the counter said he'd just attended his ten-year reunion and he'd seen Philip Beste there and had wondered why, since they weren't in the same class. I guess he wasn't sure about Philip's graduation status."

"Let me see if I get this right," I said. "Philip Beste attends a local upscale all-boys' Catholic school, then hangs around the neighborhood for ten years, eventually becoming a contract killer. I thought contract killers went to New York or someplace, you know, like actors do."

"That kid was no killer," said Maud. "I could see it in his eyes."

"Oh, yeah?" I said. "And how many killers' eyes have you looked into?"

"At least one," she said, giving me a knowing look.

"You think *I'm* a killer?" I said. I noticed the guy sitting to our left look up from his paper and I dropped my voice a few decibels. "Any killing I've done, besides myself, that is, was completely by accident."

"It doesn't matter," said Maud. "That boy was no more a killer than I am. But he obviously knows someone who *is* a killer. The person who sent him here. Did you recognize Juan's voice as the one on the phone?" I thought about it for a few seconds.

"I really don't know," I said. "I'd have to hear them both again. I'm not especially auditory."

"I'll tell you what I think," said Maud. "I think whoever the real killer is sent that boy. Whoever the real killer is wasn't about to expose himself publicly like that. So he sent a proxy." I digested that for another moment while Maud sipped her coffee.

"It still doesn't seem right," I said. "If you're going to send a proxy, as you call him, why send someone with such a high likelihood of being recognized? That's almost as bad as showing up yourself. We have a name and something of a history for this kid. I mean, it won't be hard to find out more about him."

"Right," said Maud. She took a couple more gulps of her coffee. "Come on," she said. "We have some research to do."

We decided to go over to Maud's gallery. There seemed to be no reason to lead whoever was trying to monitor our every move right back to my house. Maud's gallery was no secret anyway. Let whoever might be following us sit around for a while. They might just get bored into a lapse of attention.

At the gallery, we went into her office where she pulled up a chair next to hers and we both sat down facing her computer screen. After a quick search on Google, we found the Brother Ignatius High School Web site. After another minute or two of navigation, we found the list of alumni, conveniently arranged both alphabetically and by decade. She went to the 1990s heading first, clicked on it, and scrolled through the names until she came to Philip Beste.

"It's with an 'e,'" I said.

"Just like Mr. Greene," she said, smiling at me.

"So," I said, "this confirms that Philip Beste attended and apparently graduated from Brother Ignatius High School. It still might not be the right guy. The guy at the coffee counter may have just *thought* our friend Juan was this Philip Beste."

"I don't think so," said Maud. "He seemed pretty sure. I wish they had photos, you know, like old yearbooks."

But they didn't. I noticed as Maud scrolled through the names that many of the students shared surnames, probably because siblings attended the same school. And maybe parents. Multigenerations.

"Go back to the alphabetical listing for a moment," I said. Maud hit the back button. "Scroll down to Mr. Beste," I said. She did so, actually going through different pages. There seemed to be a dozen pages of surnames beginning in "A" alone.

There were three Bestes listed. In addition to Philip, there was a Jordan and a Charles.

"Jordan's probably a sibling," I said. "Charles sounds more like an earlier generation, don't you think? I mean, does anyone call their kid Charles anymore?"

"What do you think," said Maud, "nineteen-sixties?"

She clicked on the 1960s heading without waiting for an answer. She started scrolling, but before she could even get to the "Bs", we saw a familiar name roll by.

"Robert Astrachan," I said, pointing at the screen.

"This is getting exciting," said Maud. Yeah, right.

Along with Astrachan, we eventually located Charles Beste and Barry Justice.

"They all knew each other," said Maud, sitting back in her chair.

"So it would seem," I said.

"If I were Charles Beste, I'd start worrying," said Maud.

FIFTEEN

HOMAGE TO PETER GABRIEL

We had taken the rental car back to the hotel, exchanged it for Maud's Jaguar, and collected our "ballast" bags. The question of whether "Juan" was going to be following us was probably moot. He had those casual hostages, after all.

Maud was driving and, while she wasn't in evasive mode, she was still speeding. The tires actually squealed a couple of times on turns and she kept trying to inch her way through every red light that stopped us, as if she could intimidate the light into turning green.

By the time we got back to my house, I was ready for a beer. Maud decided she wanted to go for a run.

"You already did that."

"I often run twice a day. It relaxes me."

"Is it wise, I mean right now?" I said. Maud shrugged.

"I'm addicted to running. You keep me cooped up in here without letting me run, I'm going to be very difficult to live with."

"Stick to the main road," I said. She ignored me and went upstairs. A few minutes later, she returned in her running apparel. She started to pull her earmuffs over her ears.

"Take your cell," I said. She held the earmuffs poised over her ears.

"I don't like to carry things when I run," she said.

"How long will you be gone?" I asked.

"About an hour," she replied. "By the way, this concern is really touching."

"And legitimate," I said. "I really don't like this. Can't you go to the gym or something where there are other people?"

"I'll be fine, Dad," she said, letting the earmuffs close over her ears, signaling an end to the discussion. I watched her pull the door shut behind her and followed her with my eyes as her long, smooth strides took her down my driveway between the mounds of plowed snow and out to the street, where she took a left turn and was gone.

I got a beer from the fridge, took a sip and decided that I'd tasted a lot worse. Then I sat down at the computer, went to Google, typed the name "Charles Beste" into the search box and hit return.

Turns out, there were a lot of entries for Charles Beste, including a bio confirming that he was indeed the Charles Beste who had attended Brother Ignatius High School in the sixties. The reason there were so many entries was that Beste was an active businessman in the Detroit area, which kind of surprised me because I thought I knew all the movers and shakers in Detroit. Beste had made his money in real estate development. Most of the entries involved references to Beste's efforts to revitalize the really awful Detroit neighborhoods with proposals for low-to-moderately-priced housing projects.

One story from a local business magazine called him "Detroit's Savior-in-Waiting." The story included a photo of Beste, one of those shots taken from waist level looking up. It showed a slightly pudgy man with a double chin that I don't imagine he found flattering, and I wondered if the photographer was trying to say something about Beste in some subtle way by using this perspective. Beste wore a gray suit with a dark blue tie and stood with his arms folded across his chest, looking down at the camera. He had thick features—a wide, fleshy nose, heavy brow, jowls. He looked, in fact, like an aging boxer. He wasn't exactly smiling in the photo, but he had a smug expression. I immediately didn't like him. Of course, my relationship with his offspring might have had something to do with that. It occurred to me that "Juan" must have taken after his mother, because I saw almost no resemblance to his father.

The article concerned Beste's efforts to win bids for housing developments in the inner city. The most recent article was from 1999. There was no indication that Beste had won any of the contracts he had bid on and I wondered if the story, along with others like it, was just puff a piece secured by Mr. Beste's public relations consultant.

The bio on Charles Beste was not exactly impressive. He'd graduated from Northern Michigan University in 1970, served in the Michigan National Guard (no doubt to avoid being drafted), attended law school at the Detroit College of Law (there was no indication that he had actually graduated from law school), started a construction company in the mid 80s, then got into real estate development in the early 90s. He had developed several condominium complexes, mainly in the northwestern suburbs. He sat on several boards, belonged to the Detroit Chamber of Commerce, served on a mayoral task force on urban redevelopment. The bio said he was married and had three kids, but it didn't give his wife's name, nor those of any of his children. In short, he was just like hundreds of relatively successful, second- or third-tier businessmen trying to aggrandize themselves through civic pomp and low-wattage publicity. This guy, I thought, had spawned a hit man?

I read several of the stories about Beste, then found myself, like millions of others, doing some mindless surfing. When I looked at the little clock at the corner of my computer, I saw that it read 3:55 p.m. Maud had been gone for almost an hour. It wasn't time to panic yet, though. She had said "about" an hour, after all. And she wasn't that familiar with the area.

I went back to the Google home page and entered Robert Astrachan's name. As I expected, he had lots of entries. Presentations at conferences, citations in medical literature on dependency and substance abuse, quotes in stories about addicted celebrities. The guy was, or had been, a publicity hound. I scanned quickly through the entries, my attention somewhat diluted by my growing anxiety about Maud not being back from her run. It was now 4:15. Well past an hour.

I went to the front door, opened it, and stood on my front porch looking down the driveway. It had warmed up considerably—it was probably close to sixty degrees now, and most of the snowfall of a few days ago had melted from the paved surfaces, leaving only a layer of the stuff on the lawns along with the piles at the curb. I jumped off the porch and walked down the driveway to the street, which I looked up and down in vain for a glimpse of the errant Maud. I saw no cars parked on the street and no pedestrians. A neutron bomb could have gone off. It seemed that still and lifeless. The home of my nearest neighbor sat about two hundred yards to my right. That house, too, looked lifeless, although it was no doubt just unoccupied for the time being. People do have jobs, after all.

Back inside, I went to the refrigerator for another beer and decided to distract myself with a little TV. I flipped aimlessly through the stations, my mind increasingly preoccupied with bad thoughts about what had become of Maud. I should not have let her go. What could I have been thinking? Even now, Juan probably had her bound and gagged in the trunk of his car, taking her to whoever it was that had been "worried" about her.

And that was another thing. Why were these mysterious employers of Juan so worried about Maud? What kind of threat could she possibly pose to them that was greater than the threat I posed? She ran an art gallery, for Christ's sake.

Unless.

Unless she wasn't what she appeared to be, wasn't who she represented herself to be. I reminded myself not to be paranoid.

I flipped right by the face and had to go back to it.

At first I thought it might be an old station promo or maybe some file footage the station was using—why?—as part of the story about her body having been found? But then I realized I was looking at the talking head of Lashona Webber in real time, teasing the upcoming 6:00 p.m. news broadcast.

All I could think of was that she was either the consummate professional, or she had no idea that her husband was dead. Or . . . she was somehow involved in her husband's death and she was doing a good job of hiding it. I saw not a twitch of grief or distress.

"... and we'll also have the latest on the shocking murder of a prominent local psychiatrist in a hotel room in San Diego. This and more at six. Join us, won't you?"

Her eyes went down to her desk and she made a pretense, at least, of editing news copy or something. The announcer's voiceover followed up Lashona's invitation with his own exhortation to the audience to join Brock Jamison, Lashona Webber, Tyson Reed and Carmella Fiore at six for news, sports and weather.

Damn. Lashona was alive. Not only alive, but back on the job. Perky but intense, like she'd just returned from a vacation.

The six o'clock news was more than an hour away. And Maud was getting to be close to an hour overdue. I definitely wanted to catch that 6:00 p.m. broadcast, and I definitely had to find Maud.

I dug the keys to the Jag out of her purse and started to the door, then realized that she might come back while I was out looking for her. I returned to the kitchen table, found paper and a pen in the drawer and wrote Maud a note telling her to stay put if she got back before me. Christ, I *did* sound like her father.

I was about to head for the garage when the doorbell rang. It had to be Maud. Nobody rang my doorbell unless I had invited them over. Nobody walked door-to-door in this neighborhood. The houses were too far apart and the residents frowned on such solicitations in any event. Fed Ex or someone like that might show up with a package, but since I hadn't lived at this address for five years, such a delivery was highly unlikely. I pictured the look on Maud's face when I told her about seeing Lashona on TV. Boy, was she going to be surprised.

I opened the door to find not Maud, but a cop. I looked for a police car over his shoulder, but I couldn't see one. He smiled and extended his hand as if he was about to shake mine. I started to say something, but before I could get a syllable out, my body seemed to collapse within itself. That's the only way I can explain it. My vision failed, my legs crumbled, and I sprawled to the floor right there on my own threshold.

I realized, in the several moments it took for me to recover, that the cop had not meant to shake my hand at all. I should have known better. Cops don't shake hands. What he had actually done was hit me with a Taser. The effect was to put me into a state of temporary confusion and paralysis, which the cop used to cuff my hands behind my back and roll me on to my stomach. He didn't say anything to me during this time, but I did hear him talking on his cell phone. Unfortunately, my brain wasn't yet working well enough to process what he said.

While I was incapacitated, the cop disappeared for a few minutes. He didn't leave the house, but I assumed he searched the interior well enough. By the time he reappeared, I had recovered enough to lift myself into a sitting position. This lasted long enough for the cop to put his foot against my chest and gently push me down on my back.

"What do you want?" I managed to say, my field of vision taking in nothing but the ceiling of my living room. The paralysis and confusion were almost gone, but I still felt woozy, certainly too weak to take on my assailant physically. He didn't answer, and I twisted my head around to find him looking at my computer screen.

"What's going on?" I said. Still, he said nothing. He hit a couple of the keys on the computer keyboard and regarded the screen with interest.

"Hey," I said. "Do the words 'police brutality' mean anything to you?"

His eyes lingered on the screen for another moment. Then he moved to the coffee table where he had placed his Taser. He picked it up and advanced toward me.

"What are you doing?" I said, trying to prevent the panic from leaking into my voice as he stood over me.

"One more word out of you and we play shock the monkey again," he said.

Shock the monkey? A Peter Gabriel fan? I almost spoke, but the prospect of another indeterminate stretch of spazmatic, tractionless brain activity deterred me. The cop went back to my computer, took out a little pad from his back pocket and made a few notes.

Things were getting clearer, and I tried to focus on the cop's face. He was about thirty, with longish blond sideburns and a blank face and tan skin. His eyebrows were very light blond and he had a diamond earring in the lobe of his left ear. I wondered if they allowed cops to have piercings these days. Not that I really believed this guy was a cop. He looked more like one of the younger members of the PGA tour. He probably just wore the uniform so that I would open the door for him.

He flipped his notebook closed and stood up. He walked over to me and used his foot to roll me on my stomach again. I heard the tinkle of keys.

"I'm going to take the cuffs off," he said, like a dentist might tell you he was going to give you a shot of Novocain. "Keep your face in the carpet. If you move, I hit you again with the Taser." I felt the cuffs come off and I tried to stay as still as I could. But he hit me with the stun gun again anyway.

SIXTEEN

JUST STUNNING!

By the time I had recovered from the second hit, the cop was gone. I felt like someone had infected me with an accelerated flu virus and then had thrown me down several flights of stairs just for the hell of it. I made it to the bathroom, still slightly disoriented, where I just managed to get the toilet seat up before I vomited. Jesus, I thought, when I had finished and was sitting on the cool tiles of the bathroom floor waiting for my head to stop spinning, what the hell was *that* all about? Was this assault connected to our interview with Juan? Was any of it connected to the deaths of Barry Justice and/or Robert Astrachan?

And where the fuck was Maud Gonne?

I got to my feet and looked for a toothbrush to get the taste of vomit out of my mouth. I couldn't find a toothbrush, but I did find an old bottle of Listerine, which I used liberally.

I walked to the kitchen, where the clock on the wall read 5:45. The news would be on in fifteen minutes. I walked to my front door and peeked cautiously through the glass pane to the porch. Seeing no renegade cops, I opened the door and ventured out to the porch. I saw nobody. No cop, no Maud, no vehicles. How had the cop gotten here? Maybe he had parked his car around the corner and walked to my house. A cop walking down the street would be conspicuous in this neighborhood, but, like I said, there weren't a lot of people around during the day. Or maybe someone had dropped him off and circled the block a few times.

I went back into the house and retrieved the keys to Maud's Jag. A few minutes later I was cruising the neighborhood, looking for Maud and hoping I wouldn't find her lying in a ditch somewhere, not that there were a lot of ditches in the subdivision. I drove around for almost half an hour, but I couldn't find her. I began to imagine all kinds of horrible scenarios involving Juan and the PGA golf cop—probably the psychic aftereffects of the stun gun trauma. I decided to return home and see what would happen. Maybe even now I was missing a ransom call from Maud's abductors.

I tucked the Jag back into the garage, walked back into my kitchen and realized that the water was running somewhere in the house. The upstairs shower. Maud, I thought. It couldn't be anybody else. Unless the cop stopped back to freshen up before assaulting his next victim. I took the stairs two at a time up to the bathroom and knocked on the door.

"Maud?" I said. "Is that you?"

"Who else would it be?" I heard her yell. Jesus. It *was* her. She was safe. I felt a rush of relief surge through me, then, a moment later, a rise of anger. I pushed the door open into the bathroom before I even realized what I was doing. Behind the glass panel of the shower stall, Maud stood facing the spray of the shower, washing her hair. Stunned by a combination of my own boldness and the arresting sight of her beautiful naked body, I stood for a moment as short-circuited as I had been by the cop's Taser an hour earlier. Maud turned to looked at me, but didn't bother to go into any hysterical fit of modesty.

"You know," she said over the noise of the shower, "if you want to spy on your houseguests, there are more subtle ways of doing it. Hidden cameras and such."

I was still focused on her body, trying to take it all in as quickly as possible. Her flawless form glistened with soap and water. I could see the cut of her long quads and the ridge of her trapezoids as she massaged her scalp. Then, of course, there were her breasts, which swayed gently with the movements of her arms, and the swell of her buttocks, and, and . . .

"Stephen," she said, stopping her shampooing to look at me. "Either come in or go out. You're letting the cold air in."

"Sorry," I said. "I'll wait for you downstairs." I turned to leave.

"I got lost," she said. "You should have told me that there isn't one straight street in this entire enclave."

"You didn't ask," I responded. I walked out, pulling the door closed behind me. Then I opened it again. "If you hurry, you can still catch Lashona Webber on the six o'clock news."

"You're *kidding*," said Maud, freezing, her hands still in mid hair massage, then resuming with new energy. "I'll be right down."

A few minutes later, Maud was curled up in one of the chairs in my living room, a glass of wine in her hand, a robe covering her wondrous body and a towel turbaned up on her head. I sat on the couch, where there was plenty of room left if Maud decided she wanted to get a closer look at the TV. I had another beer in my hand—since I'd vomited up the other two, I'd really never gotten the full effect of them.

We watched as Lashona Webber did a very professional job of reading the news, while she intermittently traded lame jokes with her fellow broadcasters.

"Well, she certainly doesn't *seem* upset," said Maud.

"I guess she hasn't been home yet," I responded. "A mutilated corpse in your home, especially that of a beloved spouse, will tend to ruin your day."

"You're assuming the beloved part, right?" said Maud.

"Well, yeah, I guess I am."

The newscast went to a commercial.

"So, what was the dramatic entrance during my shower all about?" said Maud. "Or were you just happy to see me?"

"Well," I said, "I *was* happy to see you, but there's more." I told her about the episode with the cop and the stun gun.

"My God," said Maud when I had finished my story. "He did it to you *twice*?"

"Yes," I said. "Basically, upon arrival and departure."

"And all he did was look at your computer?"

"That's all I was aware that he did." Then something occurred to me. "You know, he walked around the place while I was still out of commission. Do you think he might have planted something, like a bug?"

"I guess it's possible," she said. "But if I wanted to plant a bug in someone's house, I would do it while they weren't around, you know, so as not to arouse suspicion." She thought for a second. "Maybe he was looking for your secret passage."

"I doubt that," I said.

"Why?" said Maud. "I think you underestimate the reading public out there. More people are aware of your eccentricities than you know, Mr. Fargo."

"No," I said. "I just didn't get the feeling he was looking for secret passages. If he wanted that information, he would have asked me."

"Would you have told him?"

"To avoid another jolt from his stun gun? You're damn right I would have. I have little tolerance for torture."

"So, then, why do you think he paid you this visit?"

"I don't know," I said. "A show of strength, maybe?"

"Maybe," said Maud, "but I doubt it."

"Okay," I said. "Why do *you* think he showed up?"

"I didn't say I knew why. I just don't think it was a demonstration of some kind. What purpose would that serve?"

I had to admit that I didn't have a good answer for that one.

"Do you think it was a real cop?"

I shrugged.

"Because if it was a real cop, it means the police are somehow involved in these murders, in a cover-up. That would add another formidable enemy."

"Unless it's the same enemy," I said.

"True," said Maud. "But what I don't understand is why we're being toyed with like this. Threatened, yes, and even assaulted if you want to call your experience with the cattle prod an assault. But it's like they're letting us go on with our lives while they just observe and occasionally harass. I don't understand that."

She paused for a few seconds, a quizzical look on her face. She removed the towel from her head and began to vigorously rub her hair dry. This went of for thirty seconds or so. The, she stopped and looked at me again.

"You know," she said. "It's almost like they're waiting for us to lead them somewhere or to somebody."

I considered that for a moment. "But why the heavy-handed approach?" I said. "Wouldn't they want to keep a low profile if they were looking for us to lead them someplace?"

"Yeah," said Maud. "I guess that makes sense. Well, whatever they're doing, if they're trying to keep us guessing, they're doing a good job of that." She stood up and threw the towel over her shoulder. "I'll get dressed," she said. "I can be ready to leave in ten minutes."

"Oh, yeah?" I said. "Where are we going?"

"What do you mean, where are we going? We're going to talk to Lashona Webber, of course."

SEVENTEEN

ON THE ROAD

The TV station where Lashona served as co-anchor was a forty-minute drive from my house. For most people, that is. Maud reduced that to twenty-five minutes. It helped that we were going against the grain of rush-hour traffic, but she still drove with an energetic style that bordered on recklessness—changing lanes frequently and with abandon, tailgating, and—one of my least favorite maneuvers—barging in from the closing lane where traffic was being reduced from three lanes to two.

"Do you understand the concept of road rage?" I said as she completed one of these graceless moves.

"What are you saying?" she asked. "I've never had road rage, if that's what you're asking."

"I was thinking more in terms of causing it," I responded.

"You're only saying that because I'm a woman," she said, oblivious to the horns blaring at her. "If a man drives like this, he's just being aggressive. If I do it, I'm inducing road rage. Is that it?"

"I wasn't trying to make it a sexist thing," I said. "Men are as capable—more capable, in fact—of causing road rage than women."

"This is the way I drive," she said. I tried to change the subject.

"Let's talk about how we're going to deal with Lashona Webber."

"What's to talk about?" said Maud. "We ask her if she's aware that her husband is dead. Then, whether she's aware or not, we try to find out what she might know about it. And Astrachan, while we're at it. And other stuff, too, like where the hell has she been for almost a week?" Maud looked at me as if to say, what else would we talk to her about?

"I know what kind of information we want," I said. "It's more a matter of how we extract it. Keep in mind that, for all we know, Lashona might be involved in her husband's death. She might be working with young Juan and Officer Stun Gun. She may already know more about this than we know about her involvement."

"So?" said Maud, apparently not impressed with my presentation. "What difference does that make?"

"Maybe I should do this alone," I said. "After all, I'm a dead man. I can just slip back into obscurity if things get hot. You're got a life here, a career."

"I have nothing of the sort," said Maud. "That gallery is not my career. That gallery is something my ex-husband gave to keep me busy. And it doesn't even do that."

"Why don't you sell it then?" I said.

"I'm thinking of it," said Maud. "It *does* give me a place to go every day. But I'm a terrible art dealer. I have no real instincts about what good art is. People advise me. Tell me that this or that artist is the next Andy Warhol. But I don't really know what I'm doing when it comes to art."

"Then why did you become an art dealer?" I said.

"I just told you why. My ex-husband bought the gallery and set me up in business. It seemed like a good idea at the time. It was either do that or become a real corporate wife. Learn to play golf, do volunteer work, that whole Stepford Wives track. You can probably tell just from the way I drive that I would have absolutely no patience for that life."

As if to emphasize the point, Maud swung the Jag around a Cadillac whose driver refused to relinquish the fast lane. Why should he? He was only doing about ten miles per hour slower than Maud's ninety-five.

"So art was, what, more fast-paced than volunteer work?"

"I had this illusion that the art world was exciting. And maybe it is for some people. For the artists, and maybe if you're in New York. But I've got to tell you, from what I've seen of the tastes of the suburban Detroit elite, they've got about as much artistic sensibility as migrant field hands. In fact, that's probably an insult to migrant field hands.

"What can I say? I didn't know what to do with myself. The opportunity of the gallery came up and when Conor asked me if I wanted to try art dealership I thought it might be interesting, so I said yes."

"You had no other career ambitions before that?" I said.

"Actually, I wanted to go into medicine. I went to U of M for two years. Pre-med. I dropped out to marry Conor. I was planning to go back, but I didn't get around to it. When I did bring it up to Conor, he wasn't too happy about his wife studying medicine, becoming a doctor. I think it threatened his manhood."

"Well, what about now?" I said. "Your ex-husband is out of the picture. You could sell the gallery and use the money to go back to school."

"I don't think so," said Maud. "It's been twelve years since I was in school. I'm a little too old to become an undergrad again. Heck, by the time I got a medical degree, I'd be pushing forty."

"Lots of people do it," I said.

"Lots?" said Maud.

"Okay," I said. "But people do it."

"Well, not me," she said. "Although I probably will sell the gallery at some point. I'm not making a lot of money with it. Somebody else could probably make a better go of it."

"What will you do then?" I said.

"Jeez, Fargo, I don't know. Maybe I'll travel. Or maybe I'll become a private investigator. There can't be too many woman private investigators around. I might be just enough of a novelty to be successful." She looked at me and smiled. "Maybe we could be partners."

I shook my head. "I'm not an investigator," I said. "I never was. I just keep falling into these situations."

"Right," said Maud. "And that should be telling you something. You keep falling into them for a reason."

Here we go again, I thought, with the faux-rational universe, "everything happens for a reason" worldview.

"That's why you came back here," Maud continued. "You know, I always knew you would. I never believed for a moment that you were dead. I'm not sure anybody believed it. It was almost what people expected from you."

"Great," I said. "So I went to all this trouble for nothing."

"No," she said. "Not for nothing. Do you want me to tell you why you did it?"

"Why would I need you to tell me why I did it?" I said. "I already know why I did it."

"Are you sure about that?" she said.

"Yes. So let's get back to Lashona Webber."

"I don't think you do know why you faked your own death," said Maud. "And I think that scares you. I think you're afraid to face the reason. That's not a criticism, you understand. I'm just trying to help."

"Maybe you should have become a therapist," I said. I tried to make it sarcastic, but apparently Maud didn't take it that way.

"I considered that," she said. "I like to give people advice. I think people want direction from others. Most people, that is. I can't stand anybody giving *me* advice. But I don't have the patience for therapy, either. That's ironic. Usually it's the client who doesn't have the patience for it."

We arrived at the TV station at about 7:00 p.m. Since we hadn't called ahead, it wasn't likely that the Guardian of the Station Lobby was going to just let us waltz right in and talk to Lashona Webber.

"So," said Maud as we sat in the car parked in the visitors area. "How do we do this?"

"We could wait here until she comes out," I said.

"Except that she might not come out for hours," said Maud. "Until after the 11:00 o'clock news."

"Right," I said. I pulled out my cell phone, called directory assistance and asked for the number of the station. After I was connected, I asked for the newsroom. Someone picked up the phone after two rings and announced that I had, indeed, reached the newsroom.

"Lashona Webber, please," I said.

"Uh, let me see if I can find her," said the man on the other end of the phone. "Who's calling?"

"Tell her it's Charles Beste," I said. I looked at Maud and she gave me just one arched eyebrow in return. I waited for maybe thirty seconds, then a woman's voice came on the line.

"This is Lashona Webber," she said. She said it tentatively, like maybe she wasn't acquainted with Charles Beste. Or maybe she was being careful.

"I have some information that might be helpful to you," I said. "It might make for a good story. I was wondering if we could meet to discuss it."

"And your name is Charles Beste?" she said. I sensed skepticism.

"Well, no, it's not. It's actually Stephen Fargo. I know your husband."

She said nothing for a few seconds.

Then: "Why did you identify yourself as Charles Beste?" She said it with a flat intonation, like she just wanted the information and wasn't particularly upset that I had misrepresented myself.

"I thought the name might mean something to you," I told her. "I thought maybe you took Mr. Beste's calls."

"Charles Beste is fairly well known in this city," said Lashona. "He's a newsmaker."

"Right," I said. "That's what I meant."

"You say you have a story?" said Lashona, just trying to move the conversation along now.

"Yes. But I don't want to discuss it over the phone. I was hoping you could give me a few minutes of your time. We're parked right outside of the station right now."

"We?"

"Ah, yeah. My girlfriend and me. She knows all about it."

"All about what, Mr. Fargo?"

"Like I said, I really can't talk about this over the phone."

Another long pause.

"I'm afraid it will have to wait until tomorrow," said Lashona. "I have to prepare for the 11:00 o'clock broadcast. If you'll give me your number, I'll call you tomorrow."

"That won't work," I said. "I'm unavailable tomorrow. If you could just come out and meet with us for fifteen minutes—"

"I'm afraid I can't do that," said Lashona.

"When was the last time you spoke with your husband?" I said. Again with the pause.

"What does this have to do with my husband?" Suspicion in her voice now.

I wasn't sure how to answer. I had no way of knowing what, if any, involvement Lashona had had in her husband's death. Her voice alone gave me not the slightest clue. And if she'd had nothing to do with it, and maybe didn't even know yet that he was dead, I didn't want to break the news to her over a cell phone call. That seemed inadequate, somehow, so impersonal. Maybe it's a generational thing. On the other hand, if she was involved in her husband's death, the less she knew about Maud and me, the better.

"Mr. Fargo?" said Lashona. "I asked you what this has to do with my husband."

"He's an acquaintance of mine," I said. "I ran into him a couple of days ago and he told me that you had disappeared. He asked me to help him find you. Now you show up at your desk for the evening news. I guess I'm confused. I'm not sure how I should report this to your husband. To Barry."

After another pause, Lashona said: "I'll be out in five minutes."

EIGHTEEN

THE CHAPTER THAT TAKES PLACE IN A BIG BOY

We sat in a booth at a Big Boy restaurant about two miles from the TV station. We were all drinking coffee. Maud had also ordered the strawberry pie, which I found absolutely shocking under the circumstances. I guess she couldn't resist.

Lashona had not said much since getting into the back seat of Maud's Jag, other than to suggest the Big Boy. She apparently went there often enough for the restaurant staff not to make a fuss over her.

Maud looked at me between bites of strawberry pie so vividly colorful that it looked artificial, no doubt wondering when I was going to get on with it. The problem was, now that I was sitting face-to-face with Lashona Webber, I didn't know how to proceed. I gave Maud a look back, which I hoped said, "See? I told you I wasn't an investigator." Lashona saved me by getting things rolling.

"First of all, Mr. Fargo," she said, "I want you to know that I didn't mean to alarm my husband by not telling him where I was. It was for his own good. If he doesn't know where I am, then he can't tell anyone where I am."

"Fine," I said. "Except that he was worried."

"Was he?" said Lashona, taking a sip of her coffee. Up close, she was even much more strikingly attractive than on TV. She wore a blue business suit with a subtle white pinstripe and a white scarf at her throat. Her hair was cut short and swept back from her face. She had prominent cheekbones, flawless light brown skin and brilliant white teeth. She looked like slightly more chiseled version of Hallie Berry.

"He was worried enough to hire me to find out what happened to you," I said.

This revelation seemed to surprise Lashona, but she recovered quickly.

"I'll tell you what," said Lashona. "I promise to apologize to him when I see him."

I said nothing. I could feel Maud's eyes on me, but I didn't look at her.

"Why do I get the feeling you don't want to tell me where you were during your absence?" I said.

"Because it's none of your business," Lashona snapped back at me. She smiled, but it wasn't a friendly smile. Everything about her looked tense, grim. She didn't seem particularly nervous, just wary. Now I *did* look at Maud. She, too, looked tense. She had stopped eating her pie and her eyes were boring into me as if she was trying to provoke me into telling Lashona what I knew. And she was right. After all, I might not get the opportunity to speak with Lashona again.

"As I told you," I began, "your husband asked me to help him find you. We met a couple of times, talked on the phone." I wasn't sure where I was going with this. "The point is, Ms. Webber, and I regret being the one to have to tell you this, the last time I saw your husband—" I could feel my heart beating thickly now—"he was dead."

Lashona's expression didn't change. She looked from me to Maud, who nodded slightly, then looked down to the tabletop.

"I don't understand," said Lashona. "Who are you?"

"I told you," I said. "My name is Stephen Fargo. I knew your husband through some work I used to do in the political field. I ran into him recently and he told me you'd disappeared and he wanted my help in finding you. I agreed. But someone killed your husband. In your home. Obviously you haven't been home."

"No, I haven't," she said. She was taking all this rather well. Or else she simply didn't believe me or was in denial.

"I'm sorry to have to tell you like this," I said. "The problem is, I think you might be in danger, too. As well as both of us." I nodded toward Maud. "We've had a couple of, uh, episodes."

"Episodes?" said Lashona.

So, I went through the story with Lashona, telling her most of it. I didn't tell her about our invasion of Astrachan's office or about the connection with the Brother Ignatius alumni group. But I told her everything else. Throughout my account, she *seemed* distracted enough to be in shock.

"Are you telling me that my husband has been dead for almost two days and nobody has contacted the police?" she said, after waiting for perhaps thirty seconds after I stopped speaking.

"I'm afraid so," I said. "See, the person who did this threatened to frame me for it, and I had my reasons for not wanting that to happen."

"Such as you might be involved in my husband's death, if he is, in fact, dead?" said Lashona. I still couldn't hear any grief in her voice, but I could now hear anger. Or maybe it was the same thing.

"Maybe it was the wrong call," I said. "But I had nothing to do with your husband's death." Lashona just stared at me coldly.

"Actually, Ms. Webber, Stephen tried to help your husband," said Maud, giving Lashona the stare right back. "And the fact is, we're not so sure *you* didn't have something to do with your husband's death."

"That's ridiculous," said Lashona.

"Oh, really?" said Maud. "It seems kind of convenient that you were gone and he dies and you don't feel inclined to reveal where you were."

"I don't have to reveal anything to you. You aren't the police."

"You also don't appear, to me at least," said Maud, "to be terribly broken up about your husband's death."

Lashona took a deep breath and looked at the coffee in her cup.

"Our marriage wasn't in the best of shape," she said. "But I had great respect for Barry. Respect and affection."

"I can tell," said Maud, making not the slightest effort to conceal the sarcasm in her voice. Lashona looked up to Maud's face and glared at her. Then she looked at me.

"I was on personal business during the last week, private business."

"That still doesn't mean you weren't involved in Barry's death," I said, taking my cue from Maud's more aggressive style. Lashona let her shoulders sag.

"I didn't kill Barry. I didn't pay to have someone kill him. I didn't tell him where I was going, true. But this wasn't the first time."

"Well, it might not have been the first time," I said. "But this was the first time he felt concerned enough to enlist my help. So why don't you tell us where you were?"

Lashona looked at her watch.

"I need to get back to the station," she said.

"I would think you need to get home," I said.

"They're the same place," she said.

NINETEEN

SIGNS

We walked outside. The air was cool, the coolness perhaps intensified by the deep-space look of the clear nighttime sky.

"So," I said, "where do we go from here?" Lashona shuddered—from the cold, I thought—and tossed her hair back from her forehead.

"I think it's my problem now," she said.

"So you'll be going to the police then?" I said. I looked past her to Maud. Maud didn't look back at me. She just stared off at the parking lot. She stood stiffly, her hands jammed into her jacket pockets, her breath visible on the night air.

"I'm sorry about all of this," I said to Lashona, not waiting for her to answer my question. I reached to shake her hand. She turned to me slightly. Then I heard her cough, and the hand she was just beginning to extend went to her chest. An instant later she crashed forward to her knees with such force that the only thing I could think of at that moment was that she must have pulverized both of her kneecaps. Then, a second later, Lashona fell face forward to the pavement. She didn't brace herself, and I heard the sickening sound of her face hitting the concrete.

Neither Maud nor I moved for another couple of seconds. I was thinking Lashona might have had a heart attack or maybe some reaction to the coffee she'd had. Or maybe this was some delayed grief reaction. She hadn't eaten anything, so it couldn't have been the food. Maud, on the other hand, *had* eaten something. And just that moment the partially digested strawberry pie she had eaten erupted from her mouth spontaneously. She bent at the waist and heaved, the stream of red issuing from her mouth. *What the fuck is going on?* I thought. Maude wiped her mouth with the sleeve of her jacket and grabbed my arm, trying to yank me somewhere. But where? And why?

"Stephen," she said. "Move. Get out of the light."

The light? I looked up and saw that I was, indeed, standing under one of the lights of the parking lot. Maud yanked me again.

"Somebody's *shooting*," she screamed. "Get *down*."

Maud yanked me again, hard this time, and we stumbled together behind the fender of a car where we crouched shoulder-to-shoulder.

"Did you hear a shot?" I asked Maud. Her face was very pale—even her lips—and she had a wild look in her eyes.

"No," she said. "But someone shot her." She motioned her head in the direction of the prone and immobile Lashona Webber. Lashona had her face turned to us slightly and I could see that her eye was open, staring generally in our direction, staring but obviously not seeing anything. I couldn't see any blood, but, without a doubt, Lashona was dead.

"This is fucking nuts," I said, because it seemed important to say something.

"We need to get some help," said Maud, her cooler head prevailing.

"Right," I said. I looked back into the restaurant to determine if anyone inside had observed what had happened. But I didn't see any horrified faces plastered against the windows. Everything seemed normal inside. I reached inside my pocket for my cell phone and called 911.

The cops arrived with remarkable speed, I thought. You hear all these stories about people in distress calling the cops and the cops not showing up for hours. But these guys showed in what seemed like seconds, but was probably more like three or four minutes. First a car with uniformed officers. They pulled up to within about ten feet of where we were crouching, but they didn't get out of the car right away. The officer on the passenger side of the car rolled down his window and yelled something at me, which it took me a minute to realize was an order to stay put until they secured the area. He also wanted to know if either of us was hurt. He could probably tell by looking that he didn't have to ask about Lashona.

We all sat there for another couple of minutes, the cop on his radio continuously until, somehow, the officers determined that the sniper was no longer in the area. Since it was dark, I wondered how exactly they made this determination, but the cops seemed sure enough to emerge from the car, although they made their way to us in an almost involuntary semi-crouch, the way people do when they emerge from helicopters with the rotors still turning. And speaking of helicopters, one was now circling above, its searchlight sweeping the area. Curious diners were starting to emerge from the Big Boy, and traffic was beginning to snarl up.

One of the cops carried a pair of bulletproof vests—they were each already wearing their own—which I considered very thoughtful. He told us to put the vests on while his partner, sidearm drawn, crept to Lashona's body and felt at her throat for a pulse. He didn't give his partner one of those dramatic, slow shakes of the head like you see in the movies. He just scurried back to where we were now hunkered down behind Maud's Jag. More cop cars had now appeared, blue lights swirling and blinking. Soon, the area swarmed with SWAT team guys. Then an ambulance arrived and the EMTs emerged from it and did their crouch-run to where Lashona lay. By this time Maud and I were in the back seat of a police cruiser. A couple of plainclothes detectives had joined the group and were talking to the cops who had first responded to my call. I saw them look in our direction a couple of times.

"They're probably going to take us in for questioning," I said.

Maud looked at me and shrugged.

"Fine," she said. "We didn't kill her. We don't have anything to hide."

"Actually," I said, "we do." She gave me a puzzled look. "The Astrachan thing."

"So, we don't mention it," said Maud.

You had to admire how cool Maud was about this. Except for the vomiting episode—and that had probably been involuntary—she'd displayed remarkable calm. No panic, nothing even close to hysterics. She seemed to be more interested in everything that was going on rather than intimidated by it.

I was anticipating some harrowing interrogation episode back at the police station—the "Law and Order" good cop/bad cop routine. But it didn't happen. They *did* take us back to the station, where they *did* ask us to tell our story. But we did it in more of a conference room than an interrogation cell. And the two Southfield police detectives who interviewed us were actually pretty civil. They didn't even separate Maud and me. Of course, making us feel relaxed might have been exactly what they wanted to do, but, try as I might—and I have finely attuned antennae for this sort of thing—I could detect no deception in their procedure.

We told them everything that had happened since my chance meeting with Barry Justice. Did I say everything? Well, of course I don't mean every little thing. We did skip over the B&E at Astrachan's office. In fact his name never came up, nor did that of Charles Beste. The detectives did seem to pay a bit more attention when I mentioned to them that, probably at that very moment, Barry Justice sat dead and, er, mutilated in his living room. And one of the detectives did excuse himself from the room at that point, presumably to scramble a black and white or two to the scene. But there wasn't the sort of drama and intrigue you've come to expect of these encounters if you've mainly experienced them in the world of fiction. In fact, it was all very businesslike, and as such, almost disappointing.

When the interview was over, the two uniforms who had first responded to my call reappeared in the conference room and a few minutes later we were once again in the backseat of their black and white, on our way back to the Big Boy. A few minutes after that, we were back in Maud's Jaguar. She was behind the wheel, and I was experiencing G-forces in her passenger seat. She was once again operating the vehicle like she had learned to drive by playing one of those video race car games.

"I would think that an experience like we've just undergone would give you a greater appreciation of the preciousness of life," I said. She didn't take the hint, swerving from one freeway lane to the other. Rather than being sobered by our experience, she seemed to be totally energized by it. I found this a bit disturbing.

"Maud," I said, venturing to put my hand on her forearm, as if that would restrain her. The muscles of her forearm were as taut as suspension bridge cables. "A woman died tonight."

Maud looked at me.

"Yeah," she said. "I was there, remember?"

"So slow down," I said.

"What does how fast I'm driving have to do with what happened tonight?" she said, exasperation in her voice for the first time since I'd made her acquaintance. Good question. Maybe a show of decorum was in order. I didn't know. Her speeding, her near recklessness, just seemed, well, unseemly, like turning a funeral cortege into a NASCAR event.

"I can't think when you drive like this," I said.

"What's to think about?" said Maud. Duh, I thought.

"Lashona's murder," I said. "Her assassination."

"What about it?" said Maud. Then, not waiting for me to answer, "It's pretty simple. The police killed her."

"The police killed her," I said, looking at her now.

"Right," she said. "Didn't you see how casually they took the whole thing? And have you ever heard of cops showing up that fast? It's like they were just waiting for us to call. It was all so—perfunctory." She let out a muffled snarl and flashed her brights at the car in front of us, whose driver had failed to relinquish the fast lane in spite of Maud's campaign of vehicular harassment.

"Maud," I said, talking to her as though she were a junkyard dog that I had to reason my way past. "Let's not allow our imaginations to get the better of us."

"What do you mean?" she said, turning to stare at me. This was just what I *didn't* want. When you drove with the kind of abandon she exhibited, you needed to do so with your full attention.

"I'm just saying we can't leap from a good response time by these cops to complicity in Lashona's murder."

"I didn't say they were complicit in it," she shot back. "I said they murdered her."

"Why?" I said, reluctantly.

"Because they had a grudge," she replied. "Or maybe she was in the middle of some new exposé and they wanted to shut her up."

"Maud," I said, "I know it's comforting to think that the police are capable of this kind of conspiratorial behavior, but the fact is, they're not.

This kind of thing would be too hard to keep secret. I just don't buy it. There's something else going on here."

"Okay," she said with a bit more defiance than was justified, I thought. "What's your theory?"

"Who says I have one?"

"Well, it's one of the rules," said Maud. "If you're going to criticize my theory, you have to come up with one of your own."

"Whose rule is that?" I said.

"Well, if it isn't a rule, it should be," said Maud. "So, unless you can come up with something better, I'm sticking with the cop conspiracy hypothesis."

I thought about this for a few seconds. After all, what difference did it make what Maud thought? She wasn't going to do anything about it, was she? Well, yeah. Maybe she was. She needed to be disabused.

"I think all these murders are related," I said. "Justice, Astrachan, and now Lashona."

"That's brilliant," said Maud. "Okay, I admit my theory makes no sense at all in the face of the unassailable logic of your theory."

"That's sarcasm, right?" I said.

"Stephen," said Maud, frustrated, "how does the fact of these murders being connected absolve the police?"

"How does it indict them?" I said, master of the rejoinder.

"Okay," said Maud, apparently unwilling to play my admittedly juvenile game. "How about this? The police decide they want to get rid of Lashona. However, she's gone and they don't know where she is. So they have to wait until she resurfaces. However, in the meantime, they realize that Lashona may have confided in the two people closest to her . . . her husband and her therapist. So, since their primary target is unavailable, they go with the two secondary targets, since they *are* available. Then, as soon as Lashona does show up, they waste no time in eliminating her. All nice and tidy. Think about it. Don't you think it's a little odd that the police didn't know about Justice being dead until we told them?"

"Not really, "I said. "Unless they were alerted to the fact of Barry's death, how else would they know about it? They'd have to wait until someone discovered the body—a housekeeper, or Lashona when she finally got home. Or they'd have to wait until someone where Justice worked called to let them know that he hadn't shown up for work for a few days. From what Barry told me, he easily might not have been missed for that long. So, no, I don't see the fact that the police didn't know about Barry's murder as evidence that they murdered him."

"*Claimed* not to know about his murder," said Maud.

"All right," I conceded, "claimed not to know about his murder."

"What about the cop that zapped you with the Taser?" said Maud.

"I have serious doubts about his being a cop," I said. "I think he may have been impersonating a cop to gain easy entrance. I mean, who doesn't open his door to a cop in uniform?"

"I wouldn't," said Maud.

"Oh, really?" I said.

"Well, I won't now. I'll need to see a warrant."

"Well, yes," I said. "In hindsight I can say that, from now on, I'll be much more careful about letting cops in the door. But you can't say that before this episode you wouldn't have admitted a uniformed police officer into your house without interrogating him."

"Oh, all right," said Maud. She swung the car around the vehicle in front of us, the one that had declined up until this point to relinquish the fast lane, and passed using the center lane, giving the driver of the car the finger on the way by and avoiding the other car's front bumper by, I swear to God, no more than six inches as she swerved back into the fast lane in front of the offending driver's car.

"I refuse to continue this discussion until we're off the road or until you regain some control," I said.

"Control of what?" said Maud.

"You know what I mean."

"The guy's breaking the law," said Maud. "He's driving under the speed limit in the fast lane. He's endangering the lives of other drivers."

"Under whose speed limit?" I said.

"I can't help the way I drive," said Maud.

"What do you mean you can't help the way you drive? Of course you can. It's not an involuntary activity. It's not like having no control over whether your stomach is growling or whether your hair is turning gray."

"What are you *talking* about?" said Maud.

"I'm talking about how reckless driving is a choice, and how ridiculous it is for you to say you can't help the way you drive."

"Driving a car is an outward expression of your inner self," said Maud.

"So, you're telling me that your emotional life is that chaotic?"

"I'm saying I'm on edge," said Maud. "All these murders, these hasty dislocations. I'm not complaining. It's sort of an adrenaline rush. But, like it or not, it's going to express itself in my driving."

Well, how was I supposed to argue with *that*? The road ahead of us looked relatively free of any offending drivers who were likely to do no more to earn the wrath of Ms. Gonne than obey the traffic laws of the State of Michigan.

"What about our friend Juan and the Brother Ignatius connection?" I said. "Juan didn't look like much of a cop to me and he virtually admitted to killing Barry Justice. How does that all fit in to your police state theory?"

"It doesn't disprove it," said Maud. "How do we know Juan isn't working with the cops? They get involved with lowlifes all the time. You know, informants and such. There's a fine line between what's legal and what isn't, after all. Cops and criminals have this symbiotic relationship thing going on."

"I don't buy it," I said. "I don't think the cops are involved. At least not in any organizational fashion. Of course, one or two bad cops could conceivably be involved, but it could just as easily be two bad priests or two bad astronauts."

"Bad astronauts?" said Maud. "Excuse me, but what in God's name are you talking about?"

"Okay, it's a bad example. But you see what I'm saying. Other than a guy with a stun gun who I'm pretty sure was impersonating a cop, we have no evidence that the cops are involved in these murders. Except, of course, they responded quickly to my 911 call, which, I don't know, I was kind of glad about. Isn't that what we want the cops to do? Come when we call?"

We rode in silence for a few miles. Maud seemed to have settled down a bit. I sensed that her early enthusiasm for the police conspiracy theory was waning, but I didn't want to open the subject again until she was ready. The truth was, I couldn't really concentrate on a discussion with her while she was behind the wheel of a moving vehicle.

"Let's talk about something else," she said.

"Okay," I said, a little too quickly. I guess I thought that whatever else she wanted to talk about would not stimulate her volatility to the extent that the discussion of Lashona's death had.

"I want to talk about why you faked your death," she said.

"Oh, Christ," I said. "I thought I told you that I'm not even sure I know why." I really didn't want to talk about this. "Let's get back to your police conspiracy theory."

"You don't have to know why you did it," said Maud. "I know why you did it. I just want to explain it to you."

"What if I don't need to have it explained to me?" I said. "I may not have mentioned this to you, but I'm one of those people who doesn't like to face up to the truth. I know that's not fashionable, to be in denial and everything, but I take comfort in denial and avoidance of the truth."

"I don't believe that for a second," said Maud.

"I'm sorry," I said, "but that *is* the truth."

"You wanted to die and yet stay alive at the same time," said Maud. "I know that sounds simplistic, but that's what you wanted. The question is why."

"If you want my help you on this, I'm afraid I'm going to disappoint you," I said.

"I'm thinking it's guilt. I'm thinking it has to do with guilt about the death of your wife. The death of Denise in Sedona."

"Are you going to bill me for this?" I said. I didn't try to hide the irritation in my voice. I really don't like it when people bring Denise's name into things. Anything at all.

"If you don't want me to get into this," said Maud, "just tell me to stop."

"Stop," I said.

"What if I told you I was an angel?" she said. "And I was sent here to save you?"

"I'd be concerned," I said. "Anybody that would even suggest that to a man like me would have to know how little traction it would have."

"I don't mean like Clarence coming down to save Jimmy Stewart from jumping off the bridge," said Maud. "Give me a little credit."

"Uh, Maud," I said. "I'm sort of losing the thread here. Can we get back to Lashona? I prefer to muse on the misfortunes of others, if you don't mind."

Angel. Jeez!

"There has to be a reason that our lives have intersected at this point," said Maud.

"Are you going to tell me that everything happens for a reason?" I said. "Because if you are, I just want to let you know that Barry Justice tried to convince me of that same fairy tale just before somebody took the liberty of removing his genitals prior to ending his life."

"I'm saying we have to pay attention to signs, that's all," said Maud.

"Signs?" I said. "You mean like crop circles and stuff?"

"No," said Maud. "I mean the fact that I grew up across the street, basically, from the Blessing house. The fact that I've known about you and the Blessings and about your wife so intimately and intensely in my own mind that I almost thought of myself as part of the family for almost two decades. And then one day I hear that you've been lost at sea, and do you know what my reaction was? He's not dead. He's not even lost. He has manufactured this stunt. Then what happens? A few years later I run into you almost literally in my backyard under the most implausible of circumstances. And it validates everything."

"I don't understand what you're getting at," I said. "Yes, our meeting was unlikely, but there's no magic involved. In a finite world, it's a wonder we didn't run into each other before this. If you want to know the truth, I can't *help* having these episodes. You asked me a few days ago how I managed to have these things happen to me, as if you considered them unusual. So why do you now find it so unusual that I should encounter you while looking for Lashona Webber?"

"I didn't find it unusual," said Maud. "I'm telling you it was inevitable."

"Are we there yet?" I said, in my best ten-year-old voice.

TWENTY

MOGGIO

For a few days, the metro Detroit area suffered a mild bout of sniper anxiety. After the experience of Mr. Muhammad and his young protégé Mr. Malvo in the D.C. area, people were leery about sniper attacks. The media, as might be imagined, allowed this anxiety to have full expression in the fears of the local population, when they weren't encouraging it.

But it all died quickly when nobody else was shot at. It became clear that Lashona's death was an isolated event, at least in terms of national sniper hysteria. But in terms of the deaths of Barry Justice and Robert Astrachan, Lashona's death wasn't isolated at all. So far, Maud and I hadn't been dragged into it, other than our initial involvement. The police didn't appear interested in us as suspects, and our names never got leaked to the media. For their part, the media had their hands full with the enticing ingredients of not only the murder of one of their own, but also the lurid details connected to the death of a former member of their fraternity, Lashona's husband, Barry Justice. All sorts of rumors flourished and the story eventually attracted the attention of the major cable talk shows, whose hosts and their rabid guests speculated on everything from sex cult murder to a violent racial statement from those prehistoric goons among us—or college administrators at Bob Jones University—who still consider miscegenation a crime against nature.

A few days after Lashona's death, the police—or someone—leaked that she had been consulting with the late Dr. Astrachan and a whole new round of rumors was launched. Now it became a love triangle, that old counter-transference thing going a bit too far between patient and therapist. Some anonymous tipster had called the TV station where Lashona had worked to inform management that their star anchor had killed her husband and Dr. Astrachan because the two of them were having an affair and Lashona had become jealous. The anonymous caller was less clear on who might, therefore, have done away with Lashona, and what the motive might have been in that case. I'd like to think that all these idiots with their crackpot theories were the marginalia of humanity, but I'm afraid folks like Bill O'Reilly and Glenn Beck share many of their charming views.

Maud returned home, and I took up residence once again in my apartment. That is, Mr. Greene's apartment. Things had cooled between us—not that they'd ever really been heated up—after the night of Lashona's murder. I think Maud was disappointed in my lack of enthusiasm for getting to the bottom of all these murders. I could see her point, perhaps, from a civic responsibility point of view. There was a killer or killers out there and I, along with Maud, knew more about them than anyone speculating in the media. I suppose I had a duty to come forth with this information, or, even more distasteful to me, run down all the clues myself.

But it seemed to me that the real killers were cutting me some slack. They were saying, "The cops don't know where to go with this, and as long as you don't give them any hints, we're prepared to enter into a truce. We won't kill you or your friend Maud or those perfect strangers, Greg Mineo and Leia Fountain, if you just stay out of it."

And, while it's not exactly noble, that was fine with me. I felt no obligation to track down and expose the people who killed Justice, Lashona and Astrachan. The three victims weren't, perhaps, the worst people in the world and perhaps they hadn't deserved to die in the fashion that they had. But I had hardly known Justice and Lashona. And I didn't know Astrachan at all. What did I owe them?

Of course, had she been there at that exact moment, Maud would be saying something like, "It's not a matter of what you owe them. It's a matter of what you owe yourself." And we'd be off on some meaningless metaphysical expedition (meaningless to me, anyway) that would resolve nothing.

Yet, even though I was convinced that Maud's iciness toward me resulted to some extent from her disappointment in the performance of my civic duty, I had a feeling that she was even more hurt by my reluctance—my refusal, really—to confide in her regarding my decision to disappear as Stephen Fargo, my refusal, in effect, to indulge the entire Stephen and Denise Fargo fantasy that she had been nurturing for years. I didn't understand it, in the first place. In the second place, I resented the intrusion, even though Maud's intentions were probably honorable. It's just that when it comes to Denise, I have this sense of ownership, almost, that I know is pathetic, but it's there nonetheless. I cannot share even her memory with another human being. And don't think that my beloved Denise would approve of this ungenerous behavior on my part. She wouldn't. She would hate my pathological attachment, my effort to quarantine a dead person in my daily memory. It's a strange thing, but since she has died, it's almost as if I've been more possessive of her than I ever was when she was alive. We were probably what you would call a casual couple when it came to our outward relationship. I've never been the most affectionate—certainly not the most romantic—specimen to walk the face of the earth. And while Denise was—with every move of her body, every world she ever spoke, even every breath she drew in and let out—the sexiest creature I have ever known, she was not what you'd call publicly demonstrative with her affections either. She was so far beyond affectionate to me that those outward displays of affection were almost an insult to her. Which is just why it was so pathetic for me to be this cranky custodian of her memory. I should have been giving her memory to the world, yet I patrolled her crypt, in a figurative way, like some twisted, hunchback from an old Hollywood monster flick.

And then, just when I thought I might skate—might avoid any serious or permanent damage as a result of my foray back into the world of Stephen Fargo—I got a telephone call from the past. Well, okay, that sort of over-dramatizes it. I got a call from the present, obviously, but it was like the past was pushing the words through the door ahead of it.

The caller was a man identifying himself as Andrew Moggio, a former Detroit police officer. He had reached me at my Stephen Greene phone, but he called me Mr. Fargo. He sounded like he was about fifteen-years-old and for any number of reasons, I didn't particularly want to talk to him.

"What do you want?" I said after he had gone through his identification ritual.

"Who says I want anything?" said Moggio.

"Sorry," I said. "Silly me. I just assumed that since you called me, you wanted something."

"I don't want anything," he said. And he didn't say it nice. He said it with attitude.

"Good," I said. "I'll be hanging up now."

"Jules Lazard asked me to call," he said. While this statement was somewhat intriguing, I wasn't about to be taken in. People, maybe not a lot of people, but some people, knew about the history between Lazard and me, going all the way back to 1981 and the Blessing adventure. So anyone trying to worm their way into my heart, or at least into my confidence, might easily drop the name of Jules Lazard as a means of getting my attention.

"Okay," I said. "When Lazard, himself, calls, I'll try to be more interested."

"Don't be an idiot," said Moggio. "Lazard can't call you on the phone."

"Why not?"

"See," said Moggio, "you've been away. Out of touch. Things happen. Life goes on. Or not, whatever the case may be."

"I'm going to hang up now," I said.

"Lazard can't call you because he's dead," said Moggio.

This information came as less of a shock than I thought it would. Lazard had been pushing seventy-five the last time I had seen him almost six years earlier. He hadn't been in poor health that I had noticed, but he was old. And old people die.

"I thought you said Lazard asked you to call me," I said. "Was this a communication from beyond the grave?"

Moggio sounded like he was chuckling softly.

"There are no communications from beyond the grave," he said.

"Then I guess I'm missing something," I said.

"I can fill you in," said Moggio, "but not over the phone. Do you know the Post Bar on Congress?"

"Sure," I said. "But I'm not going to meet you there. If Lazard had a message for me, let's hear it. Otherwise, this conversation is over."

"He said you'd be like this," said Moggio.

"Like what?"

"Paranoid, uncooperative."

"Look, Andy. May I call you Andy?"

"Actually, my close friends call me Drew. The guys at the station used to call me Mojo."

"Interesting," I said.

"Call me Drew," he said. "It'll help us bond."

"Mr. Moggio," I said, "Lazard was a friend, but I don't think anything even *he* had to say to me, posthumously or otherwise, will hold my interest. So, thanks for the call—"

"All right, all right," said Moggio. "Lazard didn't leave me any last words to pass on to you. He couldn't even talk for the last couple of years. He'd had a series of strokes that left him pretty much a vegetable."

"I'm sorry to hear that," I said. "He was a good man."

"Yeah, right," said Moggio. "That's why I need to talk to you."

"I don't think so," I said.

"What if I told you that I killed him?" said Moggio.

"You killed him?" I said. "I thought you said he had strokes."

"He did," said Moggio. "But they didn't kill him. I killed him. And that's all I'm going to say about this over the phone."

TWENTY-ONE

MOGGIO II

Andrew Moggio may have sounded like he was fifteen, but in the pasty, lumpish flesh, he actually looked about forty-five. He was a small, compact man, not overweight exactly, but slightly pudgy, the way some short guys can get when they put on a few extra pounds. He had thin, graying hair and his head gave the impression of being slightly misshapen, almost flat on one side. He wore Levi's and only a t-shirt on top, in spite of the weather. His arms were thick and full of black hair. He was one of those guys who probably wished some of his excess body hair was on his head. He was in constant motion, gesturing with his hands, cracking his neck with short movements of his head—flexing, stretching, flinching. It became a distraction about thirty seconds after I sat down to talk to him.

The Post Bar was a dive in downtown Detroit frequented mainly by hockey fans at night, but also by newspaper reporters, a few cops, bail bondsmen and constructions workers. It wasn't very cozy, and I guess the regular patrons were proud of that fact. But, come on, a little light wouldn't hurt and the tables could be wiped down, say, once a month. I had my elbows resting on our table now, and I wasn't sure I was going to be able to leave with them. Moggio ordered a Jack Daniels on the rocks and I decided on a Budweiser.

He took forever getting to the point. He seemed nervous, even beyond the constant agitation of his body. Maybe nervous was the wrong word. He seemed wary. He spoke lowly, but at a higher pitch than his bulk would have suggested. I had to keep telling him I couldn't hear what he was saying. Finally I got frustrated.

"Why did you want to meet here if you're so afraid people might hear you?" I said. "You're an ex-cop. You should know cops hang out here."

"I always talk like this," he said. "My larynx was crushed in a football accident when I was seventeen. I couldn't talk loud if I wanted to. I'm not worried about anyone hearing me." But he sounded defensive, and I wasn't sure I believed him, especially since the subject matter, at least part of it, concerned how and why Moggio had killed Lazard. Boy, so many people killing other people.

"How'd you find me?" I said.

"What difference does that make?" he replied, a bit of snarl in his voice. I was confused. Why the urgency of wanting to talk to me? I threw a twenty-dollar bill on the table.

"The drinks are on me," I said, and I stood up to leave.

"Where you going?" he said.

"Outta here," I replied. "It was a mistake to come."

"Sit down," he said. "I'm getting to it."

I sat back down. Jesus! If this was the way he had worked his cases back when he was a cop, no wonder he wasn't on the force anymore.

"I found you through one of my contacts, a cop on the Southfield force. He'd heard you'd been involved in the Webber shooting and he knew that Webber had been a client of mine and he also knew that Lazard had been a friend. So he knew who you were, and he called to let me know you were involved, like I said."

"Just to set the record straight," I said, "I was not involved in Lashona Webber's murder. I just happened to be there at the time."

"Whatever," said Moggio. "You asked how I found you and I told you."

"So, did you want to talk to me so you could get the stuff about Lazard off your chest?" I said, still hoping to move the conversation along.

"What thing?" he said. The look of confusion on his face seemed genuine enough. I began to wonder if Moggio was insane. Or maybe he was just fucking with me. Maybe he wasn't an ex-cop at all. Maybe he was just another cop impersonator.

"You said on the phone that you had killed Lazard," I said.

"Oh, that," he said as if I had reminded him that he had forgotten to pay a parking ticket. "It's not what you think."

"It's what you *told* me," I said, trying without much success to keep the exasperation out of my voice.

"It was more of a mercy thing," said Moggio, almost nonchalantly. "Lazard was like a father to me. I would never have hurt him."

Funny, Lazard and I had never really been close, but I didn't remember him mentioning a young protégé by the name of Andrew Moggio.

"So, this was an accident then?" I said.

"No," said Moggio. "I told you. It was a mercy thing. Lazard was basically a vegetable. It got to where I couldn't look at him like that anymore, so I took action."

"Action?"

"I smothered him with a pillow."

"That sounds like homicide to me," I said. I had been about to use the word *murder*.

"I told you, it was an act of mercy. Lazard didn't want to live that way."

"And he confided his wishes to you on this subject, or left a living will?"

"He didn't have to. I knew him well enough to understand his position in this regard. I told you, he was like a father to me."

"So you mentioned," I said. He looked up at me quickly.

"Lazard saved my real father's life almost forty years ago," said Moggio. "They were partners. My father got shot one night when he and Lazard were busting a blind pig downtown. Coincidentally, it was the same night that the riots broke out. July 23, 1967. I'll never forget that date. I was ten years old. My dad was first through the door of this place there were busting and somebody on the inside opened up with a twelve gauge. My dad took a full blast in the hip. Lazard took the shooter out, then performed CPR on my father until the medics arrived. My dad had gone into shock and probably would have died. He never did fully recover. He went on disability and spent the rest of his life on the couch. He died of a heart attack about ten years after the shooting, but, really, he pretty much died the night he got shot."

"I'm sorry," I said. Moggio took a Camel cigarette from the pack in his shirt pocket and lit it with an old Zippo with a Marine Corps insignia on it. Mr. Retro.

"Believe me," he said, removing tobacco fiber from his lower lip, "I'm over it. But when my dad got shot is when I decided to become a cop. I couldn't tell you why exactly. It wasn't like I wanted to take his place or that I wanted to fight the kind of evil in the world that had destroyed him." He took a drag from his cigarette. Smoking unfiltered cigarettes couldn't be good for a damaged larynx, I thought. "I think it was Lazard's influence. He became a role model for me. Took over from my father. I wanted to be a cop just like Lazard was."

"But you're not a cop anymore, right?" I said.

He didn't reply right away. Instead, he motioned to the waitress for another round of drinks.

"I sort of got into a beef," he said.

"With a fellow cop?"

"With the brass," he said. "We had artistic differences. So I quit back in '97 after twenty years on the force. Now I'm a private investigator." He looked at me through the smoke of his cigarette. "Just like you," he said. "Only I have a license."

I was about to protest that never, ever, had I claimed to be a private investigator, but the waitress arrived with another Bud for me and another Jack Daniels on the rocks for Moggio. A hard-drinking private eye. Boy, he was really playing the role to the hilt. I looked at my watch.

"Got someplace to go?" said Moggio.

"Eventually."

"Don't you want to know why I really called you?" he said. Well, that depended on whether I was going to get the answer in the next fucking decade.

"I want to know about why you killed Lazard," I said.

"I told you, he was already dead."

"Was there an autopsy?"

Moggio shook his head. "Lazard was living at my place. After his last stroke they were going to move him into a nursing home for stroke victims. He didn't have any family. I live alone and I have a pretty good-sized condo, so I took him in and hired a nurse for him. But I just couldn't watch him exist like that. So, one night when the nurse had gone home, I put a pillow over his head and killed him. It was very peaceful. He didn't struggle. I don't think he suffered. Next morning I called the hospital and told them that when I checked on Lazard he was dead. That he must have died during the night. Nobody questioned my word. I was a former cop, after all. Everybody knew I was devoted to Lazard and I stood to gain nothing from his death. And—"

"Don't tell me," I said. "He was like a father to you."

Moggio's eyes narrowed. "That's right," he said. "More like a father than my own father. You know how that is, don't you?"

"What makes you think I would know anything about that?" I said. He knocked back what was left of his drink in one gulp.

"Forget it," he said. "The point is, there was no reason for anyone to think that Lazard had died of anything but natural causes."

I took a drink of my beer and pondered how to react to this information. It still wasn't clear to me why Moggio felt compelled to confess if it wasn't that he was burdened by guilt.

"You're probably wondering why I've been so forthcoming," said Moggio.

"That's pretty good," I said. "I was thinking just exactly that."

"Well, first, I don't think you're gonna turn me in. Lazard and I didn't spend long winter nights talking about you, Fargo. But you came up occasionally."

"Should I be flattered?" Moggio made a brief snorting sound.

"Lazard really only mentioned his relationship with you when you popped up in the news for whatever reason. I remember we had a brief conversation about you about the time you got mixed up in the Blessing stuff, then later with that whole Eric Crowe mess. Then, of course, when you disappeared." He paused for a second, taking out another cigarette. He tapped it several times on the top of the table, but he didn't light it right away. "Lazard told me at the time of your disappearance that you had faked it. He seemed to have had no doubt about it."

"I guess I wasn't as clever as I thought," I said. Moggio lit the cigarette and snapped the cover of the Zippo shut.

"No, it's not that," he said. "Lazard just knew stuff like that. I can't explain it. The point is, I wasn't surprised to hear you were still alive. Although, I *was* surprised to hear your name connected to Lashona Webber's."

"Why's that?" I said. He looked at his cigarette like he'd never seen one before, or like the answer to my question might be printed on the cigarette paper.

"Lashona Webber was a client of mine," he said.

"You mean she hired you to do investigations?" I said.

"That's what I do," said Moggio.

"Well, she didn't hire me, if that's what you're worried about," I said. "In fact, the night she was shot was the first time I'd ever met her."

"Relax," said Moggio. "I wasn't worried about whether she had hired you or not. But I am interested in what your business was with her. From what my buddy on the Southfield police force told me, it seemed to have something to do with the death of her husband, right?"

"Yeah," I said. "Barry Justice."

"Right," said Moggio. "Well, it's not like I feel any special obligation to Lashona to find her killer, but it would be nice to know. And I thought if you were looking into this thing with Barry Justice, maybe we could sort of pool our resources."

"You've got it wrong," I said. "I'm not looking into Justice's death, as you put it. In fact, I'm not looking into anything." Moggio nodded and played with his cigarette.

"Lazard told me you were the shy type," he said.

"What's that supposed to mean?" I said.

"I've kind of looked into this faked death of yours," he said.

"Looked into it?"

"Just some checking. Did you know that it appears not to be a crime to fake your own death?" he said. "As long as, you know, you're not doing it as part of some other illegal activity, such as to defraud an insurance company, or to avoid paying a debt or some other financial obligation like child support or alimony or to avoid criminal prosecution. Faking one's death for those purposes is actually a lot more common than you would think. In fact, the opportunistic nature of the criminal mind being what it is, you might not be surprised to know that a number of people took advantage or our national tragedy on 9/11 to claim that they had been in the World Trade Center that day and had died."

"Is that right?" I said.

"It is," said Moggio. "I can't say much for their patriotism, but you have to admit that it's a pretty neat scam. They get someone to say that they had a meeting at the Windows on the World restaurant that morning at nine a.m.

Then, kerplowee." Moggio shrugged. "Who's to prove otherwise? They're never going to identify all of the victims of the World Trade Center disaster."

"You're probably right," I said.

"Of course, I don't put you in that category," said Moggio.

"Thank you very much."

"No, as far as I can tell, you weren't avoiding the IRS—although they might be interested to know how you've been earning a living for the past six years—or hiding from an ex-wife or anything like that. Which leads me to the question of why you would want people to think you were dead. Maybe someone threatened your life. Or maybe someone was stalking you. I don't know. But I *do* know that people do things for reasons, and people don't take the extraordinary step of faking their own deaths capriciously. Which then leads me to think that you probably have reason for people to continue to think you're dead."

He paused, perhaps waiting for me to explain my reasons. When I didn't, he tried a new approach.

"Actually, there's a long literary tradition pertaining to the faked death," he said.

"Gee, I wouldn't have taken you for the literary type," I said. He waved my statement away.

"Just stuff I picked up doing my research. There's Sherlock Holmes, of course, and that whole debacle in Romeo and Juliet. Of course, those are fictional characters. Then you have this whole subgenre of deaths of celebrities that people seem to *hope* were faked. Elvis and Princess Diana and Tupac Shakur and Jim Morrison and Andy Kaufman. Even JFK, Jr. But those don't really apply, I guess. Then, obviously, you have the most famous faked death in history."

"Obviously," I said. "Now which most famous faked death would that be?"

"Think of the world's major religions," said Moggio.

"Right," I said. "I think numerous theologians would dispute the contention that Jesus faked his death on the cross. I believe it is a major tenet of the faith that Jesus actually died and came back to life. No trickery involved."

Moggio shrugged.

"I guess there are different ways of looking at it," he said. "Anyway, I don't put you in their league. They had, what, nobler rationales for faking their own deaths."

"If you don't know why I did it, how can you make that judgment?" I said.

"Good point," he conceded. "So maybe you had a noble reason, too. I guess my overall point is, you clearly want people to think you're dead. And I'm willing to let you keep your little secret."

"For a price, right?"

"Well, yeah."

"You know, you aren't the first person who has coerced my assistance by threatening to expose me."

"Is that right?" said Moggio.

"Yes, it is. Would you like to know who the other person was?"

"I think you want to tell me," said Moggio.

"It was Barry Justice himself. And look where it got him." Moggio thought for a moment, continuing to pull on his cigarette, which had now burned down so far that it threatened to burn his lip. He looked like a stoner trying to get that last hit on the eighth-inch of a roach.

"That would actually give you a motive for killing Justice, wouldn't it?"

"I've already told the police my story on that," I said. "They know I didn't kill him."

"So, you're saying there's a curse on people who threaten to expose you? Is that it?"

"I'm just pointing out a similarity. Or a potential similarity."

He shook his head vigorously, as though he was trying to clear up blurred vision.

"I think were getting off track here. I didn't want to get into threats and recriminations. I just wanted to maybe get some information. I thought that since we had Lazard's friendship in common, we could find some common ground." It was my turn to take a pause. I could feel myself relenting, but I still couldn't figure out Moggio's angle.

"You say you were working for Lashona Webber," I said. He nodded and finally stabbed butt of his cigarette out in the ashtray.

"I've worked for her on a couple of different things," he said. "Mainly for stories she was doing. She really thought of herself as an investigative reporter."

"What were you working with her on most recently?" I said. He squinted at me.

"I'm not so sure I should talk about that," he said.

"You're not still working for her," I reminded him. He looked around the room, then back at me. But he still it didn't say anything. "Look," I said. "You want me to spill my guts to you, right? Well, it's a two-way street."

He took another quick look around the bar—even though nobody else had entered the place since he taken his last survey a few seconds ago—and leaned toward me, lowering his voice.

"Lashona was working on a story about the effects of vaccines on children." This didn't sound, particularly earth shattering. "Negative effects, I mean," said Moggio.

"You mean allergic reactions?" I said. He shook his head.

"You ever heard of Thimerasol?"

"I sure haven't," I said.

"It's a preservative that was used in vaccine vials. Thimerasol contains mercury. The theory is that the mercury given to very young children causes autism in some kids. There's really been no proof of this one way or the other, but I think it's interesting that the FDA basically recommended banning the use of Thimerasol in vaccines in the late nineties."

"And Lashona was looking into this for a story?"

"Yeah, well, partly. She also has a personal interest. Her daughter is autistic." I remembered that Justice had mentioned this. But I didn't say anything to Moggio about it.

"So Lashona was researching a story on this Thimerasol?"

"In a way. I mean, it's not like people aren't aware of this controversy. There are several class-action lawsuits in progress. And it's all over the Internet."

"So what was Lashona's angle?"

"Like I said, I think she was just looking for a story at first. She interviewed the lawyers handling the lawsuits and someone at the Centers for Disease Control and I think she tried to talk to some drug company executives. She was less successful there. She couldn't get past the PR people. I think she was about to forget the story until she got this anonymous letter from a biochemist at one of the drug companies. He claimed to have information about how the drug companies—at least the one he worked for—knew about the effects of Thimerasol, knew that its relationship to autism had some validity, but were suppressing the data. That's when she got me involved. To try to find out the identity of the letter writer, this whistle blower."

"Did you find him?" I asked. He shook his head.

"Before I even got started Lashona called and told me that she'd changed her mind. That she didn't need me to find the guy."

"Do you think she learned his identity on her own?"

Moggio shrugged.

"She didn't say and I didn't think too much about it at the time," he said. "I had told her that this kind of investigation could get pricey. This mystery chemist could have worked at any one of a dozen or more pharmaceutical companies. Or maybe even for an independent lab. We didn't have much to go on and it would have been time-consuming. I'm not in the same class as the Philadelphia lawyer when it comes to my hourly rate. But I don't work for free."

"Okay," I said. "So Lashona called you off the investigation. Why are you still so interested?"

"Because the day after she calls me off the job she disappears. She doesn't show up for work, her husband doesn't know where she is and her family won't talk. Then a few days later she's back in the studio, doing her newscast.

Then, later that night, she *is* the newscast. The sniper shot her as she emerged from a restaurant and the people she was with at the restaurant turn out to be you and another female"—here, he dug a small notebook out of his back pocket and flipped through it—"an art gallery owner named Maud Gonne. Friend of yours I take it. So professional curiosity got the best of me. Especially since you and I have this connection to Lazard. And you are presumed dead and now Lashona really *is* dead. How could I not try to learn what *that* was all about."

I had to concede that, from Moggio's point of view, the whole thing was almost irresistibly intriguing.

"Do you think Lashona's disappearance had anything to do with the anonymous chemist and her investigation into the autism story?"

Moggio shrugged again.

"I just don't know," he said. "On one hand, I really don't see this Thimerasol story being all that sinister. I mean, people with more clout and better contacts than Lashona and me have investigated this thing, and I find it hard to believe that any of the drug companies could keep this kind of information secret. On the other hand, look at the cigarette companies and how they managed to suppress internal documents linking cancer and cigarettes. Not that I believe there's any such link," he said smiling. "Fuck the Surgeon General." He pulled out another Camel and fired up. "Still, when you think about the millions of kids that have been vaccinated over the years and the marquee value of a disease like autism, the exposure for the drug companies could make these settlements with the tobacco companies look like chump change. I mean, you're talking innocent children here, who were victimized, not people beyond the age of reason, who should know better, but who choose to indulge in a questionable lifestyle choice. See what I'm saying?"

"I get it," I said.

"So you could have a scenario where Lashona could have been onto something and the drug companies facing that kind of potential liability, well, do the math."

"You mean like a conspiracy of drug companies?" I said. He gave me another one of his shrugs.

"Or just one drug company," he said. "But before we get carried away, I need to point out that Lashona disappearing, then getting killed, might have nothing to do with her investigation. Something else might be going on, which is why I got in touch with you. See, maybe you have information or insights I'm not privy to you or"—he referred to his notebook again. "Ms. Gonne. Why does that sound familiar?" He suddenly looked up at me. "Maud Gonne, I mean."

"There was a famous historical figure by the same name." I said. "Active in Irish politics in the early 20th century."

"Hmmm," said Moggio. "That doesn't sound like where I heard the name before." He smiled. "Don't know much about history."

My cell phone rang. I pulled it out of my jacket and read the caller ID display, telling me that the call was originating from the Birmingham Gallery.

"This is an interesting coincidence," I said. "Excuse me for a moment." I got up from my chair and moved toward the door out of earshot of Moggio. Then I pressed the talk button on my phone and said hello.

"Stephen? It's Maud."

"Hi," I said. "How are you?"

"I'm fine," she said. "Well, I take that back. Actually I'm not fine."

"What's the matter?"

"You remember that charming young man we met at Starbucks? Juan?"

"How could I forget?" I said.

"Well, I just opened my mail here at the gallery and I got a letter from him."

"A letter from Juan?"

"Well, not really a letter. It's a newspaper clipping."

"How do you know it's from him?"

"It's a clipping about the woman at the coffee shop. The one Juan threatened. Remember? Her and her boyfriend?"

"Yeah?"

"Well, the clipping says she was shot last night as she sat in her car in a 7-11 parking lot."

"Jesus," I said.

"What should we do, Stephen?"

"I don't know," I said. "Have you seen anything of Juan?"

"No. Do you think Juan did this? You think he's sending us a message?"

"I don't know," I said, my mind racing. "Don't leave the gallery. I'll be there in twenty minutes."

TWENTY-TWO

JUAN II

Maud would have been proud of me. I made it to her gallery in fifteen minutes. Moggio insisted on coming along for the ride, and, at first I was reluctant to indulge him, but I didn't have time to argue with him and it occurred to me that I'd rather have him *in* my sight than out of it. It also occurred to me that it might not be a bad idea if I had another ally in addition to Maud. In fact, I thought maybe I could hand off this burden to Moggio, who seemed to have more interest in it than I did, anyway. And more motivation.

On the way to the gallery, I brought Moggio up to speed on pretty much everything that had happened since I had bumped into Barry Justice in the Home Depot. He listened distractedly. He seemed like a nervous passenger.

"You've been a busy guy," he said when I had finished.

"Yeah, especially since just a little less than a week ago, I was dead."

"Maybe we can talk more about that later," said Moggio. "Right now, I'm interested in learning more about this Juan character and how he fits into this picture."

"I guess I'd like to know that myself," I said. "I'm a little concerned that he seems to be making good on his threat to kill innocent people just to keep us in line."

"You said he didn't look like a killer, right?"

"Right. But who knows what a killer looks like these days? I mean, Christ, you've got Columbine. You've got six-year-olds in Flint killing their first-grade classmates."

"Yeah," said Moggio, "the whole good and evil thing keeps getting murkier and murkier."

Maud had a customer in the gallery when we arrived. Actually two customers. One was a woman who appeared to have come directly from her daily workout in the gym. She was accompanied by what I assumed was her teenage daughter, who appeared to be about as interested in looking at art as I might be in watching "Oprah." Her heavy sighs of boredom didn't seem to break through her mother's intense discussion with Maud, though, so the girl soon turned her irritation on us. Lots of surly glances in our direction.

In an effort to make friends in the silent sort of way, I smiled at her when she caught my eye. She immediately let her mouth fall open, giving me the village idiot look, and flipped me the finger. I looked at Moggio, who looked back at me with an expression on his face that said, "Don't be surprised to read in the paper one day that this young girl had shot up her first-hour study hall, because her teacher looked at her the wrong way."

I moseyed over to the door and peeked out to the street. As usual, there were cars everywhere. That's what midday in Birmingham was all about. I checked out some of the nearby cars, many of which might very well have been black Mercedes, to see if anybody was watching the gallery, but I didn't detect any activity like that. Obviously, anybody who didn't want to be seen watching the gallery could easily find a perch that would be unobtrusive from where I stood. I turned away from the door and looked back to where Maud was conversing with the mother of The Bad Seed. Maud was smiling, but when I caught her eye I saw tension in her face as well.

Moggio pretended to look at the artwork, but I could tell by his body language that he wasn't a connoisseur. Maud glanced at him a couple of times, too, obviously having noticed that we entered the gallery at the same time and also noting, no doubt, Moggio's feigned interest in the art. We were all waiting for the customer to leave, especially her daughter. But the customer was oblivious. Finally, I saw Maud give the woman one of her business cards. Negotiations appeared to be over. As if sensing this, her daughter was already out the door, standing on the sidewalk in front of the gallery, her arms folded across her amazingly ample breasts, glaring back through the window at all the disappointing maturity contained therein. I'll bet that was going to be one great car ride back to wherever they lived.

But I'd been premature in my assumption that our customer friend was finished. Actually, she was just getting her second wind. I wandered over to where Moggio was pretending to be inspecting one of those strange paintings by Maud's favorite artist, William Bleak.

"Am I to understand that there was some urgency involved in getting here?" Moggio whispered.

"The urgency was all mine," I said. "She can't very well kick a prospective buyer out just because we show up."

"That woman isn't buying anything," said Moggio. "I know her type. She's just trying to impress the world, herself included, with her own importance."

"You can tell all that just from this brief exposure to her?" I said.

"Well, it's either that," he said, "or she's just pulling some power trip maneuver on her daughter."

I thought that the more likely case, but I really didn't care. I glanced out the front window again to the sidewalk to see how Her Majesty was taking this further delay, but she was no longer standing in front of the gallery. I wandered over to the entrance to get a better look down the street. I had no interest in keeping tabs on the girl, but something made me want to determine her location. I looked north up Woodward Avenue, but I didn't see her. Then I looked down the street in the other direction. No sign of her. Maybe she had popped into one of the stores, realizing that her mother was going to be longer than she thought. I was just about to give up on her when I caught a flash of her blonde hair above the tops of the cars cruising Woodward.

She had relocated to the other side of the street, where she stood in the entranceway of a building. She was laughing and talking, making those goofy teenage gestures that pass for, what, flirting? I realized she was talking to somebody standing close to her, someone obscured by a brick column that guarded the entrance to the building. It occurred to me that maybe she'd run into a friend, but I found myself unable to take my eyes away until I saw who it was she was talking to.

A moment later, Juan stepped out from behind the brick pillar.

For a second, the incongruity of the scene short-circuited me. Juan was the last person I had expected to see the girl talking to. I turned quickly to where Maud was standing. She perceived the abruptness of my movement and immediately interpreted it. I turned back to look at Juan and the girl. She was still talking and Juan was talking and smiling back at her, but his eyes weren't on her. He was looking at me.

When I turned back again to look at Maud, I could see that she was looking past me to the scene in the street. The color had drained from her face and she no longer appeared to be paying any attention to the blathering of her customer. Moggio was now looking back and forth between Maud and me, sensing the anxiety in the gallery. Maud seemed to snap out of it and returned her attention to the Customer from Hell, perhaps appraising her from a new perspective, as in what in God's name is your daughter doing flirting with a killer and mutilator of corpses?

Moggio sidled over to me. He casually glanced out the front door of the gallery, saying under his breath, "What the fuck's going on?"

"I'll tell you in a minute," I said. A moment later, the customer finally exited the gallery. I watched as she hesitated in front of the gallery looking up and down the block, then responded to a call from her daughter, who stood alone now on the other side of the street. Maud now stood on one side of me, and Moggio stood on the other as all three of us watched the activity outside.

"Where'd he go?" said Maud.

"I don't know," I said.

"Where did *who* go?" said Moggio.

"Juan," I said. "At least that's what he calls himself. The kid I told you about who claimed to have killed Barry Justice." I turned to Maud. "Is that a regular customer?" I said.

"Not really," said Maud. "I don't really think she was in the market for art. She told me she been an art history major in college. She kept asking me why I didn't have this artist or that artist. She seemed to just want to impress me with her knowledge of art." Well, chalk one up for Mr. Perceptive, Andrew Moggio, P.I. extraordinaire. "Do you think they actually know Juan?" said Maud.

"I have no idea," I said. "But something's going on. This can't just be a coincidence."

"I wouldn't jump to conclusions," said Moggio. "You've probably heard this before, but things aren't always what they seem." I saw Maud give Moggio a strange look.

"Maud," I said, "meet Andrew Moggio. He's a former cop and current private investigator. It just so happens that he had been doing some work for the Lashona Webber when she died."

"Mr. Moggio," said Maud, extending her hand to shake his. "Is that Moggio as in 'Got my mojo working?'"

"Sounds the same," said Moggio, who no doubt heard this about ten times per day. "Spelled differently. Call me Drew."

I could see that Moggio was taken with Maud, as any normal red-blooded American man would be. She looked particularly smashing today. She wore tight black slacks and one of those tight long-sleeved shirts, black also, with the logo of her gallery splashed in sequins across her chest. She wore high heels that seemed to be not much more than an arrangement of straps. Her toes were painted a brilliant red matching the red of her fingernails and the lipstick glistening on her full lips. She had small dangling earrings with turquoise stones in them that seemed to be almost the same color as her eyes, though they lacked the radiance of her eyes. All in all, breathtaking. But she was still a little rattled by Juan's appearance, although she was managing to cover it up with aplomb.

Moggio cleared his throat. "Just so I'm understanding this," he said. "This Juan character is the one who sent you the newspaper clipping, right?" Maud looked at me.

"I filled him in," I said.

"Yes," said Maud. "Or, I don't know. I'm assuming that's the case, who else would have sent it?" Moggio didn't answer.

"Let's see the clip," I said. Maud walked to her desk at the rear of the gallery, Moggio watching her intently all the way. He leaned toward me and said, "So, was the historical Maud Gonne a knockout, too?"

"I guess she broke a few hearts," I said. I found myself a little disturbed by Moggio's interest in Maud. Wow. Was this jealousy? *That's* an emotion I hadn't experienced for a while, not since Denise was alive, and every man in the world who laid eyes on her would step on his tongue in her presence. Maybe we didn't need Moggio around after all, I thought.

Maud returned a few seconds later with a regular number-ten business envelope, which she handed to me. The envelope was addressed to Maud at the gallery. The address and return address appeared to have been done on a computer printer. The postmark was Royal Oak, which wasn't unusual, since the Royal Oak post office was one of the largest in the area and handled a huge volume of mail. The return address was familiar.

"Isn't this Barry Justice's home address?" I said, pointing to the return address. Maud peered down at.

"I don't know," she said. "It's his street in Bloomfield Hills. I didn't even pay any attention."

"I think it is," I said.

The envelope contained only the newspaper clipping, or actually, a Xerox of the newspaper clipping, which had been neatly trimmed so that I couldn't even tell what paper it had been taken from. The headline read, *Few Clues in Clawson Shooting.*

"They're not the only ones who are clueless," I said.

Moggio was about to say something in reply when my cell phone rang. The I.D. readout said "Private." I pushed the send button and said hello.

"Hey, Fargo," said Juan, or Beste, or whoever he was. "What up?" I couldn't think of anything clever to say to that, so I said nothing. "Did I catch you at a bad time?"

"No," I said. "This is fine. I glanced at Maud and Moggio, who were both looking at me with varying degrees of expectation.

"Hey," said Juan. "I just met the coolest babe coming out of the gallery there. I assume you're still at the gallery. Well, actually I *know* you're still there. My best to Maud by the way and to your new friend. I'm not sure I've had the pleasure as far as he's concerned."

"What do you want?" I said.

"Oh, I'm just following up," said Juan. "I wanted to make sure Maud get the clipping I sent about Leia."

"She got it," I said.

"Amazing isn't it?" he said.

"What?"

"How we just saw that chick and her boyfriend not too long ago, and now she turns up dead."

"Yeah," I said. "Amazing. So what's your point?"

"I think my point is obvious," said Juan.

"We didn't say anything to the police," I said.

"Well I don't believe that," said Juan. "Now I want to be clear about this. This new chick, the one I just met coming out of the gallery there? She's on the list now, and the dead chick's boyfriend is still on the list. I see anything about your behavior or Maud's that I don't like, well, Nicole—that was the new chick's name by the way—she's never going to see her high school graduation. You know we can make good on this. We've already done it. And there are a lot more where Nicole came from. You getting all this?"

"Yes," I said. "But it was your fault we even got involved with the police. If you hadn't killed Lashona in our presence the police would never have even taken us in for questioning."

"What you need to understand," said Juan, making an effort, it seemed, to control his temper, "is that nothing is our fault." He hung up.

"It was him, right?" said Maud. I nodded.

"He's glommed onto a new victim," I said. "The daughter or whatever of that woman who was just in here."

"Did he threatened her?" said Maud.

"In his own special way, yes," I said.

"This is getting totally out of control," she said.

"It's *been* totally out of control," I said. Moggio looked back and forth between us without saying anything.

"What are we going to do?" said Maud. "This guy seems to be able to kill people with impunity."

"Him or someone else," said Moggio.

"You don't think he's the one actually doing the killing?" I said.

"I don't know," he said. "I'm just speculating this one may be Mr. Outside. Mr. Inside could be the actual killer. Did you mention Juan to the police?"

"Yeah," I said. "But I don't think we mentioned, the girl. I guess I didn't take the threat that seriously."

"What are we going to do?" Maud repeated. I didn't have any better answer this time than I'd had a few seconds earlier.

"You're the ex-cop," I said, turning to Moggio. "What do we do?"

"Go on the offensive," Moggio, smiling just little bit.

"Howso?" I said.

"First," he said, we have to find out who Juan is. "

"What do you mean?" said Maud. "We *know* who he is."

"You do?" said Moggio.

"Yes, his name is Philip Beste." Maud looked at me. "You didn't tell him?"

"Well, it wasn't like I was withholding it," I said. "I didn't have time to go in every detail."

"How'd you know his name is Philip Beste?" said Moggio. He looked, what, not confused exactly. More like frustrated.

"We talked to someone who recognized him. Someone who went to high school with him," said Maud.

"Here, locally?" said Moggio.

"Yes," said Maud. "Right here in Birmingham, at Brother Ignatius."

"And this person you talked to was positive he recognized Philip Beste? It was a positive ID?"

"He seemed pretty positive to me," said Maud. She looked at me. "You didn't tell him about the Brother Ignatius alumni list?"

"No," I said. "I hadn't gotten around to it."

"Maybe we should get around to it," said Moggio. "But let's find someplace else to do it."

"Someplace else" turned out to be Moggio's office, a modest building on Southfield Road he shared with a home security firm and a lawyer. His office had a receptionist's desk, but no receptionist. A brass sign hung above the receptionist's desk that read Moggio Investigations. It was a nice sign. He'd obviously paid a lot of money for it. Maybe that's why he couldn't afford a receptionist.

His office had a small conference room in addition to Moggio's private office. He ushered us into the conference room and asked if we wanted coffee. Maud declined, I accepted.

When he left the room Maud said, "Is this a good idea?"

"What?" I said.

"Meeting here in the office of a private detective? Juan might see this as provocation."

"We're taking the offensive, remember?"

"But what about that poor girl? Or that boyfriend of the girl that was killed? Shouldn't we warn them?" said Maud.

Well, it seemed like we should, but that was for sure going to get the police involved and was also sure to drag us deeper in than I wanted to be. Juan had said we shouldn't involve the police. Wouldn't he truly be provoked by that?

"Let's just be patient for a while," I said. "See what ideas Moggio has."

"What's his interest in this?" said Maud.

"He was working for Lashona," I said. "I told you that."

"Yeah, but Lashona's dead."

"He wants to get to the bottom of her death, I guess." Maud did not seem satisfied with this answer.

"How do we know he's for real?" she said.

"Well, we're sitting here in his office," I said. She glanced around.

"This could be anyone's office," she said.

"Where is this paranoia coming from?" I said. "Weren't you the one who was all gung ho about solving this mystery?"

"Yes," she replied. "But not at the expense of the lives of total strangers for whom I'm now responsible."

"*You're* not killing them," I said.

"You know what I mean," she shot back.

"I'm open to suggestions," I said to Maud, but apparently she didn't have any because she didn't say anything.

A moment later Moggio was back in the conference room with paper cups of steaming coffee.

"So let's talk about this Brother Ignatius thing," he said.

I went into the story about how we looked up Philip Beste on the school's web site and about how we also found his father's name on the alumni list. And how he had been the same class with Robert Astrachan and Barry Justice. Moggio did a lot of nodding and scowling. When I was done, Moggio said nothing.

"Well?" said Maud, clearly getting antsy.

"I went to Catholic Central," said Moggio. "We used to play football against Brother Ignatius. We had quite a rivalry. We were pretty much a blue-collar group, even for a parochial school and Brother Ignatius was full of children of wealth and privilege."

Well, I had no response for this, but Maud did.

"How is that relevant?" she snapped.

"I guess it's not," he said. "I'm just making an observation." Maud turned her attention to me.

"I don't think we should be wasting time," she said, "while Juan is out there stalking innocent people."

"Don't worry," said Moggio. "We're not wasting time. All of this is pertinent."

"Even your reminiscences of the class struggle?" said Maud.

"Oh, yes," said Moggio. "That's the most pertinent of all."

I was about to ask him how, but he had moved on to something else.

"Our first objective is to have a little conversation with Juan. But on our terms, under circumstances that we control."

"Uh, is Juan someone we necessarily want to irritate?" I said. "He himself is perhaps not much more than a piss-ant little nuisance. But he's working with someone who seems to enjoy his work."

"What did you think I meant when I said were going to go on the offensive?" said Moggio.

"Oh, I'm fine with that," I said. "It's just that there's a risk, you know, to people having nothing to do with this." Moggio shook his head.

"That's because Juan and whoever else he's working with have the upper hand at the moment. We need to change that." He turned to Maud. "You see ma'am, I know the kind of people who send their kids to schools like Brother

Ignatius. They might be capable of murder, but they can't withstand the kind of conflict we can give them. They have no stomach for war."

"Jesus," I said. "Who said anything about war?"

"I did," said Moggio. "That's what we have to confront Juan and his friends with. Total war."

"I'm not sure I'm up to *total* war," I said.

"Well, that's something we need to talk about," said Moggio "You're in the middle of this thing. You can walk away, but Juan and his friends are never going to have a high comfort level where both of you are concerned. Of course, *you* can go off and die again, go to that Big Witness Protection Program in the Sky. You can, too, ma'am, if that's what you're interested in. I'm interested in ridding the world of scum like Juan and the people who killed Lashona Webber. I know that's a cliché, but, hey, we all need a purpose in life. And I've made it my life's purpose to eliminate as many bad guys his I can."

"Where's your cape? "I said.

"I don't have one," said Moggio. "Don't have a secret identity or superpowers or a Batcave someplace. I've got this dump—he waved his hands around the conference room—my police pension and a crusader complex."

TWENTY-THREE

Q'S & A'S

The first part of the plan was to capture Juan.

"I think if we got him alone, he won't turn out to be very tough," said Moggio. "Besides, he's the only one of our adversaries that has identified himself, showed his face."

Twenty minutes later the plan went into action. The idea was for Maud and I to get in the Jag and start driving. Anticipating that Juan was watching Moggio's office building and would go into pursuit mode when he saw us drive off, Moggio would follow Juan and grab him as soon as the opportunity presented itself. It was a weak plan in my estimation. It failed to account for too many contingencies, like what if Juan wasn't even watching Moggio's office building?

But at least it gave us something to do.

Maud and I drove Moggio to his car back at the Post Bar. I had glanced repeatedly at the side view mirror on the way there, but I hadn't noticed anyone following us. By the time we got to the bar, I had just about made up my mind that this wasn't going to work.

"Just keep driving after you let me out," said Moggio. "I'll be behind him."

"What are you talking about?" I said. "He's not following us. This isn't going to work."

Moggio looked at me quizzically. "He's been following us since we left my office. Haven't you seen him?"

I looked at Maud, who just shrugged.

"The tan Jeep Liberty," said Moggio. "He's pulled off to the curb now, about a hundred yards behind us." I looked in the side view and rear view mirrors, but I didn't see any tan Jeep Liberty.

"Are you sure?" I said.

"Yes."

"He had a black Mercedes before," I said.

"Well, he's changed rides," said Moggio, a bit more edge to his voice. "Makes sense, right? You start looking for a black Mercedes, he changes to a tan SUV." He slapped the top of my seat. "We got him," he said. "Just keep moving till I tell you different. I'll keep in touch by cell."

"Why don't we just lead him somewhere specific?" said Maud. "What good is it going to do to keep driving around?"

That actually seemed like a pretty good point to me, and I could see that it was giving Moggio some pause, too.

"Do you have any place in mind?" he said. Maud said nothing.

"How about my home in Clarkston?" I said. "Juan already knows where it is, so we won't be revealing any secrets."

"Okay," said Moggio after thinking it over for a few seconds. "Head for your house. Don't worry about me. I'll be right behind you. Well, not right behind you, but I'll be out there."

"What kind of car do you have?" I asked, expecting him to be driving some piece-of-shit crop duster like Colombo used to drive.

"Black Mercedes," he said, deadpan as hell. Then he broke into a small grin. "Hey," he said. "What can I say? It's a great car."

He got out of the Jag and I turned the car into the street and headed for the freeway entrance that would take me home. The thirty-minute ride to Clarkston started out uneventfully, if you didn't count Maud's misgivings about the plan—and about Moggio.

"He's not very imaginative, is he?" she said, as though I'd made a poor hiring decision.

"He's all we've got for the moment," I replied. "And he *is* a former cop. So I imagine he has some expertise in this stuff."

I kept looking in the mirrors for a tan Jeep Liberty. But I couldn't see one. I also didn't see a black Mercedes. Maud seemed ill at ease; part of it seemed to be the residue of fear and shock that Juan's appearance and the death of Leia had provoked. Part of it seemed to be her lack of confidence in Moggio.

"I wanted to apologize for my behavior the other day when we were driving home from the police station," she said.

"Don't worry about it," I said.

"I'm not *worrying* about it," she said heatedly. "Will you just shut up and let me apologize?" I saw anger in her face. "I came on way too strong about that whole police conspiracy thing, and I really have no business cross-examining you about your life. It's none of my business if you want to play dead. It's none of my business what you do."

I'm slow on the uptake, but I could see now that she was talking about "us;" this had little if anything to do with the murders of Justice, Astrachan, or Lashona Webber. It also had little to do with Juan or Leia or Moggio. Maybe it never had. I felt the need to say something.

"I'm not really trying to hide my reasons for—"

"Stop," said Maud. "Let's just drop, it shall we?" Her voice was cold and decisive. I felt terrible.

"But I want to explain," I said.

"There's nothing to explain," said Maud. She pulled a tissue from the pocket of her coat and wiped tears and she blew her nose with alarming ferocity. "And these are not tears of sadness," she said. "Don't think I need sympathy. Yours, or anyone else's."

"I wasn't thinking that at all," I said. "Look, I'm sorry I got you into this."

She shot me an icy stare.

"You know," she said, "that's just so typical. Who do you think you are to presume that you got me into anything? In the same way I don't need sympathy, I also don't need your protection."

"I didn't mean to imply that you did," I said lamely.

"You think you're the fucking center of the universe, Stephen," she said vehemently. "You need to get over yourself. Oh, sure, you have this self-deprecating act working, this false sense of humility, this feigned sense of not wanting to be noticed, but the fact is just the opposite. The fact is you crave attention. You crave responsibility. Like this faked death stunt. You'd like to think it's a matter of desiring obscurity, but it's not that at all. If that were the case, you'd have had the courage not to return. Or to just kill yourself outright. But that's not what it's all about. It's all about wanting attention. And what better way to get attention—especially for someone who thinks that everything that happens in the world is somehow related to him—than to disappear? It's like a magic trick for you. Look, everybody, look how clever I was in making myself disappear. Now let's have a big hand for me."

I was going to say something about how I thought we were going to drop this topic, but some instinct for self-preservation compelled me, for once, to keep my mouth shut. Man, she was seriously pissed.

"Face it," she said, apparently by way of summary. "You love the fact that people have acknowledged this resurrection of yours, that they've dragged you back into these intrigues and mysteries. I'm not buying your reluctant participation act. I never did."

I did not want to validate her challenges with my silence, but I really didn't know what to say.

"Why did you even bother to call me when you got the newspaper clip?" I asked her. "If you're so disappointed in my behavior, why not just let it go?"

"I should have," she said. "And I guess that's mainly why I'm angry at myself. Believe me, I'm no better than you are. I've been living a delusion for way too long."

I didn't ask her what she meant. I assumed it had something to do with her fantasy life as part of the Blessing story.

"I want to make love," she said.

Wow. Did *that* ever come out of left field.

"I want you and me to make love," she said as though she had thought my lack of response to her previous declaration required clarification.

"I don't understand," I said.

"What's not to understand?" she said. "I assume you don't find me totally unattractive. All my parts work. I guess I'm assuming yours do, too. We take our clothes off, engage in some foreplay, then there's some penetration involved." She looked at me, the hint of truculence still in her eyes. "Are you saying that you haven't felt any urges in that direction?"

"I haven't said anything at all," I replied. "I don't know what to say."

"Well, don't allow yourself to be too flattered. I want to have sex with you because I want the truth out of you. I'm sick of your pretense and evasions, and, and, I don't know what you would call it, your layers. Layers of half-truths, layers of self-deception." She poked me in the ribs. Not playfully. "I want to know if there's a real person there, if you really have come back from the dead."

I don't know if I've ever been seduced with such ferocity and, well, I hated to say it, discipline. Nevertheless, I found myself being aroused by Mistress Gonne. But she wasn't done with me yet.

"Even this playing-hard-to-get attitude of yours is all about you. You don't want to mislead, you don't want to deceive. You don't want a woman to get hurt. As if anyone cared."

We were close to my house, now. Just a couple of blocks away. I still couldn't see a tan Jeep Liberty or a black Mercedes behind us, although Juan would no doubt be a little more careful following us in a residential neighborhood, where he'd be easier to spot. Assuming he cared about whether or not he was spotted.

"Are you going to be this abusive while we're making love?" I said, not looking at Maud.

"That's what you want," she said without hesitation. I looked at her now. She was looking straight ahead, out the windshield. But I could see a small smile on her lips. So this was my problem? I'd been into S and M all my life and I'd never known it?

"What about Moggio and Juan?" I said.

"What about them?" she replied. The woman had an answer for everything. And I didn't.

We pulled into my driveway and I got out of the car and surveyed the street in both directions. No SUVs or luxury cars of any description. I walked to the side door and unlocked it, pushing the door open for Maud to enter. When we were inside, I moved to the window and parted the drapes slightly to check the street again.

"You're stalling," said Maud. I turned around to see that she had already removed her clothes down to her bra and panties. They seemed to be a matching set—pale yellow, very frilly, very see-throughish.

"Do you want to go upstairs?" I said, feeling that I had to say something.

"No," she said immediately. "Right here on the floor."

I began taking my clothes off as Maud slipped out of her bra and panties. She had a stunning body, with narrow hips and high breasts with those pinkish, puffy kind of nipples. I took off the last of my clothes and stepped to her, taking her in my arms. She moved her hand down between my legs and grasped my erection.

"See," she said softly in my ear. "This doesn't lie." Then she moved her hand to her vagina and a few seconds later she brought her moist hand up to my nose. "And this doesn't either."

I kissed her wet fingers, then kissed her on the mouth. Her tongue pushed against mine and I could hear her breathing more quickly through her nose. A moment later she pulled me down to the floor. She rolled me on my back and straddled me, pinning my arms to the floor with hers and bringing her face close to mine until we were looking directly into each other's eyes.

"This is what I call taking the offensive," she said.

For a while, we forgot all about Moggio and Juan and all the evil in our little world. But we couldn't forget it for long. At least Moggio had to the decency (or sense of timing.) to wait until our lovemaking was over. It had been a pleasant enough experience, although I had to discount it a little because Maud had positioned it as a test of some kind.

"So," I said, "did I pass?" I was propped up on my elbow looking at Maud's face. She had her eyes closed, not, I thought, in an expression of ecstasy, but perhaps, just trying to shut out the external world.

"Oh, you can't tell by one test," she said, smiling a little, but not opening her eyes. "You need to confirm, validate. All that good scientific stuff." She opened her eyes and looked at me. "The start was promising, though."

I lay back down and stared up at the ceiling. Our attempts at humor were lame and self-conscious. The entire sexual episode, although pleasurable, had not been what I would call satisfying. There was something wrong with it, some lingering tension, suspicion, even. I tried to put it out of my mind.

"We shouldn't dilly-dally," said Maud, sitting up and reaching for her bra. "Your new friend Moggio could knock at the door at any moment."

"He's not my friend," I said. "And isn't it the male of the species that usually can't wait to move on to other things once the sex act is completed?" I was still trying to pretend we were in a quasi-scientific mode here, but Maud didn't seem to be playing the game anymore. She reached out for some more clothes and when she had rolled back toward me, she had my jeans in her hand. Without looking at me, she let them fall so that they were partially draped over my face. I guessed post-coital cuddling wasn't required in this instance.

I was just pulling my shirt over my head when my cell phone rang. It was Moggio.

"I think we've waited long enough," he said. I tried to determine by the tone of his voice if he knew what Maud and I had been up to. There was no reason he should know. Maybe he just suspected. In any event, his statement didn't give anything away one way or the other.

"What's happening?" I asked him.

"Nothing," said Moggio. "That's my point. He's just sitting there in his car, the tan SUV, occasionally glancing at your house. He made a couple of calls, but I haven't seen any indication that he is going to get out of the car."

"Maybe he called for reinforcements," I said. "And they could be on their way now."

"Reinforcements to do what?" said Moggio.

Well, I didn't have a good answer for that. And Moggio wasn't waiting for one anyway.

"I got a gut feeling about this," he said. "And my gut tells me we're not working with a large crew here. Two or three guys, tops."

"Okay," I said, although I felt like pointing out that a miscalculation in this regard could be perilous. "What do you intend to do?"

"He hasn't made me yet," said Moggio. "I'm pretty sure of that. I think I'll wander over to his car and invite him in for a little discussion. You got any problems with that?"

"Invite him in here, you mean?"

"Yes," said Moggio. "Where else?"

"I don't know about that," I said.

"He's not going to do anything," said Moggio. "I got a gut feeling about this guy. I think he's a wimp."

Well, I felt like saying, what if he's not a wimp? What if we're underestimating Juan? What if he comes in here guns blazing, or maybe wired up with explosives? Maybe he's a suicide bomber, although that seemed unlikely. What then, Mr. Gut Feeling? But I didn't say any of these things. I didn't want to look like a wimp to Moggio after all. And we were on the offensive, right? We had all agreed to that. And, finally, I guess I did want to confront Juan at close quarters in a situation where we had some control, instead of vice versa.

"Okay," I said. "What do you want us to do?"

"Just open the door when we get there," said Moggio. "I'll be holding a gun on this guy, and I don't want to be standing around too long on the front porch for any curious neighbors to see us and call the police."

"Okay," I said. I hit the button to end the call and informed Maud that visitors were imminent. She had finished dressing and was moving to the bathroom with her purse.

I moved to the front door, where I looked through the peephole. Nothing but a vacant porch and the quiet street beyond. Maud emerged from the bathroom a few minutes later. She had freshened up a bit, but she didn't look particularly elated. She didn't have that afterglow of sexual pleasure. It was beginning to settle in on me that the sex thing really hadn't gone very well. I wondered if I could get another opportunity. Or, maybe I really *was* dead. Maybe this was how sex felt when you're deceased.

This unpleasant and, let's face it, self-indulgent contemplation was cut short by two quick, sharp raps at the door. I looked back through the peephole and into the unhappy face of Juan. I opened the door, hoping that Moggio was also somewhere in the vicinity. Turns out he was. He was standing behind Juan and, when I opened the door far enough, Moggio pushed the young man through, then followed him into the foyer. I shut the door behind them and turned to see that Moggio had a very large handgun jammed into the small of Juan's back. This handgun was along the lines of Dirty Harry dimensions, and I wondered how Moggio had managed to keep it concealed.

"I trust everybody knows everybody," said Moggio. Then he prodded Juan again with the .357 Magnum or whatever it was, moving the young man into my living room.

"Have a seat," he said, and Juan dropped to the couch and looked back up at Moggio, a sullen expression on his face. Moggio took off his coat, shaking one side off at a time and changing hands with the gun. Apparently he didn't trust me to hold it for him. Which was just fine with me. Juan watched Moggio go through this maneuver, then he looked at me. Then over to Maud, who stood sort of on the periphery of things staring at Juan, her arms crossed tightly over chest. For some reason the nagging discomfort of our sexual encounter took hold of me once again. Well, the circumstances hadn't been ideal, after all. It's hard to be romantic when you know that a murderer is casing your home, right?

"You're dead," said Juan, just to get things started, I guess. "You're all fucking dead." I almost mentioned that, strictly speaking, I might metaphorically be the only one in the room who actually fit that description, but the moment didn't seem to call for lame-ass wit.

"Well," said Moggio, "if we're all dead anyway, why don't you bring us up to speed on what's been going on? We won't be able to tell anyone anyway."

"So you die ignorant," said Juan. He was trying to sound tough, but I could tell that some of the swagger he had exhibited during our first meeting at Starbucks had gone out of him. He looked more like an adolescent now than he had during our first meeting, although he was clearly older than that. Well, maybe that's what going on the offensive will do for you. Take a starch out of your adversary.

Moggio took two steps towards Juan and in a move that was so quick and unexpected that its stunned me—and Maud as well, as her short scream indicated—Moggio whacked Juan across his left ear with that monster handgun of his. Juan grunted and both his hands flew up to the injured area.

Moggio flipped the gun again this time catching Juan on the other ear. Then, before the kid could react, Moggio was pushing him back against the couch and jamming the barrel of the gun into his mouth. Juan's eyes were streaming tears and they were wide with terror as he focused on Moggio. I never would have predicted this kind of brutality from the man, which just goes to show you what kind of a judge of character I am.

"See," said Moggio almost spraying the word in Juan's face, "when I was a cop, I was never allowed to use any of the more intense interrogation techniques, so now I kind of get off on them." He put some pressure on the handgun, forcing it a little deeper into Juan's mouth. It hurt the back of my throat just to watch. "Now I'm just going to keep this here until you're ready to talk. Hey, want to hear my impression of Clint Eastwood doing his speech on that most powerful handgun in the world thing?"

A stain suddenly began to spread around the crotch area of Juan's gray slacks. I looked back at Maud, perhaps for some counsel on what to do, but she was no help. Her eyes were as wide as Juan's and she had both her hands clamped over mouth. Apparently the "going on the offensive" strategy wasn't looking as appealing as it had a few minutes earlier.

"Hey, Drew," I said to Moggio, "is this necessary?" Juan's eyes darted over to me for instant, then went back to Moggio, who ignored my question.

"When you're ready to answer some questions just blink your eyes twice," he said to Juan. I could smell the odor of urine now and blood was dripping from one of Juan's earlobes. I guess I was going to have to buy a new couch, which probably wasn't a bad idea, anyway. This one had been purchased sometime during Ronald Reagan's first term. I saw Juan blink his eyes several times quickly, but Moggio still didn't remove the gun from the kid's mouth.

"Was that two blinks, or three?" said Moggio.

I wasn't sure who he was asking. I thought he was just fucking with Juan, but, after all, I had just met Moggio myself. I couldn't tell you about his sense of humor.

"Two," said Maud, her voice recovered. "Definitely two."

"Good thing we have an interpreter here," said Moggio. He slowly withdrew the gun from Juan's mouth and stood back from him, the gun still pointing at Juan's head. "So now that we've decided to be a little more sociable," said Moggio, "let's start with some introductions. What's your name? And don't tell me Juan."

"Beste," said the young man. It came out like a hoarse grunt. "Philip Beste."

"Good," said Moggio, with enthusiasm, glad to see that the object of his abuse had become so cooperative. "That's a good start. Now, suppose you tell us why you're bothering these nice people."

"I'm not bothering anybody," said Beste, almost poutish.

"Well, they certainly *feel* like they're being bothered."

"Can I get a towel or something?" said Beste. He had moved both of his hands to his crotch to cover the pee stain.

"No, you can't," said Moggio. "This ain't the Plaza fucking Hotel. We're through being nice. You need to answer some questions before we start breaking out the amenities."

Beste looked at him in confusion.

"I'm answering your fucking questions," he said. "I'm *watching* them, I'm not bothering them."

"Okay," said Moggio, "why are you watching them?"

"Some people got worried about him," said Beste, motioning with his head in my direction. "He got in the middle of something, let's say, and these people were concerned, let's say, about where he might go with it."

Moggio looked at Beste for a moment, tilting his thick head like a dog might. It kind of went with the habitual growl in his voice. He seemed to have forgotten that Maud and I were even in the room.

"But this is not what we're looking for, let's say," said Moggio. "More specificity, let's say, is what we're looking for."

"I can't do that," said Beste. "They'll kill me."

"Well, hell, *I'll* fucking kill you," said Moggio "I have two witnesses here that you threatened to kill them after confessing to the murder of Barry Justice and Lashona Webber. In fact, you were just about to kill them when I showed up on the scene. All I had time to do was slap you around little bit, then shoot your punk ass. It will be self-defense all the way. Or maybe justifiable homicide. In either event, you will be dead. So you see, you need to be worrying about the immediate situation here and not so much about what might happen later. You need a little Zen. My advice? Focus on the task at hand."

"I didn't kill Justice or his wife," said Beste. Moggio shook his head in frustration.

"You don't get it do you?" he said. "I don't care if you killed them. It will be enough that we say you told us you did. Now, I don't have all fucking day for this." He started to put the gun back into Beste's mouth.

"Okay, okay," said the kid, drawing his head back from Moggio's approach. "I really don't know who killed the woman, I mean Justice's wife."

"Okay, who killed Justice?" said Moggio.

"I *was* going to kill him," said Beste. "But somebody beat us—me—to it."

"This is getting tedious," said Moggio.

"I'm *serious*," said Beste.

"Then why did you tell these folks here you killed him?" said Moggio.

"I don't know," said Beste. "I wanted them to know what I was capable of," he said.

"But you're really not capable of it, are you?" said Moggio. "You're just a sniveling little prick who's been playing a role here, right? You've never killed anyone in your entire miserable life. See, I've known a few killers in my time and they don't piss their pants 'cause somebody gets a little rough with them."

"People know I'm here," said Beste, which seemed to be a change of subject as far as I could tell.

"Yeah," said Moggio. "But they're not going to do anything about it, are they?"

Beste said nothing.

"You got one, maybe two other punk kids in on this with you. Maybe a couple of old high school buddies. Saw an opportunity, right? An opportunity for little shakedown maybe? Except you're so fucking incompetent you don't know how to go about it, right? What were you going to do? Work your way up to a little extortion of my friends here? First you had to make your threat sound credible by killing that little girl in the 7-11 parking lot, right? But you couldn't even handle that. That had to be the work of one of your buddies, one who has a couple more balls than you have, right? The fact is, you had nothing at all to do with Justice or his wife or any of this stuff except for the Leia girl."

"You're wrong," said Beste.

"About what?" Moggio snapped back at him.

Beste said nothing, just looked at Moggio petulantly, like a teenager who had just been told he couldn't use the car tonight, as if any teenager these days even had to ask a parent for the use of a car.

Just as I thought Moggio might be ready to re-insert his gun into Beste's mouth, the kid spoke up.

"I need some assurances," he said.

Moggio looked over to Maud and me with an expression on his face that said, *Do you believe the nerve of this little bastard?* Then he returned his attention to Beste.

"Okay, I assure you that it's going to be raining brains here and about five fucking seconds."

"All right, all right," said Beste. "I was working for Justice." Nobody said anything for ten seconds, until Moggio broke the silence.

"Working for him doing what?"

"As muscle," said Beste. Moggio grinned.

"Muscle, huh?" He said. "Who'd you ever muscle?"

"Justice thought his wife was having an affair with her shrink," said Beste. "He wanted the shrink to disappear."

"Disappear as in die?"

"No," said Beste. "Just lay off his old lady." Moggio smiled again.

"Lay off her, huh? I like that. He sure will be laying off her now."

"We didn't have anything to do with killing him," said Beste, energetically, even pulling himself up into a more erect sitting position on the couch. "We just discouraged him."

"Where did this happen?"

"Here in Birmingham. We went to the shrink's house and roughed him up a little bit, basically just tried to scare him."

"So did he lay off Justice's wife after that?"

Best shrugged. "I guess so," he said.

"What do you mean, you guess so?" said Moggio.

"I mean, right after that, Justice's old lady split. A couple days later the shrink's dead."

"So who killed the shrink?"

"Not me," said Beste, crossing his arms over his chest.

"Okay, who do you *think* killed him?"

"I don't know," said Beste. "You're the cop, aren't you?" The opportunity to engage in conversation and the relative lack of threat from Moggio in the past few minutes had apparently emboldened young Mr. Beste. He was edging back into smartass mode. Moggio tried another approach.

"How did Justice find you for this job?" he said. "I wouldn't take you for muscle, if I just saw you walking down the street." Moggio accompanied this comment with a little nudge to Beste's bicep with the barrel of his gun. Beste looked at the gun like it might have a life of its own, like it was a trained snake or something.

"Justice knew my father," said Beste. "He told my dad about his problem."

"And you're dad recruited you for this job?" Moggio asked. Beste shrugged. "What the fuck kind of family you got? You the Sopranos of Birmingham, Michigan, or something?"

"Maybe," said Beste, in a manner that the thought might give us some pause in our treatment of him, or, I should say Moggio's treatment of him. For Maud and me, this was more like very intense dinner theater.

"So when you let these folks here believe that you killed Justice, that was just an exaggeration, right?" said Moggio.

Beste shrugged again.

"So, any thoughts on who *did* kill Justice?"

Beste shook his head.

"Why did you say you were going to kill him?"

"He refused to pay us."

"So you were gonna kill him for that?" said Moggio. Then, without waiting for an answer, he said, "Why did he refuse to pay? You guys fuck up the job?"

"No."

"Then why?"

"He said he didn't have to. He said he thought his wife had run off with the shrink, so, whatever we did or said to the shrink didn't work."

"What did you say or do to the shrink?"

"I told you, we roughed him up a little bit."

Something occurred to me.

"Wouldn't Dr. Astrachan recognize you?" I said. "He knew your dad, right?"

"Not like friends," said Beste. "Besides, we wore masks. Ski masks."

"Ingenious," said Moggio. "What did the shrink say, when you told him to lay off Justice's wife?"

"Just what you'd expect him to say, I guess." said Beste. "That he had no idea what we were talking about, that it was against the rules to get involved with his patients. All that bullshit."

"I take it you didn't believe him?"

Beste had another shrug for us.

"It didn't make no difference to me. I guess we expected him to deny it."

"So after you and your buds rough up Dr. Astrachan, what, you just left him to think about it? Is that it?"

"Right," said Beste.

"Then Astrachan leaves for his conference out west and you go back to Justice, demanding payment and he refuses."

"Right again," said Beste.

"Then, before you know it, Justice and Astrachan are dead and you're out your fee and even more awkwardly, implicated in two murders."

"No," said Beste. "I told you, we had nothing to do with killing the shrink or Justice."

"Or Lashona Webber?" said Moggio.

"Her either," said Beste.

"You sure?" said Moggio. "A little revenge maybe?"

"I told you," said Beste. "Nobody even knew where his wife was. She had disappeared. How was I supposed to kill her if I didn't know where she was?"

"But you knew where she was by then," said Moggio. "She was back on the job. All you had to do was go to the TV station where she worked and wait for her to come out. Then follow her. You see her walk out of the restaurant with my friends here and, bang, bang. She's dead."

"Sorry, man," said Beste. "Looks like you're gonna have to work a little harder. It just didn't happen that way." Moggio looked at me.

"You got any beer?" he said. Having been all caught up in the drama of this interrogation, I was taken aback by this request.

"Uh, yeah, sure," I said.

"We could be here awhile," said Moggio, by way of clarifying his request, I guess. I headed for the kitchen.

"Ms. Gonne," Moggio said to Maud. "Perhaps you could find some napkins or paper towels." He looked back to the blood- and pee-stained Philip Beste.

Maud followed me into the kitchen.

"I'm beginning to think this kid is telling the truth," she said, when we were out of sotto voce range. I opened the refrigerator and took out three cans of Bud, offering one to Maud.

"Thanks," she said, accepting the can, then offering it back to me. "Could you open it, please. These cans are murder on my nails." She smiled and I smiled back at her. I opened the can for her and gave it back.

"Juan, or Beste, may be telling the truth, but the fact is he or one of his twisted fellow cretins killed that girl Leia. So I'd go easy on the sympathy."

"I'm not sympathizing," she said. "What I'm trying to point out is that if Beste here isn't the bogeyman, someone else is, someone probably a lot scarier and a lot more competent than this slacker out there."

This, of course, was obvious. But I had to admit to myself that I hadn't given it a lot of thought.

"There was actually some security in thinking that Juan, I mean, Beste, was our villain, you know? At least he is a known quantity. Now—" she trailed off. She took a drink from the can of Bud. "Who is killing these people?" she said. "And why?"

"I don't know," I said. "Maybe this love triangle thing is correct."

"Yeah," said Maud. "Except that it would have to be a love square or rectangle, right? The fourth person? The one who's doing the killing?"

"I guess so," I said. "If that's the motive."

But I really didn't believe that was the motive. It had been my sense all along that the marriage between Barry Justice and Lashona Webber had not exactly been a love match and it bothered me now as it related to Beste's story. Basically, I wasn't buying the fact that Justice had hired this loser to threaten Astrachan. On the other hand, Moggio was right. Beste wasn't a killer. He might be acquainted with killers, might even be related to killers, but he was no killer himself. My impression of Beste was that he was a timid young man trying to act tough. Moggio was right again. Real tough guys don't piss their pants like a puppy the first time somebody waves a gun at them. Or even the first time someone sticks the gun in their mouth. Like the independent operation of male genitalia, weak bladders don't lie.

"Do you think Moggio is thinking along the same lines we are?" asked Maud.

"I don't know," I said. I put the two remaining cans of Bud on the counter and opened them. Then I drank about half of one of them down. I realized my throat had been very dry and I was sweating rather copiously under the arms. This thing was taking almost as much out of me as it was out of Beste.

"I don't know Moggio well enough to understand what he's doing."

"He has a peculiar approach to interviewing people," Maud acknowledged.

"He seems to be making progress," I said, but without a lot of enthusiasm.

"We should get back," said Maud. "No telling what kind of torture he'll inflict if we're not around as witnesses."

"That might be an argument for staying here," I said. She gave me a strange smile, one I couldn't read, but which I guess I would have called seductive under different circumstances. "Uh, the lovemaking thing," I started to say. She put her fingers to my lips.

"That was my fault," she said. "I made totally the wrong call in that situation." I wasn't sure what she meant by this. Then she clarified. "It'll get better," she said. "Much better." Then she kissed me hard on the lips, and, guess what? She was right. It would get better. It was getting better already.

I knew even before we returned to the living room that something was wrong. I guess it was the sense of quiet. Somebody should have been saying something, even a pause in the conversation should have had some volume. What do they say in the movies? It was too quiet?

We found Moggio lying at the foot of the chair that Beste had been sitting in. That chair was now empty and its occupant had disappeared. After a few frozen seconds, I rolled Moggio over on his back and felt for a pulse at his neck. It was there and seemed to be strong enough, but he seemed unresponsive to my untrained eye.

"Is he all right?" said Maud in a whisper, as if Moggio's assailants were still within earshot.

"He's alive," I said. "If that's what you mean. I don't know about all right."

"We need to call 911," she said, and she was right. I couldn't have Moggio just expire there in my living room. How would I explain that? Especially on the heels of having been three feet away from Lashona Webber when she had been killed. On the other hand, how was I going to explain Moggio's injury to the police who would undoubtedly accompany the emergency medical people?

"Did they shoot him?" said Maud.

"I don't know *what* happened," I said. "I don't even know who they are."

I hoped Moggio would cooperate by coming to. But that wasn't happening. We had to do something quick. Beste was out of our control now and no doubt dreaming up nasty forms of retaliation.

"How did this happen without our hearing it?" said Maud. "We should have heard something, even if it was only Moggio falling to the floor."

"I don't know," I said. I inspected Moggio for wounds, as much as a person with my level of squeamishness was able to. It was purely a visual examination. I wasn't about to touch anything. After all, I didn't know where Moggio had been. "I don't think he was shot," I said. Maybe someone just hit him with a blunt object."

Professor Plum in the library with the candlestick.

Maud got up and headed for the kitchen.

"Where are you going?" I said.

"To call 911. We can't just let the poor man lie there without medical attention."

Moggio still hadn't regained consciousness by the time they loaded him up for the hospital. A uniformed cop of the Clarkston Police Department had arrived at about the same time the ambulance had. This was beginning to be something of a habit for Maud and me, being on the scene, that is, in the presence of victims of violence. First Lashona Webber. Now Andrew Moggio. In my own case, I could add Barry Justice to the list, although, of course, there had been no ambulances or police in that case. But it was still weird. It was like someone was performing these acts of violence for our entertainment or edification.

We told the cop what had happened without omitting anything. Maud and I agreed in advance that it would not be a good idea to lie to the police at this point. The cop made a couple of calls after talking with us, one of which was to confirm Moggio's occupation as a private investigator and former cop. He probably learned of this through some cop grapevine. He also put out an alert for Philip Beste based on the description we gave him, warning his brethren that Beste was the likely assailant and that he might be traveling in the company of others who could be armed and dangerous.

Luckily, the cop did not think it was necessary for us to go downtown for interrogation purposes. I wouldn't have been up to that. I don't think Maud would have either. The cop did recommend that we stay put and told us that he would have patrols go by the house on a regular basis, although he pointed out it was unlikely that the culprits would show up at my place again that night. That seemed reasonable to me. The cop explained that Moggio had been taken to a hospital about twenty miles up the road in Grand Blanc—which apparently was the nearest trauma facility—and that, since Moggio didn't appear to have any information on emergency notification, they would be contacting us to report any changes in his condition.

"It doesn't sound like Moggio has anybody he's close to," said Maud after the cop had left.

"I guess not," I said. "The person he was probably closest to the past couple of years was probably Lazard."

"Jules Lazard?" said Maud in astonishment. "*The* Jules Lazard? The detective?"

"That's the one," I said. I hadn't had a chance to mention my discussion with Moggio at the Post Bar. Things had been hectic.

"You say it like Lazard's dead," said Maud.

"According to Moggio, he is," I replied. "And it gets even weirder. Not only did Moggio tell me that Lazard was dead. He also told me that he had killed him."

"Killed Lazard?" said Maud. "What, in some kind of accident?"

"Not exactly," I said. "It was more like a mercy killing as far as I can tell."

"Moggio told you that?" said Maud. "And you still allowed him to get involved in this?"

"You make it sound like he's a criminal," I said. "Which he's not."

"Oh yeah?" said Maud. "Tell it to Jack Kevorkian."

She had a point there. Even at that moment, Dr. Death was serving a prison sentence for murder somewhere in the Water-Winter Wonderland that is the dreadful State of Michigan.

"Hey," I said, "he didn't have to tell me that he killed Lazard. He could have just gone with the official version. I wouldn't have been any the wiser."

"Okay," said Maud. "So that's a point in his favor, but I still don't like him. He's got a sadistic streak. I'm sure you've noticed."

Well, yeah, that had been troubling. But didn't the fact that he was lying unconscious in a hospital bed right at that moment suggest that his particular form of the "going on the offensive" was justified? It was preemption, after all. Hey, it was good enough for Dubya.

"All I can tell you was that having him along seemed like a good idea at the time. He's already involved to some extent, through his work for Lashona Webber. And he's a former cop. He might, in fact, he definitely would, know more about solving crimes than you or I would."

"I wonder why whoever disabled Moggio didn't just shoot him. And us in the bargain," said Maud. It was a very good question.

"Maybe they weren't armed," I said.

"Well, someone shot that Leia girl. So *someone's* armed. I understand it's not difficult for criminals to acquire weapons."

"Well, I don't know why they didn't kill Moggio—and us. Maybe they had no reason to."

"Except that we're on to Beste now." Neither of us said anything for a few minutes. Then Maud said: "I wonder if Moggio got a glimpse of his attackers?"

"Okay, it's something to wonder about. I tend to doubt it, my evidence being that he's still alive. Probably someone got the drop on him, hit him from behind."

"So, they didn't have to kill him."

"Right," I said. "Whoever did this isn't stupid. Why complicate their lives by killing an ex-cop, if you don't have to? I guess any time you commit a crime you increase the chances that you'll be caught."

"You think they're that smart?" said Maud. "I have my doubts about anyone who would ally themselves with Beste."

"Beste isn't necessarily stupid," I said. "Maybe just inexperienced. Almost certainly he wasn't born criminal. Somebody may have just been using him." Maud thought about it.

"Which makes him expendable, right?"

"Right," I said. This gave me pause. "We may have seen the last of Mr. Beste after all."

Maud pondered that for another couple of seconds, then said: "Who *are* these people?"

Well, I had to admit that I didn't have the slightest idea.

"Moggio mentioned that the last thing he had been working on for Lashona Webber was some investigation she was doing on drugs connected to autism in children. Vaccines, I think he said."

"You think these drug people could be involved?" said Maud.

"Who knows?" I said. "Even if they were involved in Lashona's death, would they risk killing Justice and Astrachan, too?"

"Maybe," said Maud. "If they had the same information she did."

"Well, according to Moggio, there wasn't any secret about the story. He said it was all over the Internet, but he also mentioned that Lashona had gotten some kind of message from a chemical engineer or something, who claimed to have some smoking gun evidence that would provide a link between this drug and autism, and that this information could just rain down a shit storm of grief on the pharmaceuticals. We would be talking some serious liability here."

Maud put her index finger to lips and looked past me. "And some serious motivation," she said. "Hey, I like that even better than my police conspiracy theory."

"Yeah," I said. "A woman like Lashona, with all the stuff she was into, there's no telling how many hypotheses you could come up with."

"The mind spins," said Maud. "It reels."

I woke up in front of my TV. It was on and tuned to MSNBC, which I had been watching before I drifted off to sleep after my third or fourth beer. Time was it would take a lot more beers than that to put me out. But I don't drink quite as much as I used to. Also, it had been a pretty fatiguing day, what with all the excitement of encountering Moggio, then all that adventure with Philip Beste and the sexual exercise with Maud and the attack on Moggio and the police. And Maud's and my speculation on who the über criminal was behind all the mayhem we'd been witness to. Certainly enough to wear out a middle-aged dead man for one day.

Maud wasn't around. And I kind of remembered her saying that she was going off to bed as I sat semi-conscious, half watching the interminable news about Iraq and the guy who allegedly killed his pregnant wife in California, etc., etc., etc. The little time stamp in the corner of the TV picture indicated it was 5:08 a.m. It was still plenty dark and the house felt cold. Then I remembered that the heat was turned down to save money, since nobody had actually been living at the house until now. I got up and stretched, then made my way to the thermostat on the living room wall. It glowed at me, letting me know that the temperature was a brisk sixty-two degrees. I cranked the thermostat up to seventy and a few seconds later I heard the furnace kick in. I assumed that Maud had gone to sleep in the guest bedroom, but when I clicked on my bathroom light I heard a soft moan of protest from my bed. Maud lay under the covers, which were pulled up to her neck. I had been planning to take a shower in the master bathroom. Instead, I grabbed clean underwear and socks from my drawer and retreated to the shower off the guest bedroom where I stood under the hot spray for no less than half an hour.

I had thought this gallantry on my part would allow Maud to get some much-needed sleep. But when I walked into the kitchen after my shower, I found that Maud had already started coffee going and she was on her tiptoes, rummaging through my kitchen cabinets. She wore what I guessed was one of my white dress shirts—which I myself had probably last worn about 1994 or so—and apparently nothing else. I don't think I'd ever been in the company a woman dressed in this fashion, although I must have seen it in a movie someplace. It was definitely a good look on Maud. Standing on her toes like that emphasized the muscles of her calves and hamstrings. Not to mention her glutes, which were quite impressive there against the fabric of my shirt.

"The freshest box of cereal you have in here has an expiration date of September 1999," Maud announced as soon as I entered the room.

"Sorry," I said. "It's hard to keep stocked up on perishable goods when you're dead." She turned and smiled at me.

"I forgive you," she said, "but I can't begin to tell you how hungry I am. I can't run until I get something in my stomach and I can really get the day started until I've had a good cleansing six-mile run."

"It must be a terrible burden," I said. "Your life, I mean."

"Stephen," she said with a little pout, "I haven't eaten since breakfast yesterday."

It occurred to me that I hadn't either. In all the excitement of the day before, eating had not been a priority. Maud was right. I was hungry, too.

"We could try to find a restaurant. They should be opening soon. Or I could see if the supermarket is open." Maud didn't exactly jump at either of those options.

"I don't know if I can wait that long," she said.

"Hold on," I said. "I'll be right back." I headed off for one of the stock rooms where I sorted through some of the MREs that I'd stored there in case *World War III: The Terrorist Edition*, commenced. While the shelf life of some of these treats was longer than most civilian equivalents, they still didn't last forever, and most of the meals had expired. However, I was able to find three breakfast entrées that were still good, based on expiration dates on the packages. I trotted back to the kitchen feeling rather proud of myself.

"Meals, ready to eat," I announced to Maud when I returned. She was now standing at the kitchen table drinking her coffee. I would characterize the look she had on her face as dubious. I read off the contents of the packages. "We have one each, omelet with sausage and potatoes and one only corned beef hash."

"You really know how to show a girl a good time," said Maud.

"Hey," I replied. "If it's good enough for our boys in Iraq . . . . "

Well, either military rations didn't deserve the bad reputation they had or we were really, *really* hungry, because we managed to polish off all the food. We were so hungry that we hardly spoke during our feast.

"We should check on Moggio," I said when we had finished. Maud nodded.

"I had a weird dream last night," she said. "You were in it and Moggio and even the late Detective Lazard."

"Really?" I said. "Lazard?"

"Yeah," said Maud. "And I never even met the man. I guess my dream concept of him was based on your portrayal. But he was as real as you are right now."

"Did he happen to impart any wisdom?" I asked. "Something that will give us any kind of handle as to what's going on?"

"Sorry," said Maud. "But he did have something to say about your wife. I mean Denise, of course."

I don't know if Maud was expecting me to try to drag this out of her but I wasn't inclined to, so I said nothing. I may have mentioned that I don't like to talk to people about Denise and I don't like dream conversations. They're creepy. I'm not superstitious, but I *am* suggestible. I tend to be a living, breathing agent of the self-fulfilling prophecy, that is, when I'm not dead.

"You don't want to know what Lazard had to say about Denise?" said Maud, a hint of skepticism in her voice.

"Well, it's not like you'd be reporting an actual event," I said. "This is your dream, okay? It's a product of your imagination."

"Is that what dreams are?" said Maud, feigning astonishment.

"Look Maud. Can we just talk about the task at hand, which, I guess, is getting to the bottom of whatever's going on here?"

"Oh, so now you *do* want to get involved, is that it?"

We had been having such a nice romantic morning over a couple of incomparably tasty military rations, and some admittedly stale coffee. And now look where we were—on the verge of an argument over a dream. How any couples managed to stay together was beyond me.

"I've come to the conclusion that we need to do something, yes."

"Well, if you're expecting my participation, you're going to have to listen to my dreams. There won't be that many. I hardly ever remember my dreams. Even my most vivid dreams start to dissipate the second I wake up, so for me to remember a dream in any measure of detail or continuity is something we can't ignore."

"In dreams begin responsibility," I said.

"What does that mean?" she said.

"Forget it. Your dream doesn't have anything to do with solving this mystery—"

Maud brought her fist down hard on the table, causing both of our coffee mugs to jump. I still had almost a full cup and its contents spilled over onto the tabletop.

"It has *everything* to do with this mystery," said Maud.

"I just asked you if Lazard had provided any insight into this situation and you said no," I told her. Jesus! This was crazy. We were talking about Lazard and Denise like they were on a trip to Vegas rather than deceased individuals. Maud seemed to collect herself for a moment.

"I'm going to go for my run," she said finally. "While I'm gone, you'll have time to think about whether or not we are going to continue to do this thing together, whatever this thing is. I know that's what I'm going to be thinking about. My running as a way of clarifying things for me. Maybe you could employ whatever ritual you're partial to to achieve the same result. Then, when I get back we can compare notes." She stood up and drained the remaining coffee from her cup.

Out of spite, perhaps, I didn't immediately give any thought to where we were going with "this." I calmly finished my coffee and even had another cup. I did think about other things. Mainly, I thought about myself. When I had told Maud that I didn't know why I had faked my own death, I hadn't been exactly telling the truth. I had a rough idea, although I couldn't have explained it to anyone in any detail.

First let me say that, although I put on a pretty glib front about this whole death thing, I am absolutely terrified of dying. Terrified and outraged. I know about all the religious rationale and philosophical justifications for death. But I don't buy any of them, and I don't know anyone who does, or at least wouldn't admit that they didn't if you got them alone.

The death of Denise hit me hard. Not so hard I wanted to join her, but hard enough. I guess I had survivor's guilt. I had *something* anyway that made me feel as though someone had opened my chest and pumped one of those turkey basters full of tar into my heart. I felt like I walked around toxic, like anyone I might touch would immediately vaporize right before my eyes. Toxic Man.

In a nutshell, I felt like shit. But I didn't feel so bad that I wanted to die. And you would have thought that if ever there was a time that I might sail off into the sunset—or actually into the sunrise as the case was—it might have been at that low point in my life. I'd actually managed to climb a little bit out of that black hole, the color had returned to my heart to some extent and I had been getting back into the flow of things when I made the decision to fake my own death.

The decision was one thing; the execution, however, was another. The approach that I decided on—apparent loss at sea and death by drowning—required some planning. You can't just swim to Bermuda from thirty miles off the coast of North Carolina. That meant that I would have to recruit a co-conspirator, and, since I had no confidants or close friends, I would have to pay somebody for not only their assistance, but also their silence. The co-conspirator I eventually settled on was illegal immigrant from Esmeraldes, Ecuador, who worked in the small boat harbor in Florida where I had taken sailing lessons. The immigrant's name was Pablo something or other. I didn't especially want to know his last name, and he sure as hell didn't want to give it to me.

He seemed like a good choice. He had been a fisherman in his native country and he seemed to know his way around a boat as far as I could tell. He made about five dollars an hour cleaning up around the marina—washing boats, cleaning fish for the tourists, chopping up bait for the fishing charters. Someone told me that he lived on one of the boats, maybe a boat that he owned, and that he saved his money and sent most of it back to his family in Ecuador. He was clearly in need of extra cash.

But what I really liked about Pablo was his immigrant status, that is to say, undocumented. It gave me something on him. I never directly threatened to give him up if he revealed my secret to anyone, but I think the threat was understood. And since Pablo didn't appear to have any immediate plans to earn his citizenship, I wasn't too worried that he'd become less vulnerable to my implied threat anytime soon.

Ultimately, all of this may have been moot. He didn't seem interested in giving my secret away. When I had approached him with the idea—we had met at a local bar near the marina—he had acted as if people asked him to help them fake their own deaths every couple of weeks or so. He didn't appear surprised or alarmed or disgusted. He seemed more concerned with the logistics of the thing. He had no confidence in my ability to navigate, so he was unclear as to how we would be able to effect a rendezvous in the middle of the ocean. And he was right. The classes I had taken had provided some basic seamanship, including navigation, but there was no way I could find my way to Bermuda, let alone some watery coordinate where we could meet to pull this off.

"Can't you just follow me at a distance?" I had asked him. "Then, when we're out far enough to sea and nobody else is around, you just run your boat up along side of mine and I hop on."

He pointed out that this would be a good idea if he had a power boat, but all he had was a small sailing skiff, a vessel that might not even be able to keep up with mine, let alone rendezvous with it. There were too many variables. And, he pointed out, it wasn't as desolate and unpopulated at sea as most people thought. He would need a fast boat that could make a rapid approach and a quick getaway. After all, if someone saw him approach my boat they would certainly be interested in talking to him after I disappeared.

"I can get the boat we need," he told me. "I will tell the owner that I am taking some tourists on a fishing trip. It will not be a problem."

Well, not for him. For me, the problem was that it would cost another two grand for the rental and security fee for the boat in addition to the five thousand I had agreed to pay Pablo for his part in this little charade. But what was I going to do? I couldn't go to anyone else at this point. Before you knew it the word would get out that some batshit gringo was trying to recruit someone to help him pretend to get lost at sea. And what Pablo said made sense. A faster boat would be better.

So I gave Pablo forty-five hundred dollars—half of his fee and the money for the boat rental. I told him that I needed to take care of some business that would consume about ten days. We agreed to the day of my disappearance—August 3—a date with no special significance, if you don't count the fact that Lenny Bruce and Flannery O'Connor, a more interesting couple than you might immediately consider them, both died on that day of the month.

We also agreed that we wouldn't meet again until we were on the bounding main. I told him that, if we were a go, I would set sail from the marina at 7:00 a.m. on August 3 and that he should be prepared to follow me at that time. If he didn't show up within three hours, I told him that I would return to the marina, but that the deal would be off and he would forfeit the balance of his fee. He told me not to worry, that he was awake with the sun every day and that he was very dependable. The only problem would be if he couldn't get the boat for that day. He thought it wouldn't be a issue, but in case it was, he would leave a note to that effect on my boat the night before.

I returned to Detroit and saw to the details of wrapping up my life as I had known it. Then I flew back to Florida and did my best to live the life of a carefree tourist until the fateful day. No suggestion of moroseness or doom about me. I cut a dashing figure in the local bars, but was careful not to overdo it, lest I give off some bi-polar whiff. In truth, as the day approached, I felt more and more giddy. I felt, I don't know, a sense of power that I had never experienced before. Basically, the sense I had was not that I was putting one over on the rest of my fellow human beings, but that I was pulling a fast on one Death itself. It was my revenge for Denise.

Of course, in hindsight, I can see that my behavior and my glee were pitiful. Who cared, after all? As Moggio had so adroitly pointed out, unless I was faking my death for some fraudulent purpose, I wasn't doing anything that was going to upset anyone. Was somebody supposed to be entertained or intrigued? Who would that be? But I was caught up in this thing at the time, and none of these very reasonable thoughts occurred to me.

What it boiled down to, I think, is that I was taunting death, and thereby trying to earn some immunity. Doesn't everybody think this way?

Pablo and I managed it without a hitch. It was so anticlimactic that some of my exuberance left me even as I stepped off Pablo's boat at a marina south of the one where I had parked my boat. This marina was larger and much busier. We had chosen it for that purpose. Who would notice me hopping off Pablo's boat and be able to connect me with the disappearance that would become news the next day when they found my empty boat? In fact, our plan worked, I believe, because it was so mundane. It drew no attention to itself for its ingenuity. No mystery writers would want to recount the tale in a book. I would not be the subject of cable news speculation for days and days. Everybody would simply think I was dead, and that was the point, wasn't it?

But, now, here I was, back alive again and caught up in this very strange net of circumstances and occurrences surrounding the lives of Barry Justice and his wife, Lashona Webber. Is this what I was resurrected for? I felt the malevolent presence of someone—whoever was behind this mischief—but I was more at sea than I had ever been in my little boat en route—albeit in abbreviated fashion—to Bermuda back in 1998.

Before I had time to reflect on this further, I heard the side door of the house open and close, then some foot stomping. Maud entered the kitchen, her cheeks red, a dusting of snow on her shoulders.

"It should be against the law of nature to have snow this late in the season," she said. I, of course, had not bothered to look out to see if it had been snowing.

An awkward pause ensued. Maud, I knew, wanted to ask me if I had thought further about "things," but her run had, figuratively as well as literally, cooled her off. Still, the suspension was there, the anticipation that somebody needed to say something.

"Well," said Maud, finally. "I'm going to shower. Have you given any thought to today's agenda?"

"Not much," I said.

"How's your friend Moggio?"

"I was just going to try to call," I said. Maud lingered for another moment. Then she smiled, bent down to me and kissed my forehead. "You're a crazy person, you know that?"

"I think I do," I said.

While Maud showered, I called the hospital to check on Moggio. He was not only out of danger, but he was well enough to talk to me—energetically and lucidly.

"Somebody hit me from behind," he said, referring to the cause of his injury. "I never saw them. In fact, the instant it happened I had a brief thought that you or your girlfriend had hit me. That's how quiet whoever did it was."

I assured him that neither I nor Maud had hit him, which he assured me, he already knew.

"Do you think it was Beste's accomplice?" I said.

"I doubt it," said Moggio. "I have a feeling we've seen the last of Philip Beste. I have a feeling everybody has seen the last of Philip Beste."

When Maud got out of the shower, I filled her in on my conversation with Moggio.

"I'm not going to the gallery today," she said. "I'm not going to the gallery until we get to the bottom of this."

A pretty rash statement, I thought. She might never see the inside of that place again.

"They're releasing Moggio this morning," I said. "Apparently, he didn't suffer any permanent damage."

"He's got one of those head's that doesn't look too easy to damage," said Maud. I nodded.

"Anyway, he'll be here sometime this morning. Whenever they let him out." Maud didn't appear thrilled by this information, but she didn't protest. She poured what was left of the coffee into her mug and looked out the kitchen window.

"I can't believe it's snowing," she said. She turned to me abruptly. "While I was running I was thinking about your encounter with the Barry Justice at the Home Depot. I guess it was the snow. I started thinking about how he told you he saw footprints in the snow leading away from the house. That's what he said right?"

"That's what he said."

She returned her gaze out the window. "Do you remember what Justice was buying at the Home Depot when you ran into him there?"

"No," I said. In fact, I remember that I was so rattled at the time that I didn't notice what he had purchased. It had to be something small, though. I mean, I would have noticed a load of two-by-fours.

"I don't know," said Maud. "From what you've told me about Justice. He just doesn't seem like the kind of guy who would hang out in a Home Depot. Not a handyman, you know?"

"I'm not a handyman, either. And I was there. He could have stopped in there for anything, well, not anything, but lots of those everyday needs we all have. Home Depot's really just a glorified hardware store, right? We all need to go to hardware stores at some point in our wretched lives. I mean, unless you're born in the Kennedy family or you're Paris Hilton."

"I realize that," said Maud. "It's just that the coincidence of his running into you there. Well, I'm having trouble with that. That Home Depot is not near where he lives nor where his office was."

"I feel another theory coming on," I said. Of course, I could have gone into *my* theory—actually Chance Summers'—about the likelihood at any given time of anybody running into anyone. Instead, I said, "Well, look at *our* meeting. What about the coincidence of that?"

"That was destiny," she said, smiling. "There's a big difference between destiny and coincidence." It seemed to me that that would be a matter of interpretation, but I didn't push it with Maud.

"Okay," I said. "Let's hear it." She slid the chair out across from me and sat down.

"Just bear with me on this," she said enthusiastically. "We're kind of running off in all directions, because, well, mainly because we've been into reactive mode. I mean, something happens, we respond."

"What else would we do?" I said.

"Please," she said, holding her hand up, forward in the "stop in the name of love" gesture. "Let's assume for a minute, that Justice's chance encounter with you at the Home Depot wasn't so random after all. Let's assume he wanted you to *think* it was a chance encounter, so he contrives a run-in with you at the Home Depot. I mean, he could have contrived to meet you anywhere, but the Home Depot is so, what, middle-American, you know? It's unexpected, yet, it's expected, you know?

"The problem we have then," she said, "is why Justice would do this?" She looked at me. "And, okay, I don't have an answer for that at the moment. Do you have any ideas?"

"First," I said, "what led to your speculation that Justice went through this charade with me?"

"I told you," she said. "I just can't picture the guy in a Home Depot."

"Well, we've covered that. It's not like we ran into each other in Victoria's Secret, which truly would have been a coincidence of galactic proportions. What is Victoria's Secret, by the way?"

"What do you mean, what is it? It's a woman's lingerie store."

"I know that," I said. "But what's her secret?"

"Very funny," she said. "I'm glad to see that you're taking all this life-and-death stuff so seriously. Can we get back to Barry Justice?"

"Sure. As I was saying, maybe Justice needed a tube of Superglue or one of those little screwdriver gadgets to repair eyeglasses. Or maybe he wanted an air freshener for his car. I think you can buy all that stuff in a Home Depot. I just don't see any reason for him to pretend to have bumped into me. If he had learned somehow that I was alive, he could have just called me on the phone or knocked on the door of my apartment. And what about everything else? What about the deaths of Astrachan and Lashona Webber and Justice's own murder? What about Lashona's daughter and all that stuff with Juan—I mean, Beste?"

"One thing at a time," said Maud. "I'm still working on this Home Depot coincidence."

"Okay," I said. "For the sake of argument, let's say Barry planned to bump into me and wanted it to appear to be coincidental. Why would he do that? What does it mean?" Maud puzzled over that for a moment.

"We need more coffee," she said, as if that would lead to the ultimate resolution. "I have trouble thinking when I'm just sitting down. I think better when I'm moving."

My cell phone whistled and I answered it. It was Moggio.

"They're releasing me at 8 a.m.," he said. I looked at the clock hanging on my kitchen wall, which informed me that it was 7:10 a.m.

"Cool," I said.

"Yeah," said Moggio. "The problem is I don't have a car, remember? I need a ride."

"Oh, yeah, right," I said. "I'm on my way."

"I've got some new thoughts on all this," he said before I could hang up.

"I can't wait to hear them," I told him.

"Any word on Beste?"

"You mean have we heard from him?"

"Oh, you won't be hearing from him. I was just wondering if you've heard anything *about* him."

"No," I said. "I haven't."

"You will," said Moggio. "I'm sure of it. See you at eight."

I hung up and relayed Moggio's portion of the conversation to Maud.

"I'll be ready in ten minutes," she said, forgetting all about making more coffee.

Moggio looked bleary-eyed, and his face looked a little blotchier than usual, but other than that he seemed to be in pretty good shape.

"I don't know if I was comatose or just sleeping or what," he said as he sat at a table at the Little Daddy's restaurant we'd stopped at not too far from the hospital. Moggio's first priority had been food. I just had coffee, but Maud ordered a full breakfast—three poached eggs, bacon, hash browns and toast. How she maintained that breathtakingly svelt figure of hers was a mystery. I mean, she did run regularly, but she also ate like a horse. Moggio went for the huevos rancheros, which I thought was a gutsy choice in a Greek restaurant.

"Anyway, in whatever semiconscious state I was in the ideas just started the flow."

"You two ought to put your heads together," I said to Moggio. He stopped chewing and gave me a quizzical look. "Maud had a dream, too."

"This wasn't a dream," said Moggio. "This was clarity."

"Okay," I said. Whatever.

"Here's the deal," said Moggio. "I don't think Philip Beste was a killer. I think he was acting tough because he was trying to protect somebody. I think his act was just that—an act."

"What about Leia Fountain?" said Maud.

"Who's that?" said Moggio.

"The young girl we saw in the Starbucks. The one Beste threatened to kill. Excuse me, the one he *did* kill in the 7-11 parking lot."

"Funny thing about that," said Moggio. "I called a couple of my contacts at the Clawson and Madison Heights police departments. It turns out, nobody knew anything about a woman being shot in the 7-11 parking lot. Not in Clawson anyway, or Madison Heights or Warren or Troy or any other city in the entire metropolitan area. Not for the past week."

"But what about the clipping?" said Maud.

"We don't even know that it was an actual clipping. It was a copy, right? Beste could have made the whole thing up. I'm pretty much a goddamn computer illiterate, and I could probably have come up with something that looked like a copy of a genuine newspaper clipping. Kids nowadays, they can probably come up with a reasonable copy of the Declaration of fucking Independence on the computer.

"I bet if you could find this Leia Fountain and her boyfriend, they *know* Philip Beste. They're probably friends of his that he planned to meet at the coffee shop just so he could put on that little performance for you."

Even Maud remained silent in the face of this information, which could only indicate that she could see the plausibility of it.

"It's not that I'm so smart," said Moggio. "It's just that I have the benefit of clarity. You two have been all caught up in this, so you've experienced things from a different perspective."

The food arrived and Moggio dug into his huevos rancheros. Maud looked her breakfast over and decided to send her bacon back for further crisping.

"It should looked like slices of charcoal," she told the waitress.

"So," I said to Moggio, whose entire focus now seemed to be on how quickly he could hoover up his breakfast, "who is Beste trying to protect?"

"*Was* trying to protect," said Moggio. "Beste is dead."

"Did this information come during your episode of clarity, too?" I said. Moggio looked at Maud.

"Is he being sarcastic?" he said.

"Could be," said Maud. "He's gifted that way."

"No," said Moggio, redirecting his remarks to me. "My information about Beste came via one of my contacts. I made a few calls while I was waiting to be discharged. Beste's body turned up last night. The Pontiac police found him in his car. The tan Jeep Liberty we'd seen. The car was sitting in the parking lot of the Silverdome and Beste was sitting behind the wheel with a bullet in the back of his head."

"I guess he was telling the truth when he said somebody would kill him if he talked to us," I said.

"The question is," said Maud, "who killed him?"

"I asked first," I insisted. "The question, as I see it is, who was he trying to protect and why?"

"That's two questions," said Maud.

"Maybe the answer is the same for both questions," I said. Moggio stopped chewing and looked back and forth between me and Maud.

"You two talk like this all the time?" he said. Maud and I shrugged at each other.

"Only when we visit Earth," I replied. Moggio shook his head and resumed chewing. It was clear that, with his priority on finishing his meal, our discussion wasn't going to get far. The waitress returned with the coffee carafe in one hand and a plate bearing what was left of Maud's bacon order in the other. Maud inspected the bacon critically as though she still might return it for more treatment.

"They apply anymore heat to that," I said, "and it will no longer qualify as an organic substance." Ignoring me, Maud accepted the plate. The waitress refilled our coffee cups, then retreated. Moggio burped, rather loudly, and declined to excuse himself. But he did manage to use a napkin to wipe his mouth. He then pushed his plate to the side.

"Can I smoke in here?" he asked. I actually didn't know. The hostess had not asked us our smoking preference. I looked around and didn't see anyone else smoking.

"I don't think so," I said.

"I'll take that as a yes," said Moggio. He lit his cigarette. If Maud objected, she didn't say so. Besides, anyone who ate bacon that looked like strips of asphalt roofing shingles—which she was, indeed, devouring with relish—wasn't about to concern herself with secondhand smoke.

"My gut tells me that Beste was protecting his old man," he said.

"Protecting him from what?" I said.

"Well, that's the real question. I did a little checking into Beste's father while I was waiting for you guys. He used to be kind of a hotshot around town. He was tight with some of the people in Coleman Young's administration. Back in the late eighties. He was also one of those guys who moved easily back and forth between the law enforcement community and the criminal element. He had cop friends—some of them pretty high up on the food chain—but he also came up the ranks in construction and that particular vocation's unfortunate reputation for having ties to organized crime is sometimes deserved."

"He was Jack Ruby kind of guy," I said.

"Bingo," said Moggio, shooting at my head with his finger. "Then back a few years ago when the department was going through that embezzlement scandal—remember—when the Chief of Police was convicted? Well, Beste was involved somehow. I'm not sure how or to what extent, but after Chief Hart was jettisoned Beste became persona non grata around city hall. And his business fortunes suffered."

"One of the stories Lashona Webber uncovered had to do with the police," said Maud. "Maybe there's a connection." Obviously, she still hadn't given up on the police conspiracy angle.

Moggio shook his head.

"That was a different issue," he said. "I was still on the force and I remember that story. That was all about police brutality, all the shootings."

"Well, there could still be a connection," said Maud a little petulantly.

"I don't see it," said Moggio. He took a drink of his coffee and a drag from his cigarette. "But I think Beste, Senior, is definitely hinky, and I think, whatever he was into involved Justice somehow."

"Not Lashona? I said.

"Maybe," Moggio. "But I don't think so."

"Do you think it involved Astrachan, too?"

Moggio shrugged.

"I don't rule it out," he replied.

TWENTY-FOUR

MAN OR BESTE?

After we finished breakfast, Moggio insisted upon being taken back to his car.

"Nothing personal," he announced when we'd climbed into the Jag, Maud behind the wheel, "but I can't be a passenger in an automobile for more than a few minutes. I don't know why. I have to be driving if I'm in a moving vehicle."

"Does that extend to flying?" I asked.

"I don't fly," said Moggio.

It seemed to me that Maud had been on her best driving behavior on the ride from the hospital to the restaurant. So I tended to think that it wasn't anything specific that she had done to make Moggio yearn for the comfort and security of his own car. Maybe he was telling the truth. He just didn't like being in a car that someone else was driving.

"I made a couple of other calls, while I was waiting for you," he said, without any prompting from me or Maud. Jeez, how many millennia had he waited for us? "First," he said, "the Southfield police have nothing yet on Lashona Webber's murder. Almost nothing, anyway. They do have a bullet, obviously, a 7.62 round and they have the general direction that the shot came from, but not much else." He paused, perhaps waiting for either of us to ask a question or comment upon or challenge what he had said.

"You said you made a couple of calls," I said.

"Yeah," he said. "I also called the TV station where Lashona worked. I kind of let on that I was a police officer. So I'd appreciate it if that little tidbit of information didn't get out."

"Mum's da woid," I said

Moggio smiled a bit, then fidgeted some. He was sitting in the backseat of the Jag, right in the middle of the seat. I thought he might be on the verge of asking. "Are we there yet?"

"It turns out that Lashona's whereabouts during the past few days weren't all that mysterious," he said instead. "Her producer knew where she was." We were at a stoplight, and when it changed, Maud took off a little too quickly, causing the car to fishtail in the snow.

"I don't know why I bought this car," she said. "Well, I mean, I know why I bought it. I just don't know why I keep it. It's terrible in the winter. No traction it all." Moggio looked at his watch. Maud's comment on her car's performance wasn't helping his mood.

"So," I said, "did Lashona's producer tell you where she was?"

"Florida," said Moggio distracted. "A family thing. It had nothing to do with a story, her family situation—well, let's just say when you look in the dictionary under the word dysfunctional, there's a group shot of the Webber clan."

"Did her producer tell you specifically what she was doing in Florida?" Moggio shook his head.

"Not specifically, but I think it had something to do with her daughter."

I thought about this. Justice had mentioned that Lashona's daughter had been autistic. Or at least suffered from some mental ailment. And that she lived with her mother and brother. From what I'd learned about them, they didn't seem to be ideal choices as caregivers.

"If you had an autistic daughter, would you pawn her off on your relatives a thousand miles away?" I asked no one in particular.

"Everybody's different," said Moggio. "Some people take to parenting differently than others. We think that mothers are good parents just because they're mothers, but that's not always the case."

"Hey," I said. "I know that. I saw *Mommy Dearest.* My point was, why not just park her daughter in an institution if you're going to abandon her anyway?"

"Lashona may have been conflicted," said Maud. "She had this very successful public career. But she also may have had enough feelings for her daughter that she couldn't just warehouse her someplace. Anyway, do we think Lashona's relationship with her daughter or anyone else in her family had anything to do with her getting killed? And why didn't she tell her husband that she was going to Florida to visit her family? She told her frickin' producer."

"This producer is like, was like, this dear friend, maybe her closest friend, from what I can gather," said Moggio. "Lashona didn't tell anyone else at the station where she was going. And to answer your question, I don't know if her family situation was a factor in her death. If it was, how are Justice and the shrink involved?" For a few moments, all of us seemed to be stunned into silence by these questions.

"It's just all over the map," Maud finally said. "I told you we should have made that trip to Florida."

"I work strictly in the Detroit metropolitan area," said Moggio.

"I was talking to Fargo," said Maud.

"Well," said Moggio, "it may still come to that. But right now, I think we need to work the angles here."

"It may come to what?" I said.

"You might have to go to Florida," Moggio replied.

"What do you mean, I might have to go to Florida? Why don't *you* go to Florida? I hate Florida."

"I told you," said Moggio, "I work strictly here in the Detroit area. And I don't fly. Driving all the way to Florida would take too much time. It's impractical."

"But it's okay for me to go?" I said.

"Don't worry about it," said Moggio. "We haven't even begun to exhaust all the possibilities here. You might not even have to go."

"Thank you," I said.

We were almost back at my house. The snow had continued to fall. The salt trucks hadn't yet had an opportunity to get out and the streets were beginning to clog up with traffic.

"I wish I *did* fly," said Moggio, looking out the window. "I hate snow."

"So," said Maud when we had reached my house, "what do we do now?"

"We need to make a couple of calls," said Moggio.

"To whom?" I said.

"I phoned Charles Beste from my hospital room, but he wasn't in yet," said Moggio. "I left a message on his voice mail, but I told him I'd call him back. We need to talk to him."

"He's probably taking care of the arrangements for his kid," I said.

"Maybe," said Moggio. "But the way people are disappearing, I think we need to talk to Mr. Beste before he joins his son."

This time when Moggio called, Beste was in. Maud and I listened as Moggio explained who he was and that he and a couple of his associates would like to meet with Beste to discuss a few things.

"Great," said Moggio. "We'll be there in an hour."

"There," turned out to be an office building in Livonia where Beste Development Inc. was located. I wondered if they pronounced it "beast" in this context.

"He's *working*?" I asked after Moggio explained to us that we would be meeting Beste of his office. "*Today*?"

"He didn't seem terribly broken up about his son's death," said Moggio. "But people have all kinds of ways of responding to loss. Maybe his way is through his work."

Maybe, but I didn't think that was the case.

"He probably feels safer in the office than at home," I said.

"There's that, too," said Moggio.

"So what do we hope to accomplish by this interview?" I said.

"At a minimum we might be able to find out why Philip Beste was trying to protect his father. Or from whom he was trying to protect him."

"Assuming that was the case," I said.

"I already told you that was the case," said Moggio. "My gut tells me it's so."

Beste's office was among a suite in a low-rise building in a strip of commercial sites along the I-275 freeway northwest of Detroit. The building directory indicated that, in addition to Beste Development, the structure housed a Web design firm, an events management company, a limousine service and something called Cleartec, which could have been anything.

"Maybe they use lasers to zap acne," I suggest to Maud. "You know, like those electrolysis places?"

"Maybe," said Maud, rolling her eyes. In the lobby of Beste Development, we reported to the receptionist, a woman who looked like she was going straight from work to a Marilyn Monroe look-alike contest. She had the same platinum hair with that flippy wave on the side, sparkling blue eyes and bee-stung mouth covered in luminous fire-engine red lipstick.

"Look at her," I said. "She looks like Marilyn Monroe," I said.

"Hardly," said Maud.

Moggio was looking at a photo on the wall, one among lots of them. Several appeared to be reprints from magazine covers, probably showing homes built by Beste Development. There were also plaques recognizing Beste Development for various community and civic deeds. And a few photos of Charles Beste—at a groundbreaking event with the Coleman Young, shaking hands with Donald Trump, and others with people I didn't recognize.

The phone rang at Marilyn's desk and she listened briefly, then said, "I'll send them right in." I was hoping that she was going to come out from behind her station and escort us into Beste's office, not just because I wanted to see her body, which would have been okay by me, but also because I wanted to see if she had that Marilyn Monroe walk down, too. But it wasn't to be.

"Mr. Beste will see you now," she said, smiling. Maud and I got up, were joined by Moggio and approached the door that Marilyn indicated, which opened when we were about three feet from it. The timing was so impressive that I wondered if Beste had access there in his inner sanctum to a security camera monitoring the lobby. Beste wasn't smiling, but he was polite enough.

"Please come in," he said, sweeping his hand in a gesture toward his office, a gesture that seemed a bit theatrical to me. "Can I get you folks anything to drink?" Maud and Moggio declined, but I took Beste up on his offer, asking if I could get a cup of coffee. Then we had to go through the "regular or decaf" routine and the question about how I wanted the coffee.

"Just Equal, if you have it," I said. Beste looked at Marilyn.

"That's the blue stuff right?" she said. "I think we only have the pink stuff."

"That's okay," I said. "Black will be just fine."

This all seemed pretty natural to me, but when I looked at Maud I could see that she wasn't pleased. I think she could see right through my little performance. I think she knew that I had only asked for the coffee because I assumed that Marilyn would be serving it and I would get a glimpse of her in action. Specifically, Maud's look said, "Grow up, Fargo, you asshole."

Beste had a small conference table in his office around which he invited us to sit and where he himself pulled up a chair and sat down, crossing his legs and picking what looked like a cat hair from his gray slacks. In addition to the slacks, he wore a black mock turtleneck shirt that appeared to be silk, black socks and black alligator shoes buffed to a brilliant shine. He wore a Rolex watch on his left wrist and one of those bracelets that golfers wear on his right wrist. He also had added an ear accessory since the photo that had been taken of him for the cover of the business magazine, a diamond post in his left earlobe. He still had a roll around the middle, but he didn't look nearly as heavy as he had in the photo. He had lost a considerable amount of weight. That was good, because there's something about fat guys with earrings that just doesn't work for me. His face was still saggy, but in that way that people's faces get when they lose weight. He had enormous hands, the kind of hands you would expect someone in the construction business to have.

Moggio had just expressed, for all of us as far as I was concerned, his condolences on the loss of Beste's son, when Marilyn wriggled into the room with a white mug of coffee, which she placed in front of me. The coffee mug had a Beste Development logo on it, a line drawing of an A-frame with the words "Only the Beste" under it. Not very imaginative, but with a receptionist like Marilyn, who needed imagination? And I guess it answered how the name of the firm was pronounced.

"Thank you, Lindsay," said Beste.

Lindsay? That was her name? Like Lindsay Wagner, The Bionic Woman? Lindsay Lohan? Or, wait, Lindsay was a man's name, wasn't it? I didn't dare look at Maud. I didn't want to see the triumph in her expression. I was gratified to see that Lindsay indeed had The Walk, though, those mincing little steps that Marilyn Monroe used to take.

"So," said Beste when Lindsay's performance was finished and she had pulled the door closed behind her. "You mentioned that you had some information about my son's death?" Moggio looked sidelong at me. I took a drink of the coffee, burning my lips. She must-have zapped the stuff in the microwave. It was so hot that I couldn't even taste it.

"Actually," said Moggio. "There might be just a slight misunderstanding. We were hoping *you* could shed some light on what happened to your son." Beste blinked at each of us. Just once, moving his head to face each of us in turn.

"I have no idea," said Beste. "What makes you think I would?"

"Something your son mentioned," said Moggio. "To my associates here." Moggio had told Beste our names, but he hadn't seemed to pay much attention. Now he took a closer look at me and Maud.

"How do you people know my son?" he asked. Moggio looked at me and seemed to gesture in a fashion that said "Take it away. It's all yours." So I did. Once again, I ran through the story, starting with Barry Justice asking for my help in finding his wife and ending with our interview with young Mr. Beste the night before and his escape or abduction from my house.

"You know the rest," I concluded. "They found your son in his car."

Beste had listened without interrupting me and without much change of expression. I was finished. He didn't say anything for thirty seconds or so.

"The idea that Philip was protecting me is a laughable," said Beste, not laughing.

"You may have been unaware of the threat," said Moggio. "But that doesn't mean Philip didn't perceive a need to protect you from someone."

"You tell me you met my son," said Beste. "If that's so, you can't possibly believe that what he said to you or hinted to you about killing other people or protecting me has any basis in reality. Philip is a very weak person, physically and mentally. When he was younger, I thought he might even be gay. I should point out that Philip is my stepson. I adopted him when I married his mother. I was never close to Gabby's children. Hell, for most of our marriage, I wasn't even close to Gabby. That's Gabriela, Philip's mother."

"I take it you're not still married." said Moggio.

"Not to Gabriela," he said. "She died in 1994. Cervical cancer. Same year Philip graduated from high school."

"Yeah," I said. "Brother Ignatius, right?"

"Right," said Beste.

"Same place you graduated from," I said.

"Same place," said Beste.

"And," I continued, "the same place, Barry Justice and Robert Astrachan went to high school. In your class, as a matter of fact. I assume you're aware that Dr. Astrachan, like Barry Justice, was murdered recently, out in California."

"Yeah," said Beste "I'm aware of that. So what?"

"So it just seems coincidental that they were both high school buddies of yours and they both get murdered within a few days of each other."

"We weren't buddies," said Beste.

"What about your other stepson?" said Moggio.

"Jordan? What about him?"

"What's he up to these days?" said Moggio.

"I couldn't tell you," said Beste. "Last I heard he was living in Mountain View, running some high-tech startup. He did pretty well in the dotcom frenzy of the nineties and then didn't do so well when the bottom fell out. For all I know he's still out there trying to hustle up venture capital."

"So he was older than Philip?"

"Yeah," said Beste. "He'd be in his middle thirties by now."

"What did Philip do for a living?" said Moggio.

"That's something of a mystery," said Beste "a mystery, by the way, that I have no intention of solving. He was in a band for a while. He did something with video."

"He never had any interest in the construction business, I take it," said Moggio.

"Not that he mentioned to me. That would have been too much like work for Philip."

I was beginning to wonder why Beste had even agreed to meet with us. If he wasn't that close to his stepson and if he wasn't worried about any threat that Philip was allegedly protecting him from, why talk to us? It occurred to me that he did it just to see who we were and how much we knew. In other words, he was gaining as much information as we were, maybe more, because we certainly weren't getting much.

"So how's business going?" said Moggio.

"What do you mean?" said Beste.

"Your business, Beste Development. How's it doing? "

"It's doing fine," said Beste. "Is that why you came here? To ask me about my construction business?"

"It's just that I had heard you'd had some problems, some falling-out with the city fathers."

Beste looked at his watch.

"You're not a cop, right?" said Beste. "I don't have talk to you at all. I agreed out of courtesy, but now I think we need wrap things up." He put his hands on his thighs and prepared to stand.

"What did your son have on you?" said Moggio. I looked sidelong at Maud, who was looking intently at Moggio.

"We're done here," said Beste standing up. But Moggio didn't appear to be ready to leave just yet.

"I'm not the police, Mr. Beste," he said. "But some of my best friends are cops."

"Is that right?" said Beste. "I don't care of much for cops myself." He was smiling, but not in a nice way. He started towards the door to usher us out of his office. Moggio still hadn't risen from his seat, and, taking our cue from him, Maud and I remained seated as well. Beste turned back to look at us, a bemused expression on his face.

"Was there something else?" he said. He was being the perfect gentleman, but he was doing all he could to control himself. It didn't appear to be anger he was fighting as much as impetuosity. It was like at any moment he might pick a fight with us, just because he liked the action. In addition to looking like a boxer, he probably had *been* one at some point and probably during that time his basic form of social interaction had been pounding the hell out of people. If Maud hadn't been there, he might have challenged Moggio and me to a fistfight right there in his office and he probably would have kicked both our asses. I stood up.

"Thanks for your time, Mr. Beste," I said."

"Fuck you," said Beste, still smiling.

Maud was on her feet now. But Moggio still sat there as if pondering another question. Unfortunately, this wasn't police headquarters and Moggio wasn't in control. I was just about to say something to him when he jumped up and walked right past Beste without a word. He opened the door and stomped through the lobby to the glass doors at the front without even turning back to see if Maud and I were following. I nodded sort of awkwardly at Beste and followed Maud out of his office. As I stepped into the lobby area, I saw one of the other office doors close quietly. But before it closed I caught a glimpse of the person who was closing the door. I couldn't tell if the person had seen me, but the furtiveness with which he closed the door suggested that he knew we were there and knew who we were. At least knew who *I* was.

And I knew who he was too; Mr. Shock-the-Monkey himself. The phony cop who had zapped me with the stun gun in my own home.

TWENTY-FIVE

DESMOND I

"Things are starting to make a bit more sense," said Moggio.

We were back at my house after our ride from Beste Development in Moggio's car, during which he had asked us not to speak while he thought things through.

"You didn't say anything about a vow of silence when you suggested we all ride together in your car," Maud had said. "We could've taken two cars."

"It's just that I can't think when other people are carrying on a conversation within earshot," Moggio had replied.

"Well, excuse me," Maud had said. She stared silently out the window for the rest of the ride home.

I, too, deferred to the quirky Mr. Moggio and kept my mouth shut, not even mentioning who I had seen in Beste's office. I saved it. It would make a nice surprise.

"You're kidding right?" said Maud in response to Moggio's assertion that things were starting to make a little more sense.

"A little faith, please, Ms. Gonne," said Moggio.

"Faith in what?" she shot back.

"In the process," he said.

"What process?"

Sensing that things could degenerate into a quarrel, I decided at that point to jump in with my revelation.

"When we were leaving Beste's office, I saw the guy who zapped me with that Taser," I said. They both looked at me.

"Saw him where?" said Moggio.

"In the room next to Beste's office. He was just closing the door as we were walking out."

"You sure it was him?" said Moggio. This information had taken him by surprise and interested him intently.

"Positive."

"Things still making sense?" said Maud. Moggio ignored her. Why couldn't we all just get along?

"The only reason Beste agreed to see us was to get a sense of what we knew," said Moggio. Well, even I had figured that out.

"Knew about what?" said Maud.

"Knew about his involvement in all this."

"Which is?" said Maud.

"Which is at least that he killed his own son. Or had him killed."

"I assume this is one of your gut feelings?" I said. "Because I was there, and I didn't get that all. I mean, the guy's definitely weak in the paternal devotion area, but to jump from that obvious deficiency to murder is a stretch, don't you think?"

"What bothers me more is the appearance of the phony cop in his office," said Moggio.

"I agree," I said. "The fact that Mr. Shock-the-Monkey works for or with Beste means—well, I guess I'm not sure what it means."

"That was kind of careless," said Maud. "Wasn't it? I mean letting himself be seen like that in Beste's office?" Moggio looked at Maud with new appreciation.

"Careless or intentional," he said.

"Or maybe he didn't know we were there," I said. "Or maybe Beste is unaware that one of his employees or associates, or whatever he is, is moonlighting as Zapman."

Moggio's cell phone sounded and he answered.

"Yes?" said Moggio. Then he said "yes" several more times. Then he said nothing for a few minutes, although he did look into both my eyes and Maud's with what appeared to be significance. "No," he said, finally. Then he listened a bit more. "No," he repeated. "I want you all to stay right where you are. I can be there in an hour. Does anyone else know you're in town?" He waited as someone answered his question at some length.

Maud looked at me with an expression that said, "Who in God's holy fucking name is he talking to?" I shrugged back at her.

"What's the room number?" said Moggio, reaching for his pad and pen. "Okay," he said. "I'll call you again when I'm in the hotel. I'll let it ring twice and then I'll hang up. You hear two rings and no more, you'll know it's me and I'll be knocking on your door a few minutes later. Don't pick up the phone. No more phone calls out, either. I'll have a couple of people with me—a man and a woman." He paused to listen to what must have been a protest from whomever he was talking to. "No, they're cool," said Moggio. "They're with me. They're involved in this thing, too." He listened again. "I'll be wearing a black baseball cap with the Red Wings emblem on it," he said. He paused again. "It's a red logo thing, looks like a car's tire with wings attached to it. It's red." Moggio looked at me and rolled his eyes. "An hour," he said. "And remember. No phone calls and no leaving the room."

He flipped his cell phone shut and smiled at us, letting the drama build, or smolder, depending on your POV.

"So?" I said. "Who was it?"

"That," he said, "was Desmond Webber. He and his mother and Lashona's daughter just checked into a room at the Airport Westin."

"I don't understand," I said. "Why did he call you?"

"Apparently, Lashona gave him my number and told him to contact me if anything happened to her. The Southfield police contacted Lashona's mother after the murder. The old woman insisted she had to come up here. Apparently Desmond couldn't talk her out of it, so the whole clan's here. Obviously they couldn't leave the daughter alone down there, but old Desmond is scared shitless, believe me. He didn't say why, but I think he's afraid that whoever took out his sister out wouldn't mind doing the same to him. He already thinks he's seeing people."

"What people?" said Maud.

"He wasn't clear on that," Moggio reply.

"Do the police know they're here?" I asked.

"Nobody knows," said Moggio. "That's the beauty of it. We can talk to them first, before the cops get to them." Moggio stood up. "We need to move," he said. "This Desmond doesn't sound like the sharpest knife in the drawer. I told him to sit tight, and he's scared, but the guy doesn't even know what a Red Wing insignia looks like."

"He's from Florida," I said. "He's probably not a hockey fan."

"This is the 21st century," Moggio replied. "They even have hockey in Florida now. Two professional teams even. One of them, the Lightning, is right in his own backyard in Tampa."

"Can we take two cars?" said Maud.

TWENTY-SIX

EN FAMILLE

We did take two cars. Moggio said he'd be leaving the hotel to go directly back to his office anyway. I rode with Maud in the Jag. Obviously, I was the kind of guy who craved a cheap thrill. She drove with her usual disdain for everyone else on the road, all the while complaining about Moggio.

"We were doing just fine without him in the picture," she said.

"I think you're jealous," I said. She responded by snaking between two semis at about 90 miles-per-hour.

"I think he's full of shit," she said. "Just because he used to be a cop doesn't mean he's a good investigator."

"He was Lazard's partner," I said.

"Yeah," she replied. "Until he murdered Lazard."

"If it comes to it, I wouldn't put it to him just like that," I said.

"Oh yeah?" said Maud. "Why not? What's he going to do?"

"I don't know. I just think it's a sensitive point with him."

"How far would we get, criminal justice-wise, if we worried about the sensitivity of murderers with respect to their crimes?" said Maud.

"But my point is, he's not a murderer. He told me it was a mercy situation."

"Yeah, right."

"Anyway," I said, "think of this. Would we be driving right now to talk to Desmond and his mother if it weren't for Moggio? Desmond wouldn't have called me."

"I told you we should have gone to Florida to see him," said Maud.

"The guy's scared out of his mind," I said in exasperation. "What makes you think he would've talked to us?"

"You're selling yourself short," said Maud. "Even worse, you're selling *me* short."

We rode in silence for a few miles.

"Let's see how it goes with Desmond," I said. "We can always cut loose from Moggio after that."

"Fine," said Maud in that way that let you know it was anything but fine.

We got to the hotel first—no surprise there—and parked in the short-term parking lot, then made our way to the hotel lobby, where we waited for Moggio. He arrived about ten minutes later, sporting, as he had promised Desmond, a black baseball cap with the Red Wing insignia on the front.

"Nice disguise," I said as he approached.

"I was thinking on the drive over," he said, ignoring me, "that maybe I should do the talking." Maud turned to me.

"He really does come up with brilliant ideas alone there in his car with no conversations to distract him," she said.

"Look, Drew," I said, "we'll be cool. But we didn't drive over here to sit around like dummies."

"Okay, okay," he said responding more to Maud's sarcasm than to my protest. "But let me at least take the lead. These people are scared and they've been told at least by implication that I'm the only one they can trust."

"Great," I said. "You take the lead." And he did, marching off towards the elevators.

We emerged into the hallway on the third floor. Moggio pulled out his cell phone, dialed, asked for Desmond Webber's room number, waited a moment, then flipped the phone shut. When Moggio knocked at the door of room 302, it opened so fast that I thought Desmond might have been standing there at the peephole since the moment he had hung up from talking to Moggio.

"Mr. Moggio?" said Desmond, opening the door wide even as he said it. Trusting soul. He gave me and Maud a quick nod as we followed Moggio into the room.

Desmond Webber was a tall, lanky man, probably close to six-four. He wore a baggie Hawaiian shirt and loose khaki pants, which accentuated his slim frame. He wore only sandals on his feet. Definitely underdressed for Detroit in March. The TV was on, tuned to a soap opera. A woman who appeared to be approaching the century mark—Lashona's mother, no doubt—sat in front of the TV and didn't look up when we entered the room. She was hooked up to one of those portable oxygen tanks, tubes in her nose. She, too, appeared to be very thin. Must have run in the family. I couldn't see the daughter, but I could hear another TV on in another room of the suite, and from the sound of that, it was tuned to one of those lame sitcoms like "Full House" or something. Laugh track, the cute voices of adolescent children, laugh track.

"This is Stephen Fargo and Maud Gonne," said Moggio, gesturing in turn to me and Maud. Desmond nodded again, but didn't say anything for a few seconds. He appeared not to know what to do with us. He stepped over to the desk, which had a bottle of Popov vodka sitting in the middle of it.

"Offer you a drink?" he said, apparently to all of us, hoisting the bottle up to display it.

"No, thanks," said Moggio. "We're good." Desmond poured himself a drink into a plastic cup and drank it right down. Then he poured himself another, and screwed the cap back onto the bottle.

"That's me and Lashona's mother," he said, gesturing towards the woman watching TV. We all looked at the woman, but she still didn't look away from the television. "She don't like to be disturbed when she watchin' her stories. We had a stop ever' day at a hotel at one in the afternoon. She woont a been any fun at all, if she missed them shows."

To me, the woman looked like she hadn't been fun for twenty or thirty years, but who was I to judge? Desmond regarded his mother for a moment.

"She goes into her story trance 'bout three hours a day and Venetia, she don't talk at all. So, I spend lots of time with my own thoughts, you know?" He took a drink from the plastic cup, then regarded it pensively for a few woeful moments.

"You mentioned that it was your mother that insisted you come to Detroit," said Moggio. It seemed weird for us to be discussing this woman like she wasn't even there, when she lay there six feet away from us.

"She wanted to see her daughter," said Desmond with great solemnity. "She said, 'Lashona need us now.' I tried to tell her that Lashona don't need nobody no more, but she don't listen. Got her stone face on and says 'We goin'.' So here we are." He took another drink. Desmond didn't appear to be drunk, but half the bottle of vodka was gone. I saw Moggio watch intently as Desmond took his drink. I imagined that Moggio was thinking he had to get what he could out of this man before he got too shit-faced to make sense—probably another thirty seconds. Desmond looked at us expectantly. He had watery yellow eyes and wet lips. He looked to be in his mid-forties and I could see a slight resemblance to Lashona. Same skin tone, same high cheekbones. But Desmond, here, had done some hard time with the bottle, there was no doubt about that. He had that perpetual half-smashed look about him.

"These the folks with Lashona when she shot?" Desmond asked.

Moggio nodded. Then Desmond nodded. Moggio paused a couple of beats, then said, "Mr. Webber, I'm very sorry for your loss." He waited, but Desmond didn't acknowledge the expression of condolence. "We'd very much like to find out who did this," he continued, "bring your sister's killers to justice." A look came over Desmond's face that was part wince and part sneer.

"They ain't no fuckin' justice," he said.

"Okay," said Moggio. "Maybe not. Call it a personal thing for me then. Lashona was a client of mine and I don't take kindly to having my clients killed out from under me in the middle of an engagement, if you know what I mean."

If Desmond *did* know what that meant, he didn't give any indication, although I was kind of wondering about that "out from under me" reference. I wanted very badly to glance over at Maud, but I restrained myself. Desmond reached for the vodka, then must have decided he needed to remain relatively sober for this, and returned the bottle to the tabletop. Instead, he switched to another vice, pulling out a pack of Pall Mall's and lighting one. I wondered how this worked with his mother's breathing problem, but she seemed to take no notice of the suddenly befouled air.

"Mr. Webber," said Moggio, "you mentioned that you may have seen some people who you suspect may have been involved in your sister's death." Desmond looked at his mother.

"We goin' downstairs to the lobby for a few minutes," he announced to her, raising his voice. "I got my key, so don't be openin' the door for nobody."

Desmond's mother did not respond. Desmond motioned with his head towards the door and started to get up. Following his lead, all of us advanced towards the door. I felt myself almost tiptoeing, as though if I trod too hard, I might bring Lashona's mother out of her trance. For some reason she appeared to me to be the type of woman you just didn't deal with if you didn't have to.

When we got out into the hallway, Moggio asked: "Mr. Webber, are you sure this is a good idea? If you have seen someone who might not have your best interests in mind, perhaps we should stay in the room." Webber shook his head.

"They's things she don't need to know," he said. "They's a bar downstairs. A public place. Should be safe enough."

Right, I thought. He was interested in the bar for the safety it afforded.

The elevator arrived and we all entered. Desmond even brought his lit cigarette along. Luckily, the ride was a short one.

As we stepped off the elevator and headed for the bar off the hotel lobby, Maud grabbed my arm and pulled me back.

"Is Moggio kidding?" she whispered to me.

"About what?" I asked.

"This guy barely has motor skills, let alone any insight into his sister's death. I think he's drunk."

"I think you're probably right," I replied. "But since it's pretty much a natural condition for him, I don't really think it will impair his ability to tell us things. Besides, what else would we be doing?"

"I could think of several things," said Maud, but she didn't elaborate and we fell into tow behind Moggio and the slightly unsteady, yet weirdly dignified figure of Desmond Webber.

The bar was full of customers and we were lucky to find a small table next to the wall.

The crowd offered the usual mix of travelers—businesspeople, some in suits and ties, but an even greater number in business casual, whatever in the hell that meant. Then there were a few of the young, backpack types. There was even a young family with two small children, a boy and a girl no more than six years of age, whom the parents were having a hard time keeping seated at the table. I didn't see anyone who looked like a hit person, but these days you never knew, right? Hell, one of the kids could be a killer.

The environment of the bar removed the inhibitions that Desmond had exhibited in his room. He ordered a Stoli on the rocks. Moggio ordered a Budweiser and, not wanting to appear antisocial, I followed suit. Maud, the paragon of reason and propriety, ordered a Diet Coke, which I was actually glad to see. Her driving was a harrowing enough experience without adding alcohol to the mix.

Desmond drank about half of his vodka down the minute the waitress lowered it to the table. After a few seconds of silence, Moggio said:

"Do you know who killed your sister and her husband?"

"I know some people wouldn't *mine* they dead," said Desmond, pulling out another Pall Mall.

"And they want you dead, too?" said Moggio.

Desmond lit his cigarette, then blew out his match with a stream of smoke.

"Hell," he said, looking very grim indeed. "They want *everbody* dead."

"Who's they?" I said.

"Aint like I know they names," he said. "Lashona, she workin' on some story for her job, somethin' havin' to do with vaccines and how they's hurtin' kids, you know, like Venetia."

"Vaccines that cause autism," said Moggio.

"That's what I'm talkin' about," said Desmond. "She tole me they was some kinda paper or report was gonna prove some vaccine made lotta kids like Venetia sick and she was gonna git holt of it and do a show on it, maybe even take it to '60 Minutes,' see if they was interested."

"And, so, somebody who didn't want Lashona to go public with this information found out about it and threatened her?" said Moggio.

"She never said they threatened her," Desmond replied. "But the potential was there, understand?"

"Your sister was an investigative reporter," said Moggio. "She worked on lots of controversial issues that might get her in trouble with the wrong kinds of people. How can you be sure it was the vaccine people that killed her if she never mentioned a specific threat?"

"Cuz nobody Lashona ever investigated stood to lose as much money as the vaccine guys. We talkin' Fortune 100 here."

I was impressed. It had not occurred to me that the Fortune 100 would be on Desmond's lo-res radar screen.

"Did Lashona give you any ideas what the nature of this threat was?" said Moggio.

"I *tole* you," said Desmond. "She warn't that pacific."

"She ever mention a guy named Charles Beste?" I said. Desmond paused.

"Yeah," he said, slowly. "Yeah, I remember that 'cause of the way it sound, you know, like a animal."

"But you don't know if she mentioned the name in connection with this vaccine thing?" said Moggio.

Desmond thought some more, squinting his left eye against the smoke from his cigarette curling up into it.

"See, I got me some cognitive problems," he said. Whoa, Desmond, I thought—cognitive? "It interferes with my thinkin'. It's 'cuz a Gulf War Syndrome."

"You getting any treatment for that?" said Moggio.

"I *was*," said Desmond. "At the VA."

Obviously, the treatment was less than effective. So, we have the well-armed, respirationally-challenged matriarch of this family so addicted to soap operas (and, if Barry had been correct, dog races) that it severely restricted her social skills, an apparent case of autism in the junior member of the clan and the one somewhat able-bodied male had "cognitive problems" due to Gulf War Syndrome.

They would make great witnesses in an eventual trial.

"I could get better treatment," Desmond continued, "if I had me some money."

"So, you're broke?" said Moggio.

"Fuckin' a," said Desmond. Moggio thought for a moment.

"If you want to go to the police," he said, finally, "I'm pretty sure the county will find a place for you and your family to stay, at least until some determinations can be made with respect to how they will proceed legally." Desmond didn't jump at this. Instead he regarded Moggio dully.

"I got me some problems with the poh-lice," he said. "Cuz a my condition."

"What kinds of problems?" said Moggio. Desmond shrugged.

"DUIs, shoplifting. A home invasion. See, I'm on probation now, so I'm really not spose a be here."

"I see," said Moggio. "So, what would you like us to do?"

"Thought *you* would know," said Desmond. "Ain't that why Lashona said to contact you?" Moggio looked helplessly at me and Maud, then back to Desmond.

"Mr. Webber," he said, "If it's money you want—"

"Is they a will?" said Desmond.

"Well, I don't know," said Moggio. "I assume Lashona would have made some provision for her daughter at the very least."

"Right," said Desmond. "Ah been thinkin' the same thing."

"Well, I can't answer your question with any degree of certainty," said Moggio. "I could look into it. If Lashona left a will, she must also have named an executor. Of course, the logical choice for that would have been her husband. And he's dead, too."

"I gotta get back," said Desmond grimacing as though he had stomach cramps. "Mama's shows be over soon and Venetia be needin' her medicine."

"Who's paying for your room?" said Moggio. "And for Venetia's meds?" I had been wondering the same thing. Usually you had to hand over a credit card to hotels at check-in. And the room had definitely been upscale.

"Venetia still got her pills from the last time the prescription was filled," said Desmond. "And I got me a credit card for the room. Lashona gave it to us. Problem is, it only got a two-thousand-dollar limit on it. For emergencies and such. And it real close to that limit right now."

Moggio pulled out his wallet, took two hundred dollar bills from it and handed them over to Desmond.

"No, see, Mr. Moggio, this ain't right," said Desmond, shaking his head mournfully.

"It's a loan," said Moggio. "You can pay me back when you're able."

"It ain't right," said Desmond, still shaking his head. But he stuffed the two bills into the front pocket of his khakis. Moggio then threw a twenty-dollar bill on the tabletop for the drinks.

When we were back at the elevators, Moggio reminded Desmond once again not to leave his room.

"I'll see what I can find out about any will or insurance money and get back to you," he said.

"Is they a funeral?" said Desmond. "Mama will wanna know."

"Right," said Moggio. "I'll find out about that, too." Desmond gave us a solemn, hangdog nod, then shook each of our hands in turn. He had a very soft, dry handshake, almost no grip pressure at all.

"You take care of your mother and niece," said Moggio. "I'll try to call you by tomorrow with some news." The elevator arrived and Desmond stepped in, turning to look back at us dolefully. The door stayed open.

"You need to push the button for your floor," said Moggio. Desmond looked at him uncomprehendingly, and Moggio reached in and pushed the button for him. The door closed and the car lifted off to Desmond's floor.

"Pathetic," said Moggio, shaking his head.

"I'm going to check into what's going on with Lashona's body. And if there's any will," he said when we had reached the lobby doors. It had started to snow again. I could hear a jet roaring through its takeoff, but I couldn't see the plane. The snow was falling that heavily.

"I'm having trouble seeing a connection between this vaccine/autism scenario and Charles Beste & Associates," I said.

"I know what you're saying," said Moggio. "On the surface, the motive questions seem worlds apart." He looked out at the snowstorm, his finger pressed to his lip. "I've got a couple of contacts in the health department. They might be able to provide some insight into this vaccine thing. I'll make a few calls on that, too. Where will I be able to reach you?" He said it kind of to both of us.

"My cell phone," I said.

"I'd keep away from Beste," said Moggio. "He gives off bad vibes."

Listen to Moggio, I thought, Mr. 60s. Mr. Counterculture.

TWENTY-SEVEN

SUBTERRANEAN HOMESICK BLUES

The snow cramped Maud's driving style, which didn't improve her mood. She said nothing until we had been driving almost half an hour.

"Ah, you angry at me for some reason?" I finally asked her.

"Not at all," she replied. She looked at me and smiled. "I was just thinking."

"What about?"

"About how downright strange all of this has been. I mean, doesn't it bother you? How strange it all is?"

"It does, actually," I said.

"I know I can get a little intense sometimes," she said. I tried to understand how this fit into the discussion about how strange things were.

"Are we talking about the Lashona Webber/Barry Justice case? Or something else?" I asked.

"We're talking about everything," she said without hesitation. "We're talking about Lashona and Barry and Moggio and Desmond with his whole Diane Arbus-slash-Florida-gothic family life and we're talking about you and me." This kind of took me by surprise.

"What about you and me?" I said.

"Oh, I don't know, where we're going I guess. I usually don't like to speculate on the fate of my relationships with men. That hasn't been productive in the past. But I have wondered about us, if there even *is* an us."

"Well, of course there's an us," This seemed a funny way to talk.

"You think so?" she said, looking at me.

"Well, isn't there?" I said. She shrugged.

"I'm not sure there's even a me," she said. It didn't seem to be a lament, just a flat statement.

"Maud," I said, trying to look for the right words, "I'm probably not salvageable."

"Who said this is a salvage operation?"

"I don't know," I said. "You always seem so disappointed by my behavior."

She laughed.

"That would assume that I had some expectation about your behavior," she said. "Don't worry. I don't. I have frustrations. I'm an impatient person, perhaps you've noticed that in my driving."

"I did notice that," I said, smiling back at her.

The snow was beginning to let up, but the storm had added another two or three inches to the stuff we already had on the ground. Maud had pulled the Jag off the freeway and was making her way towards my house on surface streets, which were less congested, but more treacherous, since the salt trucks and snow plows consider the freeways their first priority.

"Don't look now," said Maud. "But we're being followed."

"Somebody would actually try to follow us in this shit?" I said, not allowing myself to turn around for a peek.

"He's been with us since the airport," said Maud.

"Why didn't you say something?" I said. She shrugged, nonchalant.

"People can be behind you for miles on the freeway and doesn't mean anything. I didn't see a problem until we got off. He stayed right with us. A black Mercedes. Didn't we have a problem with that particular model previously?"

"Yeah," I said. "I thought that's what Juan—Philip Beste—had been stalking us with."

"Apparently they've already found his replacement," said Maud. "What do you want me to do?"

Good question. I turned around to look at the car behind us. It was indeed a black Mercedes, although the windshield glass was so darkly tinted that I couldn't make out who was behind the wheel.

"Why the hell would someone be following us?" I said. "By now, I thought everyone knew where I lived. Do these people understand that we aren't a threat? I mean we don't even know anything."

"Yeah," said Maud. "But *they* don't know that. They might think Lashona or Barry told us something or that, through our own hard work, we are on the brink of some revelation."

"Maybe," I said.

We were a couple of blocks from my house. I was beginning to think this was nothing more than a threat display of some sort, a show of force. But as I was about to utter something to that effect, Maud stomped on the gas and swerved the car to the far right side of the road as the black Mercedes sped up to get even with us. I looked past Maud's head and saw the passenger-side window of the Mercedes slide down. In the driver's seat sat the young man from Charles Beste's office, the one who had impersonated the cop and zapped me with the Taser. This time it wasn't a stun gun in his hand. It was the real thing. He raised it and pointed at us.

"Look out," I yelled. Maud hit the breaks and spun the wheel, sending the Jag into a spinning slide, so that we were actually moving broadside down the street. Simultaneously, the side window next to Maud's head exploded, sending glass shrapnel throughout the interior of the car. Maud remained cool. All those hours of aggressive driving were paying off. The car slid to a halt and she spun the wheel, pointing the car back in the direction we'd come. Several oncoming vehicles swerved to avoid us as Maud wove her way back through traffic. I looked through the rear window of the Jag to see the black Mercedes' break lights go on and the car beginning to slide. We had a head start on him. But not much of one.

"Ha," said Maud. "You think just because I'm a girl I can't drive this thing? I was into evasive maneuvers before you were born, you little fuck."

I guessed this was the adrenaline speaking.

It was snowing inside the car, now, as the wind howled through Maud's shattered window.

"Where to?" said Maud, turning my way so that I could hear her better. Blood was running from several small wounds in her cheek.

"You're bleeding," I said.

"Where *to*?" she repeated. I turned to look again out the rear window. The black Mercedes was once again in pursuit, but several of the cars that spun out avoiding us were now blocking the road in front of it.

"My house," I said.

We pulled into my driveway and I jumped out to open the garage door for Maud to pull the car in. Just as we emerged from the garage and ran through the door in the kitchen of Redundant House, the black Mercedes slid up and over the curb and onto my snow-covered front lawn. Zapman was immediately out of the car, running across the lawn towards the side door of my house, gun drawn.

"Come on," I said, grabbing Maud's hand.

We ran through the kitchen and down the hall to the underground passageway that led to the defunct Stephen T. Mason Elementary School. I stabbed the code into the keypad as I heard Zapman burst through the side door in pursuit. The door to the passageway slid open and we walked through it. A second later the door slid closed, just as I caught a glimpse of Zapman, his face a smear of rage, turn the corner and head towards us.

"What do you think he'll do?" Maud whispered.

"I have no idea," I replied. "Maybe hang around long enough to figure we're not coming out any time soon."

"How long do you think it will take them to figure out where this leads?" said Maud.

"I don't have the answers to all these questions," I said. "I've never actually had to use this."

"We could use your cell to call the police," said Maud. "The guy did have a gun in his hand. He *did* shoot at us. I wonder why, by the way."

"Add it to the list of things to wonder about," I replied. "I'm not calling the police. You may be right about them, after all." I tugged her by the arm towards the stairs leading to the passageway.

"So, is this going to be like a sleepover?" Maud whispered. I felt her hand squeeze mine.

"Uh, something like that," I said.

We made our way through the passageway and to the doors that opened into Stephen T. Mason Elementary School. The interior of the school was dark, but I thought in wouldn't be a good idea for the lights to suddenly come on in an abandoned school building, not right at that moment anyway, with Zapman out there prowling around. We made our way to the remodeled teachers lounge in the interior of the building, where it would be safe to indulge in a little illumination. I turned the lights on and opened the refrigerator.

"Can I offer you a beer?" I said.

"Hey," said Maud. "This really does sound like a date."

"Do you want a beer or not?" I said. I wasn't sure I wanted to enter into this playful banter with her right at this moment. I needed to come up with a plan first.

"Absolutely," she said.

I took the two cans of beer out of the refrigerator, popped them open, and handed one to Maud.

"I can't say that I've ever been entertained by a man in his safe house," she said.

I kind of toasted her with my beer can in mock appreciation of the statement and took a drink. She responded similarly, wrinkling up her nose a little bit. Then she put the beer down on the counter and moved closer to me.

"I know this is going to sound weird," she said, a look that I could only call sultry coming into her eyes, "but that whole episode with Mr. Zapman, as you call him, I found it very arousing. Why would that be?"

I shrugged and was about to say something when she put her arm around my neck and pulled my face to hers, kissing me forcefully on the mouth. I could feel her tongue moving against mine as she moaned just slightly. I still held the beer in my hand, but I managed to wrap my arms around her and hold her tightly. She pulled her mouth away from mine and moved it to my ear.

"And this is going to sound even weirder," she whispered. I could feel her lips brushing against my ear and her warm breath as she said the words. "But I'm in love with you. I think we need to make love right now."

"Not plan our next step?" I said, overcome now by the force of her presence.

"It *is* our next step," she replied.

This time, the sex was much better. Why either of us should have felt so relaxed about it under the circumstances was something I couldn't answer, but for the moment, all the concerns about Zapman and the fate of Lashona Webber and Barry Justice and the status of Charles Beste and the three generations of Webbers at the airport receded way into the background.

We lay down on the bed next to the wall that I had designated as the sleeping area of my little hideaway in Stephen T. Mason Elementary School. I tried to kiss every inch of Maud's body, literally. I kissed her eyelids and her tiny scratches from the glass and her elbows and the soles of her feet and her belly button, and, well, lots of stuff. It apparently all worked because she began to go into spasms and finally pushed my head away from her.

"My God," she said. "I don't even want to think about how long it's been since that happened." She pushed me over to my back and straddled my hips. "I'd tie you up," she said, smiling. "But we might have to move quickly." Then she bent down and kissed me long and hard, reaching around to find my now very rigid erection and pressing it against her wet labia. Then she sighed and settled down on me slowly, and, well, I guess I don't remember much of anything after that. Okay, just kidding. I really do. I would not be likely to forget.

"I am the last woman you will ever fuck," she whispered to me when we were done and she still lay on top of me. "And I mean that in a good way."

"That's the way I took it," I said.

Maud slid her body off mine and lay beside me, looking into my face, her head propped up on her elbow. She looked absolutely like the sexiest creature on the face of the earth.

"Going forward," she said, "I want you to promise me a few things." She must have planned this. Get me into this vulnerable state where she has just given my body the most pleasure I could remember since, well, since Denise was alive, then lie there looking like a brunette Charlize Theron. I would have promised her anything.

"Shoot," I said.

"Bad choice of words," she said, punching my arm. "First, no more faked deaths."

"Agreed," I said. That one was easy. It's more of a strain on you than you might think, this whole faked death thing.

"You agree so easily," she said. "That makes me suspicious."

"You want me to think about it for a while?"

"No, I guess not. We *are* in crisis mode, or we should be."

"My thinking exactly," I said. "Tempus Fugit. Or is it Tempo that Fugits?"

Maud didn't respond, not that I blamed her. My habit of lapsing into juvenile humor in times of stress is not everybody's cup of tea. "So, is that it for the promises?"

"Not hardly," said Maud. "You also need to promise me that you'll see this thing through to the end."

"What thing?" I said.

"This thing about Lashona Webber and Barry Justice."

Well, I planned to see it through to the end anyway. I was so deep into it now, what with Zapman graduating from stungun to semiautomatic pistol, that it was a matter of survival. But I felt I had to ask anyway.

"Why is it so necessary that I see it through to the end?" I said.

"Because it's going to be your enlightenment."

"Enlightenment, huh? Like nirvana, that kind of enlightenment?"

"I mean it's going to clarify things for you, make your life more meaningful. Well, maybe not meaningful, but more acceptable. You won't want to go off on solitary boat rides."

"I already told you I wouldn't do that again," I said.

"I'm being allegorical."

"You're so sexy when you get metaphysical like this," I said, raising myself up to kiss her. But she pulled away.

"I'm serious," she said.

"Okay," I said. "I promise to see it through to the end. Whatever *it* is, and assuming I have that many years left."

"It's not going to be years," she said.

"Is that right?" I said. "Do you know something about this case that I don't?" I could feel the old paranoia creeping into my bones, like arthritis on a cold day.

"Not any more than you do, at least in terms of facts," she said. "But there was something wrong with that whole Webber diorama or tableau vivant or whatever it was we were invited to witness today."

"Diorama? Tableau vivant." I said in wonder.

"Hey, you forget I'm in the art game. I know all sorts of technical jargon like that."

"You thought it was all being staged for our benefit?" I said.

"Well, duh," said Maud.

"Yeah, I had the same sense, now that you mention it. But why?"

"I have no idea why. At first I thought it was a play for sympathy, you know, Desmond showing us how burdened he was by domestic responsibility. And that might be all it is."

"Or they just might *be* some archetype of the Florida gothic," I said. "See, I know technical terms, too."

"Those aren't technical terms," said Maud. "And what is the Florida gothic?"

"That's the term you used," I said. "In the car."

"Oh, yeah, right."

"Does sex obliterate your short term memory?" I was trying to make a joke, I think.

"Did we have sex?" she said. Funny.

"Also," said Maud. "I don't think they just arrived from Florida."

"I can't wait to hear your rationale," I said. Maud smiled and poked me in the side.

"Don't misunderestimate me," she said.

"I wouldn't think of it," I said. "So what makes you think they didn't just arrive from Florida, or more likely, from Mars?"

"The smell," said Maud.

"Excuse me?"

"The odor of recent travel," said Maud. "They didn't have it."

"What are you, part bloodhound?"

"There is a certain odor that people get when they've been on a plane for a while. Maybe it's the recycled air or the stale coffee smell or the solvents they use to clean the planes. I don't know the source of the odor, but I know it when I smell it. And they didn't have it."

"Maybe they showered when they arrived," I said, then regretted it immediately.

"Did personal hygiene look like a priority to those people?" said Maud. "There would have to have been a TV in the bathtub for Grandma, and Desmond, well, I'm willing to bet the most valuable painting hanging in my gallery that he hasn't bathed in a week."

"Okay," I said. "Then maybe they've been here long enough for the smell to dissipate."

"I don't think so," said Maud. "Plus they're all cooped up there in that tiny hotel room. No, it would reek of recent travel odor if they'd arrived anytime in the past twenty-four hours."

"So you've actually calibrated this," I said. This time Maud's poke in the ribs became a punch.

"I know I'm right about this," she said.

"Okay," I said. "So once again, my question is 'Why?' Why would Desmond want us to think that he just got here? What difference does it make if they just got here today or two days ago?"

"I don't know," said Maud. "*You're* the famous detective."

"I never made such a claim," I said.

Something else bothered me.

"Desmond seemed to indicate that they had driven here," I said.

"I don't remember that," said Maud.

"Well, he didn't actually say that. It was when he was talking about his mother's devotion to her soap operas. He said that they had to stop every day at the same time to watch them. I took that to mean that they had to stop wherever they were on the road and check into a motel. Do you think it was a slip?"

Maud lay back down on the bed.

"Have you ever thought about the subterranean motif in your life?" she asked, still looking at the ceiling.

"Is this part of the same discussion we were just having?" I said.

"No, new topic," she said. "A little digression."

"Okay, what is the subterranean motif in my life?"

"Well, you were buried alive in *Our Father*, right? And there was that whole archeological dig scene."

"Okay," I agreed, tentatively.

"Then in that other book about your adventures with that right-wing radio talk show guy."

"Eric Crowe," I said. She was referring to a book that, I'm happy to say, I had no part in producing. It was called *The Big Island*, and it was written by a man with the unlikely name of Paul Hall. A pseudonym, no doubt. The weird thing was, he told it from my point of view, using the first person narration. At least that's what I've heard. I haven't read the book. I thought of suing, but the book came out when I was dead, which would have been a problem.

"Right," said Maud. "In that book you go through that Underground Railroad tunnel to catch Eric Crowe in the church. And now, here we are, not exactly underground at the moment, but we had to go underground to get here, right? And the whole faked death thing has a subterranean aspect to it."

"That would be submarine, I think," I said.

"You know what I mean," said Maud.

"Is there a point to this observation?"

"Not that I care to discuss right now," said Maud. "It was a digression, remember? And, as you've pointed out, we do have someone trying to determine our location for the purpose of ending our lives."

"So are we back on the promises, then?"

"No. I'm all done with the promises. Just those two."

"Great," I said. I got up and put my pants on. If I had to be ready for action, I wanted to be dressed.

"Do you have a shower in this place?" said Maud.

"Are you kidding?" I said. "This used to be a school."

"Yeah, but you said it was an elementary school. I don't remember that we had showers on my elementary school. The trauma to all those young psyches would have been too much of a liability on the school district."

"What trauma?"

"All that prepubescent nudity," said Maud, definitely not prepubescent herself. She got out of bed and stood there waiting for me to direct her to the showers.

"You're right," I said. "They didn't have any mass showers here. But they did have one in the basement. I guess the janitor must have used it."

"*Yuh*-uk," said Maud.

"Don't worry," I said. "I've upgraded. I don't believe I've even ever used it. It's probably in pristine shape."

"I probably shouldn't walk the halls naked," she said.

"I'll be right back," I said. I moved across the hall to where the administrative offices of the school used to be. I had converted them into a storage area—plenty of closets and drawers in the wall. In one of the closets, I found a robe, which didn't smell bad at all, and in the drawers I found towels. I also found brand new underwear—still in the package—new socks, several shirts and other changes of clothes. The place was stocked with both men's and women's clothes, but I had bought the women's clothes—my wife, Denise, would not collaborate in my delusions at the time—so I imagine Maud wouldn't find them exactly styling, assuming they would even fit. Nevertheless, I congratulated myself on my foresight, even though at the time I had stockpiled this stuff I really had no intention of using it. In hindsight I wondered if I hadn't gone slightly out of my mind during that period of my life, but, hey, I couldn't complain now. It had probably saved our lives.

I took the robe and towels back to the teachers lounge, along with some underwear, and two new denim shirts and two new pairs of jeans.

"The Bobbsey Twins Play Detective," said Maud when I offered her one of the shirts and pairs of jeans, along with a robe and a towel.

"It's your choice whether you want to wear them or not," I said.

"I think I'll go with what I already have," she said. "It's not like I've been wearing these clothes for a week. I just put them on this morning, although I have to admit that this morning feels like about three days ago."

"Suit yourself," I said.

"Cute," she replied, with a look.

I escorted her to the elevator that led back to the basement of the building, where I showed her to the functional but almost sparkling clean bathroom.

"I'm impressed," said Maud. "Care to join me?"

"I think you'll find that shower stall is pretty small," I said.

"That could be fun," she said.

"I'll take a rain check," I said. "I don't think this is the right time for both of us to be fooling around down here in the shower. I'm going to keep an eye out upstairs. And I'll give Moggio a call, bring him up to speed on our adventure. Do you need anything else?"

"Do you have a masseuse down here?"

"Just me," I replied. Maud smiled and turned towards the shower curtains.

"If I'm not back up there in two hours, come and get me," she said. I smiled back at her.

On the way back to the teachers lounge, I stopped at the electrical closet that housed the security system and confirmed that it was still on. No reason it shouldn't be. I had left instructions that it should be left on constantly. The only way to disarm it was by calling the security company. If I entered the building from the outside with my key, the security system automatically disabled for two minutes, but if I didn't reset it during that time, an alarm would automatically trip at the offices of the security company, and the local police, fire department—who knows, maybe even the National Guard—would descend on the building within seconds. I had sealed off all but two of the entrances to the building, not counting the one that came directly from my house. That one was not connected to the security system at all on the assumption that I or someone I revealed the entrance code to would be the only ones coming through that entrance.

I felt pretty secure. Unless Mr. Zapman was up on his history of Stephen Fargo, famous paranoid (and Zapman didn't seem like the kind who would be up on that or any other kind of history), he wouldn't even be aware that my secret passage was there. He probably figured I was holed up in a safe room. He'd probably go back and report as much to Beste before taking any drastic action—such as a C4 charge on the door lock. I didn't have neighbors close by, but this was still a residential neighborhood. An explosion would register.

On the other hand, if he did figure out the secret passage thing, he would soon realize that the school was the most likely terminus of the passageway. It was the only building in the neighborhood that wasn't a residential structure, and, though you couldn't see it immediately, it was only a hundred yards from my house. A quick scan of the neighborhood would reveal its presence. Luckily it was one of those low-profile brick-style schoolhouses of the late fifties and early sixties. No second floor, so that, if you weren't looking closely, you might not even realize that it was there.

I did a quick tour of the building, which mainly meant that I walked the hallway circuit, which, given the size of this school, took all of about two minutes. At a few points along the route, I took a peek out the windows to see if I could spot any suspicious cars loitering around, but I didn't see anything. It was starting to get dark. Snow was falling again—not heavily, but enough so that I could see it cutting through the occasional porch light or the light of residential lamp post fixtures. Everything looked peaceful enough.

I phoned Moggio, but halfway through the ringing of his phone, mine beeped for a few seconds, then went quiet. Once again, I had neglected to charge the battery. I found the landline in the kitchen area of the old teachers lounge and picked up the receiver. The dial tone was there. Even though there was no reason for it not to be there, I still marveled that it was. Nobody had used this phone for more than six years or so, and yet it still sat there, obedient, ready.

I got Moggio's voice mail and left him a message asking him to call me back, giving him the landline number. He called back within minutes, just as I was beginning to wonder what Maud and I were going to eat. We had not eaten since breakfast, and frankly I wasn't looking forward to another MRE. It had occurred to me to order a pizza, but how weird would it look to the pizza guy? Delivering a pizza to a mothballed elementary school that hadn't hosted students for more than twenty years? Not to mention how suspicious it would look to Zapman and any of his associates who might be lurking out there, just waiting for something like that to happen so they could learn of our whereabouts.

I told Moggio of our encounter with Zapman and of how we had escaped him by fleeing to the old school.

"You have a secret passageway leading out of your house?" said Moggio, incredulous.

"Doesn't everybody?" I said.

"I think the royal family might still have a few out of Buckingham Palace," Moggio replied. "Do you have a bomb shelter, too?"

"That's kind of a personal question, isn't it?"

"Would you like me to come and pick the both of you up?" said Moggio.

"Not at the moment," I said. "If Zapman is still out there, I'd rather not disclose this location to him. I might still need it."

"Okay," said Moggio. Trouble was, he said it as though I had just told him about my trip to Alpha Centuri. "Anyway, I did a little digging while you guys were on your field trip."

"Funny," I said. "What did you find out?"

"I found out that Lashona's body is still on ice at the coroner's office," said Moggio. "Nobody from the family has come forward to request its release."

"Does that surprise you?"

"Not really," said Moggio. "Familial devotion isn't the Webbers' forte, I don't think."

"Which brings us to the will," I said. "I think Desmond might be devoted to *that*."

"Right," said Moggio. "And there is one, a will, I mean. But we kind of figured that. I wasn't able to find out what or who was in the will, of course, only that there is one."

"Barry had mentioned a pretty substantial insurance policy," I said.

"And Lashona probably made pretty good money," said Moggio. "So Desmond is sniffing up the right tree."

Maud walked into the lounge, wearing the white robe I had given her and drying her short black hair with one of the towels. I pointed to the phone and mouthed the word "Moggio" to her. She rolled her eyes a little and opened the refrigerator door, immediately frowning at the contents, or lack thereof. Great minds, as they keep insisting, think alike.

"So, where do we go from here?" I said.

"Well, there isn't much more we can do tonight," said Moggio. "Tomorrow I'll see what I can do about learning who the executor of the will is and maybe see about talking to Desmond, see what he wants to do."

"It sounds like it won't have anything to do with police," I said.

"Sounds that way. You two sure you'll be all right there for the night?"

I tried to read something into the way Moggio had asked the question, but it seemed innocent enough.

"We're probably as safe here as anywhere. Maybe tomorrow you could swing by my house. We could emerge from there once you've checked out the place to make sure nobody's lying in waiting."

"I could do it right now if you want," said Moggio. "You guys could find a hotel room someplace until things cool down a little. I could pay another visit to Beste tomorrow, let him know that we know who his friend is that's taking shots at you."

"Let me check with Maud," I said. "I'll get back to you within the hour."

I hung up and looked at Maud, who still had the refrigerator door open, undoubtedly waiting for something edible to materialize.

"I'm starved," she said, before I could say anything. I didn't have the heart to offer her another MRE.

"Me, too," I said.

"What are our options?" she said.

I told her about Moggio's offer to pick us up back at my house and take us to a hotel. Maud frowned.

"They could be waiting for that," she said. "Then they could just follow us to wherever Moggio takes us." I, of course, had thought of that.

"Our options beyond that are not particularly appealing," I said. "I've got some more military rations around this place, but they've got to be closing in on their expiration dates."

"As charming as breakfast was," said Maud. "I think I'll pass on the army food."

"Moggio could be our only hope, then," I said. "Unless you want to call the police." Maud gave it some thought.

"I can't believe someone is trying to kill us," she said.

"Well, you had to know it would come to this," I replied. "We've obviously gotten too close to something."

"I don't feel like we're close to anything," said Maud.

"I know what you mean," I said. "But maybe that just means we're closer than we think."

"You're making my head hurt," she said. "And I already have a headache from lack of food. I have a very delicate blood sugar balance to finesse all day long."

"I say we call Moggio to come and pick us up, then," I said. "I'm not equipped to deal with the kind of exotic medical emergency your blood sugar situation might erupt into."

"How gallant of you," she said. "Okay, let's call him."

"This is a good decision," I said. "You'll be glad you made it."

"You make it sound like I've just agreed to a heart transplant," said Maud. "Can we just call him already? I'll go put some clothes on." She turned to walk away. I picked up the phone and waited for the dial tone.

"Dress quick," I said. Maud turned to look at me, alarmed by something in my voice. "The phone's dead."

TWENTY-EIGHT

NOCTURNE

"I thought you had alarms," said Maud as she dressed hurriedly. She had decided, after all, to wear the denim shirt and jeans I had given her. They looked a little big on her, but they looked better on her than they did on me, Bobbsey Twin Stevie.

"I do have alarms," I said. "And the bad guys would have activated them had they tried to break in. The good news is they probably realized that and didn't try to break in for just that reason. But they probably thought they could terrorize us by cutting the phone lines, which, unfortunately they can apparently get to without tripping the alarm."

"Or maybe you just didn't pay the bill," said Maud.

"We should only be so lucky," I replied. "I don't suppose you brought your cell phone with you."

"It's in the car," she said. "We abandoned it in a hurry, remember?"

"I realize that," I said. "I wasn't criticizing you. I was just asking."

"It sounded like a criticism. Next you'll be scolding me for seducing you when we should have been planning what to do about Zapman."

"I will not," I said. "Besides, we're okay. Like I said, they just cut the phone lines. There's no need for us to panic."

Maud zipped up her jeans. "I wish I had more sensible shoes," she said, looking down at her high heels.

"I think I have a pair of Asics in stock, but they're men's eleven-and-a-half. Probably too big for you," I said.

"I'll be all right," said Maud. "What's the exit strategy here?"

"My guess is they're going to try to wait us out," I said.

"That could be a while," said Maud.

"They might not be in a hurry," I replied. "They may assume that sooner or later we'll panic, having no access to the outside world."

"How would they know that? Why wouldn't they think we had cell phones?"

"I don't know," I said. "But why cut the phone lines if they assumed we had cell phones? What would that accomplish?"

"Like you said, it might make us panic."

"I have another theory," I said.

"I can't wait to hear it," said Maud.

"I'll tell you on the way," I said. "We shouldn't linger here." I grabbed Maud's hand and started pulling her out of the teachers lounge.

"Where are we going?" she said.

"You'll see," I said.

We walked back downstairs to where we had entered the school from the passageway leading from my house. Maud started to head for the door.

"Not there," I said. She looked at me, confused.

I pulled her hand and led her another twenty feet or so to another door, marked "Emergency Exit." Next to that door was another keypad. I hit the code and the door clicked unlocked.

"Seriously?" said Maud. She looked at me in astonishment. "You really *are* paranoid," she said.

"That would only be true if we had not found it necessary to use this," I said. "You know the old saying, 'Sometimes people really are out to get you.'"

"So, where does *this* lead?" said Maud. "A helicopter pad? A chalet in Switzerland?"

"Actually, just to the pumping station on the edge of the property," I said. "I had a lot of money at the time, but even I couldn't afford another safe house."

"Or you would have bought one?"

"Can we talk about this later?" I said. "My theory is Zapman and friends think we're holed up in my house. They cut the phone lines, and maybe they cut the power, too. They'll try to wait us out."

"Your phone lines in the house are connected to the phone lines here?" asked Maud.

"I don't know," I said, feeling exasperation rising within me. "I'm not real good on phone technology."

"What about my excellent point on the cell phones?" said Maud.

"Remember that power outage we had, when there was no power for a day and a half or so?"

"Yeah."

"My cell phone didn't work that day after about two hours. I had let it run down."

"Mine worked," said Maud.

"Okay," I said. "Maybe my theory is off base. But I still think they're watching the house, and not the school."

"Why not just go out from the school door, then?"

"Why take the chance?" I said.

"I think you just want to show off your insufferable ingenuity," said Maud. "Or paranoia."

"Fine," I said. "Can we go now?" I pushed the door open and nudged Maud ahead of me through it.

"Is there another secret passage to somewhere else when we get to the pumping station?" she asked. "An endless series of secret passages?"

"An intriguing thought," I replied. "But no. This is the last of them."

"It's sad, a little bit, you know?" said Maud. I pushed her with a little more force.

If anything, this corridor was more ill-lit and claustrophobic than the one leading from my house to the school, which made sense, since it was almost an afterthought.

Maud might have been right. At the time I built these things, I might have been just a little bit around the bend.

After a walk of about a hundred yards, we came to another door with the inevitable keypad. I hit the numbers and, once again, a door clicked open.

"You're lucky all this stuff still works," said Maud. "It wouldn't be any fun being stuck in this tunnel."

"We wouldn't be stuck," I said. "I have backup systems, sensors. I can even communicate with the security company from here."

"Why don't we then?"

"Well, we could. But that would mean contacting the police. Believe it or not, I've come around a little bit to your way of thinking on the police. I'm not exactly sure that they're involved in Lashona's death or the deaths of Barry or Astrachan, either. But something about the police reaction bothers me." I shrugged. "It's just a feeling."

"That's good enough for me," said Maud.

We entered the pumping station, a cold, concrete and cinderblock enclosure whose function I had never really understood. All I knew when I had installed the passageway to it was that it was no longer in use—no longer actually pumped anything. The county had been about to dismantle it when I bought it from them.

"Where are we now?" said Maud.

"On the edge of what they call a mixed-use complex," I said. "Which is, basically, the middle of nowhere, especially without a car."

"*Now* you think of this?" said Maud.

"There are public phones at the comfort station not too far from here," I said, not dignifying her sarcasm with a response. "You got any change?"

"No," said Maud.

"Okay, no problem." I looked down at her feet. "The snow and terrain is going to make it difficult for you to walk in those."

"But I look good," said Maud, smiling.

"Right," I said. "I'm going to call Moggio. I'll call him collect, tell him to pick us up at the entrance of the park. You just wait here. I'll be right back to pick you up."

"Yes, Sir," said Maud, saluting.

I opened the door and walked out into the cold evening air. I could see the silhouette of Redundant House from the pumping station. There were no lights on, and I tried to remember if we had turned the lights on before we fled for the school. I couldn't see anybody watching the house, but from my vantage point I could only see the backyard and the rear of the house. Anybody watching the house would likely be in a car sitting in the street in front of the house.

I started jogging to the area of the park where I knew the comfort station was. A couple of minutes later I was standing inside the station, the cold receiver of the pay phone at my ear. I dialed the operator and told her that I wanted to make a collect call to the office of Andrew Moggio. She asked me for the number and I told her I didn't have it. She didn't seem to like that too much, but she managed to dial the number anyway. It rang several times, and I was just about to assume that Moggio wasn't there, when I heard him pick up. The operator asked him if he was willing to accept the charges for a call from Stephen Fargo and I heard him say yes.

"Go ahead, Sir," the operator told me.

"I can't remember the last time I got a collect call," said Moggio. I could almost hear the astonishment in his voice. "They're like something out of the nineteenth century, what with cell phones and such."

"Listen," I said. "Can we postpone the whimsical contemplation on communications technology? I've got a situation here."

I explained everything that had happened to Maud and me—well, almost everything—since we had left the airport.

"So, we need you to pick us up," I concluded. "As soon as possible. It's not getting any warmer out here and Zapman might just start expanding his surveillance perimeter."

"Who?" said Moggio.

"The guy who assaulted me with the stun gun."

"Okay," said Moggio. "I'll need about an hour, though. It might be quicker, but this snow has snarled things up a bit. And we're at the tail end of rush hour."

"I understand," I said. "We'll look for you in about an hour. Flash your lights when you turn into the parking lot so we'll know it's you."

"How many times?" said Moggio.

"Jeez, Moggio, I don't know. A couple of times." Did I have to think of everything?

I made my way back to the pumping station where Maud stood in the middle of the room where I had left her, not that she had too many options.

There were no chairs or benches and the concrete floor would be mighty cold this time of year. She was shivering.

"Moggio won't be here for an hour," I told her. "Maybe we should go back into the tunnel. At least it's a little warmer in there."

"I'm fine," she said. "Just hug me."

I took her in my arms and hugged her to me. I could smell the hint of shampoo in her freshly washed hair.

"You're warm," she whispered in my ear. Then she kissed me. "I don't know why I'm so horny. Crazy, huh?"

"You're fine," I said. "Men just love horny women, believe me." We hugged for a few more minutes in silence.

"I lost my father and my brother on the same day," said Maud. I had no idea where this was coming from, but I had enough sense not to ask.

"I'm sorry," I said.

"We were up north for Christmas," said Maud. "It was cold, just like this. We had a cottage near Charlevoix. It was 1980. I was fourteen. My brother was sixteen. He had gotten a snowmobile for Christmas and he and my father were riding on it. It was stupid, really. They hit a log and both of them were thrown from the snowmobile. My father broke his neck and died instantly. My brother lived for about twelve hours, then he died of a closed head injury. I thought for sure he would live. I knew my dad was gone, but I thought there was no way they could both die like that. Not on a snowmobile. Not on a snowmobile he had owned for exactly one day."

Have I mentioned that I am not good with things like grief and consolation? Not that Maud appeared to be inconsolable. This had taken place more than twenty years ago, after all. Still, I said nothing, just hugging Maud closer.

"My mother never recovered," said Maud. "She was like a 1950s corporate wife, you know? Lifelong devotion, totally supportive of her husband, totally focused on the family. She couldn't survive the shattering of that unit. I mean emotionally. She survived physically, but we would go entire days without even talking to each other. I used to think she blamed me. You know how kids take on everything. But she was just stunned. Just lost. She died two days after I graduated from high school. Breast cancer. But, you know, I have a theory about disease. Sometimes we just let it in. Not just that our immune systems are compromised. We invite disease in. It's a form of suicide. It's like when one half of a couple that's been together for many years dies and the spouse dies a few days or weeks after that. I know this is not a brilliant new theory on my part, but I believe it. And it says something about willpower and illness." She moved her head back to look at my face. "Speaking of death, I'm boring you to that extent, aren't I?"

"No," I said. "I'm sorry about your father and your brother." I could feel her shrug.

"Not to get all psychological on you or anything," she said. "But I'm telling you this because you kind of filled a gap for me, well not you specifically, but my fantasy of you. My fantasy of you as father-brother-protector. From your book."

Maud paused, maybe for me to make some sort of contribution to this story, but I had absolutely no idea what to say.

"It was a combination of things," said Maud. "The fact that we lived virtually across the street from the Blessings, the focus on fathers in your book, my identification with the Denise character."

Maud must have been able to feel that I was getting tense. She moved her head away from my chest to look at my face.

"I'm scaring you, aren't I?" she said. Then she laughed. "Don't worry, I'm not a psycho about this. But I do feel that it's right, somehow. I know I can be a little aggressive sometimes. But I'm not a whack job."

"That's reassuring," I said.

"Not to the extent you are, anyway," said Maud, smiling.

"We should start heading over to the park entrance," I said a little while later. It had probably been close to forty-five minutes since I had called Moggio, much of which Maud and I had spent clinging to each other as she told me about her life after the death of her father and brother.

"This place could be downright homey with a few improvements," said Maud. "Like a toilet, for example."

"We can stop at the comfort station," I said. "It's on the way to the park entrance."

The snow was deep enough to cause Maud some problems in her high heels, but we managed to make it to the comfort station in about five minutes. While I waited for Maud to use the restroom, I scanned the surrounding area. The park appeared to be deserted, but it was so dark it was impossible to tell. I still could see no lights in the general direction of where I thought my house was, and, as yet, I could see no car lights at the entrance of the park. I could see the streetlights beyond that and an occasional pair of headlights traveling down the road that paralleled the park.

I started to wonder what we would do if Moggio didn't show up, but just as I did, I saw a pair of lights indicating that a car had pulled into the park entrance. A few seconds later, I saw them blink.

Maud was still in the restroom—why exactly does it take women so long to go to the bathroom?—so I didn't want to leave. But I also didn't want Moggio to leave. I walked to the door of the women's restroom and knocked.

"Our ride is here," I said, trying not to say it too loudly. There was no answer. "Maud?"

I felt something press into my back.

"Shut your fucking mouth and move into the bathroom," said a male voice.

"Who are you?" I said, refusing to move. I felt a sharp pain at my right ear as something hit me there. It hurt so bad that I saw lights.

"Didn't I just say 'shut your fucking mouth?'" said the voice. He pushed me through the door and into the restroom as I tried to smother the pain at my ear with my cupped hand.

Maud was being held from behind by what looked like a teenage boy, some character out of an Eminem video. He wore a tight knit watch cap and small brass hoops hung from each of his ears. He had one of his gloved hands over Maud's mouth and his other arm was wrapped around her chest, pinning her arms to her sides. Maud appeared to be unhurt, but her eyes darted around the room. I heard her try to moan something as I walked into the room. The person behind me gave me a shove in the direction of Maud and the guy who had been holding Maud let her go and moved to his partner's side.

"You okay?" I asked Maud. She nodded, breathing hard.

"You're bleeding," she said. I touched my ear. When I pulled my hand back, it was covered with blood.

I looked at our captors. They really were just kids. They were dressed similarly in those loose sort of athletic apparel that urban rappers favored. Both of them also had guns. Jeez, we were almost two counties away from Eight Mile. What was going on here?

"Who are you?" I said.

"Who the fuck are *you*?" said the kid who had hit me.

"We're nobody," I said. "We stopped to use the bathroom."

"You stopped at the wrong fucking place," he said.

"Look," I said. "We've got someone waiting for us. We don't have any money. And we don't care what you're up to. We just want to get out of here."

"Did I ask what the fuck you wanted?" said my captor, who seemed to be in charge.

"I was telling the truth when I said someone is waiting for us," I said. "He just pulled into the park. If we don't show up in a minute or two, he's going to start looking for us."

"Then he's gonna find your ass dead if you don't shut the fuck up," said the kid. "If I thought you was cops, you'd already be dead." I found it hard to believe that this kid had ever shaved, let alone killed anybody, but in this day and age you could never tell.

A knock sounded at the door. Jesus, I thought, Moggio already. I was about to shout out a warning to him when the door opened and two more kids pimprolled their way in. Had Maud and I walked into some Stephen King teenage vampire novel? The two new arrivals looked at us, but didn't say anything. The kid who had done all the talking to us whispered something in his partner's ear and turned to talk to the two kids who had just entered. The kid who remained with us raised his gun to eye level and pointed it at my head. He didn't tell us not to move or to keep our mouths shut, but we got the message.

The business between the kid who had been talking to us and the newcomers transpired quickly. They went through some urban rapper rituals of departure—all chest bumps and gestures and complicated handshakes and then the two kids left.

Our captor returned and looked at both of us.

"We're set," he said to his partner. His partner did not lower his gun, which I took as a bad sign. "The bitch comes with us," he announced to me. "Gonna have a little par-*tay*." He smiled at Maud. "I like mature pussy," he said. "Just like fuckin' the old lady."

"Be the *last* person you ever fuck," Maud hissed at the kid. Wait a minute. Hadn't she just said the same thing to me?

"You've obviously overdone the Ecstasy," I said. "She's not gonna be partying with you. We're both leaving."

I started to reach for Maud's hand. The kid started to swing his gun up. I moved my head back and kicked with my right foot, just like I was punting a damn football. My foot caught him squarely in the crotch and he let out a loud grunting moan and fell to his knees. He had dropped his gun and was holding his groin with both hands. A second later he vomited.

His partner seemed frozen, which allowed Maud time enough to stomp on his foot with enough force that her spike heel appeared to go right through his Air Jordans. I picked up the gun that the kid on his knees dropped and swung it at the other kid, hitting him in the temple. He went down like the floor beneath him had turned to ice and lay there with his eyes open, but clearly too stunned to move.

I turned back to the kid I'd kicked in the crotch, who was still writhing on the floor, a tight grimace on his face.

"I'll fucking *kill* you," he managed to tell me, his voice straining.

"Not today," I said, and I hit him hard on the temple with the gun. He let out a sharp gasp and fell sideways onto his shoulder, just as I heard the door to the restroom reopen. I swung my gun in the direction of the door and at the person standing in the doorway.

"Don't shoot," said Moggio, raising his hands in the air. "I give up."

"What was that all about?" asked Moggio when we were back in his car.

"I have no idea," I said. Moggio had given me his handkerchief and I was holding it to my ear. "Maybe a drug deal."

"Nothing to do with this other stuff?"

"Like what?" I said.

"I don't know," said Moggio. "I guess I just assumed this was connected to our investigation into Lashona Webber."

"What made you go into the restroom?" I asked Moggio. He shrugged.

"I waited few minutes. Then I saw these two kids coming out of the restroom. I called to them to ask them if they'd seen you, but they started running. So I went over to check it out. Looked like you didn't need my help anyway."

"You're telling me we just coincidentally walked into a drug deal?" said Maud from the back seat.

"That would be my guess," I said. "Aren't you glad now that you weren't wearing sensible shoes?"

"Little bastards," said Maud. "How old were they? Fourteen?"

"Old enough to know the business end of a gun," I said.

"They grow up quick these days," said Moggio. "My last couple years on the force, we'd be picking up twelve-year-olds for drive-bys."

"Anything new to report?" I asked Moggio.

"Nothing," he said.

I stared out the windshield, waiting, perhaps, for an answer to materialize there. I felt tired and, well, outwitted. Instead of things making more sense, they were making less. I felt no closer to understanding what had happened to Barry and Lashona than I had on the days they had died. And now Maud's life and mine were in danger for reasons that I couldn't understand, we were at least temporarily homeless, and I was clueless. I had come back to life for *this*?

I felt Maud's hand massage the back of my neck and I reached around to squeeze it. She pulled my hand with the handkerchief away from my ear and looked at it. I saw Moggio look at us.

"My recommendation is that we just step back for a few hours," he said. "Today was hectic. We can regroup tomorrow. In the meantime, you two can stay at my place. I've got plenty of room." He smiled. "But you have to promise to behave yourselves."

TWENTY-NINE

THEORETICALLY

Moggio lived in a high-rise condo in the city of Southfield, not too far from his office. We didn't take much of a tour of the place when we arrived. All of us were exhausted, and, even though it wasn't even nine o'clock yet, we were all ready for sleep.

Maud took Moggio's guest bedroom and, observing some code of decorum that I can't even imagine, I pretended that Maud and I had not been intimate just several hours earlier and took the couch in Moggio's living room. I had mentioned to Moggio that it was likely his condo was being watched and they might have seen us enter, but he wasn't worried about it.

"We've got great security here," he said. "The company's run by an ex-cop friend of mine. A virus couldn't get in this place."

Next morning, I was the first one up. It wasn't quite dawn yet and I stumbled around a little until I found the kitchen and turned on the light. The digital clock above the stove read 5:38 a.m. I found the coffee maker on the shelf and the coffee itself in the refrigerator. I brewed a pot of the stuff and was on my second cup when Maud walked sleepy-eyed into the kitchen at 6:21 a.m.

She poured herself a cup of coffee without saying anything, took a drink, then walked over to where I was seated, bent down and kissed me on the top of the head.

"Morning," she mumbled. She was wearing a pair of men's pajamas that were too small for her. "I can't wait to wear my own clothes again," she said. "Speaking of which, you don't suppose Moggio has anything I can run in."

"He doesn't look like much of a runner," I said. "Are those his pajamas?"

Maud looked down at them. "I don't know," she said. "I don't think so. These were in the closet. The room had a kind of a hospital bed in it. And a hospital smell, actually."

"Must be where Lazard was," I said.

"You mean I slept in the same bed where Lazard was murdered?" she said.

"Ixnay on the murder references with respect to Lazard," I said. "Moggio's been kind enough to show us this hospitality. And let's not forget that he picked us up last night."

"My hero," said Maud, rolling her eyes. She looked down at the pajamas she was wearing. "These are probably Lazard's. It can't be good that I'm staying in the house of a man I just met wearing the pajamas of a dead man."

"*I'm* here," I said. She bent over and kissed me on the lips.

"What are your thoughts on morning sex?" she asked.

"I always liked it," I said.

"Me, too," said Maud. She yawned and stretched. She had only buttoned one of the front buttons on the pajama shirt and when she stretched I could see her ribs and her smooth stomach, right down to her belly-button pin.

"I'd kind of like to get back to some of my normal routines," she said. "Do we have any plan for that? And don't tell me you're open to suggestions."

"Well, I am," I said.

"Okay," she said. "Here's my latest theory. Charles Beste killed Barry because he, Beste, was having an affair with Lashona and she wouldn't or couldn't leave her husband. But when Lashona finds out that Beste killed her husband, she goes ballistic and threatens to go to the police, so Beste has her killed." She stopped abruptly.

"That's it?" I said.

"You said yourself that it wasn't a marriage made in heaven, not that any of them are," said Maud.

"Lashona seemed to be pretty surprised that her husband was dead when we told her," I pointed out.

"She could have been faking it. Maybe she just wanted to find out what we knew."

"Why didn't she tell us that Beste killed Justice, then?" I asked.

"She had no reason to trust us. For all she knew, we might have been working for Beste."

I thought about this. It still didn't seem right.

"Okay then who killed Astrachan?" I asked.

"Beste could have killed him, too," said Maud. "People having marital problems go to psychologists. They tell them they're having affairs. Beste might have just assumed that Lashona told Astrachan about him and killed him just to make sure he never went public with the information."

"But we never found anything about Beste in any of the session notes," I said. "Besides, I'm pretty sure that mental health professionals can't ethically go public with that kind of information."

"Yeah," said Maud. "Well, that is a problem." She drained her cup and got up to replenish it. "Anyway, it's just a theory. We need to be looking at all the possibilities."

"I've got another one for you."

Both Maud and I turned to the sound of the voice and saw Moggio standing in the doorway to the kitchen. Neither of us had heard him approach. He was fully dressed and he held a burning cigarette.

"Another what?" I said.

"Another theory," he said. He got a coffee cup from the cupboard, hoisted the coffee carafe as if inspecting the color of the liquid it held and poured himself a cup. He took a long drag from the cigarette and knocked the ash off into the sink.

"So," I said. "Let's hear it."

"I'll tell you on the way," he said. "You two need to get dressed."

"Where we going?" asked Maud.

"The airport," said Moggio. "Desmond Webber called me this morning. Lashona Webber's daughter disappeared last night."

"So, what's your theory?" I asked Moggio as we rolled along the freeway west of Detroit toward the airport.

"About Lashona or Justice?" said Moggio.

"Wouldn't they be covered under the same theory?" I asked. "And Astrachan, too?"

"See, I think that's where we might be looking at this thing wrong," said Moggio. He was smoking another cigarette and he had cracked his window a sliver to let the smoke out, not that it was doing much of a job of that.

"Okay," I said. "Who do you have a theory about?"

"Well, I'm closest to the Lashona situation. I did a little research on the Internet this morning. I got a little more information on Lashona's daughter, Venetia."

"Venetia?"

"Yes, Venetia," said Moggio. "It turns out Venetia may not suffer from autism after all, although she certainly suffers from *something*."

"You mean, like a disease?"

"Or abuse," said Moggio. "Two years ago when she was sixteen she attacked one of her teachers with a nail file. That wasn't the first time she'd attacked a teacher. She's definitely got a problem with male authority figures."

"This kind of information is available on the Internet?" I said. Moggio pushed his cigarette out through the crack in the window.

"If you know where to look," he said, blowing a stream of cigarette smoke out into the wind behind the discarded cigarette. "And subscribe to the right services. Hell, nowadays, a private investigator would never have to leave his office if he didn't want to. His or her office." He looked in the rearview mirror and nodded at Maud.

"So, let me jump ahead here," I said. "You think Venetia killed, who, Barry?"

"Well, I don't think she killed Lashona. She doesn't have access to that kind of ordnance and she doesn't have the training for that. Her violence is more along the irrational striking-out variety—spontaneous, the crime of schizoid passion thing."

"Okay," I said, trying to absorb all this. "You're suggesting that Venetia killed Barry and someone else killed Lashona and they might not have anything to do with each other."

"I guess I'm just pointing out that Venetia has a history of violent behavior. A documented history. And from what I was able to gather from Lashona, she also had mental problems."

"I guess I could see her lashing out at Barry," I said. "But that whole castration thing and the frying pan. That seemed twisted to me beyond the lashing out of an adolescent girl."

"Just barely adolescent," said Moggio. "She's eighteen or so, at least chronologically."

I nodded. My conception of Venetia all this time had been of a child. I turned around in my seat to look at Maud.

"What do you think?" I asked her.

"I told you they didn't just arrive from Florida," she said.

THIRTY

BESTE & CO.

We had to go through the same routine of calling Desmond from the lobby of the hotel. This time, when we got to his room, the door was already open. Desmond was standing in the doorway, holding a large white Styrofoam coffee cup, wearing the same clothes he'd had on the day before.

"She gone," he said, raising the hand that wasn't holding the coffee cup. "She just gone," he lamented again, letting the hand slap against the side of his leg.

We entered the room, which this time did not contain Desmond's mother. The door that connected to the bedroom was closed.

"You mean Venetia's gone, right?" said Moggio. "That's what you told me on the phone."

"Right," said Desmond. He took a drink of coffee from his cup. I had to believe that there was more than coffee in the cup. The place reeked of vodka, although I couldn't see the Popov bottle.

"Where's your mother?" said Moggio.

"Sleepin'," said Desmond, motioning with his chin towards the closed bedroom door.

"So what happened?" said Moggio.

"We went downstairs to the lobby this morning for coffee," said Desmond. "Me and Venetia. And while I was buyin' the coffee, she just wandered off."

"She do that often?" said Moggio. Desmond shrugged.

"She like the snow," he said.

"The snow?" said Moggio.

"Yeah," said Desmond. "She never seen snow livin' in Florida. She like to walk in the snow and see her tracks."

I didn't spin around and flash Maud a significant look, but I sure felt like doing so.

"So, you think she went walking outside in the snow, is that it?" said Moggio. "I mean, was she dressed for it?"

"No. Had nothin' on but a sweatshirt and jeans."

"She couldn't have gotten far," said Moggio. "She's probably just lost here in the hotel someplace."

"Or in the airport," said Maud.

"Right," said Moggio. "Or in the airport. But she won't be wandering around outside too long. It's too cold. Do you have a photo of Venetia?"

Desmond shook his head.

"Okay," said Moggio. "What does she look like?"

"She tall," said Desmond. "She good lookin' like Lashona." Not especially helpful.

"You said she was wearing a sweatshirt," said Moggio. "Did it have a logo or anything on it, the name of a school, maybe?"

"Yeah," said Desmond, coming to life a little bit. "She had a Florida State University sweatshirt on that her mother give her. That's where Lashona went to college. Florida State University. FSU."

"Well, that's helpful," said Moggio. "What color was the sweatshirt?"

"Red," said Desmond. "But dark red, you know."

"Like maroon or burgundy?" said Moggio.

"Yeah, like burgundy," Desmond agreed.

"I think it's actually garnet," said Maud. Both Moggio and I turned to look at her in semi-amazement.

"That's one of their school colors. Garnet and gold."

"Okay," said Moggio, after a short pause. He looked at Desmond. "You stay here. We're going to take a look around."

"Why I got to stay here?" said Desmond. I would like to think that he said this out of concern for his niece, but I didn't think that was the case. I had the feeling that he didn't want us to be alone with the kid. We might get to talking to her and she might tell us something that Desmond didn't want us to hear.

"Somebody has to be here if she comes back," said Moggio. "She didn't have a key with her, did she?"

Desmond shook his head.

"Mama's here," he said.

"Yeah, but she's sleeping," said Moggio. "Besides, what if this triggers some sort of medical emergency with your mother. Somebody needs to be with her in case that happens." Desmond nodded reluctantly.

"Okay," said Moggio. "Call me on my cell phone if Venetia shows up." Desmond nodded again, and we left him standing there in the middle of the room with his laced coffee and displeased countenance.

I shot Maud a glance as soon as we were in the hallway, and Moggio noticed it immediately.

"What?" he said.

"A couple of things," I replied. "First, Venetia won't be in the airport terminal. You have to have a plane ticket for the day of your flight to get through security, remember?"

"Right," said Moggio. "I told you, I don't travel on airplanes. What's the other thing?"

"When Barry told me his wife was missing, he mentioned that he had seen footprints in the snow in the backyard, leading away from the house. None returning, just leading away. And he also told me that he didn't think they were Lashona's. Lashona didn't like being out in the cold. That's how the Florida influence affected *her*, I guess."

Moggio stopped in the middle of the hallway and stared intently at the floor, gnawing at the fingernail of his right index finger. He looked up at us and said nothing for several seconds.

"You think those were Venetia's footprints?" he said, finally.

"I don't know," I said. "But when you put it together with Maud's contention that the Webber clan didn't just arrive in town and your information about Venetia's violent history, well, I don't know, a new picture, as they say, starts to emerge."

"You think she wandered off outside?" said Moggio. He paused again, a pained look coming over his face. "But, man, she'd freeze her ass off."

"I'm not sure what to think," I said. "If she's fascinated by the snow, maybe that overrides the cold. Besides, it's cold, but it's not *that* cold. It's probably mid-to-high-thirties. She could survive that for a while."

"But there's no place to walk around here," said Moggio. "We're at a fucking airport. She can't just stroll around on the runways."

"She must be in the hotel," I said. "Maybe just wandering around the halls. Who knows? I have no idea what her state of mind is."

"If she's wandering around outside, the police will pick her up sooner or later," said Maud.

The elevator bell rang to indicate the car's arrival. Reflexively, all of us looked up to see who was getting off, thinking it might be Venetia.

Boy, was it *ever* not Venetia.

There, standing in front of us with guns in their hands, were Charles Beste and his young protégé, the ubiquitous Zapman.

They seemed surprised to see us, but not so surprised that they forgot to raise their guns and point them at us. A smile was spreading out on young Mr. Zapman's face that said, "How fucking lucky am I?" Beste had a bit of a more serious demeanor, but he, too, seemed highly pleased to have run into us like this.

"Here to visit the Webbers?" he asked.

"Relax," said Moggio in his rasping near-whisper.

Beste looked at his companion, then back at Moggio.

"I believe we *are* relaxed," he said. "*You* folks seem a bit tense.

"We were just leaving," said Moggio.

"Ahhh, I think you all better stay, Mr. Moggio," said Beste.

"If we don't, what, you'll just open up on us right here?" said Moggio. "You gonna kill every guest who opens his door to see what's going on, too? And what about the security cameras?"

"I don't see any cameras," he said. "And by the time anyone opened their door to see what was going on, we'd be long gone, and you all, well, you'd be long gone, too."

"We're in an airport," said Maud. "Security rules here. You'd never get away."

Beste broke into a big smile now. He looked at Maud.

"You're kidding, right?" he said. She didn't respond to him. He motioned with his gun that we should turn around and head back in the direction of Desmond's room. "Let's take this out of the hallway, shall we?"

Well, making a break for it, notwithstanding Maud's faith in airport security and Moggio's faith in the courage of innocent bystanders, didn't seem like a prudent move. We turned around and headed back to Room 302. When we got there, Beste knocked on the door. We waited for a few seconds, but nobody answered. Maybe as addled as he was, Desmond Webber wasn't *that* stupid.

"What makes you think he's gonna answer the door?" said Moggio.

"I'm just trying to be polite," said Beste. He nodded to his companion, who put his gun in his pocket and took out his wallet, from which he extracted one of those hotel keys that look like a credit card. He stuck the card in the slot above the handle and the little green light came on indicating that the door had unlocked. Zapman turned the handle and slowly pushed the door open with his left hand while retrieving his gun with his right.

"Yo, Dez," he said. When nobody responded, he poked his head in the room.

"Check it out, Jordan," said Beste.

Ah, I thought, Jordan, brother of Philip, no doubt. Jordan disappeared into the room while the rest of us stayed in the hallway, not speaking. I snuck a look at Beste. He didn't appear nervous, but I thought I detected impatience in his furrowed brow and tight lips. He kind of rolled on the balls of his feet, again, emphasizing the boxer aura that he projected. A few seconds later, Jordan was back in the doorway.

"No one here, Pop," he said. I didn't know anybody had called their fathers "Pop" since "The Adventures of Ozzie and Harriet" went off the air.

"Well," said Beste, "maybe they stepped out to get some air. Why don't we all step in and get comfortable and wait for them to return." It was not as much of a suggestion as it sounded.

Once inside, Beste asked Moggio for his weapon, which Moggio surrendered without hesitation or rancor. Almost matter of fact.

"Pretty neat trick with that key," said Moggio. "I'd be interested to know how you were able to get it."

"I'd like to tell you it was magic," said Beste. He took off his coat and did a slow-motion version of that neck swivel that boxers do in the ring. "But the fact is they gave me the key because I reserved the room. And paid for it."

"Mr. Webber didn't mention that," said Moggio.

"I'm not surprised," said Beste. He pulled the desk chair away from the wall and sat on it, spine forward, feet splayed. Jordan Beste remained standing at attention, blocking the door. Moggio plopped into the armchair across the room from Beste and pulled his cigarettes from his jacket pocket.

"Please don't light that," said Beste. "I'm allergic to cigarette smoke." Moggio shrugged and put the cigarettes back in his jacket pocket.

"So, what are we doing here?" he asked Beste.

"Waiting for the Webbers to return," said Beste. "I thought I made that clear."

"Yeah," said Moggio, "but what happens then?"

"I haven't exactly worked that out yet," said Beste.

"Did it occur to you," Moggio said to Beste, "that the Webbers might not return? Not if they know what's good for them."

I was wondering how they'd gotten out without our seeing them.

"And you may know less than he does," said Beste, motioning with his head toward me.

"Okay," said Moggio. "So why don't you enlighten us?"

"I'd tell you," said Beste, a broad smile breaking out on his face, "But then I'd have to kill you." Jordan chuckled at this. Just a couple of goofs.

Maud asked to go to the bathroom, but Beste told her to hold it. After that, nobody said anything for several minutes. Then Jordan's cell phone rang and he answered it with "Yo."

He listened for thirty seconds or so, then said, "I'll get back to you." He flipped his phone shut and walked over to his father, bending down to whisper in his ear.

"Outstanding," said Beste, getting to his feet. He clapped his hands together once and held them like that, looking in turn at each of us. "You folks have a choice," he said, and I almost thought I could see a twinkle in his eye. "You can either accompany us quietly to the limo waiting in front of the hotel, or we can execute your sorry asses right here."

Needless to say, we went with door number one.

We took the elevator down to the lobby. When we got there, I looked around for anything resembling an agent of law enforcement, but, of course, I couldn't see one. Usually at the airport, especially post 9/11, you couldn't swing a dead cat without hitting a Wayne County Sheriff's deputy. But that wasn't the case this morning. We moved in this sort of human clump toward the hotel doors and out into the cold morning air. I'd had an instinct to run during our traversing of the lobby, but the thought of a bullet ripping into my back as I sprinted away from the group deterred me. That, and, yes, the fact that I couldn't leave Maud. Moggio I could have left. So call me a hopeless romantic.

The white limo was roomy and warm. A young man I'd never seen before was sitting behind the wheel and the fact that he showed almost no surprise at all when Maud, Moggio and I tumbled into the car ahead of our two armed escorts led me to believe that he was Beste's regular driver. The driver looked expectantly into the rearview mirror.

"Just get rolling, Bryce," said Beste.

A chauffeur named Bryce? What kind of a name was that? Wasn't that a canyon somewhere out west? A national park? Who names their kid for a national park?

"Head west on ninety-four," Beste continued. I-94, which he was referring to, would take us toward Ann Arbor, *not* in the direction of Beste Development, or even more important, the home of myself or Maud or Moggio's office.

"Can I ask where you're taking us?" said Moggio.

"No sense being anxious about that," said Beste.

Jordan's cell phone rang again. He mumbled into it for a few seconds, then, once again, handed the phone over to his father. Beste listened intently to whoever was on the other end of the line. After about thirty seconds, he flipped the phone shut and looked at me.

"You should have stayed dead," he said to me.

"No kidding," I replied. "But this has been kind of fun."

"Surprised that I know who you are?" said Beste, looking like he was feeling awfully proud of himself.

"I'm not surprised anymore that anyone knows who I am," I said. "But I guess I wouldn't mind knowing *how* you know who I am, although I think I have a pretty good idea."

"Oh, yeah?" said Beste. "Well, we've got a bit of a ride here, all of us together. Why don't you tell me what your pretty good idea is?"

"It's not a great revelation," I said. "It just seems to me that Barry Justice must have told you about me. You two guys were buds, right? Knew each other from high school. He probably got you some ink over the years, some media exposure and I imagine you returned the favor."

"From what I've heard about you," he said, "you've got quite an imagination."

"Well, I do," I admitted. "But sometimes it's prophetic, you know?"

"No, I don't know," said Beste, smiling at me evenly, but with it just a touch of anger in his eyes. I don't think he particularly cared for me.

"So," said Moggio, "you guys killed Justice? Is that it?"

"Why don't you ask Mr. Fargo," said Beste, not taking his eyes from me. "He's the clairvoyant in this vehicle."

Moggio turned his head to look at me. I looked steadily at Beste for a few seconds.

"No," I said finally. "You guys didn't kill Justice."

Beste smiled broadly now and looked at Jordan who smiled back at him. The limo suddenly decelerated slightly as Bryce noticed a dark blue Michigan State Police cruiser on the side of the road a couple hundred yards ahead of us.

"Let's not do anything foolish," said Beste evenly, still smiling. The guy liked to smile, you could see that. He wasn't exactly an attractive man, but he must have had some work done on his teeth. They were brilliantly white and he seemed to like to show them off. "There's no reason for anyone to get hurt," he said.

I slid my hand over to Maud, but she didn't seem to be in a handholding mood. She seemed to be seething—no fear, just anger.

"I don't care if you didn't kill Justice," she said. "You obviously killed somebody." Beste gave her a bemused smile.

"Kind of a strong accusation, don't you think?" he said.

"Accurate is more like it," I said.

Beste shook his head slowly, almost as if to say, boy, are these attempts at deduction ever feeble. You call yourselves worthy adversaries?

"My sense is that you killed your old buddy, Dr. Astrachan," I said. Beste kept the smile on his face, but it seemed to grow more tense.

"I say we shoot them now, Pop," said Jordan. "Throw them out on the side of the fucking road."

I caught Bryce's eyes in the rearview mirror. They didn't seem to register any surprise.

"Maybe not you personally," I said. "Maybe Jordan here. He knows the lay of the land out in California, right? Then, of course, there's the problem with Philip. He got, what, a little greedy?"

"If you had any confidence in this fairy tale, I'm sure you would have gone to the police with it," said Beste. "I think you're just in speculation mode."

"That doesn't mean I'm not right," I said.

"And what exactly would be my motive for killing Dr. Astrachan?" said Beste leaning forward.

"I haven't figured that out yet," I replied. "You want to tell me?"

"I didn't have one," he said, sitting back in his seat. "So much for your theory."

"So, back to my original question," said Moggio. "Where are we going?"

"Don't be concerned," said Beste. "Despite your accusations, I have no intention of harming you. We just need to get you out of the way for a few hours—a day or so at the most."

"I have to water the plants back at my house," I said.

"If you want to give me your house key, I'll have that taken care of for you," said Beste. "By the way, we're still marveling at how you and Miss Gonne eluded us on that one. Nobody saw you leave your house. That's why I was smiling on one of those phone calls. The people I have watching your house have reported that you still haven't left. But then, I run into you at the hotel. Imagine my surprise. Care to tell me how you pulled that off?"

"Maybe you need to hire more alert people," I replied. He smiled at me again.

"I'll keep that in mind." He turned his attention back to Moggio. "I own a farm, just south of Ann Arbor," he said. "Although I am sorry to say, I won't be owning it for long. But that's another story. I bought the place a few years ago thinking that the growth in the area and the renovation of the airport would drive the price of real estate up. Unfortunately, that hasn't happened in this particular area."

"When your financial situation goes bad, it goes bad across-the-board, right?" I said. Beste shrugged.

"The point is, I own the place until they don't get their next payment." He looked at all of us with a magnanimous smile and spread his arms. "And I want all of you to be my guests."

"This is kidnapping," said Moggio. "You realize that, right? People saw us leaving the hotel together. They almost certainly have security cameras in the lobby and you're a pretty well known guy in the Detroit area. Do you really think you can get away with this?"

"I could kill you, if you prefer," said Beste with almost fetching amiability. Moggio laughed. Not a confident laugh. More like a derisive laugh with just a hint of panic in it.

"What makes you think it will be any easier to get away with murder than with kidnapping?" he said.

"Your logic would be unassailable," said Beste, "if you had the slightest idea what you're talking about. See, I'm kind of taking a page out of Fargo's book. By the time the police track you down to the farmhouse, my boys and I will be residents of a new country, one I prefer not to identify, if you don't mind. We'll have new identity's, new lives, basically. You'll understand if I don't get into specifics."

"That's a lot easier for one person to do than for three," I said.

"Hey," said Beste, "Bryce and Jordan and I, we're family. Nothing more sacred than the family unit."

THIRTY-ONE

COOLER HEADS PREVAIL

Beste's use of the term the *farmhouse* more than did justice to the shack our limo pulled up in front of. The place appeared to be about 600 square feet of A-frame covered in grungy white aluminum siding that was curling up and yellowing at the corners and buckling at various places along the seams, revealing black Visqueen. There was rust around the rivet holes and along the gutters. A downspout made it only halfway down the side of the house and a rusted light fixture swayed from the small roof that covered the concrete slab porch. A folding patio chair lay overturned on the porch, next to a weathered wooden cable spool that had apparently served as a table at one time. A large oak tree dominated the front yard. A thick rope with frayed edges hung from one of the branches and stirred in the cold breeze. Presumably a tire had been affixed to it at some point to serve as a swing. The overall effect suggested Norman Rockwell gone over to the dark side.

If the outside—underscored by the bleakness of the weather—was dreary, the inside was downright depressing. There were no indications that anyone had lived in the place for years. The Venetian blinds on all four of the windows were shut, but they were in such disrepair that their function was negated. The interior walls that had once partitioned the place had been knocked down. As a concession to privacy, a shower curtain had been strung on a rod screwed into the ceiling, which then could be pulled across to block the view of the commode. An ancient stove stood on one side of the room, next to refrigerator, one of those old 1950s-style models with rounded edges. You couldn't have paid me enough to open that refrigerator.

"Make yourselves at home," said Beste, as he entered the room behind us, the room and the house being one and the same. He rubbed his hands together. "I apologize for the lack of heat," he said. "I think I forgot to pay the last bill." Jordan sniggered. I decided that if I was ever able to catch up to these guys, I was going to enjoy bitch-slapping Jordan Beste around some.

"I've decided that I don't want to kill you," Beste announced. "However, I am going to ask you to give me your cell phones and," here he nodded at Moggio, "I'll need to hold on to your weapon." Moggio shrugged. "So, you see?" said Beste. "That's it. Your situation isn't so desperate after all. Just a little inconvenient, a little uncomfortable. You're about ten miles from the nearest civilization so to speak. And you're about fifteen miles from the freeway. So you can easily walk for help. And I figure that the time it will take you to do that and proceed to mobilize the authorities—although, I don't have the sense that you are interested in getting them involved—should give me, *us*, ample time to take care of our business and take our leave." He looked at each of us in turn, perhaps waiting for us to congratulate him on his generosity.

"What are you talking about?" said Jordan, looking at his father in disbelief. "We can't let them go." Beste smiled indulgently at his son, but said nothing. "Well if we're not going to kill them, we at least need to make sure they stay put for awhile," said Jordan.

"What are you suggesting?" said Beste, cocking his head and looking at his son in what almost seemed to be amusement. "I'll fucking *show* you what I'm suggesting," said Jordan. He swung the gun he was holding in the direction of Moggio, who was standing closest to him. The gun discharged and Moggio instantly let out a howl, grabbed his left knee, and fell to the floor, where he lay writhing in pain.

Nobody reacted for a few seconds. I found myself hoping that Beste didn't find this an excellent suggestion by his son. Eventually, Maud knelt to the floor next to Moggio as though she were getting ready to assist him, although I couldn't imagine how, with the injured man still rhythmically grunting in pain and rolling back and forth as he grasped his injured leg.

"Are you out of your mind?" Beste said to Jordan.

"What?" Jordan responded, petulantly. "He'll live."

Beste stepped over to where his son stood, took the gun from his son's hand and with his other hand slapped his son across the face.

"Go wait in the car," Beste said. "*Now*," he growled when his son didn't respond quickly enough. Jordan rubbed his face, turned, stomped to the door and slammed it behind them as he exited.

"I'm truly sorry about this," said Beste. "I want you to know that what I was saying about killing you was all for effect. He looked down at Moggio, who appeared to be in too much pain to hear what Beste was saying. "It was not my plan to hurt anyone."

"You're son seems to have different plans," I said. "And now this man needs medical assistance." He looked down again at Moggio. "I'm sure it's painful Mr. Moggio," he said "but my son is right when he says you'll live." He was still standing near to Moggio, bent over slightly and looking down at him.

Suddenly, from her crouch, Maud swung her leg in a sweeping maneuver that caught Beste in the backs of both of his knees, so that he fell on his back instantly, without even the opportunity to brace himself or utter a syllable of shock, amazement or anything else. He hit the floor hard, with a sharp exhalation of breath, his head banging loudly against the concrete slab a split second later. In a continuous fluid movement, Maud completed her spin and brought her elbow down sharply into Beste's Adam's apple. All this had happened in about a second.

Beste was either stunned or dead. He certainly wasn't moving and he didn't appear to be breathing. His eyes were still open and stared straight up at the ceiling. Maud replaced her elbow with her knee to Beste's throat and went through his pockets until she found his gun and Moggio's. Then she wrenched Jordan's gun from his hand as well and handed all of them back to me. She jumped quickly off Beste as if she had been holding down a calf she had just wrestled to the ground in some rodeo maneuver. Not that her caution was necessary. Beste wasn't going anywhere anytime soon.

"Is he all right?" I asked Maud.

"Do we care?" she replied.

"Will you marry me?" I said, awestruck.

Within a minute or two, it was pretty clear that Beste was, indeed, alive. At least I could see his chest rising and falling. But he didn't sound good.

"I think you damaged his larynx," said Moggio, his voice, nevertheless, betraying the stress of his injury. "Believe me, I know that sound. Nice spin move. You've had some training." Maud shrugged.

"Just in a few defensive moves, really," she said. "I picked them up at a battered woman's group during my divorce. How's the leg?"

"I can't walk, if that's what you're asking," Moggio's face had drained of color and he was actually tearing up from the pain. "But he's right. I'll live."

Beste made some sort of groaning noise, and tried to raise himself up.

"Can you talk?" I said. Beste shook his head. I handed one of the guns to Maud and walked to where the kitchen had once been and started going through the cupboards. There wasn't much, but I found a rusted steak knife, which I used to cut through the electrical cord at the back of the refrigerator. Returning to Beste, I pushed him back down to the floor with my foot and rolled him over on his stomach. He didn't resist. I tied his hands behind him. Then wrapped the remaining length of cord around his feet and pulled tight, so that he was basically hogtied from behind.

"What about Beavis and Butthead?" said Maud.

"You want me to go out there and get them, or do you want to go?" I said.

"Probably better if I go," said Maud.

"Just tell them Beste wanted them back in here and didn't tell us why. But try not to stand too close to them in case they do something stupid."

Maud smiled at me.

"Hey," she said, tucking the gun I had given her behind her back and under her jacket. "I can take care of myself."

"I noticed," I said. "Help me move Beste behind the bathroom curtain."

When we had stashed Beste behind the curtain Maud went out to the limo to retrieve his two offspring.

"This could be dicey," said Moggio. "You should give me one of the guns."

"I can handle this," I said. "Besides, you keep forgetting that I'm legally dead. I can't get into any trouble."

"I just wouldn't depend on their devotion to the old man," said Moggio. I thought about that for second and then handed Moggio his gun. He put it in his belt behind his back.

I heard the car doors slam shut and the sound of footsteps crunching their way through the snow. I held my gun behind my back as first Maud entered the room, followed by Bryce and then Jordan.

"Yo, Pop," said Jordan. I stepped behind him and lowered the gun to the back of his knee and fired. Jordan went into almost the same gyrations that Moggio had gone through several moments earlier. I immediately swung the gun up to Bryce's face.

"Nobody knows we're here," I said to him. "They might not find your bodies for months." Bryce raised his hands and stepped back from me.

"Hey," he said. "I'm cool."

We used their belts and strips from the shower curtain to tie their hands and feet.

"I need a doctor," Jordan moaned.

"You give me the right information, maybe I'll send one out here," I replied.

"What fucking information?" Jordan spat at me. He was sweating heavily, his lips were pale and quivering, but he was putting up a macho front.

"Who killed Barry Justice?" I said.

"I don't know," said Jordan. I looked at Bryce.

"I mainly just drive the car," he said with a sickly look on his face. He bore no resemblance whatsoever to Jordan, and I wondered if this was another half brother.

"I hate to interrupt," said Moggio. "But my leg really hurts."

Moggio insisted on being driven to Henry Ford Hospital in Detroit, even though it was a good hour's ride from the farmhouse. We had retrieved our cell phones from Beste, while making sure to relieve Beste and his sons of theirs. In the limo on the way to the hospital Moggio made a few calls. He stretched out in the back and Maud made him an ice pack from the limo's bar. I asked Maud to pass me up a beer while she was at it, which she did, reluctantly. I *was* driving after all.

"One beer," I said. "My nerves are gone. I just shot a man. Have a little sympathy."

"Yes," she said, handing a bottle of Samuel Adams to me. "Was that absolutely necessary?"

"I was trying to get information," I said. Hadn't she ever seen Dirty Harry? "You had already made it impossible for us to get anything from his father by shattering his voice box."

"I didn't hear you complaining at the time," said Maud.

"Children," croaked Moggio, now off the phone, "can we stop the bickering and move on to more urgent matters?"

"Such as?" I said. He winced as he readjusted the position of his leg on the seat.

"I just spoke to a couple of cops, friends of mine. They're going to pick up The Beastie Boys."

"Hey," I said, turning back to look at Moggio, "that's pretty good, for a man with an untreated gunshot wound." He ignored my impertinence.

"We should have just left them there," said Maud. Moggio ignored her, too.

"I think we need to find the Webbers," said Moggio. "Or you two will have to. I don't think I'm going to be doing a lot of walking for a while. We'll get what we can out of Beste, and if any of that is useful to you, I'll let you know. I'm also going to have to let the police know about Desmond and his mother and niece. They're gonna find out about them sooner or later anyway, and I don't want it to look like we're withholding evidence."

"What evidence?" I said.

"I'm not sure," said Moggio.

A couple of Moggio's cop buddies met us at Henry Ford Hospital and saw to getting him checked in in that expeditious way that police have. The last I saw of him, he was giving me and Maud the thumbs up sign as they rolled him into the ER. The cops also insisted on impounding the limo, which meant that Maud and I didn't have a ride. One of the cops offered to drive us back to my house, but I declined. I didn't feel like being interrogated and I wanted to talk some things through with Maud alone.

Before I could bring anything up, though, Maud said, "Do you have any idea what's going on?"

We were sitting together in the back seat of the cab, as it rolled towards the northern suburbs and Redundant House.

"I think it may have something to do with blackmail," I said.

"Blackmail?" said Maud.

"Yes. I think that's what Beste was talking about when he was referring to retirement in Monte Carlo, or wherever his destination was." Maud considered this.

"Okay," she said. "But who was he blackmailing? Anybody with money appears to be dead. Justice, Lashona, Astrachan. Who's the blackmailee?"

"I'm not sure yet," I said. "But who's the next of kin?"

"What, you mean Lashona's next of kin? Well, it can't be her daughter. And neither Desmond nor his mother looked particularly affluent."

"It may be more of a timing thing," I said.

"You mean the will?" said Maud. "But wills take a while. You have to go through all the legal mumbo-jumbo."

"Assuming we're talking about a traditional will," I said. "But what if Lashona set up a will in her daughter's name. Barry told me they had just taken out large insurance policies. Maybe at Lashona's death the money went directly into this fund."

"Yeah, but Venetia doesn't sound like she's competent," said Maud.

"How do we know that?" I replied. "More important, how does the insurance company know that, especially if Venetia has lived in Florida her entire life? And if nobody has challenged her competency, and even if she isn't competent, Lashona may have set up a trust for her with an executor."

"Yeah," said Maud, "except that the executor would likely have been her husband, and Justice is dead, too. And what in holy hell does Astrachan have to do with any of this?"

Well, that was a good question. I had to admit that he didn't seem to fit in anywhere.

"Coincidence?" I said. Maud gave me a look.

"You *believe* that?" she said. "I mean *you* believe that?"

Well, no, I didn't. My head was beginning to hurt, which is usually what happens to me when I have only one beer in the middle of the day. And think too much. Then I suddenly realized that hunger—low blood sugar—was probably a contributing factor.

"We should get something to eat," I said.

"Will everything make sense if we do?" said Maud.

"I can't think on an empty stomach," I said.

When we rolled up to Redundant House, I looked around for any suspicious vehicles before paying the cabbie. Then we exited the cab and nearly sprinted to the door. I unlocked it, we entered, and I hit the code on the keypad to let the people at the alarm company know that this entrance was authorized. In the kitchen, I picked up the phone, which offered no dial tone in return. See? I'm not so paranoid. Maud retrieved her cell phone from her purse, but it, too, was dead.

"I guess we can't call for a delivery," I said. "And since I think you know how slim the pickins' are here, we should probably go out. We can charge my cell phone in my car if it needs it."

"Sounds like a plan," said Maud. "Now that you mention it, I am hungry. What has it been, like forty-eight hours since we ate?"

"It only seems that way," I said.

"I'm going to try to freshen up a little bit," said Maud. She headed for the master bathroom. I stood in the middle of the kitchen for a few seconds, wondering if Maud's freshening up would involve enough time for me to have a beer. I decided, as I always do in these situations, that I had plenty of time. I opened the fridge. There was one beer left. Right next to the severed head of Charles Beste.

I jumped back in sort of an involuntarily delayed reaction from the grizzly sight of the head sitting on its bloody stump of a neck and slammed into Maud, who was standing behind me. I turned to see a look of horror on her face.

"There's a note on the bathroom mirror," she said, speaking almost in a tone of awe after she'd recovered from the impact of my crashing into her.

"It says to check the refrigerator and not to call the police." Then, as if she'd suddenly just come to the realization, she said, "My God, that's Charles Beste."

"Jesus," I said. "Who's cutting these people up? What are we dealing with here?"

Maud just shook her head.

"What else did the message say?"

"It had a phone number."

I grabbed Maud's hand and we walked down the hallway to the bathroom. On the mirror over the vanity someone had written in red lipstick, "Check your refrigerator. Don't call the police." Below that, was, indeed, a telephone number.

"What's the 941 area code for?" I said.

"I don't know," said Maud. "I'm now convinced," she said. "This is definitely a job for the police." She had recovered some of her poise.

"The note told us not to call the police," I said.

"I thought Beste was the bad guy," she said in a characteristic non-sequitor.

"Except that his son, Philip, was killed, too," I said. "Maybe Beste's desire to get a new life wasn't just because he wanted to disappear with someone's money. Maybe he was afraid for his life."

"Justifiably so, I would say," said Maud.

"Anyway," I said, "we need to get out of here."

"You realize, don't you, that someone is probably watching the house," said Maud. "Whoever got in here with the head. So much for your security system, by the way."

That *was* baffling. Had Jordan Beste been able to get the code numbers somehow after he had stunned me? But didn't that mean that Jordan would have been the one who deposited his father's head in my refrigerator? I had sensed the usual father-son generation gap irritations between the two of them, some differences of philosophy (such as should they have killed us), but there hadn't been the undercurrent of hostility that would account for Jordan's decapitation of his father. And Jordan should right about then have been under sedation someplace, shouldn't he? Hadn't Moggio said that the cops were on the way to pick up the Beste clan? Besides, this decapitation seemed connected—so to speak—to the castration of Barry Justice. I was no criminologist, no experienced homicide detective, but I had a gut feeling that the same hand was involved in both these mutilations.

"If someone wanted us dead," I said, "I think we would be dead. That's the whole idea behind these body parts demonstrations. Somebody's trying to shock or frighten us into something or away from something."

"Well, it's working," said Maud. "I say we get in the car, plug in your cell phone and call the police on the way to the station." She'd certainly done a complete one-eighty on her police-involvement theory. But I guess that's what the presentation of a severed head will do to your frame of mind.

"Get your stuff together," I said. I grabbed a pad of paper and a pen from the drawer and went back to the bathroom to copy down the number.

"You're not really going to call that number, are you?" said Maud. In truth, I hadn't made up my mind.

"Even if I don't," I told her, "the police will still want it." Then something else hit me. "You leave any lipstick in the bathroom?" I asked Maud. She shook her head.

"I never let it out of my sight," she said. "Could it have been Denise's?"

"That's possible," I said. "But I doubt it. I don't ever remember seeing lipstick in the bathroom. Certainly not since Denise died."

"Think hard," said Maud. "This is important."

She was right about that. If whoever had written that note had used her own lipstick to do so, well, gee, we were either dealing with a woman here, or a transvestite. In either case, I had not the slightest clue who it was. Some silent partner who had been working with Beste, maybe? Maybe some kind of *Double Indemnity* double-cross? My head was spinning. My brain, wherein, it is said, there is no pain, seemed to be on fire.

"It wasn't Denise's," I said to Maud. We gave each other one of those sort of Hollywood significant looks like "Omigod, we're in so far over our heads that we have to look up to see the bottom."

"Let's go," I said, grabbing Maud's hand and heading for the garage.

THIRTY-TWO

DESMOND II

My car did us the huge favor of starting right up. I found the cord for recharging my cell phone in the center console, right next to the dead phone itself, and plugged it in. The phone immediately started in with its rebooting process. I pulled out of the garage and down my driveway to the street. I saw no suspicious vehicles, but it was entirely possibly that we were being watched from some distance away, so my comfort level didn't exactly jump off the charts.

I started in a direction that I knew would bring us to a corner not too far from Redundant House where there was some human activity.

"Where are we going?" said Maud.

"Someplace public," I responded. Within three or four minutes we had reached the intersection I had in mind, a small commercial enclave with a Blockbuster Video store, a few fast food places, a liquor store, a Rite-Aide drugstore and a few other small shops. I parked the car in front of the Blockbuster Video store. I could see inside the building, which appeared to be moderately active. A few customers walked through the rows of videos, several employees in their trademark blue shirts. Nobody seemed suspicious. Same with the people making their way to and from their cars in the parking lot.

I grabbed my phone, which had only partially recharged in the few minutes since I'd plugged it in, and said, "Come on," to Maud.

"Why don't we just stay in the car?" she said.

"I want better cover," I replied. "Don't forget that Lashona was killed by a sniper."

"But you just said back at your house that if they wanted us dead, they could have killed us already," said Maud.

"The problem is," I said, "that I don't know how many different threats we're dealing with here." Maud thought about it for a moment.

"My God," she finally said. "You mean there might be more than one?"

"It's just that, for me, the severed body parts don't fit with the more antiseptic sniper thing. It bothers me. So I don't want to be sitting in one place too long. Like this car, for instance." Maud's head suddenly turned reflexively to look out the window, as if she might see that bullet that was even now twisting its way through the air toward her head. "Don't run," I said. "But move quickly." She nodded.

We opened our doors simultaneously and walked to the Blockbuster entrance.

"I'm sorry," Maud said once we were inside.

"For what?" I said.

"For goading you into this mess," she replied. "Excitement is one thing, but this is almost intolerable. I thought my heart was going to explode just walking from the car to the door."

"That's my fault," I said. "I scared you."

"No," she said. "You were right. We have no idea what we're dealing with here and we need to be careful. But if you don't mind, I'm going to need to find a bathroom like within the next fifteen seconds."

"Go," I said. "I'll wait for you over there by the new releases."

Maud walked quickly off to find the restrooms, and I walked to the new releases area. I'd chosen this spot because it was at the back of the store, farthest away from the windows. As Maud had pointed out, there was no reason to be careless. I took out my phone and looked at the display area. The power level indicator showed only one bar out of three, which told me that there wasn't a lot of juice available. I also noticed that I had a little envelope icon showing on the screen, indicating that I had a voice mail message. Not knowing how much power I actually had, I decided to call the lipstick number first, then deal with the voice mail message. They might be the same person, after all.

I looked around one more time. A young couple was arguing quietly over their choice of entertainment for the evening—would it be chic flick or action-adventure? Several other customers cruised the aisles, scanning the video titles. I stepped toward the shelves and pretended to read a couple of DVD jackets. When I was sure that no one was taking any special interest in me, I dialed the lipstick number as nonchalantly as I could. I continued to pretend to scan the shelves as I waited for someone to answer. I might have been trying to look calm, but my heart was in extreme fast-forward.

"Hello, Fargo," said a voice on the other end of the phone. It was a voice I didn't recognize. A man's voice—clear, calm. So much for my theory of a woman being involved.

"Who am I speaking to?" I demanded with as much indignation as I could summon.

"All you need to know right now is that you're speaking to the person who left the little token of appreciation in your refrigerator," said the voice. He paused. "The appreciation was in advance," the voice said. "For the assistance I know you are going to provide to me."

"I'm not doing anything until you tell me who you are," I said. "Including staying on the line." The man on the other end of the line let out a sigh.

"This is Desmond Webber," he said. I was speechless for about ten seconds.

"You don't *sound* like Desmond Webber," I said.

"Dat's cuz Ize usin' my uppity voice," said, well, Desmond. I heard the voice I had heard earlier in the hotel room, the one that sounded like it announced Gulf War Syndrome brain damage with every syllable. I heard several quick beeps and looked at the display area of my phone, which kindly informed me that my battery was low and that I should recharge it soon. Thanks.

"Sounds like you're running on fumes there," said Desmond, in his non-minstrel-Negro voice. "I'll be brief. There have been some personnel changes in my organization, which has left me without the resources I need to complete some plans that I'd made. I require your assistance in completing these plans. I don't want to hurt you or your lovely companion, but unless we can come to some kind of agreement here, you'll find Miss Gonne's pretty head next to Beste's on your refrigerator's trophy shelf. Am I getting through?"

"Yeah, I hear you" I said.

"Now, before your little brain starts spinning plans for spiriting you and your woman to safety, let me tell you that my associate has a knife to her throat right now. All I have to do is give the word and it's say hello to Mr. Ginsu for your girlfriend."

Was this possible? Could everything have happened this fast? And was it possible that Desmond had so completely fooled us with his Stepin Fetchit routine? I had an impulse to dash out the door and into the parking lot to see if I could spot Maud, but I restrained myself.

"What do you want?" I said.

"I want you to get in your car and plug in your phone. Get on I-75 and head south. I'll call you with additional instructions." I started to protest, but my phone abruptly beeped again three times in quick succession, then went dead.

"Fuck," I said loudly enough for several customers to glance at me. I looked in the direction that I had seen Maud walk toward looking for the restrooms. I walked quickly to the checkout counter and asked the clerk where the restrooms were.

"I'm sorry, sir," said a thin blond woman with some kind of chain tattoo encircling her neck. Exactly what message was *that* supposed to deliver? "We don't have a public restroom. There's one next door at the McDonald's . . ." She kept saying something, but I was already scanning the premises, looking for Maud's short, blue-black hair. I didn't see her anywhere.

"Did you see a good-looking brunette leaving?" I asked the blond. "She had a leather jacket on. She came in with me and we were standing over there together by that used video sales rack."

"Uh-uh," said the blond. "Sorry." She seemed confused. Or alarmed. Something. I was starting to create a scene, which probably was not what Desmond wanted. And who the fuck was his associate, by the way?

I left the video store and jogged to my car. I got in, started it up and plugged in the phone, which rang about two seconds later. Desmond was obviously watching me. I twisted around in my seat, but I couldn't see him anywhere, or anything else that looked out of the ordinary. Most important, I couldn't see Maud. I hit the send button and before I could say anything, Desmond said: "What, did you have to stop and rent a motherfuckin' DVD on the way out the motherfuckin' store?"

I started to stumble through some lame answer.

"When I tell you to do something," said Desmond, "you do it without hesitation, understood?"

"Understood," I said.

"Take seventy-five to Eight Mile," he said. "Get off at Eight Mile heading east. When you get to a street named Sherwood, you turn to your left, heading north for about a half-mile. I'll call you again at that point. I won't call you until then, so if I see you reach for the phone, or if I even see your fucking lips move, I'm gonna assume you're talking to some unauthorized person, which would be anyone but me, understand?"

"Yeah, yeah, I understand," I said. I hated it when people were constantly asking me if I understood.

The phone went dead, then almost immediately rang again. Thinking that Desmond had forgotten some part of the instructions, I picked up the phone and hit the send button.

"What the fuck did I just tell you?" said Desmond.

"I thought you might have forgotten something," I said.

"No," he shouted with some significant ferocity. "You're the motherfucker forgetting something. You pick up that phone again before you get to Sherwood, we're gonna cut your lady friend here. Not enough to kill her, but enough to end any thoughts she might have had of a modeling career on the side. Now, do you understand?" He enunciated these last four words with a tone of forceful clarity that indicated it was more than a rhetorical question this time.

"Yes," I said. "I understand."

"Good," he said. The phone went dead again. It rang several more times before I reached the interim destination Desmond had given me, but I didn't answer the phone. I didn't event look at it. I didn't even talk to *myself.* I wondered if the calls were from Desmond just trying to fuck with me again, or, maybe it was Moggio. Not too many other people knew I was even alive, let alone knew my telephone number.

It took me about twenty-five minutes to get from the video store to Sherwood Street. Along the way, I tried to imagine what Desmond's role in all this was, not that I thought this information would be helpful when I finally confronted him. And I definitely couldn't imagine what favor I could do for him. I didn't have the kind of money all these people seemed to be scrambling after and I didn't have any access to anybody else's money, such as Lashona Webber's or Barry Justice's.

As soon as I turned onto Sherwood Street, my phone rang. I picked it up and hit send.

"About a half-mile down on the left-hand side of the street," said Desmond. "It's a white, two-story cinderblock building with a for-sale sign on it, right on the corner of Eliot and Sherwood. Turn on Eliot and wait for the garage door to open. Then pull your car in and shut it off. And stay in the fucking car until you're told otherwise."

The phone went dead. Well, at least he didn't ask me if I understood this time. I could see the building coming up on my left, some kind of combination office building/warehouse. A concrete sign on the front lawn read Webber Office Supply, but another sign had been partially draped over that, indicating that the building was for sale. The building looked unoccupied from where I sat, but, I couldn't see through walls, could I?

I turned onto Eliot Street. As I did so, I saw one of two large garage doors begin to roll up. I turned into the driveway and drove under the door. The driveway from there sloped down to what appeared to be a loading area for trucks. Shipping and receiving. I pulled my car up to the loading dock, shut it off, and, as instructed, sat in my car waiting for further instructions. In my rearview mirror I saw the door slide closed behind me. I had been sitting there for perhaps a minute when I heard the second roller door begin sliding up and I saw a white Ford Econoline van with rusted wheel wells and faded lettering stenciled cheaply on the side of the van which read "Webber Office Supplies." The van came to a halt beside my car and the roller door behind it shut. There was no movement or noise for a few seconds, then my phone rang again.

Well, what was I supposed to do now? Was this an authorized call or an unauthorized call? I started to reach for the phone when I saw the driver side door of the van open and Desmond Webber stepped out. He wasn't holding a phone. I quickly hit the send button to let the call through, but didn't answer it. I put the phone in my jacket pocket, opened the car door and started to exit the vehicle, as the police would say.

"You don't listen," said Desmond. For a second I thought he might have seen me fooling around with my phone. I stopped and gave him my best quizzical look. "I told you to stay in the fucking car," Desmond explained. I started to sit back down. "Forget it," he said. "Just stay still right the fuck there." He further encouraged compliance by pointing a gun at me.

I started to raise my hands. That's what you're supposed to do when somebody points a gun at you, right?

"Still," said Desmond. "Man, what the fuck is wrong with you? Don't you understand the fucking English language?"

As he said this, Maud moved into view, in the company of a woman I didn't recognize. She was young, probably in her late teens and she had African-American features, but her skin color was very light. She had a pleasant enough countenance, but a blank look on her face that gave it the effect of being masklike. The kabuki look was enhanced by an amateurish smear of lipstick that had wandered a bit astray of the mark. She wore loose fitting khaki pants and a yellowish shirt that looked like something a military dictator in a Third World country might wear. At a rakish angle on her head sat a cap that looked like it might be Muslim headwear, but I was no expert. She also had brand spanking new white athletic shoes. My overall impression was that someone else had dressed her and that someone had no more sense of style than she did, and didn't care. It was all very bizarre. It was even more bizarre when I noticed that a couple of streaks of brownish red on her shirt were not part of the fabric's design, but were, in fact, bloodstains.

"You okay?" I said to Maud. She nodded stiffly.

"She's any way we want her to be," said Desmond. "And don't forget that." He gestured with his gun in a swirling motion that I should turn around. "Up the stairs to the right," he said.

The steps he was referring to led from the oil-stained concrete floor of the docking bay to the actual unloading area which would have been level with the bed of a semi's cargo area. From there, another set of stairs led up to the second floor, where I could see a light on. I climbed the first set of stairs, then, after looking back to Desmond to confirm that I was on the correct path, I started up the second flight as well. I could hear the footfalls of the others on the metal stair behind me and could feel the vibrations of their steps. Every sound and vibration seemed amplified in the empty warehouse.

At the top of the stairs I encountered a row of several offices.

"First door on your right," said Desmond. I was hoping that whoever was on the other end of my cell phone line was getting all this. Or that they were even still on the line. The problem was, they wouldn't know exactly where we were anyway unless I could somehow get around to the address.

"Was Webber Office Supplies a legitimate business or just some front?" I asked Desmond.

"None a your fucking business," said Desmond.

"I just ask because it doesn't look like there's been a lot of activity around here lately," I said. "Is this place really for sale?"

"Didn't I just tell you it's none a your fucking business?" said Desmond.

"Yes, Desmond," I said. "I seem to recall that you did say that." I wanted to zero in more specifically on our location, but I was sure that to do so would tip my hand. I had gone about as far as I could and I could only hope that Moggio would be able to put two and two together—quickly.

I found the first door on the right and turned into it. It was a drab office with just a desk, chair, sofa and a file cabinet. A large white board on the wall had apparently been used for scheduling, because there were dates, times, cities and some other data listed on it in black grease pencil. The most recent date was May 2002—quite some time ago. I turned around and watched as Desmond, Maud and the girl escorting her entered the room.

"Sit down," said Desmond, motioning to a wooden chair next to the door. "You, too," he said to Maud. Desmond pointed to the couch and Maud moved to it, the girl staying at her side, but not holding on to her anymore. Desmond remained standing.

"Who's your friend?" I said to Desmond. "She doesn't seem to talk much."

"Yeah, but she listens," Desmond replied. "Which is a hell of a lot more than I can say for you." He didn't seem interested in answering my question.

"Her name wouldn't be Venetia, would it?" I said. As I said the name, I looked for any hint of recognition from the girl. I got none.

"You're a pretty smart guy," said Desmond.

"Apparently not smart enough," I said. "You had me fooled."

"Don't take it personally," said Desmond. "It's easy to fool white folk. They bring their preconceptions to every situation where a black man is involved. And if the white people have any guilt, which most white people do, even if they've transformed it into bigotry, they want to believe you're a no-account, brain-damaged imbecile nigger."

Gee, he sounded bitter.

"Especially if you say you sustained your injuries in a white man's conflict like the Gulf War," I said.

"I got no political ax to grind with nobody," said Desmond. "We just got a problem that needs fixing, and you're the only one who can help us with that."

"I'm listening," I said.

"Well, I haven't seen any evidence that you listen *good*," said Desmond.

"Why did you kill Charles Beste?" I said.

"See," said Desmond, "you're still not listening."

"You killed Barry Justice, too, right? Same MO, seems to me, I mean in terms of the mutilation of the bodies."

Desmond stared hard at me for a second. Then he swung the gun up and pointed it directly at my head.

"Stand up," he said. I did as he said: "Now empty your fucking pockets."

Oh, shit. This was going to be an issue for Desmond, I just knew it. I took everything out of my pockets, including the phone from my coat. Item-by-item, I dumped everything on the desktop: phone, wallet, pen, change, car keys. Desmond went right for the phone, first inspecting the display area, then holding the phone to his ear.

"You get any calls recently?" he asked. I thought it best not to lie about this.

"I got one, but I didn't answer it," I said. "Just like you said." Desmond continued staring at me for a moment.

"Just throw it away," said a new voice. I looked in the direction it came from and saw Desmond's mother in her wheelchair, framed in the doorway. Desmond removed the battery and threw both sections of the phone into a wastebasket. His mother rolled into the room and positioned her wheelchair so that she could see all of us.

The old woman hadn't changed in appearance much since I had seen her at the hotel, except perhaps that she was more engaged at the moment, more alert to her surroundings. Someone had affixed a tube of some sort to her wheelchair running vertically up the side. I could see the barrel of a rifle protruding from the tube. Holy Christ! Were we going into combat?

"He may have had the phone on," said Desmond to his mother. "Somebody may know where we are."

"You were supposed to search him before you brought him here," said Desmond's mother, or, rather, wheezed his mother. Apparently her breathing affliction, at least, was not an act. Her oxygen mask hung to the side, connected to a bottle that lay in her lap.

"The way it went down," said Desmond, "wasn't no opportunity."

"What do you say, Mr. Fargo," said the old woman. "Is somebody on their way to rescue you and your girlfriend?"

"I hope so," I said.

"But you don't know?" she said.

"No, I don't know." Desmond's mother said nothing for a few moments. She closed her eyes and appeared to be meditating. Nobody in the room seemed inclined to intrude on it, whatever it was.

"I've gone on my instincts my entire life," she said, finally, opening her eyes. "And my instincts tell me that no saviors are on the way. At least not yet. We have time."

"Mama," said Desmond, sounding as if he were ready to launch into a protest, but was halted by his mother's raised hand.

"We have time," she repeated.

I now had to admit to myself that I had absolutely no idea what was going on. It seemed that the entire Webber clan was not what it had appeared to be. I had assumed that Desmond was in charge, but that was clearly not the case. Was this old, withered, rasping and barely living fossil of a woman sitting in front of me the author of all this butchery and mayhem? She hardly looked the part. She looked like an old Incan mummy, swathed in a brown blanket, her upper lip and chin sprouting a few longish hairs. I looked at Maud, and she gave me a look back that said "Go figure."

"Venetia, baby," said the old woman. "Come here." The girl who had been sitting next to Maud got up and walked to the old woman's wheelchair. I saw no change in expression in the girl's face, even after she had sat on the floor next to her grandmother, who had draped her arm lovingly around the young girl's shoulders after stroking her cheek with a hand that looked more like the talon of a vulture.

"Mr. Fargo, we need somebody to act as an intermediary for us in a transaction," said the old woman. She said it slowly and with perfect articulation, as if to make a point about her mental faculties.

"I assume this in an illegal transaction," I said.

"That's not important at this point," she said.

Gee, it was kind of important to me.

"Well, I can't do it then," I said. "Sorry."

The old woman smiled. She looked at Venetia and hugged her a little closer.

"My granddaughter here has two passions in life," said the old woman. "The poor thing really hasn't much of a brain to think with and hardly knows what's going on around her. Been that way since birth, some defect of her gestation. Lashona thought she was autistic for a time. Even tried to blame it on measles vaccines the child had received. But that wasn't the case. Venetia was born the way she is." The old woman gazed lovingly at the profile of the young woman's face. "Do you know what her two passions are?"

"I sure don't," I said. The old woman looked at me for a few minutes, then seemed to go into another of her trances. Again, nobody interrupted her.

"Well, maybe we'll talk a little more about that later," she said, finally coming out of it. "The issue right now is that Lashona made provision for her daughter and unless we can get help in securing that provision, her daughter's future is bleak. And so is yours."

"Mine?"

"Yes, yours and your friend's here."

"Look," I said. "We don't know what's going on. We are no threat to you. Let us go and we promise not to go to the police."

"We can't depend on that," said the woman. "And anyway it's not negotiable. You are the ones to handle this assignment."

"What assignment?" said Maud.

"Maud," I began.

"No," said Maud. "I want to know what the assignment is. What can it hurt?"

"A wise young woman," said Desmond's mother. I myself was not thinking along those lines at all.

"All you have to do is make an exchange," said the old woman. "At a time and place yet to be determined, you hand a package to a person and he or she will hand one back to you. Then you deliver the package to us and we set you free. That's all there is to it."

Somehow I didn't think that was all there really was to it.

"What if I ask what's in the packages?" I said.

"I wouldn't tell you."

"What about if I asked the name of the person I would be meeting for this exchange?" I said.

"Does it make any difference?" said the old woman. "You'll find out soon enough."

"Why me?" I said, thinking that a change in topic might yield better results. "Why us?" I nodded in Maud's direction.

"Well, you have only yourselves to blame for that," said the old woman. "You stumbled into this. You happen to be available. You also happen to be useful."

"And clueless," Desmond added with a sneer. But his mother didn't appear to appreciate his contribution to this conversation.

"Desmond," she said. "I want you to make sure that the truck is ready." She looked at him and he looked right back, without giving any immediate indication of obeying her in whatever way getting the truck "ready" meant. Finally, he started for the door. "Don't be so glum, Desmond," she said, scolding him almost as though he were a child. "Everything's going to be fine."

"This can't be about an inheritance," I said when Desmond had left. "Lashona didn't leave you any money at all, did she? She had made her husband the beneficiary of her insurance and the executor of Lashona's trust fund, but she didn't leave a dime for you or Desmond, did she?" The old woman said nothing. "Why is that, I wonder?"

The old woman continued stroking her granddaughter's cheek. For her part, Venetia seemed not to have any awareness of what was going on around her. She gazed straight ahead, only stopping to look up at her grandmother when the old woman paused in her caresses.

"The young lady will ride with us in our vehicle," said the old woman, looking toward Maud, ignoring my questions. "You'll drive your car."

"Is this your building?" said Maud. Having been acknowledged by the old woman seemed to provide the permission she needed to re-enter the conversation.

"It is," said the old woman. "My former husband ran his business out of this building until he died. He left the building—there wasn't much of a business left—to Desmond."

"I love what Desmond's done with the place," I said. The old woman did not appear to take offense.

"We've been trying to sell it for almost a year now, but my ex-husband's creditors have other thoughts about that. Seems they know something we don't know about the value of this here real estate going up. Whatever. They are holding up the sale. But it's convenient for the moment."

This was downright chatty, coming from the old woman, but I failed to see the relevance. Desmond reappeared in the doorway.

"We're ready," he said.

"Wonderful," said the old woman. She said it like we were all getting ready to go to the Dairy Queen.

"Time to go, Vee," she said to Venetia, who got to her feet and stood there waiting to be told what to do next.

"Mr. Fargo," she said, "you and the Missy go first. Back down the stairs, please."

We retraced our steps to the garage. Desmond's mother rolled off a few feet by herself to take the elevator. By the time she joined us near the vehicles in the garage, she was clearly suffering from the exertion of maneuvering her wheelchair, even though it had only been a couple of feet that she had been required to propel herself. She fitted her oxygen mask over her mouth, which muffled her voice to such an extent that I couldn't make out what she was saying. Desmond, however, had apparently had lots of practice and needed no interpretation. He opened the roller door behind my car.

"Pull out," he said. "And wait. Remember, we've got your girlfriend."

As if I was likely to forget that.

THIRTY-THREE

CHARGE!

I got in my car, fired it up, and backed it out of the garage. When I was clear of the door, it slid down and, simultaneously, the other door next to it began to roll up. I watched as the van backed out and stopped once it, too, had cleared the doorway. Desmond was driving. Maud sat next to him. Although I couldn't see them, I had to assume that Venetia and Grandma were in the back seat and I also had to assume that a gun was aimed at the back of Maud's head. Desmond rolled down his window and indicated that I should do the same. When I did, he handed me a cell phone.

"Keep it on," he said. "And try to keep up. If we lose you and if I can't reach you on the cell, your girlfriend's not coming back from this field trip." I nodded and rolled up my window.

So, we were playing Phone Tag on Wheels again. I followed the van back to Eight Mile Road, then east for several miles until we got to the I-94 freeway. At that point, the van turned onto the westbound lane of the freeway, and I heard the cell phone go off—a rap number of some sort. I was becoming nostalgic for when phones announced their presence with that old familiar universal ring.

"We're going to Belle Isle," said Desmond when I had picked up the phone. "No detours," he reminded me. "And no random phone calls." He hung up.

I hadn't been on Belle Isle in years. The place was basically an island park in the middle of the Detroit River just east of the downtown area. It was a popular place for picnickers in the summer. It contained, as I recalled, a small zoo, an aquarium, a garish fountain, a small golf course, a beach, a marina or boat club and a few playgrounds. This time of the year, as I also recalled, Belle Isle would be much less populated than during the summer months. While it was a popular place among the locals, it also had had its problems. Few white people visited the island anymore, essentially out of fear and bigotry. It had a reputation, probably undeserved, for crime.

The Webber clan had probably chosen the location, or at least agreed to it, because it would be relatively deserted and open enough to be able to see clearly what was going on around them, lessening the opportunities for ambushes or double crosses. Presumably, someone could hide someplace with a rifle, but there weren't a lot of elevated vantage points, as far as I could remember, for concealing a sniper.

I followed the van as it exited at Van Dyke Road, then made its way over to East Grand Boulevard. Moments later, we were crossing the MacArthur Bridge to Belle Isle.

I followed the white van as it made its way around the south side of the island, from which the city of Windsor was visible. I had seen a couple of cars, but, as I had suspected, the island was pretty much deserted. My phone did its hip-hop number again.

"I'm going to pull over up ahead," said Desmond. "When I do, I want you to pull up behind me about twenty feet back. And stay in the fucking car until I tell you different. You think you can handle that?" Where was this attitude coming from?

"Yeah," I said. "I think so."

A few seconds later I saw the van pull to the side of the road. As instructed, I pulled behind it and waited.

"We're gonna switch vehicles," said Desmond. "We got about twenty minutes before the exchange goes down, so we got time to do the switch now."

I didn't ask why. That seemed obvious. They didn't want to be driving around in a highly distinctive vehicle with their own name imprinted on the side of it after whatever went down went down. Still, there seemed to be a highly improvisational feel to this "plan" of theirs. I mean, how long was it going to take for me to contact the police and tell them that the Webbers had stolen my car? But I told myself not to underestimate these people. I had done that once already and look where it had gotten us.

"Get out the car and open the tailgate so I can load Mama's wheelchair," said Desmond. "Leave the cell in the car. Once you've got the tailgate open, just wait outside the car, got it?"

I replied that I did, in fact, get it. I hit the button to unlock the tailgate, then got out of the car and walked around to the back to open it up. Then I walked to the driver's side door and stood outside the car, waiting. A few seconds later, I saw the side panel of the van open and a ramp slide down from the opening. Shortly after that, the wheelchair emerged with Grandma sitting in it, being carefully rolled down the ramp by her son. When they reached ground level Desmond lifted the ramp back into the van and closed the panel door. He then walked around to the passenger side of the vehicle. I could see that he carried his handgun, but he was at least trying not to be too obvious about it, holding it flat against his thigh.

From my angle, I couldn't see what was going on on the far side of the van, but a few seconds later Maud and Venetia strode into view, followed by Desmond. Maud walked stiffly with her head down. Venetia's gait was more casual and I saw her glance a couple of times in the direction of the Windsor shoreline. Maud and Venetia kept walking in my direction, while Desmond veered off to pick up Grandma. A few seconds later we were all standing next to my car. Passersby would probably have given us a second look. A third look, maybe.

"Give me the keys," said Desmond. I handed him the keys. "Venetia," he said. "Get in the car." The young girl hesitated for a few seconds, then moved to the rear passenger door of my Jeep, opened it, and got in. "You two, just move back a little," Desmond said to Maud and me. "That's far enough," he said, after we had backed up about ten feet. He handed the gun to his mother.

Then he opened the driver's side passenger door. He walked back to the wheelchair, lifted his mother from it and carried her to the door and deposited her gently in the back seat. I only hoped that someone was watching this and would think it was strange enough to call the police. I wondered why he hadn't just insisted that I take the van from the deserted office supply building in the first place. Why go through all this?

After stowing the rifle and the collapsed wheelchair in the back of the Jeep, Desmond returned to where Maud and I were standing. He handed me the keys to the van.

"Let's go," he said, motioning with his gun back toward the van. "You," he said to me, "behind the wheel, and you," he said to Maud, "shotgun." Maud and I did as we were told. When we were in our seats, the panel slid open and Desmond stepped in and pulled the door closed.

"Why didn't you just have me drive the van from the warehouse?" I asked Desmond. "You had Maud. You knew I wouldn't run."

"It was Mama's idea. She don't much like to be separated from Vee. Maybe she thought it would be more comfortable this way. I don't ask Mama why she do things she do. Guess what I did in the Army?"

This transition, or lack of it, was so abrupt that I couldn't follow him for a second.

"I have no idea," I said.

"I was an explosives expert," said Desmond, almost beaming. Already, I didn't like where this was going. "Mainly I disarmed them," he continued. "But my training basically ran the gamut. Plus, I've continued to keep up with developments in the field, if you know what I mean. I think they call it continuing education."

"So," I said, "are there explosions in our future?"

"Don't *have* to be," said Desmond. "Mostly it depends on you. Y'all heard of ANFO, right? Well, this here van is packing enough, well, to easily destroy this vehicle and its contents." He looked from me to Maud. "That would be y'all." He smiled. "Mama's got the RC sitting in her lap right now. She pushes a button, this van jumps about twenty feet off the ground and by the time it comes back down, the inside of the vehicle looks like the inside of a microwave oven where a pizza exploded." He looked at his watch. "Now, in about five minutes, a black Mercedes is gonna pull up to the van. Me and Mama and Vee are gonna mosey on down the road a bit. Find us an inconspicuous spot to watch the fun. Someone in the Mercedes is gonna ask you for this briefcase." He patted a brown leather briefcase he had pulled up from the floor. "He thinks maybe it's full of money, but, hey, do we look like we have the kind of money they'd be expecting?" I thought this was a rhetorical question, but Desmond appeared to be waiting for an answer.

"I don't know," I said. "I don't know what they would be expecting."

"Well, my friend," said Desmond, "that is a longer story than I have time to get into at the moment. They're gonna give you a package in exchange for the briefcase."

"Which doesn't contain what they're expecting," I said.

"Right."

"So what happens when they ask to see what's in the briefcase?" I asked.

"They gonna be pissed," said Desmond in mock horror. "They gonna throw one of them hissy fits like you see on them daytime TV talk shows. They probably ain't gonna want to give you the package y'all are expecting. That's where your job comes in. You're gonna tell them that we—Mama and me—we're scared. We've never dealt with any criminal elements before and we's afraid they wouldn't keep their word. That's why we recruited y'all for the job." He smiled.

"I gotta be missing something," I said. "How is this going to make these guys any happier?"

"Because you're going to agree to take them to the money, which, you explain is at a location here on the island, not too far away."

"But what makes you think they'll agree to that? I mean, nobody would agree to that."

"You're gonna insist that they keep the package they have for us until they get their money. And—" he looked at Maud—"you're gonna agree to leave your girlfriend with one of them as a hostage."

"I don't think so," I said.

"You're not understanding," said Desmond, sort of waving his gun in our direction, his seriousness now underscored by his upscale usage of the language. "This is not a negotiation. It's an explanation of what y'all's gonna do. Now, once you get one of the guys in the van, you just turn the cell phone over to him. I'll take it from there."

I took a close look at this man, Desmond Webber, brother to Lashona, veteran, devoted father and uncle, con man, idiot-savant. Then I despaired at my own ignorance, my lack of perception and sensitivity. I had not seen any of this coming. See, this is why I died in the first place. To rid myself of these burdens. Instead, I was sitting in a fifteen-year-old van with an insane man from an insane family and a woman I could be in love with and the van packed with ANFO like the jaw of a baseball player packed with chewing tobacco.

"What if it doesn't work?" I said, wearily. "What if he won't get in the van?"

"We're talking some serious greed, here, my man," Desmond replied. "Motherfucker'll *get* in the van." He looked at his watch again. "Show's about to start," he said. "Y'all break a leg." He slid the panel door open, climbed out of the van, and shut it behind him.

"I say we run," said Maud the second Desmond was gone. I didn't say anything for thirty seconds or so. I saw my car go past us, the impassive face of Venetia staring at me from the back seat. "They aren't going to blow this truck before they get what they want," Maud persisted.

"Run where?" I said. "They have my car, we'd be on foot. I'm certainly not going to stay in this van any longer than necessary. How far are we going to get?" I looked around. I could see no place closer than a quarter mile away that afforded any cover or protection.

"I'm not going to sit here and wait to be turned into hamburger," said Maud. So many food references in violent contexts, I thought. I mean, what did that say about us as a culture? "He could be bluffing about the bomb," said Maud.

"Could be," I said.

"You're taking this very calmly," said Maud.

"I've already been dead," I replied.

"Okay, that is getting very old," she said. "It wasn't even very clever in the beginning." I think she was about to get into a significant critique of my recent behavior, but she was cut short by the arrival of, you guessed it, a shiny, black Mercedes S600 sedan of recent coinage.

"You know, I wouldn't mind if I never saw another black Mercedes again as long as I live," I said. "I mean, doesn't a model like that go for, what, eighty-large or so? Somebody who can pay for a ride like that, what do they need with more money?"

"I'm still wondering why we just didn't make a break for it," said Maud.

"What exactly would we be making this break for?" I said. We were getting into an argument. I'm telling you it can happen anywhere, anytime.

The Mercedes pulled up alongside the van and the driver's window slid down. The face of Philip "Juan" Beste stared back at me.

"Phil," I said. "I didn't know dead men could obtain a drivers license in this state."

"Look who's talking," said Philip Beste.

"Sorry about your dad," I said.

"You got the briefcase?" he asked.

"Well, yes and no," I replied. I was trying to see who the second man was, who was sitting in the passenger seat, but I couldn't see past Philip Beste.

"Let's see the fucking briefcase," he said. "You bring it out, Little Miss Muffet stays in the van." Little Miss Muffet? Maud wasn't going to be happy about that.

"Okay," I said. I grabbed the briefcase from the back seat and opened the door. "Be back in a minute," I told Maud. I opened the door, exited the van and walked over to the Mercedes. As I got closer, I could see that the reason I had been unable to determine who was sitting in the seat next to Beste was that nobody was sitting there.

"Get in," said Beste, motioning with his head to the back seat. He wore dark sunglasses with black frames and a dark suit and tie. I was almost impressed. He looked like one of those agents in *The Matrix*. Maybe I had been reincarnated in an endless movie retake.

I opened the door.

"Hey, Fargo," said Andrew Moggio. He had a smile on his face, a brace of some sort on his injured leg, and a gun in his hand, which he pointed at my chest.

"Should you be up and around so soon?" I said to Moggio, sliding in next to him in the backseat of the Mercedes.

"I didn't want to miss any of this," he replied.

"Are you really an ex-cop?" I asked.

"That part is true," he said, raising a finger theatrically. "But listen, I really don't have time to get into all of this right now. Do you have the report?"

"Report?"

"What's in the briefcase?" said Moggio.

"Just tell me this," I persisted. "You really didn't know Lazard, did you?"

The smile wasn't quite as unrestrained on Moggio's face now. It was being propped up just a little bit. But my question about Lazard seemed to revive him just a bit.

"That's where I really snagged you, wasn't it," he said. "I mean, I thought if I threw out Lazard's name, I would at least get your attention, but the real stroke of genius was in telling you that I helped him put an end to his life. A mercy killing. That got you didn't it? See, I know about you guilt-ridden types with death fantasies. You probably felt like you had abandoned the old guy after your whole faked death experience. You were just waiting for someone like me to come along with the story about putting him out of his misery."

I had to admit to myself that I had gone for Moggio's Lazard story hook, line and solid lead sinker.

"So," said Moggio, "the report." He nodded at the briefcase.

"I don't know what's in this thing," I told him. "Desmond hinted strongly that it was money. Just not money in the amount you're thinking of."

Moggio slid the briefcase across the seat toward him and opened it without taking his eyes off me.

"Your friend didn't trust me did she?" he said. "I could tell. You know, you could learn a lot from that woman. She's got better instincts than you do." He got the briefcase open and looked at the contents. I saw him pull out a couple copies of the *Detroit Free Press*. He looked at me and said, "Okay, what's the deal here?"

I told him what Desmond had told me.

"This is between you two guys," I said, when I had finished. "Why not just let us go? You know we're not going to follow up on this. I just don't care and I can convince Maud not to care, either." But Moggio was already shaking his head.

"Let's just let this play out according to the script," he said. "Philip will stay with Maud. You can drive me to wherever Desmond is. We'll make the swap and everything will be cool." I wondered if I should tell Moggio about the ANFO, if, in fact, it was in the truck. I waited for Philip to vacate the front seat, then replaced him there as he walked across the road to the van and got into the driver seat of the vehicle.

"He won't try, well, to amuse himself with Maud while we're gone, will he?" I asked.

"Who?" said Moggio. "Philip? Oh, if you mean sexually, I very much doubt it. He's not interested in women." I looked in the rearview mirror at Moggio.

"So," I said, "Are you two . . .?"

"Just drive the fucking car," said Moggio, pointing the gun at my head.

Since Desmond had neglected to tell me just exactly where he would be waiting, I simply did a u-turn and headed in the direction that I had last seen my car traveling.

"So, what's in this report?" I said.

Moggio didn't respond. I think he was nervous. This change in plans didn't sit well with him. I decided to try a different approach.

"That Webber family is something else, isn't it? And Desmond is a real piece of work. He's got a fucking career in Hollywood if he wants it." Moggio just snorted. "He had me going with that whole cognitive disabilities act of his."

"He's an asshole," said Moggio. Encouraged by his response, as minimal as it was, I pushed for more.

"So, who killed who?" I said.

"We're not going to get into that," said Moggio. He looked past me through the windshield, scanning the horizon for any sign of my Jeep. "Where the fuck is he?" he said.

"I don't actually know," I replied. "I'm just following directions here. Desmond is big on people following directions." Moggio snorted again.

"Desmond Webber couldn't pour piss out of a boot if the directions were written on the boot's heel," he said. Moggio seemed to be in a bad mood all of a sudden. So I thought it was probably best that I not point out that to Desmond seemed to have us where he wanted us.

"Okay," I said. "At least tell me what that whole charade with Philip was about. Why go through all that effort to fake his death?"

"You got a problem with faking deaths?" he said, giving me a weird smile.

"This isn't about me," I said.

"You're involved," said Moggio. He paused for a moment, seeming to reflect. "I mean, imagine my surprise, when I saw you with Barry Justice."

"Hey," I said, "believe me, that was an accident."

"There are no accidents," said Moggio.

"Well, I'm here to tell you that that was an accident. I ran into Justice in a Home Depot, of all places."

"I know exactly where you met him," said Moggio. I didn't understand.

"You mean you were working with Justice?" He ignored my question.

"Where the fuck is Desmond?" he demanded. No sooner had the question issued from his mouth than I saw my Jeep parked on the side of the road up a hundred yards or so.

"There he is," I said. I pulled the Mercedes up behind my Jeep and reached for the keys to cut the engine.

"Keep it running," said Moggio. He shifted uncomfortably in his seat and I could tell that the wound to his leg was giving him problems. We watched as Desmond got out of the car and began to approach us. I didn't see a weapon in Desmond's hand, but that didn't mean he didn't have one. He walked to the passenger side of the car and Moggio rolled down the window.

"Where's the report?" said Moggio.

"Nice to see you, too, Mr. Moggio," said Desmond, a broad smile on his face.

"Cut the shit," said Moggio. "My leg hurts, I need to get into a prone position and I didn't bring enough pain medication with me. So I'm starting to feel a bad mood coming on." He pointed the gun at Desmond. "What I'm trying to say, here, is that my patience is running a little thin."

"Well, I'm sorry to hear that," said Desmond. "You got my package?"

Moggio gave a big old theatrical snap of his fingers. "I knew I forgot something," he said. Desmond wasn't smiling anymore. "I left it with Philip back at the van," said Moggio.

"Funny thing," said Desmond "that's where I left the report." They looked at each other for a moment. "Okay," said Desmond, "we'll send Fargo here back for both of them. You can stay here with me." Moggio was already shaking his head. My, my I thought, such a gloomy atmosphere of mistrust.

"It hurts too much getting in and out of the car," said Moggio. "Why don't you climb in and we'll all ride back together?" Desmond looked back up the road to where my car was parked.

"See," he said, "I don't like to leave Mama and Vee alone."

"Then we all go back," said Moggio. Desmond hesitated a moment.

"All right," he said. "Just hold on a minute." He walked back to my Jeep and got into a conversation with his mother, which lasted for several minutes and seemed to get heated.

"Still think Desmond is the brains behind the operation?" said Moggio. He looked at me for a second and began shaking his head back and forth slowly as though I was as stupid as they came. I may *be* stupid as they come.

"It's the old lady," said Moggio. He laughed. "You really aren't much of a detective, are you?"

"That's what I've been trying to tell everyone," I replied. "Do you actually have this package that Desmond's looking for?" I didn't remember Philip leaving with a package in his hands.

"It's a very small package," said Moggio. He pulled a set of keys from his jacket pocket and jiggled them.

"What, it's a key?" I said.

Moggio smiled.

"Yeah, " he said. "The key to a safe-deposit box."

"And this safe-deposit box, let me guess, it was Lashona's, right?" A look of surprised appreciation came over Moggio's face.

"Very good, Fargo," he said. "I underestimated you."

"So, there's cash in this safe-deposit box? Is that it?" I asked.

Moggio shrugged.

"Could be," he said. "I think it's more likely that there are instructions and how to get cash in the safe-deposit box. I suspect we're talking about a lot more cash than would actually fit in a safe-deposit box. Or it might be a series of keys to other safe-deposit boxes. I don't know. I know Lashona was a clever woman. Takes after her mother."

"Is this insurance money?" I said. "The inheritance Desmond was talking about?"

"No," said Moggio. "This is actually hush money."

"Hush money for what?" I said.

"I've probably said too much already," he said. "That's why they call it hush money. Hit the horn. This is taking way too long." He readjusted his position once again, his face twisting into a tight grimace as he did so.

"If it makes you feel any better, I think the young man who shot you, won't be doing it anymore. I know the old man won't. Beste, I mean. I didn't want to say anything in front of Philip, but his dad's head is sitting in my refrigerator."

"Really?" said Moggio almost bored. "Philip will be just devastated. That young girl likes to slice and dice, doesn't she?" I didn't get this for a second.

"You mean Venetia?" I said. "You think she cut off Beste's head?" Moggio shrugged.

"She cut off Justice's balls, didn't she?"

"She did?" I said.

"Rumor has it," said Moggio, shrugging again. Man, this was all coming just a bit too fast. Venetia had decapitated Beste? And castrated Justice? It just didn't seem right at all, if that was the case. My miscalculation about the Webber family was approaching orders of magnitude.

The tirade between Desmond and his mother had finally come to an end and Desmond was walking back toward the Mercedes. He didn't appear happy. He walked around to my side of the car, opened the door to the back seat, then got in next to Moggio.

"Okay," he said. "Let's go." I was beginning to wonder if either party had really thought this thing all the way through. So okay, once again, I pulled a U-turn and headed back towards the van.

"I think with a little more trust you two could probably accomplish this switch without quite so much mileage involved," I said. That's when I found out that Desmond still had his gun with him, because he rapped me with it in the back of the head, delivering such a sharp pain that my ears rang and my eyes started to water immediately.

"Just drive the fucking car," said Desmond. Like I said, he wasn't in a good mood. And it wasn't about to get any better.

I saw a figure walking toward us along the side of the road. The closer we got the more familiar the figure got. It was Philip Beste hoofing it in our direction, vanless and hostageless.

"What the fuck is he doing?" said Desmond.

"Do you have a policy on picking up hitchhikers?" I asked Moggio eyeing him in the rearview mirror.

"You want me to smack you in the head again?" said Desmond. "Stop the motherfucking car."

I pulled the car over to the side and waited as Philip approached. He didn't seem to be in any hurry. I didn't think he had good news. I didn't like the looks of this. What had happened to Maud? If this little bastard had done anything to hurt her, I made up my mind that I was going to run him down with his favorite vehicle. I didn't care how many blows to the head I had to take in the process.

Philip walked to Moggio's window and Moggio slid it down.

"She took the van," said Philip.

"Fuck," said Desmond.

"What do you mean, she took the van?" said Moggio.

"She told me she had to go to the bathroom," said Moggio.

"Jesus," said Desmond. "And you fell for *that*? Why didn't just tell her to piss in the back of the van? Or piss her damn pants, for Christ's sake."

"She didn't have to piss," said Philip, almost plaintive. "She said this whole thing was literally scaring the shit out of her, man. What was I supposed to do?"

"Fucking idiot," said Desmond.

"Get in," said Moggio. Philip got in the passenger seat next to me. He wiped his bloody nose with his sleeve. Then pulled the visor down to look at himself in the mirror affixed to it.

"Fucking cunt," he said.

"So where's my fucking van," said Desmond.

"I drove her to a public restroom back up the road," said Philip. "I went in with her to make sure there was no other way out of the place, then waited for her outside by the door. But she didn't come out. I called her couple of times and got no answer. So I went in after her. I pushed open the door of the stall she went into and I see her hanging there by her arms. And she kicks me in the head with both of her feet. I wake up a few minutes later, at least I thought it was a few minutes, and I'm laying on the floor and my gun's gone. So I got up and walked out of the bathroom and the van's gone, too. So I start walking."

"Shit, said Desmond. "She could be off the island by now."

"Let's not panic," said Moggio. "I don't think she'd leave the new man in her life, would she Fargo?"

"What, do you think she's stupid?" I said. "Of course she left."

"No, I don't think she did," said Moggio. Desmond still hadn't brought up the ANFO. Maybe it was something he didn't want Moggio to know about. Maybe it had been meant for Moggio and his young protégé. "Can we contact her?" said Moggio.

"She's got Desmond's cell phone," I said. "Remember, Desmond? And the ANFO, remember?"

"ANFO?" said Moggio, looking with interest to Desmond in the back seat. "As in explosives?"

"Yeah," I said. "According to Desmond here, the van is rigged with the stuff like a Thanksgiving turkey and Grandma's got her finger on the button."

"Well, that's interesting," said Moggio.

"Insurance," said Desmond. "Protection. I didn't want Fargo, or his girlfriend driving off with the van."

"So, now, the report that I came for is in the van with Miss Gonne, along with the package you want in exchange for the report."

"Seems that way," said Desmond. "Thanks to your partner here."

"But the woman doesn't know these valuable items are in the van. She's got to be more worried about getting out of the van at the first good opportunity, thinking you might blow it up, right?" Desmond gave a grudging not of his head.

"I guess," he said.

"Which means," said Moggio, "she probably didn't drive it very far before abandoning it. So, we drive around until we find it. Or her." He pulled a cell phone from his pocket. "And maybe we can even expedite this process. What's the cell phone number?" Desmond told him the number and Moggio punched it in. He waited a few minutes, frowned, then snapped the phone shut. "Start driving," he said to me. "Maud apparently doesn't feel like talking at the moment."

I pulled the car back onto the road and Moggio's phone rang. He opened it, listened for a moment, then handed the phone up to me.

"It's for you," he said. It took the phone from him and said "Hello?"

"Stephen?" It was, of course, Maud. "Are you all right?"

"I'm fine," I said. "Are you okay?"

"Yeah," she said. "I take it you found Philip."

"He found us," I said, looking at the blood smearing and dried on the side of Philip's face. He looked like he was about twelve years old now.

"Tell her to give us the van and we'll let both of you go," said Moggio.

"Tell her to give us the fucking van or your brains will be on the windshield," said Desmond.

"Can't both of you see I'm on the phone?" I said.

"Stephen," said Maud, "what should I do?"

"I can't talk right now," I said. "I'll call you back in five minutes." I hung up the phone and, once again, pulled the car to the side of the road. I shut the car down and turned around in my seat to look at Moggio and Desmond.

"I think the leverage has shifted here a bit," I said.

"Like I said," said Desmond, "I'm gonna shift your brains to a new location."

I heard the gun go off, and, for a split second, I expected to see in the last possible instant of my existence my brains splattered over the windshield and dashboard in front of me. Instead, the window next to what was left of Desmond's head was suddenly splattered with his blood and chunks of his skull.

"Jesus fucking Christ," said Philip, sitting up in his seat, horrified and fascinated at the same time.

"I don't see that we need to deal with him any longer," said Moggio. The smoke was still issuing from the barrel of the gun he had just killed Desmond with. "You were saying something about leverage?" He smiled at me and turned the gun in my direction. Well, of course, I had *thought* the advantage had shifted to me, but, once again, I had underestimated my adversary. I cleared my throat, which took some exertion.

"The point I was going to make was that we, Maud, that is, has what you want."

Moggio considered my statement for a moment.

"And we have what she wants," he said.

"I think that's overstating the case," I said.

"Fargo," said Moggio, "you underestimate yourself."

"Well, I don't underestimate Maud's intelligence. You mentioned it yourself."

"And you know what, Fargo? I like you. I really do. I have no wish to harm you or Maud, but I've gone to a lot of trouble to get what I want. I just killed this fool to make sure I get what I want. I'm in deep. I'm willing to do things that I might not have been willing to do in the past. Like kill you and Maud."

"Okay, okay" I said. "I get it. You're serious." As if Desmond's slumped and steaming corpse hadn't made that clear already. "What do you want me to do?"

"I want you to call Maud, tell her to bring the van here. We'll take what we need from it and get out of your hair."

"You won't be tempted to eliminate us? I mean, we *are* witnesses."

"To what?" said Moggio.

"For one thing," I said, "Desmond's murder."

"Murder?" said Moggio. "From where I'm sitting, I saved your life. Desmond was about to blow your brains out. I'm an ex-cop. I think I know a credible threat when I hear one. Philip here will back me up."

"Yeah, but there's something else going on."

"The less you know about that the better."

"I guess," I said. "But if you know anything about me at all, like you claim to, you know that I can't live with knowing less."

Moggio smiled and shook his head.

"You're too much, you know that? What, do you want to die? This would be the real thing, not some vacation."

"How about if you tell me and I promise not to tell the police."

"Maybe you'll write another book, huh?"

"No, no more books."

"Call Maud," said Moggio, the casual joviality disappearing from his countenance. "Tell her to bring the van now. Cops patrol this island. Hell, they've got a post on the island. We can't be sitting here with a dead body." He pointed the gun at my head. "Or two dead bodies." I glanced quickly in the rearview at the carnage behind me. Yeah that was what dead looked like all right. And I decided I didn't want any part of it. I took out the phone and went through the incoming calls menu, highlighting the most recent call and pushed the talk button. Halfway through the first ring Maud answered.

"Stephen?" she said.

"Yes," I said.

"I found an envelope in the van and opened it."

"Maud," I said. "You need to drive the van back to where it was before."

"No way," said Maud.

"Uh, Maud, I've got a situation here."

"I think I found what Desmond's trading," she said. "It's a scientific report of some kind. All I read was the executive summary, but I think it's what you might call a smoking gun memo."

"Maud," I said, "you need to bring the van back."

"Or what?" she said.

"Or Moggio might shoot me," I replied.

"Moggio," said Maud. "What's *he* doing here?"

"Right at this moment, he's pointing a gun at my head."

"I *knew* it," said Maud. "I knew that bastard—"

"Maud," I said. "Bring the van." I hung up before she could say anything else.

"So?" said Moggio. I shrugged.

"You heard me. I told her. She's a very independent woman. She'll either bring it or she won't."

"She won't be happy if I have to go looking for her," said Moggio.

"I tried to impress that point upon her," I said. "I don't think we want to be driving around anyway. Not with all that gore in the backseat." There weren't a lot of people around, but it only took one. And Moggio was right about that police station on the island. I remembered it from my childhood.

"This place gives me the creeps," said Philip. It wasn't clear whom he was speaking to.

"It's pretty much a summer place," I said, although I'm not sure why I thought I had to explain anything to Philip Beste.

Moggio looked at his watch.

"Here she comes," said Philip.

The van was rolling slowly toward us, which meant that Maud was driving the wrong way on a one-way street. It didn't make a lot of difference on a day like this with almost no traffic. I wondered if she knew what she was doing, if she was trying to attract attention. She pulled up beside my window. I saw that hers was rolled down, so I did the same. I couldn't tell if Maud could make out the condition of Desmond's body or not. The windows were so darkly tinted that it was difficult to see through them.

"Here's how this is going to work," she said. Before she could say more, however, I felt the barrel of Moggio's gun press against the back of my head.

"The way this is going to work is that you're going to hand over what we want, right now, or Fargo is going to be in no condition to drive." She looked at me, a weak smile on her lips.

"I don't have it anymore," she said. "I hid it." The gun didn't move away from my head.

"That was not smart," said Moggio.

"Let Stephen go," she said. "We'll drive off and I'll call you to tell you where it is."

"I don't think so," said Moggio. "You tell me where it is, I'll let Fargo go." I wanted to shake my head "no," but with the barrel of the gun pressing against it, I was reluctant to move at all. "On the other hand, if you don't tell me what I want to know in ten seconds, Fargo is going to join Desmond." Moggio reached across and hit the button to lower the window where Desmond sat. As he did so, what was left of Desmond's head plopped out the window. I saw Maud blanch a little, but she didn't panic.

"Jesus H. Christ," said Philip Beste. "What the fuck is that?"

He was looking ahead of us, again, and I could appreciate the reason for his astonishment. It was quite a sight.

Venetia and her grandmother were approaching. Venetia was sort of meandering off the edge of the road, stopping every few seconds to turn and look back at the trail she had made through the snow. Then, smiling, pleased with herself, she would begin walking again, repeating the cycle. Her grandmother seemed to pay no attention to her, but stared grimly ahead, putting all her effort into propelling the wheelchair forward, making very slow progress indeed. She had her oxygen mask on her face and was making about a mile per hour.

"It's a fucking freak show," said Moggio, mumbling it to himself. "Where's the report?" he said to Maud. "Tell me right now, or I swear to God I'll kill him."

"Him," I think, referred to me.

I could see that Maud was beginning to waver.

"Oh, shit," said Philip. He was still watching Venetia and the old woman approach, probably the least vigorous and encouraging cavalry I had ever seen.

But then, the real cavalry showed up.

Who says you can never find a cop when you want one? This, unfortunately, wasn't a cop, exactly. It was a car with U.S. Coast Guard written on the door, but it was close enough. The car sort of rolled along with the old woman's wheelchair for a few yards. She appeared to be ignoring it and its occupant. Venetia was in some other world, still making her tracks through the snow and turning every ten seconds or so to admire them.

As we all watched in fascination, the U.S. Coast Guard vehicle stopped and a man got out. He wore what looked like a blue work uniform and a baseball cap with the words "U.S. Coast Guard" written on it. He began to walk alongside the rolling wheelchair, not touching it, but trying, it appeared, to get something out of the old woman.

"This is just great," said Moggio.

Venetia had now noticed the man from the Coast Guard vehicle and had ceased her frolicking in the snow. She fell in perhaps twenty feet or so behind the wheelchair, walking with her head down. I saw the man pull out a cell phone from his jacket pocket. He continued to walk, but he was also talking into the phone now.

"Any minute now," I said, "this area of the island is going to be crawling with cops. Well, maybe not crawling with them. But we'll get a few anyway." I could see that the truth of this was sinking in on Philip Beste.

"We need to get out of here," he said, turning to Moggio seated behind him. Moggio moved the gun from my head and pointed it at Maud.

"Where the fuck is the report?" he said.

"I'll show you," Maud said quickly. I was still staring at the spectacle in front of me. Venetia had closed the distance between herself and the man walking alongside her grandmother's wheelchair. Suddenly, I saw her pull a large knife from inside her coat and lunge for the man. From his reaction, it was clear that she had stabbed him. Now all of us, except for Maud, who was oriented in the other direction, were looking at the drama unfolding before us in the middle of the road. The first stab wound to the man had not been lethal, not enough to stop him. He was now trying to run away from Venetia, who was pursuing him, rage in her face, the knife, which looked to have at least a ten-inch blade on it, on high. We could see the man screaming into his phone. He was holding his back with his right hand just about a kidney level, obviously the spot where the thrust of Venetia's blade had found its mark.

The old woman had stopped. I could see her fooling around with something in her lap. She wasn't paying the slightest attention to her granddaughter's attack on the Coast Guard guy.

"Crazy bitch," said Moggio. I couldn't tell if he was talking about Venetia or her grandmother.

"Jesus, Maud," I screamed. "Get out of the van."

"Oh, fuck," said Moggio. Maud hadn't moved. I jumped out of the Mercedes.

Moggio seemed to have forgotten that he was going to shoot me. The dynamic had changed. He had other priorities. I opened the driver-side door of the van and pulled Maud from her seat. From the corner of my eye, I could see Philip Beste spill out of the car door on the other side and scramble away from the Mercedes. Moggio's door opened, but I didn't see him emerge. His leg probably prevented him from moving quickly. I yanked Maud along with me and started running up the road. We had gotten maybe fifty or sixty feet from the van when I felt the intense thermal blast of the ANFO even before I heard it. Maud and I were both thrown to the pavement. A few seconds later, debris was falling all around us. I lay on top of Maud, waiting for the fallout to stop. When it did, I turned back to see the flaming chassis of the van, still sitting almost comically on undamaged tires, but with nothing else of the vehicle left intact. The blast had been so strong that it had almost completely destroyed the Mercedes as well. Philip Beste lay on the side of the road. I couldn't tell if he was dead or just unconscious. He certainly didn't seem to be moving. I couldn't see Moggio. No doubt, he was still in the back seat of the car, consumed by the roaring flames and black smoke.

Beyond this vision of destruction, I saw Venetia and her grandmother just watching. Venetia seemed to have completely forgotten the Coast Guard guy for the moment. She stared transfixed at the flaming vehicles, the knife at her side. The Coast Guard guy was now staggering more slowly in our direction. He seemed not to be interested in the flaming vehicles, but he had other problems, after all. About five seconds after this thought crossed my mind, I saw him fall, first to his knees, then, pitching forward, on his face. Just like Lashona had gone down.

"You okay?" I screamed at Maud, my own voice sounding like it was coming from several yards away. She nodded vigorously. "Get help," I said. "Flag down a car or something." Maud nodded again and got to her feet. She seemed undamaged, except for the mental shock of the experience. She began to jog in the direction away from the cars and in the opposite direction from Venetia and her grandmother.

I got up and ran to the inert form of Philip Beste. When I got to him, I felt at his throat for a pulse, where I found what to my untrained hands appeared to be a relatively healthy heartbeat. Philip's eyes were half open and blood was streaming from both of his nostrils. I patted his clothing, found his gun in the inside jacket pocket and took it from him. I tried to get closer to the Mercedes to see if I could help Moggio, but it was hopeless. The heat was too intense. He had managed to get one leg out of the car and his foot extended to the ground from the open door. The blast had blown his shoe away. That was all I could see of him.

I stood up and started walking back to where Venetia and her grandmother were still rooted to the spot. When grandma saw me approaching, she turned her wheelchair around and started wheeling herself in the opposite direction. But her effort was feeble. She wasn't going to get far.

When Venetia saw her grandmother turn and retreat, she seemed to snap out of her fascination with the burning cars. She started moving in the direction of the prone Coast Guard guy.

"Stop," I shouted and started running toward Venetia. She ignored me, continuing to walk in the direction of the injured man. I yelled again for her to stop and ran faster. She was at him now. She fell to her knees, straddling his body. I was perhaps thirty feet from her. She grabbed the man by the hair and pulled his head back, so that the guy was looking right at me. Whether he saw me, or saw anything, I couldn't tell. He was certainly incapable at that moment of defending himself from the ferocity of Venetia's attack. She screamed savagely and put the knife at the man's throat. She looked at me for a split second, just appearing to notice my presence for the first time. Then she raised the knife as if it was a meat cleaver. Her hand started to descend and I pulled the trigger of Philip's gun.

Venetia's head snapped back and her knife rattled to the pavement. She lay stretched unnaturally back, her legs bent under her, her arms flared out at her sides.

The bullet had caught her under the chin. I stepped up to her and I kicked the knife away. A soft gurgle came from her throat. She still had a smile on her face. Not demonic or anything. Almost sweet, almost innocent. Then the life went out of her eyes.

THIRTY-FOUR

THAT'S A WRAP?

I was tired. Maud was tired. But at least we were alive. I couldn't speak for the respective energy levels of Philip Beste and the grandmother of Venetia—mother to the late Desmond and Lashona Webber. But they had also emerged from this mess alive, at least temporarily. That was more than could be said for any of the other characters in this affair.

We came to find out, by the way, that the old woman's name was Priscilla, or "Cilla," as her kids called her. Or used to call her, when they were alive. This tender anecdote was related by Cilla's defense attorney during her trial, as part of the mosaic, the detailed tapestry of legal subtleties involved in making Cilla Desmond appear "sympathetic."

Speaking of legal subtleties, can I please skip the machinations of the criminal justice system as it worked its magic on Cilla Desmond? You've all seen enough cop shows, right? You know how all this stuff works. Suffice it to say there was a trial, a media scandal-slash-circus, and, as is usually the case, an unsatisfactory resolution.

Priscilla plea-bargained down to some ridiculously innocuous crime, went through enough of a trial for the case to go to the jury, then died of respiratory failure during the jury's deliberations. They probably would not have convicted her, anyway. The only real evidence of anything against her was her ownership of the gun that was used to kill Lashona, and Priscilla's lawyers argued that her son, Desmond, had taken the gun without her permission and used it to kill Lashona without Priscilla's knowledge. Desmond, of course, was not around to refute this testimony.

Philip Beste was initially arrested on an illegal weapons possession charge, but even that was eventually dropped. The only real evidence against Philip was our testimony, which, frankly had nothing to do with his possession of a firearm. He had threatened us, of course, but it turned out that his threats were largely without substance. The "casual hostage" ploy had been nothing more than a scam, as we had suspected. Leia Fountain had never been murdered in a 7-11 parking lot; in fact, she went on to marry Greg Mineo, the young man she had been sitting with in the coffee shop. Philip Beste disappeared shortly after his trial and soon after the bodies of his quasi-siblings, Jordan and Bryce, were found partially buried not far from the "farmhouse" where we had briefly been detained by the Bestes. Apparently, it had not been his cop buddies that Moggio had called to fetch The Beastie Boys after our escape.

Some things did emerge from the trial and from the media investigations that the trial stimulated. And you probably want to know what those things are. So, here we go in, let's say, chronological order, an order from which I reserve the right to divert, often.

First, Lashona Webber.

In doing some medical research only partly inspired by her daughter's condition (about which more later) Lashona learned that a renegade scientist from some pharmaceutical company had developed a theory, which he assured Lashona he could support with facts, that there was a direct link between the use of a substance called Thimerasol—which contained lead and had for years been used as a preservative in children's vaccines such as that which prevented measles—and autism in those same children. Now, during the trial of Priscilla Webber, information emerged that this scientist's credentials and work product were marginal, and his status as a neglected and ultimately disgraced employee didn't put his motives above suspicion.

But journalism being what it is these days, that had never bothered Lashona. She had a story. An exposé. That was all that mattered. Meanwhile, the pharmaceutical company learned—through the strategic leakage of its disgruntled scientist—that this scandal was about to break loose. Realizing they stood to lose billions of dollars even if the scientist's charges proved baseless, they mobilized all of their resources—ethical and non—to counterattack. One tactic in this counterattack involved an investigation into Lashona's background, through which the drug company honchos learned that Lashona had a really interesting family arrangement.

Interesting fact #1: Lashona's daughter, Venetia, whom Lashona had produced at the age of fifteen, had severe psychological problems. We're not talking your garden-variety adolescent female complaints here. This was not mere autism or ADHD as Lashona had sort of acknowledged publicly and grudgingly. Those illnesses, of course, were bad enough. But Venetia was way beyond those.

As a pre-teen she had attacked a male health care professional at the mental health facility where she was staying for one of her periodic "diagnostic" admissions. She had "attacked" people previously, of course. Always men, always, or almost always, figures of authority. These had usually been kicking and punching episodes, with occasional thrown objects. But the incident with the mental health facility orderly escalated the attacks to a new level of ferocity and lethalness. Venetia had discovered that she liked cutlery. And she liked to use it to remove the body parts of men. It had only been a couple of fingers in the case of the orderly. He had knelt to the floor to retrieve something from under Venetia's bed, holding on to the top of the night table at the bedside for support. At that point, Venetia had pulled out the butcher knife—it was never clear where she had obtained the knife—and, in one efficient blow severed the pinky and ring finger of the man's left hand.

Subsequent attacks followed. Venetia gradually moved on to larger and more vital body parts. She was institutionalized intermittently and had been improving somewhat through massive dosages of medication. But this young lady was never going to be mainstream. So, when she wasn't in the hospital, she spent most of her time in the highly dysfunctional environment that was the Webber household, which included Uncle Desmond and Grandma Webber and, in absentia, Lashona.

Desmond Webber was three years older than Lashona and had pretty much been a fuck-up his entire life. He broke into his first home as an eight-year-old and robbed his first liquor store at thirteen. He spent time in various juvie facilities from the ages fourteen to seventeen, when he enlisted in the Marines, who for some reason conveniently ignored his delinquencies. They were happy to have him. He was bright, he had at least a superficial affinity for the order and discipline of the military, and he was a black man that looked good in the uniform. A poster child for military diversity.

He saw action in the first Gulf War as a munitions expert, so perhaps his claim to having suffered the adverse medical effects of that war were true. But what Desmond basically was was a con man of limited skill and success. His scams were usually small time and often involved the cooperation of his invalid mother, a figure who could inspire sympathy if sufficiently motivated.

A typical scam would involve Desmond pushing Cilla around a mall parking lot in her wheelchair, claiming to any poor sucker that would listen that their car had been "hijacked" by a younger relative and could the mark please give them twenty dollars for carfare. No thanks, he didn't want to call the police. This was a family matter. Desmond would deal with the little prankster when he got home, etc., etc. Really small time stuff, until . . . .

Desmond found out about the Thimerasol gig when a couple of investigators showed up at the Webber residence in Bradenton. Desmond was a criminal and a sociopath, but he wasn't stupid. He managed to get the investigators to reveal more than they should have about the Thimerasol situation—he could play dumb with the best of them, trotting out his framed honorable discharge from the Marine Corps, and regaling his visitors with his heroic service in the Gulf. And, this being right at the peak of war fever for Iraq II, he usually held forth to a sympathetic audience. Desmond, I may have neglected to point out, was a major mama's boy. When Priscilla and her husband divorced in the late eighties, Desmond had preferred to stay with his mother even though her parenting skills were almost nonexistent and Desmond's father would almost certainly have provided a better standard of living. Mama's boy that he was, he spilled the beans to Cilla about what his sister was up to.

At this point, we move to the matriarch of this little terrorist cell, Priscilla Webber. She: 1. was not happy living the precarious life of a day-to-day scam artist accomplice, and 2. had always hated her daughter Lashona for, A., her success, B., her daughter's preference for her father and, C., for saddling her with her deranged granddaughter Venetia, who could be a sweet girl and was tremendously loyal, but, let's face it, was a handful. Living with a psychotic—a paranoid schizophrenic in this case—wasn't easy, even though Lashona made it somewhat worth the inconvenience by sending a monthly check for the rent of the house they occupied. So, mom and her boy put their evil little heads together and came up with a scheme.

It was pretty basic. They planned to extort money from the pharmaceutical company. Desmond initiated the contact with the company, only to be advised that the company planned to call the authorities. *Whoa!* said Desmond. *Y'all are misunderstandin' mah intentions. What I'm doin' is troubleshootin' for y'all. I've got information about Lashona. You can use it to pressure her to abandon her investigation.*

But the pharmaceutical company wasn't buying it.

Time for Plan B. Travel north to Detroit and make themselves so obnoxious that Lashona—who obviously had her own scam working here—would pay her own family off to get them out of her life. So, it's load up the van for the drive north along I-75 to Motown.

Act II.

Dramatis Personae:

Dr. Robert Astrachan
Charles Beste
Andrew Moggio
Lashona Webber
Barry Justice

Scene: Detroit, mid-March 2004

Lashona could no longer stand Barry Justice. She wanted out of the marriage. But there was this whole community property issue. Hey, it had seemed like a good idea to forgo the prenup at the time. Barry was making relatively big bucks as a local TV legend, while she was earning just over union scale as a newbie street reporter. Of course, fortunes, as they have a tendency to, reversed. Lashona became a media darling—there was talk of her making the jump to the networks—and Barry became a major has-been. Lashona had outgrown Barry. And she had this story, which, by the way, she knew was a bullshit story. Her pharmaceutical company scientist source was a crackpot, at best, or maybe an extortionist in his own right. But he had this report and she had the attention of the pharmaceutical company management, who, though they suspected there wasn't much to the report, really didn't know. Even if it was bogus, it could cost millions—billions even—in settlements, legal fees, public relations damage control and lost sales. So, the measly sum of ten million dollars that Lashona was willing to settle for not to run with this story was, well, a bargain.

Cut to the offices of Robert Astrachan, M.D., who, if he had to listen to the whining of one more neurotic asshole sitting on his couch, was going to, no shit, jump out of his own fucking window. Today, however, Dr. Astrachan was smiling because, 1. He was boarding a flight later that afternoon for sunny, warm San Diego to give a presentation and, 2. He had just met with a couple of swell guys representing a pharmaceutical company that was being harassed by, no kidding, one of his patients, the lovely and talented and supremely neurotic Lashona Webber. The reps from the pharmaceutical company had come to him with a deal. They didn't call it that. They didn't explicitly mention a quid pro quo, but, well, what they wanted was dirt on Lashona Webber, so that they could basically threaten to destroy her career.

And, of course, Astrachan had the goods on Lashona. He knew, for example, that her daughter had graduated to, you guessed it, murder. That's right. Venetia had cut the throat of a parish priest in Bradenton, and, uh, removed his genitals. The cops thought it was some revenge thing, some altar boy getting back at the priest for molesting him. But Lashona knew different because she'd gotten a call from her brother telling her that the day of the priest's murder Venetia has slipped his custody (which wasn't hard to do) and after several hours had returned home covered in blood and with a bloody twelve inch chef's knife tucked in her belt, and a big smile on her face. By the way, there really was no deep-seated, potentially redemptive motive for Venetia's behavior. She was just fucking nuts. She didn't even know the priest.

Thinking she was protected by the doctor-client privilege, Lashona spilled her guts on this to Dr. Astrachan. She also, over the past few months, had told him of her disintegrating relationship with her husband and of her love affair with—well, who do you think? I'll give you a moment. Theme song from "Jeopardy" plays for ten seconds here. Wait for it.

It's not exactly a love match. Unfortunately, Lashona, whose father was white, had this daddy thing going with all the men in her life. Like Barry Justice, Charles Beste was somewhat beyond the prime of life, somewhat paunchy, somewhat in decline. The affair didn't last long, but Beste was around long enough to learn that Lashona was on to a potentially big score with the pharmaceutical company. Being in hock himself up to his receding hairline, he was obviously very interested.

And then there was Charlie Beste's old buddy, Drew Moggio. Beste told Moggio, an ex-cop with a drinking problem and a sorry excuse for a private investigations business, about the potential windfall. Beste didn't do this out of generosity, but because he could use Moggio's special skills. He had resources. He had access. And, maybe up until now, he just hadn't been properly motivated. You may see a theme developing here:

The Final Big Score That Will Make Everybody Well

And that would be pretty much on the money, so to speak. Anyway, Lashona tells Beste who tells Moggio that she wants to "get something" on her husband so that she can divorce him before he learns about her potential windfall.

And, in the course of tailing Justice around town, Moggio noticed that he met with me. Now Stephen Fargo was on the radar screen, which is no easy trick for a dead man. Moggio took a photo of me around to all his cop buddies and one guy who had been around during the eighties and early nineties recognized me. So now he really *is* intrigued. A dead guy of some minor celebrity returns and has lunch with Barry Justice. And I wasn't just any dead guy, but a guy with a reputation, deserved or not—well, I can tell you that it wasn't for having any mystical investigative powers. Moggio had no idea of course that my meeting with Mr. Justice was purely accidental. He thought that Justice had lured me out of deep, deep retirement to help him relieve his wife of her anticipated treasure.

Then a wrench got thrown into the works. Grandma Cilla, Brother Desmond and Daughter Vee show up at the Justice/Webber residence. Lashona tells them they can't stay there. She's leaving for San Diego on very important business. Desmond tells her all about the visit from the pharmaceutical guys and threatens to give them the information they want if Lashona doesn't cut him in on the deal.

Is everyone with me so far?

At some point during all this, Venetia wanders off, leaving those now famous footprints in the snow leading away from the house. Everyone scrambles to find her, which they eventually do, walking along the shoulder of Telegraph Road. Lashona hustles the clan off to the airport motel demanding that they sit tight until she gets back from San Diego. Solemn promises from Desmond, yes, but with the admonition that he wants to be in on the big bucks from the pharmaceutical company. Yeah, yeah. Just sit tight, says

Lashona, who then hops on a plane and heads to San Diego to murder Robert Astrachan, who, as I've said, was trying to cut his own deal.

Back in Detroit, Desmond gets antsy and decides to visit Barry Justice, see if he can expedite things. Of course, this means packing up the entire family into the family van and driving over to Bloomfield Hills.

The meeting doesn't go well. Desmond and Justice (who is really just learning about all of this and takes Desmond's insinuations about Lashona personally) get into a heated argument and then, a wrestling match. Of course, Justice's wrestling days were long over. A man in his condition should not have tried any more strenuous pinning than attaching a boutonnière to his lapel. Anyway, Justice suffers an apparent heart attack and dies. Which wouldn't have been the end of the world as far as the Webbers were concerned, except that the incident triggers a crisis for Cilla Webber, who goes into a seizure, requiring Desmond's immediate and full attention. And while he is reviving Mama, Venetia, left to her own devices—in this case the device was another chef's knife from the Justice kitchen—gets into some corpse mutilation with the body of Barry Justice. That's right. The genitalia in the frying pan. Hey, what can I say? The woman is crazy. (During her trial, Cilla Webber defended her granddaughter's actions by saying that "the poor chile was hungry." Even the prosecutor decided not to pursue *that* line of questioning any further.)

The immediate crisis with Cilla passes and Desmond comes out of the bedroom to find Justice castrated and Venetia giggling in the corner like Regan from *The Exorcist.* Well, Desmond can't just call the police now and tell them Barry had had a heart attack. Emergency procedures for heart attack victims don't include castration, at least up to the current stage of medical knowledge. Once again, Desmond loads up the truck and heads back to the motel room, where he decides, belatedly, to sit tight and wait for Lashona's return.

Meanwhile, all these comings and goings had been observed by Moggio and Philip Beste, whom Moggio had suffered to tag along with him at the insistence of Charles Beste, who was, after all, bankrolling this operation. Seeing the Webber clan leave the Justice home in a cloud of exhaust and in what appeared to be something verging on panic, Moggio and Philip Beste entered the house to find Justice looking not so healthy on his spot there on the couch. You'll recall that shortly after this discovery, Philip Beste, using his baffling alias of Juan, called me. They wanted to know what I might have learned about the prospect of Lashona getting the money from the pharmaceutical company. They had also seen me hook up with Maud Gonne, and they wondered what that was all about. So Maud and I had our famous meeting with "Juan" at the Starbucks. Meanwhile, out in San Diego, Dr. Astrachan was opening the door of his suite to admit Lashona Webber, with whom he believed he was about to have consensual, energetic, maybe even therapeutic, sex.

And we know what happened to Dr. Astrachan. However, any satisfaction that Lashona derived from her disposal of the doctor was short-lived. Unbeknownst to her, Brother Desmond, whom Lashona had underestimated her entire life, had formed an alliance with Charles Beste, although it might in fact be more accurate to say that Cilla Webber had arranged the alliance. She had at least agreed to it and it wouldn't have happened without this agreement.

Because he suspected that the Webber family had been involved in foul play with regard to Barry Justice, Beste had leverage with the Webbers. And, given the lack of familial warmth in the Webber clan, they were already predisposed to inflict harm on the one successful person in the family. So, Desmond borrowed Grandma's rifle and headed to the TV station where Lashona worked, intending to shoot her as she exited the building. He thought this was preferable to doing the deed at Lashona's home. A sniper hit at the station would probably lead to the suspicion that it was a revenge hit by someone whom Lashona had pissed off because of her investigative reporting work. But when Maud and I showed up to meet with Lashona, Desmond got, well, confused for a moment, and his opportunity at the station was gone. He recovered after a call to Cilla, however, and took out his dear sister in front of the restaurant in the very presence of me and Maud.

How much of all this was true? A lot of it was prosecutorial speculation, so we didn't really know. Just like we didn't know who really killed Jordan and Bryce, although, given the presence of Charles Beste's head in my refrigerator, there was a high likelihood that the Webber's were involved. For months after these events, Maud and I found ourselves asking each other about incidents that never seemed to have been satisfactorily explained.

"Who do you think was in Justice's house that first day you visited it?" Maud would ask, for example. "You know, when you saw the curtain move?" And of course, I couldn't say with any certainty. Philip Beste? Moggio?

"Why would Philip and Moggio go through such an elaborate charade to try to convince us that they didn't know each other?" I would say to Maud. "They seemed to me to be inflicting actual wounds."

"Maybe they really didn't like each other," said Maud.

"And maybe Jordan shot Moggio at the farmhouse thinking that he and his father and brothers could disappear with whatever they thought they were going to get from Desmond before Moggio was recovered enough to follow them," I said. Maud would shrug.

With everybody dead or disappeared, it seemed unlikely that we would ever know.

And speaking of being dead and disappeared, all of this thrust me once again into the public spotlight, although the glare was nowhere near as intense as I had anticipated. It was, in fact, a very soft, intimate sort of light, maybe even candlelight. Hold that candlelight thought for just a moment.

Some people were surprised, of course, to learn that I had not died somewhere in the Bermuda triangle. (One old friend of mine, Claude Nickle, called to say that he *knew* I had not had not been lost in the Bermuda Triangle because the universe would not forgive such a trite demise, whatever that meant.) A couple of stories ran on the local TV news about my faked death, and Mitch Albom, *Detroit Free Press* columnist and—in case you just stepped off the Intergalactic Express from Rigel Kentaurus—author of *Tuesdays with Morrie, The Five People You Meet in Heaven* and other unspeakably sentimental drivel, called to interview me for a column he wanted to write about my experience, but I declined to cooperate in that. Maybe he wanted to know if I had met my five people in fake heaven. He wrote the column anyway, something about how I had become stuck in the late 1960s, something about the allure of "dropping out" for all baby boomers, something about a charming yet pathetic romanticism, something about everyone's secret desire for anonymity and irresponsibility, something about love and loss, something about the meaning of life. I like Mitch; he's a helluva columnist and a crackerjack sportswriter, but, he's gotta lighten up. Especially with that meaning-of-life stuff. We all know how I feel about that.

Other than that, the backlash was mild, indeed. The reaction to my faked death and reappearance ranged from perplexity to amusement. And I have to say, it's a little disappointing to have everybody sort of figuratively say, "What the hell, it's Stephen Fargo. What do you expect?"

On the other hand, there were so many more important things going on in the world. The war in Iraq, the infestation of the White House by human vermin, the travails of the contestants on "American Idol," the price of gas, the collective ADHD of the American public.

It was clear that it doesn't take much to see that the problems of three little people don't amount to a hill of beans in this crazy world.

Okay, I didn't actually say that to Maud as she sat across from me, the candlelight I had mentioned earlier gently illuminating our table. We were in one of Detroit's tonier restaurants, the Opus One, the kind of place I normally don't frequent for the same reason that I don't use valet parking, don't belong to a country club: I absolutely despise privilege of any kind. I used to come to places like this when I was a political consultant. Believe me, if the public ever really learned what their elected officials did with their time and their constituents' money, the Reign of Terror would look like a game of euchre. Hey, Mitch . . . you know that whole Meaning of Life thing? It can be summarized in four words: Slopping at the Trough.

But I digress. Maud looked particularly ravishing on this night. She wore skintight black velvet slacks, a long-sleeved, pearl-colored top with sequins and a scoop neck. She'd just had her hair trimmed and styled, although styled is probably the wrong word. It looked pretty casual in a breathtaking sort of way. She'd also had a fresh manicure and pedicure and her daily hour long runs had given her a great tan. I couldn't take my eyes off her.

We had finished dinner and Maud was alternating between sips of cappuccino and Amaretto while Mr. Blue Collar and Proud of It drank Bud from the bottle. The choice of restaurant had been Maud's idea. She was particularly fond of their rack of lamb, or, more precisely, their Rack of New Zealand Lamb a la Greque. And I had to admit, having chosen the same entrée, that it was worth the trip. Maud was gorgeous and carnivorous. What more could you ask for in a woman?

"Tell me about your family," she said. "Your mother and father."

"You mean the family I grew up with or the one I'm rumored to have been part of."

"The one you grew up with. Tell me the one important thing you remember about each of them."

The one important thing. That assumed there *was* one important thing about either of them. Maud could see I was struggling.

"Okay, how about the one thing each of them taught you?" she said.

"I wasn't close to my parents," I said.

"Everybody's close to their parents," Maud replied. "Even if they don't want to be."

"Well, I didn't feel close. I think my mother hated being a mother, which I don't blame her for. My father was just, I don't know, in his own world all the time. Neither one of them necessarily neglected me. I think they sensed that I wanted to be neglected."

"I'm aware of that in you," said Maud.

"Oh, you are, are you?"

"Yes. Ultimately, that's the reason that you faked your own death. You're a neglect junkie. You thrive on it, just like some houseplants."

I didn't recall that I'd ever been compared to a houseplant before. I tried to determine if this was a criticism or just an analysis. It certainly wasn't praise.

"So this was benign neglect," said Maud.

"Have you ever seen *Apocalypse Now*? I said.

"No. I don't like war movies."

"I don't think of it as a war movie," I said. "Anyway, at one point, the main character, a soldier-assassin named Willard, played by . . . who's that guy on *West Wing*? The President?"

"Martin Sheen."

"Right. Martin Sheen. Well the Martin Sheen character says, 'Everybody gets everything they want' or words to that effect. There's some irony, some cynicism involved in the statement."

"Yes," Maud announced suddenly, loudly and with conviction. I tried to remember what question I had asked. "You don't remember, do you?" she said, narrowing her eyes a bit. I tried to remember what I might have forgotten.

"Well," I said, "a lot has happened over the past few months." I was clearly lost. Totally and irrevocably. Way more lost than I had ever pretended to be in the middle of the Atlantic. Maud took another sip of Amaretto and smiled impishly at me. Normally, I can't tolerate impishness. Impishness shares the same zip code with perversity in my book. But Maud could pull it off.

"Yes, I will marry you," she said.

Now, don't get me wrong. This did not come as unwelcome news. Granted, I had pretty much resigned myself to the single life after Denise died. Not that I had renounced marriage. It simply had not occurred to me that I would ever get married again. And I didn't remember the proposal. Had I said the words in my sleep? Had I been drugged?

"You asked me if I would marry you when I put Charles Beste out of commission with that spin kick," said Maud, as though she had read my mind.

I reran the tape in my head and, yes, indeed, I recalled that I had uttered those words. Would it be ungallant of me now to point out that my question at the time was an attempt at cleverness? Would it even be safe to make such a defense with so many sharp objects within Maud's reach? Hmmm, I thought. Gorgeous and carnivorous and highly skilled in the martial arts. A girl you could take anywhere.

"See," said Maud, "I know you thought you were just trying to be amusing when you asked me to marry you. But, on another level, you really meant it. You probably weren't aware that you meant it, but you did. I know these things. And I think we should do it. I think it would be fun."

Fun? It might very well be fun, but is that why people got married? Then I thought about it for another couple of seconds and realized that, hey, that might be the only reason.

"But I have a few conditions," said Maud. She had conditions? "First, no more faking your own death."

"I think I already made that promise," I said. "Besides, I'm pretty sure that only works once. You know, you can fool some of the people . . ."

"Second," said Maud, "we move out of Michigan. Go someplace warm, sunny."

"You ever been to Italy?" I said.

"Never," she said.

"It'll be perfect," I said. "They won't understand a word we're saying. And they're sensible there. When was the last time you heard of Italy starting a war in the Middle East, or anywhere else, for that matter? I think they got all that imperialistic zeal out of their system sometime in the 14th Century."

"What about Mussolini?" said Maud.

"The exception that makes the rule," I replied. I took a swig of my beer. For all the nonchalance of my attitude and the playfulness of this interchange, we were, after all, talking about marriage.

"Third," said Maud, "no neglect. We are not houseplants. At least I'm not."

"Should I be writing these down?" I asked.

"Fourth," said Maud, "and last. The marriage never ends. I mean, *we* don't end it. Obviously, we'll die eventually."

Well, of course, everybody goes into marriages thinking they'll never end. I didn't remind Maud of this since I was pretty sure she already knew it. But how do you respond to a condition such as that? Okay, I agree not to end the marriage. What good does that do?

"I can see you have doubts," said Maid.

"No," I said. "Not doubts."

"Or," said Maud, looking at me closely. "I've misjudged your affections."

"No," I said earnestly. "It's not that."

"Then it's nothing," said Maud. She moved the candles out of the way so she could see my face more clearly, or to make her point more emphatically. "It's time for you to take a stand. Inform your existence with some definition."

Inform my existence with some definition? Was that a mouthful for "make a commitment?" It sounded suspiciously like "give your life some meaning."

"Do I have to start going to church or couples therapy?" I said, still trying to keep it lighthearted. My own heart rate was now something equivalent to the rate of fire of, say, an M2 .50 caliber machine gun.

"You have to worship at the Church of Maud," she said. She smiled. Then she laughed. She took another sip of her Amaretto. Then she pushed the tableware away from in front of her, leaned over the table and kissed me on the lips. I'm afraid I was too surprised to respond immediately. Maud sat back in her chair and looked at me, the smile still on her face.

"I'm going to give you a couple of minutes, then we're going to try that again," she said.

"I don't need a couple of minutes," I said. I pushed the plates and cups and silverware away from me with a big dramatic gesture, which sent several of the dishes and one of the candlesticks crashing loudly to the floor. But by this time Maud and I were crushing our mouths against each other in a PDA that certainly far exceeded anything I had ever allowed myself to indulge in previously. I couldn't speak for Maud. I had a vague sense of commotion among the other diners in the vicinity and out of the corner of my eye I could see a waiter approaching.

"I think we're in big trouble," I whispered to Maud.

"Right," she said. "They'll probably never let us in here again." She smiled and kissed me again.

"Is there a problem, sir?" said the waiter, who had reached our table and had picked up the candlestick.

"No," I said. I thought about going into some clever explanation, like Maud and I both suffered from Executive Dysfunction and had simultaneous emotional control issues, and, who knew, maybe that was true, but I was through explaining away my life.

"We were just clearing a path to each other as fast as possible," I said. Maud absolutely beamed at me.

But the waiter gave me an altogether different look, one, I guessed, he hoped would make me wish I were dead.

But that wasn't going to work.

Been there, I thought to myself, recalling the saying from a few years ago that seemed to be on everybody's lips for a while. *Done that.*

EPILOGUE

JULY 2012

"Hey, Fargo," said the voice speaking to me out of the wireless ether that is the domain of the cellphone.

"Hey, Barry," I said back.

"You don't sound surprised," he said, just the slightest hint of disappointment in his voice.

"Think about it" I said.

Actually, I *was* a little surprised. But I wasn't going to give him the satisfaction. I was in the kitchen of my home—some would call it a villa, but that would not accurately reflect its more modest dimensions—which I shared with my wife, Maud. Five years earlier we had liquidated our pooled resources and bought this place in the province of Latina—in Formia to be exact—south of Rome. Speaking of pools, I was looking at ours now, Maud next to it, sunbathing in a scandalously tiny bikini, only the bottoms of which she could accurately be said to be "wearing."

We don't always just lounge around like this, me mixing up a batch of martinis and she soaking up the sun. Maud actually works here in Italy as a personal trainer—something of novelty in the region—which keeps her in demand and contributes to her success (her stunning beauty could also have something to do with it). I teach English and do translations. We don't make a lot of money, but we don't need a lot.

"Right," said Barry after thinking about it.

"How did you get my number?" I asked.

"It's the twenty-first century, Fargo, although I didn't expect you to have an Italian country code and a number that didn't look like the typical American number."

"Why would you have any expectation at all about where I might be?"

"See," said Barry, clearly exasperated now, "I thought this would be kind of a fun call and here you go killing my buzz. What did I ever do to you to deserve such shabby treatment?"

"Do you really want to get into that?"

"I'm *serious,*" said Barry. Then, after a pause, "Okay, I conned you a little bit. But you didn't get hurt, did you? In fact, look at you, living like a Greek god with that gorgeous hunk of babedom you married. And, by the way, who you never would have met if it wasn't for me."

"I'm in Italy," I said. "Not Greece. They're different countries."

"I am exquisitely aware of that," said Barry.

"So, why are you calling?" I said.

"Well, the truth is, I've been feeling kind of bad these past few years, you know, about the way I hoodwinked you."

"Forget it," I said.

"No, I'm serious. I never even paid you for the work you did for me."

"I chalked that up to bad debt," I said. "After all, you were dead."

"Hey, I was a deadbeat," said Barry, pleased with himself.

"I have to go now, Barry."

"Wait, no. I want to send you some money, really. I feel like you deserve it."

"I don't," I said. "I never earned it. I never figured anything out. Your wife was gunned down right beside me. You could even make the case that if it hadn't been for me, she would still be alive."

"Even more reason for me to show my appreciation," said Barry.

"I don't want your money," I said. "And I don't want you to call me anymore. If you do, I'll notify the police. You know, they have ways of tracking these calls."

"Jeez, Fargo, give me a little credit. Do you really think the same guy who orchestrated what I orchestrated for the payoff that I got would fuck up by using a traceable phone?"

"It's always the little things that trip you up," I said. It sounded lame even to me.

"Admit it," said Barry. "You want to know how I did it."

"Goodbye, Barry," I said, and pushed the red button on my phone to end the call. Then I took the phone apart and threw the pieces into the trash. Fuck it. What did I need a cellphone for?

"Who were you talking to?" said Maud when I set her martini glass and the pitcher down on the plastic table next to her.

"Barry Justice," I said.

She turned to look at me and tipped up her sunglasses to get a better look.

"*The* Barry Justice?" she said.

"I only know of one," I said.

She stared at me for a full thirty seconds.

"How's he getting along without his equipment?" she finally asked. "Or doesn't he need it wherever he is?"

"I guess it wasn't his," I said. I took a sip of my martini. It was, IMHO, perfect. "I mean, I never really examined the body at the time."

"So what did he want?" said Maud after a few more moments of silence.

"To gloat, I think. You have to admit the moment was gloatable."

"So, whose do you think it was?" said Maud after another pause.

"Whose do I think what was?"

"The package. The genitals," said Maud.

I quickly ran through the list of everybody involved.

"I have no idea," I said, finally.

Maud thought about that for a few moments, then said:

"But the police must have known that Barry wasn't dead, then. How come they never mentioned that?"

"I don't know," I said. "I imagine Barry paid someone off. He had a lot of contacts."

"Contacts," said Maud.

"Yeah," I said. "Contacts. Connections. Didn't you ever read *The Great Gatsby*? Connections are everything. The guy who fixed the 1919 World Series did it through connections. Didn't you ever read *Howard's End*? Only connect?

"You're upset," said Maud. "I can tell because now you're just showing off."

"It's all ego. He just wanted someone to know."

"And you, what, you don't want to know?" said Maud.

"I don't want to feed his ego."

"And whose ego does that protect?"

"Basta, okay?"

"I told you it was no coincidence, his running into you at a damn Home Depot," said Maud after a beat, ignoring my plea for an end to the discussion.

"What I don't understand," I said, "is why did Justice need me? He could have pulled off this charade—or not pulled it off—without me. That's why I don't think it likely that he planned to run into me at that Home Depot. It just doesn't make any sense."

"What I'd like to know is how he knew you wouldn't examine his presumably dead body to confirm that he was, in fact, dead."

I thought about this, trying to relive the moment that I had discovered what I had assumed at the time was the mutilated corpse of Barry Justice.

"I think I was in panic mode," I said. "I expected the police to arrive at any moment. And let's not forget that Beste had done a pretty good job of setting me up, convincing me that Justice was dead. And the other thing is, Barry was an entertainer. It was a great acting job. And he'd been something of an actor in a prior life."

"Still, it was a risk," said Maud. "And here's something else. If Justice is dead, how does he collect on the insurance? Or on anything? How does it serve his purposes to be presumed dead?"

"I don't know the answers to these questions," I said. And then I did.

"His being dead—or the right people thinking he's dead—diverts suspicion from him in the murder of Lashona. And maybe others. Yet the fact that he really is alive allows him to cash in on the insurance."

Maud gave me a skeptical look.

"But the prosecutor's case at the trial seemed pretty airtight to me. Or at least pretty plausible. And I think he came to the conclusion that Desmond Webber killed his sister and killed Justice."

"But that was all conjecture and the testimony of people, well, like me. Nobody was in a position to rebut the testimony. Desmond and Venetia were dead. Philip Beste certainly didn't have the big picture. That leaves the old lady—Priscilla. But, as you will recall, she had a stroke or something at the time Justice had his alleged heart attack following the alleged altercation with Desmond. She probably has no idea what really happened.

"So," I continued, "picture this: Barry Justice's career is in the toilet and his marriage to Lashona is dissolving. He's worried about his future. Lashona named him as the executor or beneficiary of this five-million-dollar fund, but she's probably seriously considering modifying that to name someone else, maybe, who knows, a trusted advisor."

"Astrachan?"

"I don't think she would have trusted him with that responsibility. I guess I don't know who she would have trusted it with. Maybe that was why she hadn't taken Justice's name off the document yet. However, for the sake of this little narrative I'm putting together here, let's assume she wanted to, and Justice knew it. Under these conditions, Justice could certainly perceive that the best thing that could happen to him financially is for his wife to die."

"Wait," said Maud. "They have the gun that killed Lashona, remember? So, unless Barry talked Desmond into killing his sister or lending him the rifle so that he could do it himself, I see a problem with your scenario."

"Only if Barry is dead," I said. "If he's not dead, he could be working with Desmond, convincing him to kill Lashona by promising him a portion of the pie. Remember that Desmond's prospects aren't so good at this point either."

"It's a real stretch," said Maud. "If Desmond agrees to this, he's setting himself up to take the fall for Lashona's murder."

"Desperate men, as they say," I responded. "Without an infusion of cash, Desmond's future is bleak. Mom's not long for this world and Venetia is unthinkable as a partner in crime. If Desmond gets rid of the rifle, why would anybody tie him to the crime?"

"Okay," said Maud. "I can see that."

"I actually think it might have been Justice who pulled the trigger on that one, but we may never know the answer. What I *do* think is that Barry was pulling a lot of levers, in addition to this little faked death episode. I think Barry was manipulating the Webber family and the Beste's with this Thimerasol fantasy. I think *he* was the source on that, not some imaginary biochemist. Remember, Justice was in the news business for thirty years. He knew how it worked. He had sources."

"And connections," said Maud.

"Right. And he himself told me that this Thimerasol thing was all over the Internet. He probably put together—or hell, paid some biochemist to put together—a convincing, yet bogus report."

"So, the alleged safety deposit boxes were bogus, too? Just part of the scam?"

I shrugged.

"And the insurance investigators who allegedly visited Desmond, at least according to the prosecution."

"Impersonators, hired by Justice."

Maud nodded. "Okay," she said, not sounding completely convinced. "But what I really don't get is how does Justice profit from all this? I mean, he's presumed dead, and in a very public way, given the publicity of the trial. How does he get his hands on the insurance money, or whatever money he got his hands on? In order to do so, he would have to reveal himself and that would open him up to all sorts of scrutiny."

"I don't know," I said. "I don't want to know."

"You don't, huh?" said Maud. Can a voice be said to be dripping with skepticism?

I got up late the next morning, having pounded one or two too many martinis, most likely in an effort to expunge from my memory the telephone call I'd gotten from Barry Justice. Obviously the alcohol hadn't had the intended effect.

The house, or villa, was quiet. I assumed that Maud was out for a run or at her office at the fitness club where she saw to the training of overweight Italian housewives whose husbands were probably out chasing women younger in years and smaller in dress sizes.

But as I padded to the kitchen, I could hear the soft clacking of a computer keyboard coming from the study. I poked my head in to see Maud hunched over the computer screen. She appeared to still be in her bikini, although she had slipped one of my shirts on over it.

"You're up early," I said. "Or are you here late?" I really hadn't checked the time.

"Wrong both ways," said Maud, not taking her eyes off the computer screen as she jabbed away at the keyboard. "I didn't go to bed last night."

"Couldn't sleep?" I said. I knew Maud didn't suffer from insomnia—she really didn't suffer from any chronic maladies or neuroses that I was aware of. She was the picture of perfection. Still, I felt I had to say something.

"I could have gone to sleep, but I chose instead to do a little research."

I ignored the slight tone of reproach in her voice. This, I have learned, is how marriages survive.

"Anything interesting?" I said.

"Very," she said.

"Really." I said.

"Yes. Really very interesting. It's amazing what's available on the Internet if you're persistent."

Did I again perceive a note of criticism? As in, I had not nearly been persistent enough in my use of the Internet? Of course, persistence requires motivation—or character—neither of which I could lay much claim to. I thought of defending myself against Maud's suggestion of my failure to persist sufficiently, but, again, not pursuing these battles is the secret to a happy, if not healthy, relationship.

"So what did you find?"

"I found," said Maud, finally removing her attention from the computer screen and transferring it to me, "that Mr. Justice had quite an active, if brief, career as an actor before he entered journalism."

"Right," I said. "I believe I mentioned that."

"But you didn't mention, probably because you didn't know, that he used his real name when he acted and only changed it—or actually never did change it legally—to Barry Justice when he switched careers."

I thought about this. It didn't sound right. I was about to say as much to Maud but she continued before I could raise an objection.

"His real name, or at least the name he used as an actor, was Todd Brash." Maud, theatrically, I thought, put a finger to the side of her face and tilted her head as if in deep speculation mode. "I don't know. Sounds like a stage name to me. What do you think?"

"I think it sounds like a lead singer in a punk band, or, maybe punk band-lite—like the Disney version of the Sex Pistols," I said, trying to be clever. The moment seemed to call for clever.

"Why do I get the impression that you're not taking me seriously?"

"I'm taking you very seriously. You're very sexy when you're serious. Have I ever told you that?"

"Do you want to hear my theory, or not," said Maud. Lack of sleep had clearly not improved her sense of humor.

"I'm listening," I said. "But before you start and take yourself down some long and winding road only to have to slap yourself in the forehead, you need to remember that we found Barry Justice in the Brother Ignatius yearbook. So, unless that was another Barry Justice, which seems totally implausible to me, Barry's real name was Barry Justice, and he probably only used this Todd Brash moniker as a stage name."

Maud thought for a moment, gazing over the lid of the laptop out the window to the pool.

"You're right," she said a moment later. "But," she spun at me with the alarming abruptness of someone who's just had an inspiration, "I would bet everything I have, which is basically everything *you* have, that he legally changed his name to Todd Brash and never legally changed it back to Barry Justice."

"I don't know," I said. "If he did legally change his name to Todd Brash, that might work out pretty well as a name for a news guy. Good evening," I said in my best Stone Phillips voice, " I'm Todd Brash with breaking news."

Maud did not seem amused.

"It's a better name for a porn actor," she said. "Which he was, among other things." She waved a stack of printed sheets, obviously the yield of her overnight Internet peregrinations. "You could read through all this stuff," she said, slamming the pile down to the tabletop in what I took to be a triumphant gesture. "But allow me to summarize."

She did, and I will.

In 1964, eighteen-year-old Barry Justice left Berkley, Michigan, for Southern California with, like countless hordes before him, high hopes for a career in Hollywood. He was not without talent and a certain presence. He was able to land a few commercials (he was pretty buff, apparently, in those early days and made a visually appealing extra in beach scenes, etc.). He then worked in several B movies, most of them, as Maud helpfully pointed out, horror films of the early 60s, Vincent Price variety.

"During this time," said Maud, "Barry-slash-Todd met Enrico Tomba. Do you by any chance know who that gentleman is?"

Of course, I did not, so Maud explained.

"Tomba was one of the most famous makeup and special effects experts in Hollywood," she said.

"Was?"

"Yes, was. He died, coincidently"—here, she gave me finger quotes—"in 2004. He had suffered from AIDS, so maybe his death was natural. But probably not. Anyway, he specialized in effects related to the human body, especially wounds, disfigurements—realistic blood and guts kinds of stuff. Are you beginning to see where I'm going with this?"

She didn't wait for me to answer.

"Todd Brash didn't get very far in mainline movies, so like so many other lost souls in LaLa Land, he moved on to the next best thing—hardcore pornography, both straight and gay." She paused for a second, "I guess Barry could go either way on the gay marriage question."

"Funny," I said. "Hilarious."

"Todd's love relationship with Enrico ended about the time Todd left Hollywood in the late 70s, at which point, Barry Justice re-emerges in his hometown as a local reporter on what at the time was WWJ-TV, and the rest is history." At this point, Maud gave me a penetrating stare. "I'm kinda thinking that Enrico and Barry stayed in touch," she said. "What do you think?"

I was thinking that smugness did not become her.

"So," I said, "Barry's marriage to Lashona was a marriage of convenience."

She looked at me for a moment, then shook her head a little slowly.

"And his previous marriage and all that scandal," I said.

"Scandal is mother's milk to these people," said Maud. "Anyway, it's not the scandal that's interesting. What's interesting is that I think Barry Justice re-assumed his birth name to lose the Todd Brash connection, which could prove a little embarrassing in this new life, and because Barry Justice is just a crackerjack name for an investigative reporter who covers local and state politics. But"—Maud paused for dramatic effect—"I think he kept Todd Brash as his legal name, who knows, maybe for sentimental reasons."

"Yuck," I said.

"And that," said Maud, ignoring my interjection, "is how Barry was allowed to collect the money from Lashona's trust fund, or the insurance money, or whatever it was, under the radar. I mean if Barry Justice or his representatives showed up to collect, that could be a problem, since he's supposed to be dead. But Todd Brash? Who's Todd Brash to some functionary at an insurance company?"

I thought about this for a moment. The part I liked about it was its charming plausibility—far from a certainty—but it had merit as an explanation. What I absolutely hated about this theory was—

"Don't beat yourself up," said Maud. "Anyone could have been taken in by this."

"Not anyone over the age of nine or ten," I said. "Not anyone with enough sense to walk over to Barry's body and check for a pulse."

Maud shrugged.

"If that had been the only element of the deception, you probably wouldn't have been fooled," she said. "*We* wouldn't have been. It was the entire context. And you were, well, vulnerable."

"Naïve," I said.

"Credulous."

"Gullible."

"I'm sorry," said Maud. "But I don't have my thesaurus handy."

She stood up and stretched. Then she draped her arm over my shoulder, bent over, and kissed me on the top of my head.

"I guess the only thing that bothers me," she said, "is that I hate to see Barry get away with this."

"Except that we're not even sure what he got away with," I said

"Well, you've got seven or eight murder victims," said Maud.

"Not one of which we could say with any certainty that Barry had any involvement in."

"True," said Maud, after a moment's reflection.

A few seconds later she announced that she was going to take a shower and try to get a couple of hours of sleep.

I got a cup of coffee. The faint odor of Maud's suntan oil mixed with the always stimulating natural aroma of her body still hung in the air. I slid open the glass patio doors, stepped out into the warm, mid-summer Italian air and looked out over the pool to the hint of the tranquil coastline on the horizon. I flashed back for an instant to what I had thought at the time was Barry Justice's dead and mutilated body slumped on his couch.

Then I refocused on the perfection of the morning, the profound crystalline glory of the moment.

It was good to be alive.

ABOUT THE AUTHOR

Paul L. Hall is the author of two previous novels in the Fargo series (*Our Father* and *The Big Island*) and the award-winning *Places the Dead Call Home.* He lives in Troy, Michigan.

www.ingramcontent.com/pod-product-compliance
Lightning Source LLC
Chambersburg PA
CBHW051241260626
47162CB00002B/548
9780977041503